HEARTSTONE

The Broken Coast
Noikos Fields
The River Rule
The Irian Range
Mildaresh
Felian Pass
Karlese
Senna
Marchland
West Haven
Idira
The Elgrave
The Boot
Isle of Baktah
Ciris
The Singing Isles

Calkinon
The Cranok
Forest of Ustaar
The Grove
Zondra
Calibrae
Skarfell
Ford of Elan
Jerra-bal
Pendle Ring
The Enigmata
The Kenting
Farndale
Ferridale
Bixdale
Gravelton
The River Tella
Grey Shard
Scrimpton
Mistlands
The Bruinin Forest
T'al Agria

STONES OF THE AZURI

HEARTSTONE

BY

ROBYN PROKOP

Published by Toutouwai Publications 2020
Nelson, New Zealand

First published in New Zealand in 2020

Cover design and formatting by NOKNOK Studios

Softcover
ISBN 978 0 473 55356 2

— CONTENTS —

A BOY

Like a shining black water beetle, the boat slipped into the cove. Oars sliced the water, dark and silent. Rowers bent their backs in rhythm, blowing streams of air through tight mouths. They hugged the rocks, trusting the lapping waves to break up any tell-tale wake. They had been waiting for a night like this. Only now was the tide high enough to risk the jaws of Ciris. So far, all had gone to plan. They had evaded the whirlpool's sucking mouth. Now they needed to make haste. The longer they took, the greater the risk of being dragged into the depths on their return. For now, the tide was their ally; the cove was filled to the brim, reducing the beach to a pale fingernail.

The hull of the boat hit the shelly shore with a crunch. The cliffs glowered, but apart from the curling wash of waves, everything was still. So far, so good. Skarlon nodded at the blackened faces of his team. No one spoke. As they leapt ashore he cast a wary eye along the sharp edge of the cliffs. Shift was already doing her thing. Within minutes she was halfway up the cliff face, working feet and hands into invisible holes and cracks. A black woollen hat hid her bright hair from the moonlight. No one climbed like Shift. Part-girl, part-gecko. In no time she had disappeared over the top. Seconds later a silvery rope came fountaining down. Skarlon sighed. Climbing. A young man's game.

Skarlon was heaving himself over the crest when he spotted it. A lone bat against the sky. The omen echoed the warning in his gut. He grimaced, bringing his hand to his face. Three fingers brushing three inky stars, one for each of the gods. Just a reflex. Too late to change the plan now. Shift and Miken had already vanished into the wiry scrub. They would force their way along the central ridge of the island. Bardi and Krizo were two bent backs, running low, making for the northern headland. Skarlon and the boy would head south along the bluff, then cut inland. This side of the island was a rugged wilderness. But Pharni wanted it checked, and that is what Pharni would get. Skarlon's head told him they would find nothing.

Why, then, did he have this sense of deep foreboding?

Whipping the rope from its eyelet, Skarlon stowed it in his pack. Only the sharpest eyes would detect the glinting peg. Shift had chosen the spot well. That pair of stunted trees would be easy to spot on their return. Without a word to the boy, Skarlon shouldered his pack and began to run. He kept close to the cliff edge, ignoring the shine of water far below. There was a path of sorts. Probably made by animals. It made him nervous. That, and the boy following close behind.

Skarlon had argued against bringing the boy. Oh, he was strong all right. You couldn't argue with that — they might not have pulled past the whirlpool without him. But that did not make him ready. Not for a mission. Too green. Still a stranger to the League. They could not afford mistakes, and if they did find something they would need to get out — and fast.

When the track became a firm path Skarlon followed his instincts, veering off into the bushland. Something was wrong. He felt it in his bones as they crept cautiously from tree to tree. Just a pair of shadows under the cool moons. Skarlon knew already, even before he saw the flickering torches, far below, that somebody was here. They wedged themselves into a high perch, hidden by rock and tree, to watch.

The settlement clung precariously to the hillsides. Definitely not a clamming tribe; too far inland for that. Skarlon's heart raced as he raised the spyglass. When he adjusted the lens, a frightening scene leapt into view. Rickety fortifications, spiked platforms and wooden frameworks. Were those cages, formed up around the sides? Yes. Sturdy cages, although it was hard to be sure in the dark. There was a scaffold, too — a ghastly thing, lit by flaming torches. Dark shapes swung from it like fruit.

Skarlon shuddered. There could be no doubt. At long last they had found it: the lair of Kara-fell. Passing the spyglass to the boy, Skarlon began to sketch. He worked quickly, marking anything that might be useful. When the boy tugged at his sleeve, he scowled. Following the lad's pointing finger, he saw it, too. Watchmen! A pair of them, heading away from the camp. Time to go!

Stupid to risk the path. Not now they knew who was down there. After a silent wrangle with the twisted undergrowth, they managed to cut across into open forest. There, the ground was soft with litter, mottled in the moonlight. In a split second Skarlon's mind took in the tell-tale depression.

Too late! The earth opened and bit him — hard. An agonising crunch. Bones snapping. Pain crashed through his body. In the battle to stay conscious, he was dimly aware of the boy dragging at him. Wrenching, tearing the trap apart. Skarlon's leg came free with a new surge of pain. He would not scream, no matter what it took. His voice was a strangled rasp: 'Leave me! Follow the code!' He clutched at the lad's clothes, dragging him close.

'Do what must be done — do it!' His eyes fastened on a large rock. 'I'll turn my face away. Do it, boy! You can't leave me here alive.' The boy nodded. But he didn't pick up the rock. He tossed the cruel trap to one side. Grasping Skarlon under the armpits, he hauled him into a sitting position. Skarlon stifled a bellow and cursed through his teeth. He'd been right! Stupid choice! Too inexperienced. Won't follow orders. As black spots swam before his eyes, he snarled. 'Follow the code, damn you!'

'I *am* following the code. Pharni's orders. Every warrior back safely. That's what she said.' The boy grinned then. He *actually* grinned. 'You might want to pass out — this is going to hurt.'

'No. I command you. Braig! Put me down!'

Skarlon cursed at the brave but foolish boy. At the damned ringing in his head. Then, he knew nothing but darkness.

Chapter 1

THE TRYST

There was a sharp breeze rising in Mildaresh. It taunted the edges of the hedges in Hartlin Gardens. Although they yielded little of their steadfast dignity, they did shiver slightly, unable to entirely withstand the whispering insistence of the changing season. There were plenty of signs that the long summer was finally fading. Over-ripe fruit lay unheeded on the ground, some of the leaves had abandoned themselves to a slow dance with the wind, and the afternoon light had grown pale.

A young woman was making her way through the gardens, but the tension in her body made the leisurely pace seem forced, restrained. Her thin cloak billowed out, making her feel conspicuous — perhaps it had been the wrong thing to wear after all? But what is one supposed to wear to such an assignation? She had chosen the garment for its hood, which would disguise her blonde hair, but the edges kept fluttering against her skin, releasing tendrils of hair. The movement was also distracting her eye, causing her to imagine movement behind.

Karliana had not visited the gardens since her nurse had brought her there as a child. Remarkably little had changed, although she could have sworn the statues and fountains had been bigger back then. With effort, she brought her thoughts back to the present: it was nearly the hour. Checking behind her one last time, she took the path to the grandest hot-house, with its spotty-throated flowers and shallow fish-filled ponds. Really, she could not think of a more peculiar place to meet.

Going to open the door, Karliana found it was stuck, and had to yank it open. As she entered, she had the distinct impression that time had stood still; the fish still gaped noiselessly in their ponds and the plants seemed too alive, more animalistic than they ought to be. A monk was tending seedlings at a trestle table. With his silvery hair tied back in a long braid, he looked out of place in this lush, earthy environment, and was doing a poor job of keeping his habit's cumbersome sleeves out of the dirt. Without looking up, he spoke, startling Karliana. 'You'll find what you seek in the potting area at the back, my lady.' Barely breaking pace with his work, and still not meeting her eye, the monk gestured towards a thick curtain just visible at the rear of the hot-house.

Murmuring her thanks, Karliana picked up her skirts and moved carefully through aisles of foliage.

As she neared the curtain, she began to feel breathless. It was not just the hot smell of loam making her giddy, it was the growing certainty that she really ought not to have come. With a trembling hand she pushed the curtain aside. The potting area was dark, the light attempting to penetrate the glass roof thwarted by black mould. As Karliana's eyes adjusted to the gloom, she took in her surrounds. Inside were tiers of shelves, tables scattered with empty pots, and a selection of dangerous-looking implements. As she scanned the room, her eyes flew wide when she saw a hooded figure peering through a small window that looked outside into the gardens.

The figure turned.

'Karliana! I wasn't sure you'd come.'

As he moved towards her, she understood her initial confusion; her friend was wearing the brown weave of the unclaimed priests. It changed his appearance entirely.

'Domberto, why are you not wearing the colours of your order?'

He smiled ruefully. 'It was deemed more appropriate that I return to probationers' robes. I'm being disciplined for voicing opinions inconsistent with the values and honour of the priesthood … and bringing my order into disrepute.'

'But that's not fair: you only did what was right!' It was true. And Karliana was proud of him for saving the life of that slave, although going against Maliagne Aranti of all people was also the stupidest thing Domberto could have done. Karliana still wondered what had come over him on that fateful day.

'It is unimportant.' Domberto was checking the window again. Feeling herself blush, Karliana cast her eyes downwards, unnerved not only by his furtive behaviour, but also by his close proximity. At her feet was a stand of succulents in shades of purple and mauve. Grown monstrous in their steamy netherworld, their tendrils reached towards her from cracked pots. She moved her skirts away.

He turned again, his eyes full of concern. 'I don't mean to frighten you.'

'I'm not frightened,' she lied, with a toss of her head, wondering if he could hear her heart racing. 'It's simply very hot in here. I do wish you'd explain your message. And why you suggested this ... this peculiar location for our audience.'

'Of course.' Domberto brought a hand to his heart. 'It was presumptuous, and I apologise for the intrigue. But there was no other way.' *His eyes are so blue!* Why did she always forget that? 'Karliana ... There is something I must beg of you.'

The passion in Domberto's gaze was unmistakable. Her heart raced again, like a bird beating against the cage of her ribs. Whatever was he about to ask? Surely he knew there could be nothing between them unless he was to renounce his calling? He did not speak. Parting the curtain slightly, he checked the hot-house once more, before facing her. A warm thrill swept her body.

'We dare not tarry. Father Barlon keeps watch, but I hate to think of the consequences that would follow our discovery.'

'Quite.' With him standing so close, it was very hard to keep her tone neutral.

'I need you to take a message to your father.'

Karliana gathered her breath. 'Oh?'

'You are the only way I could think of to warn him. You must tell Torland not to act against Aranti. Not under any circumstances. Do you understand?'

Karliana stiffened, her eyebrows arching. *Politics?* Was that what this was all about? He had brought her here for *politics?*

Karliana felt the colour rising in her cheeks. 'Domberto, in case you have forgotten, my father has been deposed as Mildari. And not through righteous means, as I'm sure you are aware.'

He nodded. 'Yes. But you must nonetheless tell him. He must not oppose Aranti.'

What is this? Had Domberto crawled back to Maliagni Aranti's side? To become his pet priest once more? Karliana shook her head. 'How can you ask such a thing? My father is an honourable man. A senator. It is his right — nay, his duty — to speak against injustice.' Her frown deepened into a scowl. 'You know the nature of the man, Domberto. Maliagne Aranti may be the new so-called dispenser of justice, but he must be kept in check if he abuses the role of Mildari. My father will work against him, as all good senators must.'

'Karliana, no! He must not.'

'Must *not?* You of all people should know that Torland Lendri will never bow to political pressure. How dare you! How dare you lure me here to propose such a thing! I cannot believe you do Aranti's work, after … after speaking against him.' Her words spluttered, making her even more infuriated. Preparing to sweep out of the room, she was stunned when Domberto caught her by the wrist, then grasped her other wrist, too.

'Karliana! Please! Your father's life depends on it.' Something in his eyes silenced her tongue. Her heart stilled. 'The House of Aranti has a new priest, Father Keller. But Maliagne … well … he insists on my presence.' His soft mouth trembled. 'He hates me, Karliana, and he enjoys letting me know it. But that is nothing to how he despises your father.'

'Domberto, please. Release me.'

The young priest looked down at their hands, seeming surprised that he was holding her wrists, and obeyed at once.

Karliana shook her head, not understanding his strange mood. 'Maliagne Aranti's dislike of my father is nothing new. They have always crossed swords.'

'No! This is different. Something is wrong.' Domberto seemed to be searching for words. 'Aranti is … wrong. He is not himself. Yes, he has always been ambitious, ruthless even, but up until now he's always played within the rules. I fear … I sense some change, a new darkness … a cruelty, or propensity for real evil.'

'What makes you think this?'

'I have no clear evidence, yet I suspect much.'

'What? What do you suspect?'

Domberto answered her slowly, unwillingly. 'I believe the sacred ballot was rigged.'

Karliana gasped. It was an outrageous accusation. The *gods* decided which house was honoured by the rule of Mildari. Not even Maliagne Aranti could be so arrogant, so blasphemous as to meddle with the sacred vessel. 'I don't believe it,' she whispered.

'Not only that. He has imprisoned his mistress.'

'Matapharni?' Karliana put her hand to her mouth. 'No, that can't be. He's besotted with her. Has he gone mad?'

'Madness would not worry me nearly so much. There's more. The Calkinon ambassador has been found at last. Dead in his carriage at the village of Karlese, a Mildaren dagger buried in his neck. The ambassador's last interview was with Aranti. He was supposed to visit Lady Skagali after that, but he never arrived.'

Karliana pursed her lips. It was ludicrous. What would Aranti stand to gain from such a move?

'Karliana, the man is not himself. It is as if his soul is wreathed in darkness. And your father ... your father is at the heart of his hatred. He thinks I am your father's spy. That is why you must take the message. You must—'

A sudden noise cut short the priest's plea. Behind the curtain the monk was thumping about, moving pots to a higher shelf.

'It's the signal!' Domberto hissed. 'Somebody is coming!'

They stared into each other's eyes. Stock-still. Listening.

With a loud shudder the hot-house's outer door opened. Peeping through the curtain, Karliana caught a glimpse of a man. All shoulders and chest, with arms folded, he entirely blocked the entrance. His bulk and black hair made him instantly recognisable. And one thing was certain: Rutholine Moagli had not just happened by to admire the shrubbery.

Domberto whispered: 'Stay here!' Then, as if his previous behaviour had not been erratic enough, he twitched his robes aside to reveal his hand on the hilt of a sword. Domberto had clearly taken leave of his senses: even armed, he could never beat Rutholine. She placed a firm hand on his shoulder.

'No,' she whispered. 'I will speak to my father. I promise. But this is madness. I will not let you fight Rutholine.' Sweeping up one of the plants, she called out in a loud voice. 'Father Barlon? I think I'll take this one!'

Karliana smiled merrily as she tugged the curtain closed behind her. 'Is that acceptable to you? I fear I've chosen one with a cracked pot, though.' The poor monk looked so bewildered that she actually giggled.

Feinting surprise at seeing the monk was no longer alone, Karliana exclaimed: 'Oh! Good afternoon, Rutholine! Fancy meeting you here.' She bobbed a curtsy. Surprised, the bulky young man bowed awkwardly. 'How fortuitous. I'm desperately in need of a second opinion.'

She sauntered towards him, swaying her skirts. 'You see I want an amusing gift for my dear friend, and she simply adores these plants.' She eyed the twisted specimen and giggled. *He would never believe it.* She pushed on anyway. 'The uglier they are, the better she likes them! I know this one's positively horrid, but do you think it's more horrid than that one over there?' She pointed at a draping vine with pink spotted lumps.

'I really can't say.' Rutholine's voice suited him perfectly: a growling rumble for a beast of a man.

'Oh? Well, I suppose a man like you can't be expected to know such things.' Karliana smiled up at him and tossed her curls. 'I've made up my mind, though! I will take this one after all. Do you think it could be re-potted and delivered tomorrow, Father?' The monk took the plant from her in silence. 'Wonderful! That's settled then.' Clapping her hands together, Karliana gave a childish little bounce.

Then she made her face grave. 'Rutholine, it is a little out of order, but … I don't suppose you would mind escorting me through the gardens? My companion seems to have lost her way and I find myself here quite alone.' When he agreed, with just the slightest of frowns, she fluttered her eyelashes and put a light hand on his arm. 'Thank you so very much. I hardly know why, but suddenly I don't quite feel safe.'

Chapter 2

THE KILL SHOT

Kep gathered together all of her intent and nocked the arrow. Every scrap of her purpose was focused on that thin, pinched face. She could see his hair, shining blond, like a bright flag. He was remorseless. Kep just knew it. Her jaw tightened. This was it. This was the arrow that Narsis — the one of the three gods she felt closest to — would guide, straight to Feld's heart. She drew back her arm. The long, dark bow shook as it bent, making her shoulder ache to its joints. She held her focus, training all her energy on that hated face and the scornful curve of his grin. Mastering the trembling bow took all her strength. Another burning moment. She plucked her fingers back. The drawstring snapped and she let out a snarl, even before the arrow had reached its mark.

Slumping in frustration, Kep dropped the bow to her side. Too far right, and too low. Again! Six arrows sprouted in the straw now, all at haphazard angles — all off-centre. Two had missed the target entirely, skipping away through the bare-limbed orchards towards the tall hedges. Kep scowled, chewing at her lip. Her sigh hung in the air momentarily, a billow of grey vapour.

The light was failing now, making the practice grounds even more desolate. The others had packed up their quivers long before, leaving Kep alone with her obsession. She sniffed. The freezing air stung at her eyes making them water. Despite a cloak reaching almost to her ankles and a fur cap tugged over her ears, she was starting to shiver. Her feet were frozen. Cupping her hands over her mouth, she tried to breathe some feeling back into her numb fingertips. Her gloves were designed to protect her fingers from the ravages of the bowstring, not for warmth. Making circles with her left arm, trying to ease the pain in her shoulder, she glanced at the quiver. One solitary arrow remained.

As Kep moved to pick it up, she heard a voice.

'Still too far to the right, then?'

Kep closed her eyes. How did he always manage to sneak up like that, *and* state the damn obvious? And why did her stomach, seemingly with a mind of its own, do an excited little flip whenever he appeared?

Quelling him with a scowl, Kep plucked the last arrow from the quiver.

In spite of its superior warmth and comfort, Sarin had not adopted Azuran garb. As always, he wore the clothes of the Aurum, his clan. Close-fitting garments in brown and green were matched with soft, laced-up boots. His only concession to the cold was a dark-green cloak, lined with fur. Sarin pushed the hood back, revealing his shining black hair. A band of silver ran across his forehead, standing out brightly against his olive skin. Wearing that circlet could only mean one thing: he had been hunting beyond the city, in the Enigmata. Folding his arms, he took a position at her shoulder, grinning at the target. Kep frowned sideways at him. When he caught her eye, she looked away. Why did she always feel so flustered when he was near? It was very annoying.

After a moment, Sarin held out his hand. 'Can I see that bow?'

Kep hesitated, but it would be childish to refuse. Feigning indifference, she shrugged and handed it over.

Sarin balanced the bow on his fingertips, testing its weight. Then he ran his hands over its long curves, eyes almost closed. Kep sniffed as he grasped an end and held it out in front of him, peering down its length. He frowned before putting his hand out for the arrow. Apparently not noticing that Kep practically slapped it into his palm, Sarin made a silent inspection of the fight feathers before nocking it. His golden eyes narrowed. Kep watched his lips pout, ever so slightly. Then she turned her attention to the target. Sarin inhaled, his elbow came back, and the arrow flew — all in one fluid motion. Kep felt a quick stab of envy. The arrow arced and plunged, finding dead centre. It was as if the target had drawn it. The perfect kill shot. Sarin made it look so easy. So why, by sweet Telion, was he still frowning?

Sarin made a soft clicking noise with his tongue as he returned the bow.

'This bow is not right for you. It is a proud weapon — it wants someone taller and stronger.'

Kep bristled as she reclaimed the bow. Sarin had that effect on people. She hugged it to her body.

'Daska chose this bow for me. He said it once belonged to a fine warrior. And Daska has every faith that I will master it.' She felt oddly protective, as if it was her duty to defend the weapon against Sarin's critique. Kep loved the bow's long, dark lines, even if it did take all her effort to string. 'No doubt the warrior who had it before me *was* stronger and taller.' She drew herself up to her full height. 'Well, I might not get much taller, but I am getting stronger every day … and more skilled.'

It was true. Kep had indeed been improving every day. Thankfully, Sarin could not know just how much; he had not been present during that first embarrassing session where she had failed to hit the target at all — not even once. Today's effort was hardly admirable, but it was progress. 'You just wait and see, Sarin. By the time I take the Pledge I'll be able to hit any target you want.'

Sarin's eyebrows went up. '*Any* target, Kep?'

Kep was cold. Her feet hurt. And she was not in the mood for the same argument. 'The League has only one target, Sarin: the Melk.' Her eyes flashed. 'As well you know.' It was time to change the subject. 'What about you? How did the hunting go?'

Sarin smiled and removed the silver band from his brow. At once it snapped into a bracelet. As he transferred it to his wrist Kep could not help marvelling. She had no idea how the circlets worked; she was not even sure that their leader Nirias knew, and he was Azuri. One of the Malshorne, Nirias had grown up in T'al Jazure, around a thousand years ago — as impossible as that seemed. The circlets were Azuran secrets; beautiful, subtly crafted things, wrought in a distant past by people with long-forgotten skills. Anyone venturing past the rim, where T'al Jazure ended and the forest began, had to wear one — else risk being overwhelmed by the forest's strange power. The silver bands did not entirely counteract the bewildering effects of the Enigmata, but they did keep a person from losing their way, and their mind. Sarin blew into his cupped fingers and tucked them under his armpits before answering. Perhaps he did feel the cold, after all.

He nodded. 'The hunting was good. We chased down a young hind and—' Mid-sentence, he frowned, redirecting his gaze. 'And it's just as well.' Sarin gestured with his hand, beyond the hedged perimeter of the orchards, up towards the hills. 'Looks like we'll have more company.'

Off in the distance, a small group of people was wending its way down from the foothills, towards the city. Kep squinted, guessing at perhaps eight or nine people. The larger shape at the back looked to be some sort of pack animal. They moved slowly, no doubt overwhelmed by their first sight of the city. Sarin cast appraising eyes at the sky. 'They've made it just in time, too.' He laughed at her perplexed expression. 'It's about to snow.'

Kep stared. The clouds were faintly tinged with green. Did that mean snow? She wouldn't know. It never snowed in Mildaresh, the place of her birth — only in the mountains, high up behind the city. Kep felt a quick thrill of excitement. Snow! *At last!* Snow meant Nirias would stay this time. *Finally!* The new recruits would be allocated to a jinn, and sworn to a captain. Kep's training would begin in earnest. In spring Nirias would send warriors to Mildaresh and, with the help of Narsis, Kep intended to join them.

Sarin watched the group for a few minutes longer. 'I had better go and pretend to help, I suppose.' He gave her a wink. Kep knew he wanted to look over the newcomers. 'You should come in out of the cold, too.' His expression became solemn. Waggling his finger, he deepened his voice. 'Keep your bowstring dry for another day, Kep.' His mimicry of Daska was perfect. He really shouldn't make fun of everyone so mercilessly. Yet Kep laughed in spite of herself, making Sarin grin all the more cheekily. 'Need any help searching for arrows?'

Kep made a face at him. 'I'll be perfectly fine, thank you.' She nearly told him that she was staying for one more set — just to make a point — but her arms were trembling and her shoulders ached to the bone. It would be good to get warm. Besides, she had to check on Ash. She had not seen much of him for a few days. She suspected he was laying low. And that was never a good sign.

In that disconcerting way he had, Sarin picked up on her thoughts. 'Right, I'm off to help Ash. He's probably been commandeered by the cook to dress those fowl. If I say so myself, there were quite a few.'

When Kep rolled her eyes at him, he made a little mock bow. There was one of those odd pauses, and then he wandered off. Kep watched after him for a moment. Something had changed since that stolen kiss in the Glade. But what? She stamped her feet. It was too cold to be standing there trying to work Sarin out! After a brief struggle, she managed to unstring her bow, before wrapping it lovingly in its cloth.

❧

Extracting the arrows from the target was straightforward. Finding the two strays was more of a problem. Kep spent quite some time casting about before spotting the first arrow, which had scudded into a clump of grass, burying itself. Rubbing dirt off the arrowhead, she put it back in her quiver. Perhaps the second was lodged in the tall hedge behind the target range? Could it have flown so far?

It was getting quite dark now. The air had an eerie, hushed quality. Kep peered into the hedge, pushing branches aside. Spotting what might be the arrow, she thrust her arm in, right up to the armpit. Stretching blindly, her fingers wrapped around a smooth length. In the gathering gloom Kep straightened, pulling back and revealing her find. She stared in surprise at the object in her hand: it was an arrow — just not one of hers. Its shaft was faintly blue, and thick with mossy grime. Kep sighed. It was a poor swap for the one she had lost. Still, she added it to her quiver anyway.

⁂

A stone archway set into the hedge brought Kep out of the orchards. In spite of her weariness, she felt a little thrill to see the city rising before her. T'al Jazure had its own moods. That afternoon it seemed particularly unreal; a fantasy city against a backdrop of purpling sky. As always, Kep felt that it might vanish if she blinked. The path she was following had started to glow, slowly releasing light captured during the day. Today it shone blue, like an iridescent river.

As she walked, tiny globes winked into life among the bushes, like clouds of fire-flies. In T'al Jazure, there was water everywhere, as if it were as essential as stone itself. Here, water poured in smooth sheets from tall rectangular vessels. They stood in clusters as if in conversation, their feet washed by pools of blue light. The sight chilled Kep: all this water, and not a single altar to Narsis! She sniffed and hurried on.

The next archway was her favourite, resembling a living vine, complete with impossibly detailed flowers. It glowed in the half-light like moonstone. As always, Kep wanted to put out her hand to stroke the stone, just to check that it was real.

Beyond the delicate arch was a perfectly round courtyard, half-ringed by low, curved walls, and graced by three statues of young women dancing. The sculptor had captured the figures in mid-flight, with garlands in their hair and swirling gowns, forever on the verge of taking their next steps. Kep ran her eyes over the forms, wondering if the maidens were merely the fancy of the artist, or whether they had once danced the steps for real. The trees in the courtyard were stately, bare-limbed beauties. Kep was eager to see what the spring would reveal, and whether she would recognise their varieties. She would not be at all surprised, though, if they turned out to be thoroughly alien, like so much else in the city — with bright blue leaves, perhaps.

The path went through the courtyard and on into the very heart of T'al, where clusters of spires and turrets reached towards the sky. Somewhere inside those towers were thousands of orbs like the Taelstone — or, rather, Credé's lore-stone.

Kep frowned, pressing her lips into a line of displeasure. She still thought of it as the Taelstone, and probably always would. She hated the thing, and especially the weird effect it had on Ash. All that time on their long journey from Mildaresh she had longed to be rid of it. Who could have dreamt there would be more than one, let alone thousands? She stared at the glassy spires, unable to imagine how such things might be stored. She was yet to visit that part of the city, and was not sure if she even wanted to, in spite of Nirias's promise to give the Seekers a special tour of the Knowledge Stores. She bet by now Sarin had already made his own investigation, though, probably during one of his nocturnal explorations. However, did Sarin manage with so little sleep?

At that thought, Kep was overwhelmed with longing for her own bed. Her feet were frozen, her nose a cold, red lump. So she was glad to reach yet another arch, a living one this time, formed by interwoven branches. It marked a cobbled way, which wandered off towards a more familiar part of the city. In ancient times, the area had been created specifically for the students — those who had come to T'al Jazure seeking knowledge and skills under the tutelage of the Azuri. Characterised by busy clusters of workshops, 'The Lodges' took its name from the living accommodation: three long timber lodges with expansive windows and high-pitched roofs. Each was large enough to accommodate a hundred people. The League had taken up residence in the Sable Lodge, the one nearest the heart of the city.

Kep was turning onto the path, thinking how wonderful a hot bath would be, when the first snowflake surprised her by landing on her nose. She looked up, startled. Another spiralled down. Then another.

The tiny pieces of ice seemed to fall out of nowhere, landing on her face and eyelashes, and sticking on the fur of her cap. Kep gave a cry of wonder.

It was so magical! She stood there, entranced, hands outstretched, the snow swirling about her. She laughed to see how it twirled in flurries around the lamps. When Kep stuck out her tongue, a snowflake landed on it — a speck of pure cold. The ground was already turning white!

Then, all of a sudden, something very black jumped down from a tree.

Kep gave a startled cry and scowled.

Tarlyn!

It was a surprise to see Tarlyn on her own. She usually stuck close to Ash, perching on his shoulder like a black demon. Kep frowned. If Tarlyn was here, then where was Ash? Tarlyn walked on a few paces before casting a haughty stare over one shoulder. As always, Kep was unnerved by the intelligence in those dark eyes. The creature's low growl seemed to be a command to follow. There was nothing for it but to obey. Kep sighed as she turned away from the path that led to a hot bath. What had Ash done to himself this time?

Chapter 3

THE CURING HOUSE

As the fragments of his scattered mind started to come together, Ash took small, obedient sips of the bright green fluid. He had been instructed to drink the whole thing down, and dared not do otherwise. He stared at his hand, wanting to unwrap the bandage. He didn't dare do that either: the nurse, Agnid, had such an air of command. Ash frowned as he watched her now putting items on a tray with calm efficiency. Ash had seen her for the first time only a few minutes earlier when he had regained consciousness in a bed in the Curing House. It had been disconcerting to awake to the scrutiny of a total stranger. Strange, too, that he was being tended to by someone he didn't recognise. He thought by now he knew all of the people who had arrived in T'al Jazure — at least by sight.

Agnid was dressed in a pale-blue garment of starched linen, tightly buttoned at the neck. A matching blue cloth was pinned across her brow, covering her hair entirely. Grey hair, thought Ash, judging by the lines on her large, strong hands. He ran his tongue around his mouth. The medicine was not particularly pleasant — astringent, with a gritty texture. Trying not to worry about what it actually was, he swallowed the remainder in a gulp.

Seeming to sense that the glass was empty, the stout nurse moved at once to his bedside. 'Excellent,' she said crisply. Her keen brown eyes reminded him of a bird peering at a worm. When she smiled, crinkles formed, softening the effect of a rather masculine jawline and prominent nose. 'Rest now, Ash. I'll send Pallin to check on you. Argess willing, you should be on your feet in time for the welcoming.'

Ash nodded glumly. He would much rather miss the welcoming. Just more strangers — all staring, wondering how the skinny boy with grey hair fitted in. But he could hardly blame them: it was something he repeatedly wondered about himself, after all. When the nurse bustled out through the doorway, his eyes came back to the bandage. Was there much damage? He remembered the knife slipping, piercing his flesh. But nothing more. He supposed he had fainted — again. With his uninjured hand, he felt his head for bumps. Nothing. His right shoulder was tender, though.

Ash blew out his cheeks. At least it was Pallin on duty today. Healing was an essential part of the code, so they all took shifts in the Curing House. Ash could think of worse nurses than Pallin. With freckled skin, sandy red hair and a shy smile, Pallin was different to the other warriors. Ash did not know his story; only that he was from a lake town, somewhere in the north, up towards Calkinon. He would have a story, though. Everyone involved with the League had a story, most of them terrible.

Pushing that thought away, Ash turned his attention to the silent room. The walls and polished floors were bright white. The benches shone like silver. Everything looked sharp, lit by a globe that seemed to hang in the air of its own accord, like a bubble. In one corner, an elaborate tap pouted over a porcelain sink. Alarming instruments stood on shelves or hung from hooks. Ash did not know their purpose, and had no wish to find out. The place smelt sharp, probably courtesy of the contents of all those labelled bottles. Containing coloured liquids, powders and crystals, bottle upon bottle were crowded into rows on narrow shelves. There were books, too — lots and lots of books.

Reminded of Credé's hut, Ash had a sudden horrible thought. Credé may actually have been in this very room. Yes, it was entirely possible — Nirias said T'al Jazure had been Credé's home for long years. And for a Malshorne, that probably meant hundreds of years. It was all too easy to imagine Credé mixing up one of his concoctions at the bench. Ash scowled. If it had not been for Credé and his lies, they would never have fled Mildaresh. Ash would not be the Keeper of the Song, and Braig would be alive. Ash squeezed his eyes shut and lay back on the pillows. The last thing he needed to be thinking about was Credé.

⁂

Ash fought against sleep. He could not sleep here, not when he might wake screaming. He was just so tired, though …

The sounds of boots and commotion snapped him awake. Pushing himself up on his elbows, he saw people in the hallway carrying a stretcher. Somebody limped at the rear, leaning on a crutch. There was grunting and the scraping of furniture in the room across the hall, and terse words. The group moved out of sight, except for the man with the crutch, who collapsed into a chair near the door. A broken, sorry sight, he had bloodied bandages around his torso and blood-soaked sleeves. He dragged off his cap, revealing a mane of filthy-looking brown hair. Clutching his side, the warrior leaned forward, intent on whatever was happening, in spite of his obvious pain. Even from across the hall, Ash could hear the man's dragging, laboured breaths.

The period that followed was punctuated by tense instructions from Agnid. Ash caught glimpses of another figure in pale blue — Pallin, he guessed. Then came another flurry of activity. A woman's voice cried out: 'Please! Save her! Is there nothing you can do?' The muttered answer did not carry to Ash's ears. Then silence. A heavy silence, broken by the sound of low sobbing. The fellow in the chair sank his head into his hands. He stayed there, shuddering and trembling until he was led away, taking his grief with him.

Ash collapsed back onto the pillows. His heart was racing, his stomach clenched. Forcing himself to take long, slow breaths, he stared at the ceiling, counting the patterned tiles. His heart was still scampering when footsteps announced Pallin. The young man's thin nose ventured through the doorway first, followed by the rest of him.

'Hi, Ash.' Pallin's fringe hung low over his eyes, a curtain protecting him from the world. Awkwardly tall, he walked with his shoulders stooped.

'Hi, Pallin.'

Dressed in the uniform pale blue smock, Pallin bore a tray with two items on it. One was a black notebook; the other looked to be a flat strap of metal.

'I just need to …' The young man seemed so nervous that Ash found himself smiling, nodding encouragement. With a shy bob of his head, Pallin took Ash's hand. His fingers were long and cool, slightly freckled to match his face. The metal strap wrapped itself around Ash's wrist, making him jump a little. It wasn't uncomfortable — just strange. 'It will measure your heartbeat, and check that your body is not overheated' came the quiet explanation.

Ash had no idea how that might work. He nodded anyway. Pallin's eyes did not stray from the metal band. Ash stared at it, too. When nothing seemed to be happening, he ventured a question. 'Was that … more warriors?'

Pallin nodded. 'One didn't make it.' His quiet words confirmed what

Ash knew already. Neither spoke. Both were relieved when the object around Ash's wrist emitted a high chirping noise. A series of green numbers had appeared on its surface. Pallin made a tidy note in his notebook. 'That's good.' His eyes brushed Ash's. 'Everything seems good.' By some strange magic the circlet had transformed itself into a metal strip once more. Hearing footsteps, Pallin rose. 'Your friends,' he announced from the doorway. He made his escape, and the moment to quiz him about Agnid was lost.

❦

Kep flew into the room, preceded by Tarlyn who bounded onto the bed, giving a chirrup in greeting. Ash grinned in spite of himself. Both of them looked a bit bedraggled. Kep's quick eyes took in the bandage. 'Ash! Whatever have you done to yourself now?'

Her long blue tunic was fitted. A warrior's garment; the fabric flaring from the waist and split to enable easy movement. The pieces flew out like blades when she turned. Her cheeks were pink and flushed; like her hair, they looked wet.

'I'm perfectly fine,' Ash answered carefully. 'They put everyone to bed here. I just nicked my hand with a kitchen knife, that's all.' It was not really, but Kep did not need to know that. When Sarin appeared at the door, too, Ash groaned inwardly. Was there to be an entire audience?

'I went to find you in the kitchen.' Sarin's eyes also went straight to the bandage. 'Should have known you'd be taking a sneaky lie-down.'

Ash was grateful for his friend's banter. 'Yeah, well … I knew you'd be bringing in wagon-loads of game for me to dress, so I came here. You know me — I love to shirk.' Kep rolled her eyes at the pair of them, then her gaze was drawn again to the bandage. 'Really, Kep, it's just a scratch,' he reassured her. *He hoped.*

Although Sarin raised a brow, Kep at least seemed reassured. Fortunately, she was distracted by other news. 'Ash, guess what?' She beamed at Sarin. 'You were right, Sarin! It is snowing!' Her eyes were shining, bright blue with wonder. 'You have to come and see, Ash! It's so beautiful!'

Sarin grinned. 'And quite wet, too. You do know it's frozen water, don't you?'

For once Kep did not seem to mind his teasing. Pushing her wet curls out of her face, she laughed. 'I know! It's much wetter than I thought it would be!' She skipped to the window. Sadly it offered no view of the miracle.

When Ash promised that he would be up and about shortly anyway, and would see it for himself, she threw him a happy smile. Unclasping her cloak, she cast it aside. 'It's certainly lovely and warm in here!'

Sitting one either side of his bed, Kep and Sarin shared the rest of their news — as much as Sarin had been able to glean about the newcomers. Ash contributed what he knew about the unfortunate fate of the person on the stretcher, and Sarin nodded. 'She's not the only warrior they've lost. There have been some grim stories.' Ash swallowed, staring at his injured hand. He knew.

Sarin seemed about to say something else, then changed his mind. 'One of the men looks like a Cryer.' Seeing their mystified looks, he explained: 'You know: a Cryer, someone who sings for the living.' When they still gave no sign of understanding, he added, 'A guide for mourning.' His expression was bemused. 'Don't you have such a thing in Mildaresh?'

Ash was puzzled. How did Sarin know the man was a Cryer, just by looking at him? He exchanged a quick look with Kep, who shrugged. 'No, I don't think so.' Ash had no wish to explain The Fires of Passing ceremony to Sarin. He did not want to even think about it. Not since Braig. Not since that terrible day. 'Who else has come?' he asked, diverting the conversation.

'There are nine in total. Not all warriors. Apparently the Cryer has a daughter; I didn't catch a glimpse of her. But the Cryer's companion looks like a scholar. And from their garb,' Sarin's eyes were thoughtful, 'I reckon they've come down from Calkinon.'

'From Calkinon!' Kep and Ash exchanged glances.

Sarin laughed at their worried expressions. 'Not everyone in Calkinon is a guardian out to catch runaway slaves. Don't worry, you'll meet them tonight. Everyone will be at the welcome.' As if remembering something, Sarin tilted his head. 'Who was that woman, Ash? The nurse we saw on our way in?'

Ash filled them in on what little he knew about Agnid. They were just discussing how odd it was that none of them had seen her before when Nirias appeared in the doorway.

Ash caught his expression. For a brief moment he looked harried, concerned even. He smiled warmly, however, and entered the room.

Perhaps he was just weary from his travels. 'Here are my three Seekers!' Nirias was clean-shaven, his hair was brushed, and he had even found time to exchange his travelling clothes for a fresh white shirt and a long, belted coat of blue silk, worn over loose-fitting breeches. The coat had fine silver embroidery around the cuffs and collar, and was split at the back and sides — characteristically Azuran in its style.

'I'm pleased to say that the last of those who could be gathered have arrived in T'al Jazure — just in time for the snows.' As he gave Kep a smile his hazel-green eyes seemed to twinkle, as if he knew all about her excitement. 'Now, at last, we have time to rest, and learn. To prepare ourselves for whatever trials Fate may hold in store.'

Kep was shining with barely contained enthusiasm. Sarin, although not exactly hostile, had folded his arms. If Nirias noticed the young man's coolly neutral expression, he did not let it show. Instead, he clapped his hands together, and smiled at them all. 'But tonight, our first care is to welcome the newcomers to the city.' Sweeping his eyes over Kep and Sarin, he raised his brows, leaving an unspoken question in the air.

Kep jumped to her feet at once. 'Yes! I need to wash and change. Ash, will you follow as soon as you can?'

Ash promised for a third time that he would come and find her, and see the snow for himself. Sarin stood, too, picking up Kep's cloak. She flushed a little as he placed it around her shoulders. He gave Ash a nod, which only vaguely included Nirias, and followed her out.

Watching them go, Nirias tilted his head as if considering something. Then he drew a chair right up to the bed. 'Now then, Ash. Let us have a look at that wound.' His hands were deft and careful as he unravelled the bandage. Now that he could, Ash was not at all sure he wanted to look. He feared to see a gruesome gash. When the tail of the bandage pulled away, he blinked in surprise. There was no open wound on his hand at all — just the crescent weal of a new scar, curving red around the fleshy base of his thumb. Nirias made an appreciative sound.

Drawing Ash's hand towards him, he inspected the scar more closely. To most people, Nirias would appear to be in his middle years, with just a few traces of silver showing through his brown hair. Ash was one of the few people who knew better. For Nirias was one of the Malshorne, and capable of changing his shape. While Ash was not at all sure how that worked, it made him uncomfortable to think that Nirias had chosen this face. Faintly asymmetrical, neither ugly nor handsome, it was the face of a leader: a man you could trust.

The tattoo on Nirias's cheekbone was far more distinctive. It ran in curves and spirals down from his temple in delicate tendrils. Ash was wondering again whether it had some significance, when Nirias released him. 'Agnid and Pallin have looked after you well,' he smiled.

Ash took his chance to find out more about the mysterious nurse. 'Nirias, who is Agnid? I don't remember seeing her before. When did she arrive?'

Nirias answered quickly. 'She's a healer, Ash. One of our best — certainly the League's most experienced. Indeed, I don't think there has been an injury that the woman has not had to deal with.' The line of his mouth seemed to tighten. A shadow of pain crossed his face. Tarlyn, who was curled at the foot of the bed, lifted her head. She gave a mournful murmur. 'Agnid rarely leaves the House of Curing,' Nirias went on, rolling the bandage into a bundle. 'She prefers to keep to herself, and that is something we should all respect.' He gave Ash what seemed a rather stern look from beneath his eyebrows. Although the man had not fully answered his question, Ash let the subject drop.

As Nirias leaned towards him, Ash wished he would not fold his hands together in quite that manner. For some reason it reminded him uncomfortably of Credé. 'Your physical wound is healing well.' Although the older man's expression was not unsympathetic, Ash felt pinned beneath his gaze. 'But I fear that is not the real problem.'

When Ash did not answer, Nirias waited, motionless and silent.

'I was jointing a rabbit, and … I supposed I fainted.' Nirias did not respond, so he went on uneasily. 'The knife slipping was the last thing I remember.'

Nirias's voice was gentle, at odds with the intensity of his gaze. 'What do you think caused you to faint this time?'

There was no point lying. 'Zondra.' The name caught in Ash's throat. 'I overheard Reardon telling Jaibari about what happened in Zondra — after the swarm.'

Nirias let out a deep sigh. 'It is not surprising that such talk would have overwhelmed you, Ash. It is hard for anyone to hear. The Melk swarms rarely. When it does, it leaves an aftermath of chaos, madness and suffering. With their oppressors suddenly confused and reeling, the victims turn. Some become bullies themselves. Revenge creates a new cycle of misery.

Fresh horrors. The events at Zondra were terrible, and not something our warriors have encountered before, not in this lifetime.' Something subtle behind his eyes left Ash in little doubt that Nirias was speaking from personal experiences of such terror.

Then the older man composed himself. 'It is hardly gossip for the kitchen. But do not blame Reardon. He is a young man yet, and inexperienced for all his tales. Giving voice to the horror is one step on the road to healing. An important step.' Nirias leaned forward. Perhaps he might have taken Ash's hand, had Ash not pulled away. 'That the story affected you deeply is not surprising. You are the Taelstaun, Ash — the Keeper of the Song — and you are yet to fully understand what that means, let alone be equipped to deal with such emotion, such terrible sorrow.'

Nirias's brow furrowed. 'I'm sorry. I have failed you. If only I could be in two places at once ... But now I am returned. I admit, the workings of the Song are a mystery to me, almost as much as they are to you, but we have the Knowledge Stores to help us. Together, we will find a way for you to manage the burden of the Song. You have my solemn oath.' He pressed his fingertips together. 'You have all the songs of all the world inside your head, Ash. No wonder it feels like chaos. No wonder your body rebels.'

Ash was fighting back tears, but Nirias seemed not to have noticed. He went on, almost speaking to himself. 'The Song is a burden, there is no doubt. It is a terrible burden that you never—' At that moment Tarlyn sat up and stretched. A ruff of spines appeared around her neck. They quivered in warning, then, with a shake, were gone again. As Tarlyn turned her huge, unblinking eyes on Nirias, his words faltered. He seemed to catch himself, blinked several times and sat up in his chair. A smile made its way to his mouth, if not his eyes. 'But ... Ash. What am I thinking? We have time. An entire winter. Tomorrow!'

Like a fresh shirt to cover his weariness, Nirias put on a cheerful mood. He pushed back his chair. 'Tomorrow we begin. And the first thing you will learn, Ash, is that you are far from alone in this struggle.' Nirias almost bounced to his feet. 'And you have allies, some of whom you will meet tonight. We will all help you bear this Fate.' His eyes twinkled. 'What's more ... I believe you are about to get your first sight of snow.'

Chapter 4

TREPIDATION

Shuddering with delight, Kep lowered herself into the water, sinking deeper, until it lapped just beneath her nose. Her mouth blew bubbles at the surface. Eyes closed, she aimed her chin at the ceiling, head cradled by the moulded neck rest, letting her arms float. The oil she had used to perfume the water sent wafts of lemon and lavender into the steam. T'al Jazure had many marvels, but the bath houses were Kep's favourite. It was not just the abundance of hot water flowing like magic from spouts and slots in the walls at the mere turn of a lever. There were dials to adjust the temperature and others to regulate the steam, brushes and ladles and scrapers, scented candles and pots of perfumed oil.

This room, Kep's favourite, was one of several bath houses adjoining the Sable Lodge. The space was small, only ten or so paces across, with the round polished bath at its centre. Sunken, with a ledge all the way around, the bath reminded Kep of a deep pot of cream. A wooden rack leaned against one wall, next to which were a simple wooden bench and a cubby-hole for towels. Apart from that, the space was empty. It was far from sparse, though. Every surface was tiled in mosaics featuring plants and flowing vines — it was like being inside a secret forest dell. Even the door was patterned to match, making it almost invisible to the eye. But best of all was the ceiling, which, in spite of the steam, was crystal-clear glass. Kep had been utterly astonished the first time she had looked up to see the stars winking back at her.

There were larger bath houses, too: huge decorated affairs, like halls, or temples even, with lakes of hot water, secluded nooks and deep pools where people might soak and chat together in groups. Kep found the whole idea very strange. The Azuri obviously had had very different notions about modesty than Mildarens. In Mildaresh, even the wealthiest nobles had their slaves bring hot water and stones to their private chambers. Kep could not imagine sharing her bath with other people. Still, she had never imagined having a hot bath at all — slaves made do with a quick cold splash, quicker and colder in winter. She let the water play over her fingers, then ran her thumb across the skin on her left wrist. Perhaps it was her imagination, but the tattooed marks seemed darker now. No amount of soap from the pretty bottles would make them fade.

She lay back, trying to relax. It was hard. She was excited, and curious — especially about the three newcomers from Calkinon. Sarin had said that their clothes gave them away; Kep wondered what he meant. She had seen Calkinon uniforms of course. The guardians in Mildaresh, as in all tribune cities, wore slim, tailored coats with high collars and shiny helmets. She hardly imagined that everyone in Calkinon dressed like guardians, though. With Calkinon being a city of extraordinary wealth, her people probably dressed in fine silks and embroidered gowns.

There would be new warriors to welcome, too. No two alike, if they were anything like those who had come already. Kep sighed. She hated introductions. Everyone else had proper names and titles, anchors fixing them to their family. Not Sarin of course, he was just Sarin of Aurum. He scoffed openly at formal introductions, especially if they ran on to list fathers and grandsires. The clans had no need for surnames, he said — everyone knew the kinship lines. It was not helpful. Kep could hardly just be Kep of Mildaresh. And while 'Sarin of Aurum' claimed kinship, 'Kep of the House of Aranti' was a very different thing. It bound her to her past master, as his property, and to her status as a slave.

The worst thing was that everyone already seemed to know who she was. 'Kep the Valiant.' She scowled. She had done precious little to earn the title. She had merely stood up to her master, by releasing a bird at Braig's funeral fire to save him from eternal slavery. She had simply done what was right. Yet that one action had turned her into some kind of folk hero. No wonder if the warriors were sneering behind her back. She knew Jaibari was. The fierce young woman had been scornful right from the very beginning, even before Ash had managed to unlock the hidden city of T'al Jazure.

Kep rubbed her hands over her face, letting herself sink deeper into the warm water. Deeper and deeper she sank, until she was completely submerged, looking up at the jostling plane of the water's surface, feeling her hair swaying about her. Her ears sang and her heartbeat pounded in her chest. Then, in a surge of water, she rose up. It was time. Kep squeezed her hair, letting the water flow down her body. She smiled to herself. Things were about to change.

⁂

Two surprises were waiting for Kep in her room. The first was a solid, square bag made of tan leather with large buckled pockets on each side. It had been deposited just inside the door, near the foot of the unoccupied bed. Kep had no idea to whom it belonged. But its presence could only mean one thing: she was about to get a roommate. That was not such a surprise, as most of the warriors shared a room, and this was the largest room on the women's side of the lodge.

Set at the corner of the building, the room had two slanted windows looking up at the trees and sky. It was comfortably furnished, too, with two cosy beds; it even had a couple of padded chairs. The walls were a deep forest green, featuring a variety of trees and flowering plants. The foliage was painted so realistically that it seemed to have made its way in from the garden. The timber floors, polished so they gleamed like honey, were softened by deep rugs with patterned scrolls of flowers.

Kep did not mind the idea of sharing. It was embarrassing to have all this luxury to herself. She just would have liked to have met the person before the bag. She stared at it, arms folded, wondering about the owner. The Cryer's daughter, perhaps? No. It did not seem the sort of bag a young lady would own. It was battered and scratched — a practical bag. Of course there was an easy way to find out who owned it: she could just stop procrastinating and make her way to the hall. Kep caught her lip between her teeth. Not yet. Frowning a little, she turned her attention to the second surprise.

The little casket was woven from multicoloured grasses. It was a gift — from Sarin. He must have smuggled it into the pocket of her cloak earlier. Such a strange young man. It was not the first gift. On the ledge above her bed was a polished rock, a carving of a miniature wolvern, and a leather pouch embroidered with tiny starflowers. Each had been wrapped in the same way, as beautifully as the gift itself had been crafted. The lid of the intricate casket was secured by a tiny loop, caught around a shiny brown seed. Kep was just easing it off with her thumb when she heard a faint knock at the door. She shoved the casket under her pillow and smoothed her clothes.

It was just Ash. He entered the room, his face a picture of misery. He was wearing a plain, fawn-coloured coat with matching leggings. Not grey. Why did it always strike her as wrong when Ash wore something other than grey? As always, his hair looked a bit ruffled. He avoided looking at her. It made her wonder about her dress. Was the bodice too snug? Too late to change. Who would have thought it would be so tricky choosing clothes to wear? Kep had no experience of such things; she had only ever had one choice — a tunic in Aranti green.

'You're ready, then.' Ash hugged his arms across his chest, shuffling from one foot to the other. 'That's good,' he told the chairs. 'I thought … we might go in together?'

Kep wrinkled her nose. 'We could just hide,' she suggested. 'Perhaps under the bed?'

Ash gave her a half-hearted smile. She recognised that look of panic in his eyes. Best not put it off any longer. She lifted her chin. 'Thank you for collecting me, Ash. It will be so much easier going in together.'

Chapter 5

THE CRYER'S DAUGHTER

The hall of the Sable Lodge was certainly impressive. Six tree trunks stretched upwards, supporting the roof with splayed fingers. The roof was sharp-pitched, high enough to accommodate balustraded gantries on either side. At the far end, two polished staircases tumbled down to meet on a raised platform. The effect was quite breathtaking, yet it was the window which stole the eyes. An elaborate segmented triangle, it broke the view of the gardens into shining fragments, offering different compositions depending on where one stood. Tonight, the view was eerily beautiful: blue-lit trees under falling snow.

Kep and Ash did not enter the main hall immediately; instead, hovering in the cloistered hallway connecting the common area to the private quarters. As elsewhere in the city, the archway had been decorated with particular care. This one was greystone, carved to resemble braided hair, studded with tiny flowers.

Ash paid it little attention. He was finding it hard to take his eyes from the huge window and the hypnotic falling snow. It was strange to think about it falling on the city with nobody to see it. Every living soul was here, inside the Sable Lodge. If Sarin was right, the nine newcomers would bring their total to fifty-two. Fifty-two people, in a city built for several thousand. When something brushed at his mind, Ash shivered. Realising he had been rubbing his hands against his sides in nervous circles, he tucked them under his armpits. He was grateful for Kep's silent presence beside him.

Everything in the lodge spoke of warmth and homely comforts. The hall boasted a blazing fire of course. But what a fireplace! Wholly encased in glass, it hung in mid-air like a floating lantern, its flames dancing behind glass. Rich hangings brought colour to the space, emerald greens and deep blues. Rustic in design, the textiles featured images of birds and animals. The parquet floor was themed on Nature, too. The sable timber floors, which gave the lodge its name, were inlaid with a charming motif of tiny fish. They swam in groups, around bright rugs, which were scattered on the floor like lily pads. Atop each rug was a table, low to the ground and ringed with colourful cushions. At the centre of each table stood a glowing lamp of coloured glass. The whole effect was harmonious and comfortable. It was a room designed to bring people together, to put them at their ease — precisely the opposite of how Ash was feeling.

As they watched, more people arrived. Some embraced, with hearty warrior embraces. Others exchanged wary looks and slight nods. Nobody was sitting down yet. Scanning the room, Ash recognised Jaibari leaning against a pillar on the opposite side of the hall, her arms folded in challenge. The young woman was every bit as unfriendly as she had been at their first encounter at the Stone. Ash had no idea why. Perhaps just because they were not the fierce warriors she considered herself. He avoided her uncompromising stare.

Not surprisingly, given the smells emanating from the kitchen, people were starting to congregate at the opposite end from the window wall with its perpetually falling snow. The twins were there: impossible to miss, gigantic, towering replicas, with hair shaved up the sides and dragged into topknots. Muku and Tuku were grinning, sharing a private joke.

A pair of silver-headed men stood at the edge of the group, deep in conversation. One was Daska; the other Ash had not seen before — a smaller, wiry-looking chap with long straggled hair and an air of restlessness. When the man's eyes slid to meet his, Ash looked away. The pair had resumed their conversation by the time he looked back again. He had a distinct impression they were talking about him, or Kep. It was not unusual for newcomers to stare. Unlike Sarin, who somehow managed to look as if he belonged anywhere, Ash and Kep were decidedly out of place.

Kep nudged Ash's arm, drawing his attention to a large figure who had entered from the other side of the hall. The man's head was completely bald with prominent bumps on his skull that shone under the lamplight. He wore a long grey garment and a grave expression. His eyes seemed sunken, as if he was ill. 'Do you think that's him?' Kep whispered. 'The Cryer?'

Ash shrugged. She could be right. Was a shiny bald head the mark of a Cryer?

He was trying to get a better look at the man, when somebody sang out a greeting beside him. Turning, Ash found himself answering without thinking. The young woman had tawny brown hair, which was braided from her hairline back across her crown in small plaits. The plaits came together at the back of her head, in an intricate braid that ran down her back. Across her brow, secured by a leather thong, was a silver ornament in the shape of a fox's head. Grey-green eyes smiled at them from a heart-shaped face. The woman gave a pretty laugh, and shook her head.

'I confess, that's all I know,' she explained. 'My mother was from the Singing Isles, but I never learned the tongue.' When Ash blinked in confusion, she bowed her head. 'You must be Ash. Rodine said you had the look of the Zari, and he was right.'

Ash had no idea how to respond. He was relieved when she turned her attention to Kep.

'And you are Kep, of course.' She smiled, a hint of curiosity touching her eyes. 'My name is Eliayliah Larien.' After another merry laugh, she went on: 'I know. It's just a string of vowels! My mother's fault. It's a name to be sung really, so don't even try to pronounce it. Everyone calls me El.'

Recovering from her surprise, Kep murmured a greeting. Ash could feel her looking sideways at him. El was saying she had travelled up from Ebadour in the south, with four others. She pointed out one of her companions, a blockish woman with a mop of tight red curls. El was promising to introduce her when another young woman of a similar age sauntered into the room. El's eyes flew wide with excitement. 'Pretalla!' She ran across the room to embrace the newcomer.

Ash recognised the blonde-haired warrior as having arrived with a previous group, just a few days back. He had not met her, and he was not at all sure he wanted to. A hard expression was made even more intimidating by the tattoo that ran across her face from ear to ear. She wore black paint beneath her eyes, and her hair was a jumble of braids, beads and small objects, some of which looked suspiciously like small bones. Her plaits whipped out dangerously as she swung El into a rough embrace.

Kep had been trying unsuccessfully to get his attention. Now she gave him a nudge.

'Ash, what was that?' Her blue eyes searched his face. 'That woman just sang at you. And you … you sang back.'

Ash frowned. 'I suppose I did. I'd just heard the melody before, so … I didn't think about it really.'

'So it was part of the Song.' Kep looked anxious. Everything about the Song worried her. 'Well? What did it mean?'

Ash was not sure it was anything to do with the Song. It felt like something he had known but had forgotten. When Kep pressed him, he muttered: 'May your song ring true … ? Or something like that … And the answer was something about harmony.' *Sweet harmonies be yours.* How did he know that? Ash blinked and gave Kep what he hoped was a casual shrug. 'It's funny that she would shorten her name to a slave's name, don't you think?'

Kep frowned. He could tell she was not going to be so easily distracted, and was grateful when Sarin joined them. He was chewing something, a mischievous glint in his eyes.

Ash thought he could guess where Sarin had been: in the kitchens antagonising the cook. It was a mystery why Jen-Jay had been given the job of cook — she certainly had no culinary skills. He supposed she was just too old to be a warrior. The small silver-haired woman was eternally grumpy and it seemed that she hated cooking. For some reason Sarin found it amusing to see if he could make the woman even more surly. He delighted in mocking her food, and made a hobby out of pilfering morsels, always choosing something tiny, just to see if her sharp eyes would miss it. Now he was licking his fingers and grinning.

'Why are you two skulking here? You look like a couple of thieves.' Settling one shoulder against the arch, with one foot crossed over the other, Sarin ran his tongue along his lips. He leisurely surveyed the room as he spoke. 'I know you haven't taken the Pledge, but you are allowed in, you know. You don't have to lurk here looking guilty.'

Kep made a show of rolling her eyes at him, and Ash noticed that she had gone pink. She did that a lot around Sarin. 'We're perfectly happy, thank you. We've just met somebody, called El.' Ash winced when she added: 'She sang at Ash.'

Sarin just laughed. 'Eliayliah Larien,' he corrected. 'But don't even try to pronounce it,' he said, fluttering his eyelashes, 'it's just a string of vowels.' Ash could not help snorting. Sarin was such a brilliant mimic. He had articulated the words exactly as El had done. 'Lucky you, Ash. She didn't sing at me. What did I do wrong?'

Ash laughed at Sarin's mock hurt expression, in spite of his own discomfort. 'She said I looked like one of the Zari.'

'She's right. You do.' Sarin nodded. He paused, no doubt enjoying their perplexed expressions. 'The Zari are a remnant people of the Wimsari

Empire. Their home was the isle of Baktah. And they all had grey hair and eyes, just like you.'

Kep's eyebrows flew up in surprise. She shook her head. 'By Telion, Sarin! If you knew all that ...' She clicked her tongue, exasperated. 'Why do you always have to be so sly? You could have mentioned it sooner! Especially with everyone staring at poor Ash the way they do.' Ash did not much like being referred to as 'poor Ash', but she did have a valid point. 'Honestly,' added Kep with a sniff, 'it makes me wonder what else you haven't told us.'

Sarin's golden eyes shifted. He was always hard to read, but Ash thought his expression clouded now, just fleetingly. Then the impression was gone. His shrug could not have been more nonchalant. 'Sorry, Ash. In my defence, I only found out myself last night. Read it in a book.' A teasing smile played on his lips. 'There are loads of books here, Kep.' He quirked an eyebrow. 'The one I found about the Wimsari even has pictures.' When Kep scowled at him, Sarin laughed. Then he looked Ash straight in the eye. 'The people do look like you, Ash. Exactly like you, in fact. I can show you tomorrow if you like. Assuming Nirias doesn't have plans for us all.'

The conversation had shaken Ash, but he nodded agreement. Although they shared a room, Sarin's bed was rarely occupied and he seemed to spend his nights roaming the city. It made perfect sense that the Knowledge Stores had been part of his investigation. With all the work preparing for winter, moving supplies from the labyrinth of caves, stockpiling food and organising people, there had been little time for anyone else to explore the city. Ash wondered what else Sarin had found out. He promised himself that from now on he would ask more questions of his unusual friend.

Kep clearly had questions, too, but she had to wait. At that moment a group of people entered from the opposite hallway, bringing a buzz of conversation with them. Nirias was among the bunch, walking with two men, one a full head taller than himself, dressed all in black, the other short and clad in brown. 'Aha.' Sarin nodded in their direction. 'Here's the Cryer.'

'Which one? Is he the tall man in black?' Kep craned her neck around the archway to see. 'Is there a girl with him? Can you see his daughter?'

Sarin laughed, shaking his head. 'So many questions, Kep! I'm not your guide. You have to find out your own answers.' Then he relented. 'Oh, all right. I'll introduce you to Aechon. Come on.'

To their surprise, the Cryer was not the tall, grim-looking man, but the cheery little chap at his side. Ash understood at once how Sarin had known he was a Cryer: it was impossible to miss the tattoo around his neck. The bird was worked in exquisite detail, its head and beak perfectly aligned at his throat. The wing feathers swept around his jaw, like a dark collar. Aechon was clean-shaven with a mop of curly brown hair, which, despite a whisper of grey, made him seem boyish. His asymmetrical waistcoat fitted snugly over his belly. With leggings and doublet pieced together from different fabrics, all various shades of brown, it looked as if he was wearing a pile of autumn leaves.

The Cryer broke away from the group when he saw them coming.

'Aechon, these are my friends: Kep and Ash of Mildaresh,' announced Sarin smoothly.

'I am most honoured.' The Cryer made an elegant bow. His voice was deeper than expected, and mellow. Chestnut brown eyes twinkled at them. 'Allow me to introduce my companion, Gallin.' At the sound of his name, the tall man turned, drew his heels together and gave a stiff bow. His long face was made even longer by the height of his forehead and the raven-coloured hair which framed his face like a pair of black curtains. The man had full, sensuous lips, yet creases at either side of his mouth and deep frown lines made him look quite severe. He was as different from Aechon as a man could be. Of the two, he seemed much better suited to matters of death.

Aechon dropped his voice. 'It is a great pleasure to meet you. I believe we have you three to thank for this most fortunate turn of events.' He gestured at their surroundings and beamed at them all. 'Nirias tells me that I may be of particular service to you, Ash. And I would be delighted to help in any way that I can.'

Ash swallowed. Few people knew about the Song and how T'al Jazure had been unlocked — only the three friends, and Nirias and Daska, who had all witnessed the miracle first-hand. Nirias had suggested they keep it to themselves. Ash exchanged a quick worried look with Kep as Aechon went on.

'Tomorrow I will begin the Gleaning, for the two souls who have passed. It will be a chance for us to speak further.' Ash already knew that the Gleaning was the process of collecting stories and memories about those who had died, in preparation for the Sorrow. What he did not know was what that had to do with him. He nodded anyway.

Aechon beamed around him. 'Ha! When we left Calkinon we thought ourselves destined to spend the winter huddled in caves.' He gave a happy sigh.

'It is true then? You have come from Calkinon?' Kep's eyes were wide.

Aechon nodded. 'Quite true. The wondrous city of the lake — in all its splendour.' He chuckled and cast a glance at the man beside him. 'I'm afraid we had to leave in rather a hurry.'

Gallin drew his long fingers together in a disapproving steeple. 'Because somebody cried the wrong passing.'

Aechon gave him a fond smile. 'Don't sulk, Gallin, there's a good chap. It's all turned out beautifully, after all. I'm sure the workshops here will be exquisite. Even better than in Calkinon … Ah!'

Following his eyes, they saw that a young woman had entered the room. 'Here comes my daughter, Ordelle.' His eyebrows gave a little quiver. 'Kep, I'm hoping very much that you might get along. Ordelle does not know anyone here. In fact,' his fingers patted his lips, 'Nirias suggested that perhaps you might like to share a room?'

Sarin folded his arms. Ash could guess what he was thinking. Why had Nirias failed to mention this earlier? There were still empty rooms on the women's side of the lodge. Kep was already assuring Aechon that of course she would be happy to share. Gallin's expression was blank, except for the slightest lift of an eyebrow. Ignoring whatever meaning that eyebrow held, the Cryer beamed. 'Wonderful. That's just wonderful.' He clapped his hands together, and beckoned to his daughter, who strode quickly towards them. 'And here she is. I'm sure you young people can introduce yourselves. Come, Gallin. Let us find some of that ale that Nirias promised.' And with that, he gave them a quick smile, an even quicker bow, and wandered off.

The Cryer's daughter was tall and angular. Her dark purple garments seemed to hang from her frame in pieces. She surveyed them, hands on hips, elbows poking forward. 'You've got yellow eyes.'

To his credit, Sarin did not so much as flinch. 'Yes. You've got bulging ones … and a gigantic nose.'

Ash winced, but the description was accurate. The girl's pale blue eyes did seem to bulge, and her nose was large and hooked. She nodded, as if exchanging insults with strangers was perfectly normal. 'My name is Ordelle,' she announced. 'It means hope.'

Sarin made no effort to hide his grin. He made a sweeping gesture after the fashion of his clan and introduced himself.

Ash shot a glance at Kep. Her mouth was hanging open. He completely understood why. For one thing, it was hard to imagine a less hopeful-looking young woman. Ordelle had none of her father's merry roundness. Her straight brown hair was like a helmet; chopped short to her jawline, with a fringe cut square above her eyes. An overly large mouth, turned down at the corners, completed the gloomy visage. 'You are Kep and Ash. From Mildaresh.'

Before she could accuse him of having grey hair, Ash muttered something about being happy to meet her and made a bow.

Kep had recovered her manners, too. She even made a curtsy. 'It is very nice to meet you, Ordelle.' Ash knew nothing about the intricacies of curtsies, but the attempt looked quite good. There was nothing polite, though, about the look Kep shot Sarin, who was grinning from ear to ear and bouncing on the balls of his feet. Although she looked ready to slap him, she managed a smile, as she turned her attention back to their new companion. 'Um ... Did you travel well, Ordelle?'

'Yes.' The girl's manner was most disconcerting. She either gazed about in a drifting, dispassionate manner or stared fixedly when something caught her attention.

'I think we are to be roommates.'

'Yes.'

Kep persevered, making further attempts at conversation. Each was met with flat, one-word answers. Ash stared at his feet, avoiding Kep's imploring blue eyes. Obviously highly amused by the whole awkward situation, Sarin did not offer any help either. At last Kep's attempts petered out. As they stood there in silence, Ordelle continued staring about; it did not seem to matter to her whether anyone spoke or not.

When a commotion near the kitchens announced the promise of food, Ash was grateful for the distraction and looked over hopefully. Nothing eventuated, though. Just the clatter of platters and a slamming door. Kep was opening her mouth, perhaps intending to warn Ordelle of Jen-Jay's awful food, when Gallin came to the rescue by claiming the Cryer's daughter for further introductions. Ash wondered whether the man's solemn apology was for taking her away, or for leaving her with them in the first place. Either way, he was so relieved he wanted to clap the man on the shoulder.

As the three friends watched the pair go, Sarin seemed about to speak. Kep held up a finger, her eyes flashing. 'No! Don't you dare say anything … either of you!'

⁂

The evening meal was shambolic. The meat managed to be both leather-dry and raw at the bone. Soggy, unrecognisable vegetables dripped water. The bread was so dense it required vigorous and sustained chewing. Kep learned this the hard way when a piece stuck in her gullet. Gulping like a fisher bird, she swigged at her ale, trying to wash the lump down. It did not help that she was sitting cross-legged on a cushion.

Wiping tears from her eyes, she glanced around the room. While some warriors lounged at their ease, many looked as if they would prefer the wilderness and a proper smoking fire. The laughter and conversation were undercut by an air of watchfulness.

Their own table, near the big window, was an uneasy refuge of almost complete silence. Next to Ash, folded into a muddle of knees and elbows, was Pallin. Head down, with his sharp nose and long fringe, he reminded Kep of a heron. And so shy! He made Ash seem quite talkative. Neither of the strangers were inclined to conversation. The man was gruff in his manners. Blinking rapidly, he'd told them his name was Jakarmon Pyke, and then ignored them. Only once did he lift his head from his food, to stare at the falling snow accusingly, licking his fingers before returning his attention to his bowl. Perhaps he was expecting the snow to have stopped. It had not. It was coming down even faster, in soft clumps that weighed on the branches. Watching him from the corner of her eye, Kep guessed Jakarmon Pyke had some thirty winters — it was hard to tell with that tangled beard and hair. Something about his eyes, and the coiled tension of his body made her wary of looking too long.

His companion, Heeda, turned out to be the redheaded woman whom El had pointed out earlier, whose curls hovered about her shoulders in a mass of red. She'd grunted on hearing Kep's name, and that was the full extent of her conversation. Eating only a little, she had already shoved her plate away. Over the top of her mug she stared dead-eyed at the snow. Although there was an air of familiarity between the two, they ignored each other as much as anyone else. Perhaps they were grieving for their dead companion.

Ash looked as if he was going to be sick. Kep wanted to tell him to cheer up — the food was not that bad. The air was so heavy she actually found herself missing Sarin's foolish banter. Where had he taken himself off to this time? Hunting out gossip no doubt, or tormenting Jen-Jay in the kitchens.

Kep was wondering if she could just sneak away to the room that was no longer her private refuge when a man clambered to his feet. Sarin had dubbed him Benji the Bear, for obvious reasons. His real name was Benjin Dale. The huge warrior rumbled for attention, raising his arms and encouraging everyone to clap their hands and bang their mugs. Kep added her voice to the mix. Sarin joined their table as the cheer went up. *Nirias! Nirias!*

Nirias was laughing as he made his way through the crowd. Kep thought he was about to leap up onto the staged area, but instead he sat on its edge. Leaning forward, forearms resting upon his knees, he smiled down at his band of warriors, against a backdrop of falling snow. It was almost as if he was about to tell a story to a group of children. People gathered a little closer.

Through some acoustic trick, or mastery of his own, Nirias barely needed to raise his voice for all to hear. 'My brave warriors, my comrades, my friends,' he began.

It was the most beautiful speech Kep had ever heard. Nirias spoke softly, with words of welcome and words of comfort. They were safe, he told them. T'al Jazure had no need for guards, barricades and battlements. Nobody could pass through the city's rim, even if they stumbled through the Enigmata and happened by chance upon the Stone. They were entirely safe here. Warm and safe.

Tonight, Nirias told them, was not the time for plans — though that time would come. Tonight was not the time to speak of the dangers of the future nor the lessons of the past — that time would come. Nor would he speak of those who had been lost — he simply acknowledged their names, drawing deep sighs from the crowd. Raycha and Darias, the most recent. Nirias shook his head slowly, casting sad eyes over the room. There were others, he said. Others, whom they were yet to mourn.

Kep felt as if he was speaking to her alone. She bowed her head, swallowing hard. *Braig*. And Gooel. Gooel, the tracker who had hunted her so doggedly, only to give his life for hers. Kep lost the thread of what Nirias was saying for a while as she puzzled over that fact. Why had the tracker not acted on his kill orders? Why follow her all the way from Mildaresh, if not to kill her?

When Aechon rose, bowing deeply, Kep realised she had missed the Cryer's formal introduction. Nirias was already explaining that tonight Aechon would begin the Gleaning, gathering the stories of those who had passed. A sorrowful pause followed this announcement, and Nirias closed his eyes for a moment, overwhelmed by emotion. Then he smiled a painful smile. 'But now, my friends, my kin,' he swept his arms wide, 'now is also the time for rest — for peace, for memory, and for deep, deep sorrow.' His last words were simple: 'May the Gleaning begin.' All around, people took up the phrase, repeating it under their breaths like the faint echo of a chant.

As Kep watched Nirias walking back through the crowd, putting his hand on a shoulder here and there, she felt as if her heart might burst. All at once Kep knew she was a part of something, something important. And, for the first time, they were safe. Completely safe. She had time, and she knew she could rise to the challenge. When the League returned to Mildaresh, she would be ready. Ready to play her part. A peaceful determination welled up inside her as she turned to her friends.

'Wasn't that a beautiful speech?'

'Lovely. Especially all that stuff about what he was not going to say.'

Kep spluttered. She was thinking up a suitable retort to put Sarin in his place when she caught sight of the expression on Heeda's face. The woman's eyes were smouldering, boring into Nirias's back with fierce intensity. Whatever she was thinking, it was definitely not pleasant.

Frowning, Kep turned to Ash, wanting to know what he had thought of the speech. Ash did not even hear her. He was staring at the snow again, with a bewildered expression on his face. Kep seriously doubted that he had heard the speech at all.

Chapter 6

THE LEAGUE

Karliana arched her brows. 'Fifteen piero for a measure of Mildaren musk-wine? How utterly ridiculous!'

The stall-keeper folded her arms across a grubby-looking apron. 'It's in short supply,' she countered.

'In short supply? After such a good season? *And* … if I were wearing a Moagli armband? What would the price be then?'

'Shhh!' Karliana's companion glanced at the nearby guardian. Seeing he was looking the other way, she giggled behind her fingers. 'They don't have women in the Squad, silly.'

Karliana glowered. 'Well, I refuse to patronise such robbery.' She swept away, her plans of making her father's favourite dessert of flat-cakes soaked in musk-wine completely ruined.

Her companion had to scamper to keep up. 'Oh dear! Karliana, don't be sad! You're not going to cry, are you?'

Karliana ground her teeth. 'I'm not sad, I'm angry.'

'Oh dear!' A bag of sugared nuts was pushed in her direction. 'Have a dainty.' It was Fionella Mercardi's answer to everything — so long as there was a good supply of sweet treats and pretty ribbons, everything would be fine. Ignoring the offer, Karliana looked about her, struck yet again by the compelling absence of noise. Where were those mischievous urchins who used to romp through Mildaresh long after sundown, making the adults holler and laugh? The closer it got to twilight, the emptier the streets became.

By the time they had passed into the Arion Third, most of the shutters were closed. 'Oh, Edini's is shut! We can't have spiced wine. How disappointing!' Fionella pouted at the shuttered windows. 'Nothing's the same anymore. It's all that slave's fault. That Kep. She ruined everything. Stupid slave. I hope they catch her soon and punish her cruelly.'

Karliana caught her lip between her teeth. Her father said the longer Kep stayed free, the more she would fuel the spirit of rebellion — and not just in Mildaresh. Swifts came every day, bearing fresh tidings of unrest. Karliana shivered, wrapping her shawl across her throat. Was it wrong to pray for the safety of the slave who had sparked such strife?

'Whatever are you looking so gloomy and worried about, Karliana? You're not terribly good company, you know.'

Karliana sucked in a breath, making her teeth whistle. There was plenty to worry about these days: Calkinon's investigation into the death of her ambassador; the growing power of the Moagli Squad; the curfew denying citizens the right to walk in their own streets after twilight; the confiscation of property; Aranti's unprecedented control of the Senate; beatings; executions … Surely any one of these was enough to make a person very worried indeed? Karliana frowned sideways at her companion. 'Are you not concerned about the rule of the new Mildari?'

'Of course not. Not in the slightest. Everybody says the Squad is essential in quelling the rebellion. Everything will return to normal soon, you'll see.' Popping another dainty into her mouth, Fionella giggled. 'You are a silly worry-wart.'

Karliana flushed. Being called silly by Fionella Mercadi really was the final straw.

'You stupid girl!' When a tiny piece of spittle landed on Fionella's plump, rosy cheek Karliana nearly laughed, but anger overruled the impulse. 'Can you be so brainless, Fionella? Can you not see the danger? Are you blind?'

Fionella made a gaping motion with her little mouth and tossed her ringlets. 'Well! There's no need to be rude — just because your father isn't Mildari anymore. Perhaps Aranti doesn't look as nice in his robes, but he's a strong man. And that's what's needed in these times — everybody says so.'

'Everybody says so,' mimicked Karliana, in spite of her good breeding. 'But is Aranti a *good* man? Tell me that! Does anybody say Aranti is a good man? Do they?'

She grabbed Fionella by her fleshy forearm, making her squeal. The girl's eyes flew wide. 'Karliana! You're overwrought,' she whimpered. Wisely, she did not offer more sweets.

Karliana released her grip and lowered her voice, remembering where they were. 'Yes, I'm upset! But you …' her fingers clenched and unclenched several times as she searched for words, 'you are just an empty-headed simpleton!' Turning on her heel, she marched headlong down the nearest alleyway.

Stupid, stupid, stupid! Karliana's feet flew to the fierce rhythm of her thoughts. A strong man? Pah! Her father should have spoken out, they all should have. But he had handed over the robes of office without a murmur. She marched on, propelled by anger. And now Maliagne Aranti was untouchable! None dared oppose him!

When one of Karliana's shoes lost its grip, she glared at the uneven cobbles. Only then did she slow — something wasn't right. Had she missed a turn? Nothing looked familiar until she recognised a tree. Its trunk was fitted with an ingenious wooden bench. Her hand flew to her mouth. She had been heading straight into the crooked mazes of the artisans!

In the old days Karliana had thought nothing of visiting the artisans' sector. She had loved negotiating the chaotic clutter of painters and potters, perhaps stopping to listen to a wandering musician or to buy some trinket to please a friend. Now the sector had a sinister reputation — a dangerous place for a noblewoman to venture alone. Stupid! How stupid she had been, storming off like that. Stupid … and alone!

As she turned to retrace her steps Karliana froze, for she was not alone at all. A figure in black stood there, blocking the path.

Karliana recognised the high, polished boots and slim cut of the guardian's uniform. It should have been a reassuring sight. It was not. Karliana raised her chin. Confidence was everything; if she simply strolled by, or even bid the man good evening, he might pass on. She held her nerve, and her breath. She was quite close, and preparing a polite nod when he spoke: 'Good evening, Miss Karliana.'

'Oh! Good evening.' Karliana thought he was the guardian from the marketplace, but she could not be certain. All of the guardians wore their helmets these days, making them look so much like beetles it was hard to tell them apart. Her heart gave an urgent little hop. If it was the same man, he must have followed her! How did he know her name? 'Do I recognise you from somewhere?' she asked, as lightly as she could.

The guardian bowed. 'Indeed, you might remember me, my lady.' He took off his helmet and the beetle became a man. 'Bellart is my name. I was one of your father's personal guards while he was Mildari. It was a great honour.'

'Why, yes, I do recognise you.'

The guardian's eyes creased with pleasure. 'I'm delighted to think so, my lady.' Karliana made a gracious dip of her head, waiting for him to step aside. He held his ground. 'I believe I saw you earlier with another young lady …' He looked about, as if wondering whether Fionella might spring out from a hiding place, perhaps from behind that barrel. Karliana suppressed nervous amusement at the idea. 'If you don't mind me saying so, it's not very wise to be here alone — especially after curfew.'

'No … I didn't plan to be unwise.' Karliana bit her tongue. *No one ever plans to be unwise.* Tossing her head a little, she added, 'Miss Mercadi went on ahead to her villa. I'm afraid I took a shortcut and ended up here.'

The man nodded gravely. 'Well, Lady Karliana, it's not safe to walk the streets alone, not this — not anymore.' He winced slightly, and searched her face. 'Ah, well, I think your father would want me to escort you home. Shall we walk together, my lady?'

With an inward sigh of relief, Karliana accepted the offer of his strong, uniformed arm.

If the streets had been quiet earlier, that was nothing compared with the deathly hush after curfew. Even the birds' evening chorus seemed half-hearted, as if they were wary of making too much noise. Conversation was out of place, so they walked in silence. Karliana was thankful when the glimmering lights of the Lendri estates came into view. Tonight, she decided, she would ensure that some of the drapes stayed open; she did not want the villa to close its eyes on the world. Thanking Bellart for his assistance, she promised to remember him to her father. The ornate gates closed behind her with a reassuring clang.

Pelor opened the door promptly, as if he had been waiting for her. He folded himself in half with his usual dignity. Since the new Mildari had purged his office of every trace of his predecessor, Pelor was now ensconced at the Lendri villa. Karliana was not entirely sure what his actual function was: 'supervisor of all and sundry' perhaps, with the added duty of 'intimidating the young mistress at every turn'.

'Good evening, my lady,' he murmured. His expression inferred she was late, but that such disappointments could only be expected of one so young and frivolous.

'Good evening, Pelor. Has my father taken his tea?'

'He has gone out, my lady. Shall I take your cloak?'

Karliana's heart sank. 'Do you know where he has gone?'

'I believe he has gone to visit Guardulian Skagali, my lady,' came the smooth reply. 'Will you take your tea in your chambers?'

Guardulian Skagali? How odd. Her father certainly had no love for Guardulian Skagali. Why would he be visiting him? Of course there was no point asking Pelor. 'No, thank you. I will wait.'

'Very well, my lady. And will you be keeping to your chambers?'

'Yes. Please send word when my father returns.' Only as she mounted the staircase did his question strike her as unusual.

⁂

Karliana soon regretted her decision to defer taking tea. She just could not settle, and took to strolling along her private terrace. Tonight, the view of the darkened hills and star-studded skies was powerless to still her nerves. Thinking a bite of something to eat might help, she went to ring the bell. Then she paused. What had Pelor meant: 'Will you be keeping to your chambers?' Officious little man! She decided to slip down to the library and wait there for her father instead.

She already had a foot on the sweeping staircase when she heard a crash below. Running down the first flight as quickly as her silken slippers allowed, she was startled to hear voices rising up from below — men's voices. Then came a muffled scream, like a cry from an injured animal. Karliana's heart gave a horrible hop. Leaning out over the railing, she could just see the bald top of Pelor's head. His words rang in the white space of the entrance hall: 'Quickly girl, get this cleaned up!' Then he vanished from view. Whatever was going on?

Karliana flew down the remaining stairs to the sounds of a bucket clanking. Nearing the bottom she saw the slave. On her hands and knees, she was swabbing at the white marble in desperate swipes.

'Is there some trouble here?'

The girl nearly tipped her bucket over with fright. 'Oh, no! No trouble, my lady.'

Frowning, Karliana stepped onto the marble. 'What is that? What are you cleaning there?'

'Nothing. Nothing, my lady.'

Karliana gasped. No matter how furiously the slave wiped, nothing could hide the long trail of blood. At that moment Pelor swept out from the library and glided into the space between them.

'Ah, Lady Karliana. Are you perhaps ready for your tea?' The girl at his feet was apparently invisible.

'Tea?' The word was weak in her mouth. 'Pelor, there is blood, there on the floor. And muddy footprints.' She pointed.

'Yes, my lady,' he agreed, as if commenting on the weather. 'The wisest course of action would be for you to return to your chambers.'

The wisest course of action? Karliana was not very tall, but she drew herself up to her full height. 'Pelor, I am the head of this household in my father's absence. Therefore I will decide the wisest course of action. And I have decided that you will tell me immediately why there is a trail of blood leading to the library.'

A flicker of surprise crossed Pelor's face. He blinked stiffly before dipping his head in reluctant acquiescence: 'Please come through, my lady.'

❧

The stranger lay groaning on Lord Lendri's couch. A second figure knelt at his side, attempting to staunch the blood. Karliana recognised him at once. 'Bellart! Whatever has happened? Who is that man?'

Pelor answered for him. 'This man is a colleague of your father's and he needs urgent care.'

Karliana looked from the stranger's ashen face to the blood soaking darkly into the upholstery. *A colleague? What sort of colleague?*

'He must be taken to the Curing Houses,' she commanded shakily.

Pelor shook his head. 'No. The Curing Houses have been requisitioned by the Squad; this man cannot go there. They would lock him up again.' He looked at her closely, as if to test she understood his meaning.

'He's an escaped prisoner!'

'Yes, my lady. Others will arrive soon to take him away. In the meantime we must do what we can. It would help very much if you could collect your embroidery case and bring it here.'

Karliana blinked several times before answering: 'Where is my father?'

❧

Slipping through the library door, Karliana saw that the injured man had been stripped of his shirt. Three others had arrived, making the room seem crowded. One was a nobleman judging by his attire, yet he was filthy, his hair and beard matted. To find Domberto there was a complete shock, but nothing could prepare Karliana for the sight of Matapharni. Her gown was torn and splattered in mud, her hair fell about her face in wild tresses. The slave woman was just as beautiful as ever — even as she snarled a question at Pelor.

'Does she know?'

'Some of it. I'm afraid it could not be helped.'

Aranti's mistress sniffed and returned her attention to the wounded man.

Karliana's thoughts were whirling. What was Matapharni doing in her father's library, and acting for all the world as if she owned the place? And how dare she treat Torland Lendri's daughter with such contempt? Domberto was refusing to meet her eyes — like the others, he seemed absorbed by Matapharni's quick, decisive movements.

'Quickly, girl, I need strong, thin thread and your sharpest needle.' In spite of the woman's impertinence, Karliana found herself obeying. She passed the items with shaking hands. 'Good. Now the key! The key, girl!'

Karliana gaped, wondering at the woman's meaning. Pelor cleared his throat. 'Your necklace, my lady. If I may?'

Karliana passed the chain over her head, handing over the silver key. She always wore it, in memory of her mother, thinking it just a pretty ornament. She watched in disbelief as Pelor removed books from a shelf and unlocked a secret compartment. The nook contained a number of packages, secured in red twine. Each was sealed with a button of green wax. Producing a knife from nowhere, Pelor slit one open to reveal a pale-blue powder, like chalk dust. Following Matapharni's instructions, he stirred a precise amount into a measure of water and dribbled the liquid down the throat of the wounded man.

'What is it?' Ignored by everyone, Karliana raised her voice. 'Pelor, what are you giving him?'

Matapharni gave a slight nod and Pelor supplied an answer: 'It is nathine powder. Or dream dust, as it is known by those who misuse it.' Noting her blank face, he added, 'It is powerful medicine, my lady. And very rare. Your family had a secret source.'

Karliana blinked at the information. 'Thank you, Pelor.'

Matapharni had been scorching the needle over a candle. Karliana could not help staring at her extraordinary eyelashes as she threaded the needle. When the needle pierced the man's flesh, making him hiss through clenched teeth, she averted her eyes.

'You. Priest,' said the woman inflicting the pain. 'Tell me: what did you see?'

Domberto spoke shakily. 'It all went smoothly at first. The decoy worked. The main force was drawn out and we easily overpowered the remaining guards. The prisoners were in three separate cells: two above the level where we found you. Most were in terrible shape.' He shuddered. 'They'd been tortured … Some could not walk by themselves. By the time we reached the outer wall, the first wagon had gone. So we waited … but then …'

Matapharni glanced up from her work. 'But then?'

Domberto grimaced, placing his hand over his eyes, and the filthy stranger broke in: 'They can't have been human. They just can't have … There were two … with Squad bands, like the others. But they … Their eyes …' He winced. 'Their eyes were entirely black — empty. Just holes where the eyes should be. And they fought like rabid beasts. They just kept coming. Hacking at the unarmed prisoners, showing no mercy. Their own injuries were dreadful, but they just kept coming. We killed them both … It was terrible, unnatural …' His eyes pleaded with a burning intensity. 'They can't have been human.'

Matapharni looked up, her face grim. 'No. It is as we feared. The Melk grows strong in Mildaresh.'

Karliana hardly dared speak. 'The Melk? What … ? What does that mean?'

'It means we leave the city at once.' Matapharni got to her feet. 'The stitches will hold for now.'

Domberto nodded. 'It is arranged. You will take the passage to the river. A barge awaits.'

'Good. You're coming, too.'

'No!' Domberto glanced swiftly at Karliana. 'We killed them! We overcame them.'

Matapharni laughed. 'You merely killed two hosts. Nulls at that. Aranti will know of your involvement. And,' she frowned, 'he may already be strong enough to see through his vassals' eyes. You cannot serve the League by staying here. You must flee.'

Karliana rubbed at her forehead. 'Domberto? What is the Melk?' she asked unsteadily.

At that moment Pelor crept back into the room, drawing everyone's attention. No one had even noticed he had been gone.

Pelor said but four words. They were enough to make the floor seem like liquid beneath Karliana's feet. 'Torland has been taken.'

A groan went through the group. Matapharni closed her beautiful eyes. 'His decoy was exposed then.'

'So it seems. They're alive, but the whole group was arrested. It will not go well for Guardulian Skagali, I'm afraid.'

Matapharni was already loading the remaining packages into a bag. 'We'll take these; they'll search the villa and questions will be asked. Make haste. The girl, too. The name of Lendri is implicated.'

'Come, Miss Karliana.' Bellart put his hand gently beneath Karliana's elbow. She pulled away.

'I will do no such thing! I'm not going anywhere until I get some answers.'

Domberto had moved to her side. 'It's only fair,' he said quietly.

Matapharni's eyes flashed. 'Karliana!' she snapped. 'People have risked their lives for this chance of escape, including your father. I will not waste that chance talking. You wish to know about the Melk? I fear you will soon know more than you wish. But now is not the time for instruction. Know only this: it is the most evil force you will ever encounter and, unaccountably, it is suddenly strong in Mildaresh. We fly. And we fly now!'

At her words, everyone began to move — all except Karliana.

'No.' The quiet word stopped them in their tracks. 'I'm staying. My father needs me, and I will use whatever influence I have to protect him.'

'Whatever influence! What childishness is this?'

Karliana trembled at Matapharni's expression, but she knew her mind. 'I may be young, but that does not mean I am childish or stupid.' She glanced at Pelor. 'I am the head of the house of Lendri in my father's absence. The House of Aranti stands against tyranny.' She lifted her chin, and angry tears sprang into her eyes. 'I will not abandon my father, and I will not abandon my city.'

Matapharni grimaced and sighed. 'You have your father's heart, child. It is a rash decision, but it is yours to make.'

Bellart nodded gravely.

'You will be admitted to the League.' Matapharni gathered her things as she spoke. 'And you'll answer to Pelor. He will take your oath.'

Karliana's mind was reeling. 'My oath? I don't know ...'

'It is not a choice.' Matapharni held up a long finger. 'The League's secrecy is paramount. Take the oath or die. Pelor will explain.' She was already turning away. 'Pelor, send a swift as soon as you are able: *Melk swarm located in Mildaresh. Nexus confirmed. Presence … strong.*'

He nodded. 'And shall I report where you are heading?'

'No, it's too dangerous — the game has changed. And both of you: avoid Aranti at all costs.'

When Matapharni turned again to Karliana, her tone was more gentle. 'Remember this in the darkness, Karliana, for darkness is surely coming to Mildaresh. This is a retreat, not a defeat. The League will return. You have my promise.' She nodded. 'Ready, Pelor?'

To Karliana's complete astonishment, Pelor walked to the tall portrait of her mother and lifted it off the wall. He ran his hands along the panelling and pushed. An entire section of the wall swung open. Bowing gravely, he gestured at the passageway. Domberto was the last to leave. He pressed Karliana's hands between his own, his expression soft and desperate. Nothing and everything was said in that final moment. Then they were gone.

The painting restored, Karliana gazed up into her mother's face. She had the feeling that, if she could just stay there, looking into those gentle eyes, time might stop; Fate would cease its headlong course and all would be well. It seemed to work for a moment — until the spell was broken by a cough.

'Might I suggest some tea, Lady Karliana?'

Karliana drew herself up. 'Yes. Thank you, Pelor.' She met his eyes. 'They will be here soon.'

'Yes, my lady.'

Chapter 7

A SUMMONS

They came around midnight, their boots ringing on the marble floors. Karliana was waiting in the library, poised behind her father's desk, her hands tucked into the lavender sleeves of her over-gown. A scented candle sweetened the air, its flame flickering a warning. The blood-stained furniture had been removed, of course, replaced by a chaise longue after the same fashion. Its velvet red upholstery was a good match for the room. It made Karliana think of blood. The library was stained now, stained with memory and the smell of blood — and there were not enough flowers in all the world to take away that scent.

When Rutholine Moagli was ushered in by a blank-faced Pelor, Karliana made a gracious curtsy, just as if she had issued the invitation herself. Then she arched her brows. 'Please. Be s o kind as to remove your boots, Rutholine. No matter what your orders, there is really no excuse for poor manners.' To counterbalance the censure, she gave him the warmest smile she could muster.

Rutholine shuffled a bit, but he complied — thank Telion. Karliana had no idea what she would have done had he refused. Pelor played his part beautifully. He received the gigantic boots in his arms with as much ceremony as if he had been handed a casket from a queen. Karliana controlled the urge to giggle. Rutholine was such an incongruous sight, towering, pillar-like, in her father's study, in his socks. 'I hope you will take some tea?'

One of her mother's favourites, the teapot was sturdy with a fat belly. It was perhaps a little too rustic for entertaining visitors, but then Rutholine was not really a visitor, was he? The action of pouring tea helped to steady Karliana's nerves, if not her shaking hands. Thus far, Rutholine was responding as she had hoped. To her relief, he had decided of his own accord that, since she was obviously putting up no resistance, it was more fitting to send his two men to wait outside.

Only one could really be called a man, the other was a mean-looking scrap of a lad with bright blond hair. He had been gazing at the ornaments and draperies with hungry longing — the very epitome of what she knew of the Squad members, brutal and brutalised: a wolf on a leash. The look he cast at Karliana on his way out was heavy with hatred. She was relieved to see the back of him.

Rutholine looked as out of place in her father's library as a bull kattlen would have. Karliana had to admit he did rather suit the uniform of the Moagli Squad: a long frock coat in dark brown, embellished with orange at the collar and lapels. The embroidered symbols, she believed, depicted rank of some sort. She presumed that he was outranked only by his elder brother, Castronon. And his mother, of course. Although she did not wear a uniform, Serenitia Moagli had orchestrated the whole thing; both of her sons were firmly tied to the strings of her political purpose.

Rutholine wore the traditional orange band of the Moagli Squad high on his left arm, bound tight around the bulging muscle. His broad face, with dark hair clipped short and parted in the middle, matched the rest of him. Brown eyes flickered around the room, avoiding hers. He took his chair with considerable unease. *Good.* Rutholine had his orders, but he was uncomfortable with them. It was a start.

'So.' Karliana placed her teacup on its fragile saucer where it rattled slightly. She made her gaze gentle. 'Rutholine …' She nearly added 'my dear friend', but decided against it — that was certainly pushing things. She fluttered her eyelashes instead. 'I imagine there is a very good reason for this disturbance of my nightly studies?' Her inflection turned the statement into a sweetly innocent question. Of course, she had no such routine. Ordinarily she would have been slumbering beneath silk covers. Her father was the nocturnal reader. The thought of him sent a horrible shiver down her spine. Perhaps he was in the dungeons by now, awaiting whatever vengeance Aranti might devise. She made herself smile.

With slow reluctance, Rutholine drew a paper from the breast of his coat. 'I do apologise for the disturbance, Lady Karliana. But I have orders to search and secure the property … and escort your person, for questioning, to the Squad headquarters.'

Karliana felt bright points growing in her cheeks. *The Squad headquarters indeed!* But it had never been more crucial to control her temper. She took a sip of tea. Endeavouring to keep her tone neutral, she murmured, 'Oh dear. If I am under arrest, Rutholine, I should very much like to know the charges.'

'Your father is charged with sedition against the Mildari's rule.' Rutholine ran his finger around his collar. One of his socks was tapping out a silent rhythm on the plush carpet.

Karliana forced her lips into a tiny smile. 'My father. I see. Oh dear.' She stood, smoothing her hands over her gown, letting them flow over the shape of her hips. It was hard to be sure without watching him, but she hoped his eyes followed. She had already walked a couple of paces, thinking to buy more time, when she realised her mistake. Her heart jumped to see her sewing kit, where it had been abandoned on the floor, overlooked in the hasty restoration of the room. In a swift moment, Rutholine swooped and picked it up.

'Ah! Is that where it got to?' Karliana's heartbeat skittered. Her eyes flitted, scanning the floor. Where were the bloodied bandages? Had they been missed, too? When Rutholine opened the lid, she was nearly sick with fright.

He frowned. 'There's a patch of blood here.'

'Oh!' Karliana laughed, hoping he would fail to detect the falsity of her melodious tone. 'Quite probably. You have happened upon my wicked secret. Embroidery is not one of my talents. I am forever stabbing myself with the needle.' Stepping close, she retrieved the box, brushing his hands with hers. Rutholine's black brows came together in a perplexed line. 'I'm afraid I tossed the thing aside in a complete pique. It is quite ruined. A shame … it was such a pretty thing.' She pouted a little, emulating Fionella Mercadi as best as she could. Then she made her smile sweet. 'Shall we finish our tea?'

Rutholine was still frowning as they regained their seats. Lifting her teacup Karliana took a quick sip of the tepid liquid. Time was passing, but so slowly. How much longer could she stall the man? And what if nobody came?

Even though Pelor was standing to attention near the door, she lifted the silver bell and made it tinkle. 'Pelor, please see if my messengers have returned.'

Rutholine froze, his teacup halfway to his mouth. It looked quite ridiculous in that massive hand. 'Messengers?'

As if in answer, the clattering of hooves came to their ears. Karliana tilted her head. Horses! Many horses, by the sound of it. At last she could breathe. Unclasping the knot of fingers in her lap, she turned her attention to the parchment. 'May I?'

Rising, Rutholine surrendered the paper into her hands. He refrained from going to the window, but his eyes followed Pelor, who was sliding from the room. Karliana had to admire the way in which he stood to attention in his socks. She read. Or rather she pretended to read. Her eyes caught the occasional word, 'treason,' confiscation,' 'withholding' … hard words from a hard-mouthed man. Although the Mildari's stamp graced the bottom of the sheet, there was nothing graceful about the illegality of Aranti's command. It was tyranny, clear and simple, and she meant to expose it. She made her eyes cold.

'The men you hear outside are most probably from the House of Montfane, since that is closest. But they could be from any one of the other houses to whom I sent messengers earlier. I informed them of my father's disappearance. Feeling myself vulnerable against the evils of the world, I bade them send support.' Karliana's heart lifted to hear more horses dancing up the cobblestone drive.

At that moment Pelor returned, bustled out of the way by five young men. If he was perturbed, he did not show it. Lace flourished and capes swept as the men announced themselves. Berin Skagali, Perion Bell, Archi Montfane, Alginine Daylin and Mateus Sanarson came the tumble of names. The words 'at your service' echoed, and Karliana found herself with five young noblemen at her feet, all representatives of their Houses.

It was hard not to laugh at the ridiculousness of it all, but Rutholine's eyes were upon her. 'Thank you, my friends. Thank you so much for responding so very promptly to my message.' When they showed no indication of doing so, she added, 'Please, rise.'

A rather foppish young man with flopping blond hair took the initiative. 'The House of Dunbar is delighted to lend support in your hour of need, Lady Karliana. My father sends his warmest regards and hopes for your safety. He bids me say that my men and I are at your command.' He shot Rutholine a look that said he would fight him in a second.

'And also with the House of Daylin!'

'As are mine!'

'My party is twenty-strong and willing!'

A tumult of voices rose as the young men gave ardent pledges of service and protection.

They really did look quite foolish, all bobbing and bowing like that. Karliana pushed her amusement aside. 'Again, I thank you, gentlemen. Pelor, please see that these gallant young men are housed in our very best rooms. I welcome you all as my guests.' She gave her deepest curtsey and the men took their leave, some shooting triumphant looks in Rutholine's direction.

When they were alone again, Karliana took a breath. 'Rutholine, I thank you for your patience. Please inform the Mildari that I find myself unable to meet his request this evening. As I am sure he is aware, the Moagli Squad does not have jurisdiction over the nobility. If he wishes to speak with me, I am happy to receive him here, tomorrow afternoon.' Realising that her chin had been thrust out rather aggressively, she softened her expression. 'It was very nice to see you and to take tea together.'

A very worried-looking Rutholine collected his paper and tucked it away. His dark eyes met hers. His mouth seemed painted on.

'That was well played, Karliana. But it was a dangerous move. Aranti's power is …' His eyes narrowed. 'He is more dangerous than you imagine.'

Karliana felt a little flutter of fear. The man actually did seem worried. It was most unnerving in such a mountain of a person. Clasping her hands beneath her ribs, she feigned composure. 'I thank you for your concern. However, Aranti is subject to our laws under the Calkinon Peace. He cannot order noblewomen about, according to his own whims.' She lifted her chin. 'I am sorry for your part. I understand that you must follow your orders, however ridiculous they may seem.'

As soon as she said it, she was unsure. What exactly was the relationship between the Squad and Aranti? Had Serenitia Moagli really handed Aranti full control? It seemed unlikely somehow. Rutholine was shaking his head. As he went to leave, he turned back with a soft warning.

'Be careful, Karliana. Aranti is not a man to be thwarted. There will be consequences.'

He meant her father. Karliana felt her composure slipping. She wanted to beg Rutholine for word of her father, to throw herself to her knees. She did not. Nor did she curtsey. It was all she could do to speak. 'Thank you, Rutholine. I bid you good evening.'

❧

At long last the villa was quiet. The young men were tucked into their quarters, if not their beds. Most of the horses were stabled, and promises made that the others would be accommodated on the morrow. Karliana turned to her father's clerk with a weary sigh. She rubbed at the frown which had settled into a headache between her brows. 'We seem to have rather a housefull, Pelor.'

'Yes, my lady.' The man actually allowed himself a quiver of a smile. 'At least twelve of the most eligible bachelors in Mildaresh, I think you will find. A handful more who wish they were eligible, and a couple whose tastes lean … in another direction, shall we say?'

Karliana blinked at his inference. The man was full of surprises. She barely stifled a yawn. He was right. She had landed herself a veritable gaggle of suitors, all as silly as geese.

'It is late, my lady, and the night has been long.' Pelor drew his long fingers together. 'There is an idea I wish to discuss with you, but the morning will suffice. I confess … it may not be much to your liking.'

Karliana nodded. *Not much to my liking.* Well, that pretty much summed up the entire day's events. As she climbed the stairs to her chambers, Karliana wondered if anything would ever be to her liking again.

Chapter 8

A BROKEN CROWN

Breakfast at the Lendri villa was an uncharacteristically noisy affair. The young men were continuing to tumble over themselves in competition. Karliana could hear their banter from her chambers, where she had taken her own meal in relative peace. After only a few hours of sleep, she had been more than happy to take Pelor's advice and 'hold herself aloof'.

A general invitation had been issued instead, creating quite a furore. That morning the young mistress planned to attend the Senate, and would welcome the escort of any young man who might so desire. Not a single one of them had refused. All were busy readying themselves, their men and their horses. Slaves rushed here and there, dragged from one young lord to the next, trying to satisfy a hundred demands at once. Ordinarily, Karliana would simply have walked to the Senate House, since it was not far. Today, a procession was in order. The ancient carriage was receiving a hurried polish, in readiness for a rare outing.

The Lendri custodian gave Karliana a final appraising look before adjusting a single curl of hair. It made no discernible difference as far as Karliana could tell, but the woman gave a prim nod, satisfied at last. Karliana stared at her reflection in the long glass. The gown had been passed down through the ages to her mother, who had most certainly never worn it. Its lavender skirts, just brushing the floor, fell in heavy folds, coming together in a deep pleat at the centre where the deep purple bodice plunged to a point. Buttons traversed the satin in long lines — tiny, precious sea pearls. The splayed collar was stiff with pearls, too, and studded with amethysts. Fit for a queen. And, as if all that were not enough, there was a fitted over-jacket, stiff with purple brocade and skirts that stood out in a proud ruffle about the hips. Such a costume had not been seen in Mildaresh since the city's foundations. Every embroidered symbol, every design whispered of lineage reaching back to caress those ancient times — times when royal blood had dictated who should rule.

The gown fitted Karliana perfectly. The broken crown on the bodice rose and fell with every breath. A glittering thing, split asunder at her heart. Illuminated with lustrous purple and silver thread, the image still glowed after all the long years. None would fail to recognise that symbol, nor the jewel that Karliana wore upon her brow. It was shaped like a tear, the once proud centrepiece of the crown that was broken. The reminder would not be lost on Lord Aranti, nor, she hoped, on the senators themselves. It was an audacious play. Karliana trembled as she lifted her gaze. 'So? Will I do, Pelor?'

The man's thin reflection nodded gravely and bowed. 'My lady, you will do admirably.'

Once the young suitors had recovered from their gaping, they did a magnificent job of adding to the performance. In fact, one might have thought they had been specifically asked to dress for a pageant. Many of the horses wore plumes, and their riders boasted splendid finery, giving no hint that they had been summoned under such strange circumstances, in the middle of the night.

As Karliana climbed into her carriage, she heard a whinny. Cloud, her dappled mare, was tossing her head over her stable door. She probably wanted to join the team of blacks — infected by the atmosphere, they were stamping proudly, blowing out their nostrils and shaking their manes, making harnesses jingle. Karliana turned her eyes to the front. Her spirited grey was far better left behind, safe in her stall. It was a good morning to stay behind.

The group rode slowly, taking the main routes, with a slight detour so as to pass the gates of the Feyindi villa. The carriage was open, and the wind bitter. Karliana pulled her furs tighter and fixed a wide smile to her face, waving at anybody who was there to see. People stopped in their tracks, wondering at the antique carriage and colourful array of fine young noblemen.

As calculated, the Senate was about to begin the day's proceedings as they arrived. Karliana caused quite a stir as she entered. Although several closer seats were empty, she paraded to the far end, drawing the eyes of all. Her retinue streamed in behind her, like a string of goslings. Karliana smiled and nodded. It was a delight to see Serenitia Moagli's jaw drop open, mid-sentence. A rare moment indeed, and one to be cherished.

Madalinelle Skagali was there, seated next to her sister, Anatha. Both looked pale and frightened. Of course. They would be as worried about

Guardulian as Karliana was about her father. Shoving grim thoughts of dungeons to one side — she could not afford to waver, not this morning — Karliana gave the sisters a cool nod of solidarity. The gesture would not be lost on more astute observers.

As she took her seat, she felt an icy cold sensation at the back of her neck. Folding her hands in her lap she knew Aranti's eyes were upon her. Even though he was on the opposite side of the hall, she could feel his dark gaze. She turned away and beamed, rather too enthusiastically, at the surprised couple beside her.

That morning the Senate's official business was even less riveting than usual. The entire schedule was taken up by one speaker, a dour-faced man called Gandola Esprin who was proposing redevelopment of the city's sewer. Karliana was reminded why she so rarely attended. She feigned interest, but paid him little attention. She did not plan to give an opinion. In fact, she did not plan to say anything. The only plan was to be seen — a plan that had already triumphed. Many people were returning their eyes to her, as if trying to divine the reason why she had made such an entrance, in such a fashion.

When everyone rose for the break and glasses of rosewater, Karliana chatted about trivial matters. To her satisfaction, many an eye was cast over the motifs on her embroidered gown. Some people blinked, almost aghast, to recognise the jewel on her brow. Brandol Sanarson gave her a thoughtful nod. Nothing missed his shrewd eyes. His son, a thoughtful red-haired youth, was one of those who had taken up residence at the Lendri villa. He was one of the more serious contenders for her hand, she supposed — had she, for one moment, been seriously entertaining marriage. The elder Lord Sanarson was a staunch conservative and ardent opponent of upstart aristocracy. Karliana imagined she could almost see his mind working. *Good.*

This reminder of Karliana's royal heritage, and the sacrifice her family had made, was a calculated move. Parallels could not help but be drawn to the unprecedented power that Aranti had gathered into his own hands. The Mildari was not a king, just the first citizen, yet here was Aranti behaving like a tyrant of old. Some who were beginning to fear the man's growing influence might even welcome the reinstatement of the monarch as a means to his removal. A terrible thought. Most, Karliana hoped, would be thinking of the broken crown, and everything it stood for.

Karliana waited until most people had made their way back to their seats. She had no wish to hear further of sewer maintenance. It was time to make a final point. Moving with serene dignity, drawing every eye in the room, Karliana approached the altar of the gods. Fingertips at her brow and thumbs resting on her cheekbones, she made the sign of the triangle. Her curtsy was deep — any deeper and she would be prostrated on the floor. And there she stayed. Karliana Lendri, bowing her head in humility, to the gods and to the Senate. It was done. The visitation was complete.

As she dipped a curtsy to the Mildari, she saw how Maliagne Aranti's eyes glittered. He was clutching the staff of Mildaresh for all he was worth. Hiding the plunging sensation of pure terror at what she had begun, Karliana swept a parting smile over the crowd. Then, although she wanted to pick up her skirts and run, she glided out of the Senate House with as much regal grace as she could manage. The senators might go back to discussing drainpipes and overflows, but she felt certain that everyone's thoughts had been diverted to other matters: just as dark, with equally unpleasant undercurrents.

❧

'And that,' crowed Perion Bell, tossing down his card, 'makes a captured maiden!'

Karliana feigned a merry laugh, clapping her hands in mock celebration of the still-spinning card. She had no idea if the boy's call was correct or not. She could not have cared less. Surrendering her own cards, face-down on the table, she excused herself. How exhausting it was to entertain so many adoring young men at once. The House of Lendri did not keep herati — now Karliana fully understood why others did. If she could have snapped her fingers to summon a troop of beautiful women to flirt with her guests, she most certainly would have! It was just fortunate that so many of these young men found pleasure in cards and good wine. When she caught Pelor's eye, he gave her a nod — imperceptible, had she not been expecting it. She drew closer to the window.

Seated on the highest plateau, the Lendri villa enjoyed views over most of Mildaresh. Outside, a storm was brewing, tossing the trees, sending leaves into the darkening skies. Karliana's stomach clenched itself into a knot when her eyes confirmed that Maliagne Aranti's black carriage was indeed approaching, flanked by an entourage of soldiers on horseback. From this distance it looked like an upturned beetle, carried by ants. She turned away from the sight.

Noticing that she had been clutching fistfuls of gown at her sides, Karliana picked up her feathered fan. She fanned herself for a full moment before realising how ridiculous that was. The huge reception room had been chosen deliberately for its grandeur. It was far from warm, in spite of the fires which blazed in both of the mighty grates. As Karliana returned her fan to the table, the card-players froze, exchanging horrified glances. They had not dealt her any cards.

'Gentleman,' she murmured, 'please continue your game. I'm afraid I must take my leave of you for a time. The Mildari is about to grace us with a visit.'

The boys, for really that is all they were, stood at once, pushing back their chairs.

To his credit, Berin Skagali stammered only a little before taking control. He squared his narrow shoulders. 'My lady … If you are in need of any assistance … You need only give a signal … We are at your service.'

'Thank you, Lord Skagali.' Trying not to laugh, Karliana thanked each of them by name as they chimed in with equally chivalrous sentiments, before resuming their game. Only one excused himself, and as he scurried from the room Karliana did not blame him. She wished she could run away, too. But the stage was set. And she must play her part, to the very best of her ability.

Karliana moved slowly, away from the tall bay windows, towards the opposite end of the room, trying to gauge how long it would take for Aranti to be ushered in. Every chandelier had been lit on this dim afternoon. Rose-glass clear-lights were doing their valiant best to light the lavish ceilings. Taking up an entire wing of the villa, the room had once served as a ballroom. Nowadays, since Torland Lendri had not danced since the death of his wife, the place was usually shut up, empty of all but dust motes. Today it was far from empty. Furniture, some of which had been in storage for decades, had been set out in convivial arrangements. Every table was occupied by Karliana's guests, and their own guests, some playing at cards, some lounging and chatting.

As she strolled the length of the room, a few looked up to catch her eye. Mateus Sanarson gave her a nod that seemed to say 'we are with you'. She bowed her head in acknowledgement. Archi Montfane peeped over the top of his cards. She smiled, making him blush. Yes, the young men were all playing their parts, albeit unwittingly. Everything was set.

Karliana continued her journey, past a series of bronze statues, her ancestors, posing in creamy gilded alcoves. She walked past Pelor, who was in position, his stiff back to the mighty polished doors, ready to announce the Mildari's arrival. Reaching the far end of the room at last, Karliana picked up her skirts. Three semi-circular steps took her up to a half-moon platform. Two high-backed chairs waited, one either side of an ornate table. Karliana took her seat, looking down on her guests. Behind her was a higher platform again. She could feel the presence of the single object that stood there.

Crafted in ancient times from a single piece of oak, the throne had a dark, brooding quality. Its arms were giant scrolls. Its back had been carved to resemble a mighty sea eagle, grasping a shield in its talons, a shield featuring all the crests of the founding families. The eagle's wings were outstretched. Anyone who sat there would probably look as if they had sprouted feathers. As old as the city itself, the throne was a remnant of the tribal kings who had made their way up the river those long centuries ago. It was a monstrous, hateful thing. Karliana despised it.

Once, queens and kings had sat there, now the seat was empty save for one object — the crown that was broken: a constant reminder of what her family had relinquished to safeguard the city from tyrants. The Senate was fragile in the face of events, Karliana knew it. But the city would not fall to a man like Aranti — Melk or no Melk, she just would not allow it.

'All rise for the Mildari!'

Everyone rose, folding themselves into bows and curtsies, in obeisance to the office of Mildari, if not the man himself. Maliagne Aranti's presence seemed to darken more than the mood. To Karliana, it seemed that the clear-lights dimmed when he approached, as if something about him was sapping their light. As he strode forward in his swift, arrogant manner, she gave herself a little shake. *Nonsense.* The man was intimidating enough without the fuel of imagination. The two men accompanying Aranti wore the uniforms of the city guardians. Like twin pillars, they stood to attention at the foot of the lower platform. Aranti stepped up towards her. The room had fallen completely silent, but now soft conversations resumed, as subdued as the shuffle of cards.

Karliana's spine shivered. It was as if Aranti had brought a chill with him, stolen from the advancing storm. His black eyes seemed darker than usual, if that was possible. They seemed to swallow the light.

'Lady Karliana.'

Karliana felt a flash of indignation. The correct address under these circumstances was Lady Lendri. Returning his clipped bow with a curtsy, she lifted her chin. Two could play at that game. 'Lord Aranti.' Her tone rose at the end, underpinning her refusal to call him Mildari. He just smiled, ignoring the slight.

As they took their seats, Aranti's gaze slid about the room, taking stock of the artworks and priceless treasures, which he had no doubt had designs on confiscating for himself. Not once did he acknowledge the massive throne, not even with a glance. Karliana allowed herself an inward smirk. A valiant pretence indeed. One thing he could not avoid seeing was the tapestry detailing the Lendri bloodlines. Pelor had commanded that the extravagant piece be placed directly opposite where the man would be seated. Aranti raised a displeased eyebrow, and soured his mouth. His eyes settled on her instead.

'It seems you have rather a houseful of guests, Karliana. Are these young pups,' he waved a hand, 'what lies behind your refusal to obey my summons last evening?'

'In part.' Karliana smiled a sweet smile, refusing to be baited by his use of her first name. 'After all, hospitality is the first order of the lady of the house.' Her heart beating wildly, she kept to the script they had devised. 'There also seemed to be a certain, shall we say, irregularity in the request. I concede that the Senate, in the light of a possible slave uprising, has granted the Moagli Squad extended powers. However, under the auspices of the Calkinon Peace, such powers would never extend to nobility. Such a thing would be quite unthinkable.'

Maligne Aranti made no answer. He simply leaned back in his chair, watching her with those black eyes.

Karliana faltered, her heart was fluttering. 'When ... When my father failed to return last evening, and there was no sign of his private guard, I felt myself quite vulnerable. Thankfully the House of Lendri is most fortunate in its friends.' She gestured ever so slightly at the young men seated at the nearest tables: Sanarson, Montfane, Devali. All heirs to the most powerful and wealthy Houses.

'Vulnerable.' Aranti's tongue licked out as if he savoured the word. His eyes remained fixed upon hers. Unblinking. Black beads. Like the eyes of a snake. Karliana was sure he had not blinked the entire time. If he was seeking to frighten her, it was working.

When a slave approached bearing a tray, she took the opportunity to look away. The poor man cowered at the bottom of the stair, inviting the two guardians to inspect the bottle. One broke the wax seal, nodding approval. The slave filled two goblets. With downturned eyes he crept up and offered both to the Mildari. Aranti chose the furthest from himself and waited for Karliana to taste hers before putting it to his lips. Pelor was right. The man was wary.

'You are right to feel vulnerable.' His words sent ice down her spine. 'Several prisoners were freed last night. Enemies …' Aranti's eyes glittered. 'Enemies of the city. Traitors. Those who have incited violence, through actions and words, encouraging our slaves to rebel. Sadly, Karliana, it seems your father was involved.'

Karliana shivered. Those last words were steeped in malice. Domberto was right. What had once been rivalry was now pure hatred.

Her chin had started to tremble, making it difficult to form words. 'My father is a man of peace. He is no traitor.'

Something moved in the inky depths of those black eyes — something that slithered. Karliana wanted to scream and run, but she could not move. She could not even speak.

'A daughter's presumption of her father's innocence.' Aranti's mouth twisted as he stroked the top of his glass with a finger. 'You are a child, Karliana. A stranger yet to passion … and all its devious devices.'

When Aranti turned his eyes back to the room, Karliana reeled, as if released from an icy grip. 'So you have gathered yourself a little army of consorts, Karliana. How long will they remain your playthings, I wonder? How long until they lose patience?' He made an obvious appraisal of her figure. 'You cannot withhold the prize forever.'

Karliana blushed under the frankness of his gaze. 'I have decided to marry.' She faltered a little, then found her anger. How dare he speak to her in that way? She repeated the words, more loudly to give them strength. 'I have decided to marry. In the spring.' She swallowed. Pelor would rebuke her, no doubt. She did not care. It was worth a try. 'I therefore request an audience with my father. I wish to seek his advice in my choice of partner.'

Aranti gave a lewd chuckle. 'Oh. Fear not, my dear. Your father will hear of how you are holding court, like a bitch in heat.' He leaned towards her and sniffed. 'Be careful, Karliana. You do smell … quite delectable.' His eyes surveyed the guests. 'I wonder if Torland will enjoy hearing that every mongrel in the city has sniffed out his daughter's scent.'

Karliana took a breath. She knew what he was doing. Seeking to shame and frighten her. Striking at her love for her father and her need for his respect. But knowing his game did not stop her heart from fluttering like a wounded thing. She could not speak.

'Mmm … Let us see. Your father is quite busy, you know. He is much occupied with the entertainments of his accommodation. And quite miserable I'm told … Does a lot of sobbing.' Aranti smiled, steepling his hands at his lips. 'A visit from his only daughter? Yes. That might be just the thing to lift the man's spirits.' His smile stretched. 'Hope,' he said softly. 'It is a precious thing, is it not?'

Karliana knew he was toying with her. But to see her father, to know that he was alive … Yes. She did hope for that. And she would pay almost any price. She lifted her chin. As she held his gaze, she saw a flicker of surprise. He raised his eyebrows, as if enjoying her pathetic defiance.

'Oh, very well.' When Karliana ground her teeth, determined not to look away, Aranti actually chuckled. 'I have but one condition.' Her heart pounded. In that moment she would have agreed to almost anything. 'You will extend an invitation to my son, Tindelfion, to join your other guests.'

Hot tea was brought. It grew cold, untouched, and was taken away again.

'Something a little stronger. Under the circumstances.' Karliana had never heard Pelor speak in such kindly tones. 'Drink, my lady. It will calm you.' She accepted the crystal glass, noticing that his hands were shaking, too. As he went to leave, she found her voice.

'Please. Stay.' Her body felt washed-out, exhausted, as if she had been crying. She had not. 'I'm sorry.' She felt a fool. It was weak. Collapsing like that.

'There is no need for sorry, my lady. Few people can face the Melk without going into shock, let alone a nexus as powerfully inhabited as Aranti. You did remarkably well, my lady. Your father would be proud.'

The man kept speaking, recalling the evening's events in soothing tones, sometimes circling back to ask gentle questions, mostly filling in trivialities. He spoke partly to appraise her of events — she did not recall much that had taken place after her conversation with Aranti. But mostly for the simple sake of calming her, as one speaks to a nervous horse. It is the reassurance of tone that matters. Yes. That was a good analogy. Karliana had been shivering like a frightened horse, wild-eyed, ready to bolt. As she sipped at her brandy, listening, she slowly came back to herself sufficiently to reflect on how odd it was to be chatting over sandwiches in her private chambers with her father's aging clerk.

Pelor seemed to sense that she had gathered her wits. He drew himself together, placing skinny hands on skinny knees. 'I repeat. You did remarkably well. There is no doubt Tindelfion will bring spies when he joins us, but that is unavoidable. And perhaps, it might be used to our advantage. Most importantly, Aranti will be distracted. Today the nobles have been reminded of the dangers of tyranny. The major families are vying to ally themselves with the House of Lendri.' The man's eyes almost sparkled. It actually seemed he was enjoying the intrigue. 'Now we can put plans into action.'

Karliana leaned forward. Her voice broke a little. 'A visit to my father?'

'By Telion, no!' Pelor looked quite startled at the suggestion. 'That is precisely what Aranti wants. To torment your father. To demonstrate his powerlessness to protect you.' The man's face sagged, adding to his age. 'I am sorry, my lady, I thought you understood. That must not happen.'

Karliana's heart sank another notch, to depths she had not known possible. The chance to see her father had seemed a beam of hope. 'What then? What can be done against such a monster?'

Pelor blinked, as if taken aback. 'Why we kill him, of course.'

Chapter 9

THE KNOWLEDGE STORES

Ash was listening. Listening, to the baffling silence. The hills were snowy blankets. The trees wore scarves of white. Everything felt muffled. Yet there was something, something unsettling. A note, a vibration perhaps … something Ash could not grasp. It was more than the feeling of being watched. Right from the beginning he had sensed it, from the moment he had placed his hands on the Stone. Now, in the eerie silence of this snow-drenched garden he was certain. Something was there … He just did not know what.

He raised his eyes to the cold city spires and shivered. The only human marks in this weirdly white world belonged to him: the trail of footprints leading back to the lodge. Everywhere else, the snow lay undisturbed. A terrible sense of loneliness swept through him at that thought. When Tarlyn's tail brushed his neck, he put up his hand, catching its silky curve.

'You were the one who said I had to come, Tarlyn. The Taelstaun must go to T'al Jazure. Well, I'm here. What am I supposed to do now?' Silence.

When the sound of crunching announced that Nirias was approaching, Ash sighed and turned. He was not at all looking forward to spending time with Nirias. But at least now a second set of footprints had joined his own.

❧

According to Nirias, there were seven archways at the heart of T'al Jazure. Each, he claimed, was completely unique. Ash believed him. The one they were admiring now was wrought from glass scales in different shades of red; almost orange at the bottom, deepening to crimson at the top. A glassy finial, like a feather, adorned its apex. Today it wore a tiny crown of snow. The splayed feet of the arch reminded Ash of the claws of a giant bird. The whole design was so peculiar he could not help shrinking as he stepped through.

The bizarre archway was just the beginning. The heart of the city was filled with objects of delight and imagination. Some were functional, providing seating, shade or light, while others seemed entirely whimsical. Many of the structures moved with the wind, or changed colour in the sun. As elsewhere in the city, water had been directed in cunning ways to a hundred different effects, whether it be to turn wheels or create curtains of raindrops. Crystals caught the winter sunlight, sending it dazzling in bright rainbows and prisms of colour.

The city's artists had obviously felt under no obligation to restrict themselves to rectangular portraits of great men — Ash doubted whether there even was such a thing in the city. They had painted animals and fish and birds directly onto the walls, some breathtakingly lifelike, others fantastical, the stuff of dreams. Some of the paintings were designed to trick the eye. More than once Ash realised that what he had taken to be real was in fact just a painted surface.

He stared about in wonder, aware that Nirias had gone completely silent at his side. Perhaps the man was just letting him take it in for himself. Ash stole a glance at his face. *Sadness. Weary sadness.* He realised then that it might be too painful for Nirias to speak. The Malshorne was one of the Azuri and, as impossible as it seemed, he had grown up in this city, had walked these streets as a young man. If T'al Jazure felt like a ghost city to Ash, what must it feel like to Nirias?

The Knowledge Stores were most remarkable of all. It was hard to tell if the structure was one building or seven interconnected towers. The turrets were varied in colour, texture and design. The trees and towers seemed to have grown up as one, interwoven with shining walkways, some enclosed, some not, some arching like thin silver ribbons. Gardens were perched here and there, atop impossible hanging platforms. Ash found himself gaping. When they came to an elaborate door he could not contain a gasp of awe. Nirias chuckled.

Ash reached out his fingers, not daring to touch the silver panelling. The design was moving before his eyes, like a pond stocked full of bright silver fish. At its centre the fish swam faster, in a tight circle, chasing each other's tails. It was beautiful and disturbing at the same time.

'Is it locked?' Realising he sounded like a wonderstruck child, Ash cleared his throat.

Nirias gave him a cryptic smile. 'No. Doors in T'al Jazure are never locked, Ash. Some are hidden, but they are never locked.' Ash turned the idea over in his mind. Was hiding a door any different from locking one? 'The Knowledge Stores have many entrances: this is my personal favourite. Watch.' Nirias put out his hand. As soon as his fingers touched the central motif, the fish scattered and the door swung open.

Following Nirias's lead, Ash removed his boots, selecting a pair of green silk slippers from a wooden cabinet. The carpet was deep and red. He cast a quick glance behind him, expecting to see tracks where he had trodden. There were none. Realising he had been holding his breath in response to the solemn hush of the place, he let it out slowly. Trying to breathe normally, he skipped to match Nirias's stride. The man seemed oblivious to the splendour of the curved ceiling, which was painted in ornate designs on a base of eggshell blue. Ash took quick glances, craning his neck as they strode towards the light at the end of the corridor.

Then they emerged. Two tiny figures in a cavernous hall. Ash was halted in his tracks, dazzled by the sheer majesty of the place. Nirias spread his arms wide, palms open, lifting his face to the light that poured down from a high dome. Like a man in the ecstasy of worship, he drank in deep breaths. Then, as if suddenly remembering Ash was still at his side, he turned and laughed, whether from his own joy or at Ash's bewilderment, or both, it was unclear. 'Welcome, Ash. Welcome to the Knowledge Stores of T'al Jazure!'

There were books, of course. Countless thousands of books. So many that they seemed the very fabric of the place. The leather spines stretched away in long curves, towering in stacks that could only be reached by ladders or the high gantries. There were nooks like book-lined caves, and long avenues, leading out from the centre like the spokes of a wheel. Huge reading benches were set on the ground floor, beneath giant hanging lamps. There were sequestered alcoves, too, with soft chairs and lamps on gilded stands.

Even more remarkable than the elaborately carved bookshelves were the immense transparent vessels. Some were oblong, like fish tanks, and set upon legs. Others rose towards the ceiling — giant cylindrical pillars. And every tank was filled with shining orbs. Lore-stones! Thousands of them. Some drifted, transparent like bubbles, others were packed so tightly that

Ash was reminded of fish eggs.

When Nirias beckoned him towards the centre of the room, Ash hesitated. For some reason his heart began to beat faster. Reluctant steps took him from plush carpet onto hard marble, then up to join Nirias on an engraved stone platform. It was round, like a massive dial. Ash frowned. The intricate lines etched into its face seemed familiar somehow. 'And here we are …' Nirias's words echoed in that space, like an incantation. 'We are standing at the very heart of the Knowledge Stores — the precise centre of T'al Jazure itself. And this, Ash, is the Heartstone.'

The Heartstone gave off an unnatural energy. Ash felt that if he closed his eyes he would have been able to point to it from anywhere in the room. It was very much like the Taelstone, the orb he had wrenched from Credé's dead fingers. Only this sphere was much larger, and it felt … It felt strange, like nothing Ash had encountered before. Resistant to the shafts of light that struck it from above, the sphere glowed with its own luminescence, like a small moon. Its stand was beautifully crafted, yet something about the design suggested restraint; the sphere was encircled with bright silver bands, as if the maker had feared the sphere might escape were it not tightly shackled.

All of a sudden, Ash had the uncanny sense of a moment repeating. It was as if he had stood there before, in precisely the same manner. As he studied the graven runes at his feet, and the concentric markings, his lips parted in realisation. 'It's … It's the Stone,' he breathed.

Nirias gave him a startled look. 'Indeed.' His eyes flickered and narrowed. 'It is the Stone. One and the same … Well done, Ash.' He seemed to watch Ash even more closely as he explained. 'The Stone and the Heartstone are one. They are twinned.' Then he frowned, reconsidering. 'Or rather, echoes if you will. One sits here, inside the realm of T'al Jazure, and the other outside, separated by the slightest fracture in reality, so that one … becomes two.' Nirias held up his hands, overlapping them at first, then drawing them apart as if to demonstrate.

In response to Ash's complete bafflement, he shook his head. 'I'm sorry, Ash. I cannot begin to explain the complexities of how T'al Jazure is able to exist as it does, only to say that it is just a shade removed from the time and space that we would think of as the outside world.' He paused, probably sensing — quite correctly — that Ash was no less bewildered than before.

'It is difficult to comprehend,' he nodded, 'and I understand your confusion. Perhaps if I give you the analogy that was once given to me.' He swept his hand, palm down, through the air in a line. 'Imagine reality is a plane, like a blanket,' he said. 'Then imagine a fold ... a pocket in that plane. Well, the realm of T'al Jazure is tucked into just such a pocket — into a fold in reality. But, the Stone,' Nirias held up a finger for emphasis, 'the Stone is able to exist in both. It is the link between two dimensions. Is that sufficient for now?'

Ash nodded. 'Yes ... Thank you.' He stammered under the intensity of the man's gaze. It was more than sufficient. Ash was totally confused. He just needed Nirias to stop talking.

Not only was he struggling to follow any of what the Malshorne was saying, the orb itself was wholly distracting. It seemed to pull at his attention. And it was changing. It was almost as if speaking about the thing had brought it to life. Shadows, like clouds, were gathering on its moon-like surface.

'Good!' Nirias sounded pleased as he rubbed his hands together. 'So, on we go.' He gave Ash a smile of encouragement. 'The Heartstone is exactly that: a stone that reads human hearts.'

'So, it's alive?'

'No. No. It may seem to be alive, since it acts like a mind, but no. You should think of it as a tool. A very clever and useful tool. It is our guide to the Knowledge Stores. Quite simply, Ash, the Heartstone will help you find the answers that you seek — so long as you know the questions.'

He waved his arms. 'This is just the main chamber. There are others, too. Together they contain thousands of lore-stones, all created by the Azuri themselves, or the men and women who studied here.' Nirias's eyes were bright with enthusiasm. 'The stones cover every subject you can imagine — well, almost.'

In the pause, Ash was tempted to ask him what he meant by 'almost'. But since he already had too much strange information to take in, he let the man continue.

'So! You must be wondering how it works.' When Ash gave an uncertain nod, Nirias continued. 'It is quite straightforward. You place your hands upon the orb, while framing a question in your mind.' The man's head tilted. With a knowing smile, he asked softly, 'So, what is it that you most desire to learn, Ash?'

Ash was still trying to decide whether the sphere really was changing colour, or whether it was his imagination. He blinked at Nirias. Did the man really need to ask? 'The Song,' he replied. 'I need to understand the Song.'

Nirias nodded and fell silent, his hands coming together over his heart. Something about the man's watchful expression made Ash wary as he stepped up to the orb. After a long moment, he drew a breath, grounded his feet and placed both palms on the surface of the globe.

At once the Heartstone surged, as if the thing had fully woken at his touch. Nirias darted to his side. 'Don't draw away,' he warned.

Draw away? Ash clenched his jaw. *Impossible!* His hands were fused to Heartstone's surface! His palms grew hot, as if lapped by flame. In a blink, the orb had changed. Where it had been opaque and clouded, it was suddenly clear. Ash could see a ball of energy at its heart — pulsing and coursing, it sent out tendrils to caress his skin. His flesh crawled at the licking sensation.

'Think of a question, Ash,' murmured Nirias. 'As clearly as you can.'

All Ash could think of was that the thing was alive, and searching his soul. Maybe if he could think of a question it would let go. Trying not to panic, he tried to form thoughts. There were so many things he needed to know: not least, what did Nirias really want from him? Wishing he could pull away, he put words together in a silent shout. *How does the Song work? How does the Song work?* It was a desperate plea, wrung from the core of his soul.

Ash's hands were released so abruptly that he staggered. The Heartstone was swirling wildly now, as if something had stirred its depths. Ash held his hands before his face. There, upon each burning palm, was the sharp outline of a crescent moon. Nirias grasped Ash's wrists, curiously eager. When, after a moment's study he released his grip, his voice was reverent.

'In ancient times, the moons were a mark of pride. The Heartstone adds fresh lines with each reading, you see. The moons grant the holder prestige and access to knowledge. The more intricate the patterns, the more learned the Azuri. The more trusted.' Nirias was rubbing his own palms together in an unconscious circling motion. For some reason Ash was reminded of Sarin. Then the impression was gone. 'Only those whose intentions are pure can become Azuri.'

Nirias's eyes clouded with pain and he sighed. 'Little did the Azuri know how dangerous those marks would prove. The Stone was recalibrated. But late … far too late.' His words had faded to a whisper as if he was speaking to himself. At last he shook himself free of whatever memory had made him so grief-struck. 'Oh, my boy. You need not look so worried. Your marks will fade, only reappearing if you rub your hands together, recreating the Stone's heat.'

Ash had hidden his hands under his armpits. Nirias might have warned him what to expect! Once again he reminded himself of something he must never let himself forget: Nirias was Malshorne, and kin to Credé.

'Let me show you what happens next,' said the Malshorne with a cunning smile.

Beneath the Heartstone's housing was a silver pillar. Ash had taken it to be part of the support, but it turned out to be a stack of silver disks. Nirias reached down and drew one from the top. 'Press your palm to the plate,' he instructed.

Ash stared at the object, dreading some new horror. After a long moment, he gritted his teeth and did as he was told. To his great relief, nothing happened at all.

'Good. Now, hold the plate from beneath, on the tips of your fingers.' Almost as soon as Ash had balanced the plate, it lifted into the air! It hovered there for a moment, before shooting upwards. Nirias chuckled in delight at Ash's stunned reaction. Together they watched the spinning plate fly around the chamber, higher and higher, until it stopped right near the top of one of the tall cylindrical vessels. The lore-stones seemed to shuffle and jostle in response to its presence.

Ash hurried closer, stretching his neck to see. He thought he could make out a pinkish glow among the clustered spheres. There was a flare of light accompanied by a faint popping noise. Whirring more quietly now, the plate floated down, returning to hover in front of Ash. The lore-stone glowed: a pink pearl, served to him upon a silver dish.

⁂

'Ah. Here we are. My favourite nook.' Nirias stroked the velvet wing of a crimson armchair in a proprietary manner. 'I spent many an hour in this place as a lad, mulling the stones.' He chuckled. 'That's what they called it when anyone spent long hours in the stores, flitting from one subject to another.' His eyes shone with memory. 'Mulling the stones.' He sighed deeply and settled himself into the chair.

Ash had never sat in a chair so deeply cushioned. Fearing he might be swallowed up by it, he perched on the front edge. With Nirias apparently lost in thought, Ash took the opportunity to look out of the window. A white-stone tower was framed by the arched casement. Oddly shaped, like an inverted goblet, it was ringed with balconies. Beyond that were the ranges, bright white under winter sun.

Between Ash and Nirias was a table, with indented circles that turned out to be holders for lore-stones. The pink orb selected by the Heartstone was flanked by stacks of leather tomes, all gathered by Nirias. Ash eyed the books anxiously. He could read a little, of course. Lord and Lady Feyindi insisted that their house slaves maintain the skill, for several years at least, since those with talent might prove useful as clerks and secretaries. Ash feared his skills were nowhere near up to the challenge of such vast volumes, though.

He was relieved to discover that Nirias had already browsed the pile, which only 'touched on' the subject of the Song, and was preparing to summarise what he had learned. When Ash's stomach gave a loud grumble, the Malshorne chuckled. 'I'll be as brief as I can.' Ash blushed, shifting in his chair. The others were probably taking their midday meal. He would give anything to be with them.

Nirias had already launched into what was to be a long lecture. 'Above all else, the Azuri were a people of peace. There were no weapons in T'al Jazure, nor any knowledge about how to devise one. Such things were strictly forbidden. If the Azuri touched the world beyond the city, peace was ever-present in their motives: they aimed only to foster harmony among the peoples of T'al Agria. The Song was the Azuri's most noble endeavour — their greatest gift to the world. For the Song encompassed all the histories, all the stories of the world, in perfect harmony. The Taelstaun, as you know already, were the Keepers of the Song. Men and women chosen for their gifts, and given a destiny: to travel far and wide, collecting stories, learning the songs of every people, of people within peoples — women and men, kings and cobblers, elders, children and slaves ... Yes, even slaves, Ash. However — and this is most pertinent to our problem — the Taelstaun did not merely collect stories, they wove them into the fabric of the Song. Ravelling out common threads, they built a harmony of sound and words — rooted in individuals and place and time, but flowing with shared emotion.' Nirias paused. 'Do you begin to understand?'

With panic rising in his belly, Ash could not trust himself to answer. He just bobbed his head.

Apparently satisfied, Nirias went on. 'Thus the Taelstaun were listeners and gatherers, but they were also singers. Composing melodies sweet enough to melt the hardest hearts, they created the Song anew with each place they visited, blending new stories with old, capturing memory and experience. The three Taelstaun travelled to every possible coast, crossing every boundary, learning and singing. Then, at specific moments in time, in accordance with the moons and stars and tides, they gathered here, in T'al Jazure, to sing in chorus. And hence, three became one: one Song, one story, touching all the joys and sorrows of the living world.'

Silence hung between them for long moments. Ash was hoping he had misunderstood.

'So … you mean … I …' Ash's voice quavered, and broke. 'I have to sing?'

'Yes, Ash. You are the Taelstaun. If you do not sing, the Song will drive you to madness.' Ash was struggling to breathe. Every one of Nirias's words felt like a punch in his gut. 'I believe that was Credé's fate. His failure to master the Song very probably contributed to whatever sickness ailed him. Credé was not the rightful Taelstaun. My brother was a brilliant man, but he had none of the skills …'

Nirias kept talking, not noticing that Ash had stopped listening. He wanted to howl. *I am not the rightful Keeper of the Song either!* Tucking his hands between his knees, he fixed his eyes on the hard edge of the table. Hot surges assaulted his body, roiling in his stomach, making his palms sweat.

At last Nirias faltered. Leaning forward, he blew a soft stream of air through pursed lips. 'Ash, you need not look so stricken. Credé was the Song's keeper for nigh on a thousand years. That, at least, will not be your fate.' Perhaps he thought the idea was reassuring. It was not. Ash brought trembling hands to either side of his head. Not his fate. Just one ordinary lifetime of madness for him.

Nirias seemed to hesitate, as if not quite sure how to deal with the terrified youth before him, then he ploughed on. 'I understand, the prospect is frightening. But there is really no use in evading the truth …' He gave a delicate cough. 'And I'm afraid your problem — our problem — is even worse. The Song that Credé passed to you is incomplete, at best. Centuries are missing. But, even more alarmingly, from what you've told me of your dreams …' Nirias shook his head, 'I believe Credé used his lore-stone, the Taelstone if you like, to lock the truth away. Truth that he could not face, fragments of history, indelibly stained with his own crimes.' The Malshorne gestured at the pile of books. 'These records all agree. The Passing of the Song required a second Taelstaun. Credé replaced that person with the orb, with terrible consequences. I'm sorry to say, Ash: somehow Credé's guilty, irreconcilable memories have stolen into your consciousness — through the conduit of the darkstone and the Taelstone itself.'

Ash dragged his unwilling eyes to Nirias's face. His mind went back to Credé's hut and the ceremony on the weird dark triangle. He remembered how the Song had surged, emblazoning the stone with fire, drawing energy from three points: Credé, Ash and the Taelstone. Yes, what Nirias was suggesting seemed horribly plausible.

'So, you think Credé was really there — at the fountain, in Eeroktan?' Ash had told Nirias about his recurring nightmare, those terrible images … the blood and the bodies in the water.

Nirias's eyes glittered, as icy as the winter ground. 'Yes. I believe Credé witnessed the last days of Eeroktan. Perhaps, one day, when it is safe, when you have mastered the reading of lore-stones, then Credé's stone may shed further light on those events. But Ash, for now you must avoid unnecessary contact. If I am right, then it is the repository of all his bitterness. Keep it safe, but safeguard yourself from its energy.' Ash resisted the urge to move his hand to the pocket where the Taelstone was concealed. 'Just for now … Until you are stronger.' Nirias sighed, rubbing his brow. 'And, yes, I suspect Credé was there. It seems more than likely that he watched over the destruction of Eeroktan and her dying moments. I do not know when he came to build his hut on the site of the darkstone, but perhaps he also witnessed the invasion of the Mildarens, and their enslavement of the Eerok.'

Ash felt even smaller in his armchair. There was an awful, compelling logic in Nirias's words, a logic that put a quaver in his voice. 'What must I do?'

Nirias smiled then. In fact, he gave a soft chuckle. 'Be hopeful, Ash. For you are safe in T'al Jazure — the city of hope.' Leaning forward, he plucked the pink orb from its resting place. 'Your first step is to learn to read the stones.' Holding the orb in one hand, he rubbed his other hand over the top of it, as if giving it a quick polish. He gave a little shout of laughter before handing it to Ash. To his surprise, Ash saw that the orb now contained an image. A woman's face smiled back at him.

'Ash, allow me to introduce Demara Cantoya. A delightful woman, and expert advisor on all things to do with the Song.' Nirias's smile grew wider. 'Oh, yes. A most fascinating woman, Demara.' He gave a satisfied sniff. 'I rather thought this might be one of her stones. According to the books, she trained the apprentices. You will be in excellent hands.'

***

Ash trudged through the snow, absorbed in his thoughts and oblivious to the fact that several new tracks had now appeared. Had he been less preoccupied, he might also have caught a movement at the edge of the low wall, just beyond the dancing statues. Striding along as he was, nose tucked into his collar, he did not even glance at the dancing maidens, let alone notice the peculiar fact that one now held a snowball in her outstretched hand. So the blur of white that smacked into his shoulder spraying his face with snow came as a complete shock.

As he stood gasping, another snowball thwacked into his forehead. He shook his head, blinking snow from his eyes. Tarlyn had already leapt from his shoulder. She sprang and plunged through the snow, a black arc against the white. Reaching the trees, she vanished.

Sarin emerged from his hiding place, rocking with laughter. 'Sorry, Ash,' he called. 'You just looked so serious.' Vaulting the wall, he wandered over, arms stretched out in apology but still chuckling. 'I couldn't help myself.' Sarin tried to smother a grin, to no avail. 'Seriously! You're not supposed to just stand there! I swear those statues would have moved quicker!' As Ash shook the snow from his hair, Sarin shook his own head, too. 'You didn't even spot my clue!' He laughed, pointing at the statue holding the snowball. 'Haven't you ever had a snowball fight?'

Ash wanted to point out that slaves hardly had time to frolic in snow, even if there had been snow in Mildaresh. Sarin was already patting snow into another ball. 'Come on, Ash. It's fun.' With a flick of his wrist he sent the ball hurtling towards the statues, hitting one full in the face. Sarin hooted with delight. 'Too easy! First one to smash the dancer's snowball wins!'

Ash squinted at the dancer. She was a long way off and he'd never had a good throwing arm. He scrambled for snow anyway. Before long he was flinging snowballs for all he was worth, cheering every near-miss. The snow flew, pelting the dancer from all angles. It was fun. It felt so … rebellious. Ash laughed for the sheer joy of it. The dancer remained steadfast against the onslaught, poised and graceful.

They were just taking a breather, readying themselves for a renewed volley, when a snowball whizzed over their heads. Continuing its trajectory, it dashed the prize from the dancer's hand.

With a shout, they turned. And there was Kep, brushing off her palms. She picked up her basket and strolled towards them. Ash snorted with delight at the look on Sarin's face. How was he to know that Kep had been pitching rocks at predators since she was a child? Nothing got near Kep's precious flock of bug-eye goats!

Kep laughed, too, then she blushed, totally ruining her attempt at nonchalance. 'Food,' she said, addressing Ash. 'Did you forget?'

Hot from exertion, they cleared snow from a bench and sat in the pale sunlight to share their midday rations. Kep had collected enough for all of them. Sarin did not volunteer where he had been that morning — for once it did not seem to have included the kitchens, for he ate as hungrily as anyone else. A quick tap on the bench demonstrated that the loaves were as hard as ever, but Kep had brought water to help wash the bread down, and strips of smoked meat for flavour.

Sarin swallowed a mouthful. 'You go first, Ash. Did Nirias keep you entertained?'

Ash told them about his interminable morning with Nirias. When Sarin heard his description of the way the Heartstone had reacted he seemed surprised.

'That's weird. It didn't do that for me.' He laughed at their shocked faces. 'Of course I checked out the Knowledge Stores. Who wouldn't?' He started rubbing his hands together. 'Didn't know I was supposed to ask questions; I'll try that next time. But I did find these on my hands.' He held his palms out for them to see. The crescents were faint but clearly etched. 'What else did you find out, Ash?'

Kep shuddered when Ash told them about the Song, and Nirias's theory about Credé's memories.

'I was right! I knew the Taelstone was dangerous. You are going to take Nirias's advice, aren't you, Ash?'

Ash had not told her that Nirias thought the stone held secrets, secrets that only Ash could uncover. She would only worry. He avoided her eyes and did not reply.

Sarin raised skeptical brows, then grinned. 'So, you going to give us a song?'

Ash gulped. Just the thought of singing for an audience made him queasy and his knees wobble.

Kep scowled at Sarin on Ash's behalf. 'Don't worry, Ash. We're not going to make you sing.'

Ash shrugged, hoping to look casual. 'Nirias said Aechon would help. That's what the Cryer meant last night. Nirias thinks watching Aechon go about his work might be useful.'

'Makes sense to me.' Sarin was amusing himself by piling snowballs one on top of the other. 'Composing songs for dead people. That's sure to cheer you up.'

Ash stood and stretched. Sarin was right. It would not be fun. League warriors were intimidating enough; Ash could not imagine asking them to talk about their dead comrades.

'Is that all, then?' asked Kep, brushing crumbs from her cloak. 'You were gone an awfully long time.'

Ash shrugged. 'Pretty much. I spent the rest of the time trying to read the stone. With no luck,' he added quickly, before they could ask. It was an understatement. He had spent ages staring at that stone, willing something to happen. Finally even Nirias had admitted defeat. The trick would come, he had said. You just have to calm your mind. Except there was nothing calm about Ash's mind. His brain was a boiling mess of fear and unanswered questions — and staring at a woman in a bubble did not help one bit.

'Oh!' Something fell into place, striking Ash so unexpectedly that he could not help exclaiming.

'What, Ash?' Kep put a hand on his arm. 'What is it?'

'I've just remembered. It was something Rilka said: she told me there were faces in the circle.' Sarin swivelled his head at the mention of his sister. 'I had no idea what she meant, but I think she meant the stones.'

Sarin nodded, thoughtful. 'Sometimes it takes a while to find the meaning in Rilka's visions.'

Kep was frowning and stamping her feet. 'Come on, you two,' she said brightly. 'Let's get somewhere warm.' Ash knew she did not want to talk about Rilka or her visions. He didn't either. Especially not the ones that linked him to the Melk. So they chatted about other things as they walked.

'And how are you finding your new roommate, Kep?' asked Sarin as they drew near the lodges. 'Is Ordelle proving an ordeal?' Sarin's eyes sparkled with mischief.

Kep gave him a stony look. 'Stop it, Sarin. I'm sure Ordelle and I will get along perfectly well — once we get to know each other better.'

Chapter 10

THE SORROW

Pushing the door open with his shoulders, Daska backed into the small room that Nirias had commandeered for himself. Located over the kitchens, the room was accessed by one of the gantries; useful if one wanted to keep an eye on what was happening in the hall below. It also had a private staircase, via the kitchens, for coming and going. Very like Nirias. Daska could not help but smile as he looked around. Books lay everywhere, already stacked in piles and scattered on the floor — everywhere, it seemed, except the bookcases. Nirias seemed to have that effect on every space he inhabited. He looked up from the volume which currently sought his attention and frowned. 'Why are you waiting on me, Daska?'

Daska dumped the tray on a table, making the plates jump. 'I have no idea. I am certainly no nurse maid.' He glowered. 'But the fact remains, you would waste away if I did not.'

Nirias adopted a half-annoyed, half-guilty expression and closed the book.

'Stew,' announced Daska.

'Is it terrible?'

'Not as terrible as usual. I suspect somebody managed to smuggle seasoning into it.' Daska had his suspicions about who that somebody was.

Nirias chuckled. 'We should have thought of that sooner.' When he caught Daska watching him pick up the bowl, he brandished a spoon.

'Stop your fussing, my friend. Sit. And tell me what you think about our three Seekers.'

Taking a chair, Daska brushed imaginary dust from his sleeve. 'They are children. Far too young for the business of the League. Just this morning I watched them playing in the snow.'

Nirias chuckled in between spoonfuls of stew. 'They are far from children, my friend. They are Seekers. Kep and Ash travelled all the way from Mildaresh with a tracker in pursuit. With Sarin's help they avoided slavers, fought off cessrats and evaded the clutches of Calkinon. No, they are not children, and nor are they slaves.'

Daska folded his arms. 'Hmmm. Kep has the heart of a warrior, I'll grant you that. She certainly shows determination with the bow. I expect she applies herself with that same grit to everything.' He shook his head. 'As for Sarin, he shoots better than most of our warriors, learns everything quickly and has a disturbing flair for deception. He would make a brilliant shade, even without training.' Daska grimaced as he rubbed the back of his neck — more than once he had found himself the object of Sarin's tricks. 'Whether he would follow orders, that is a different question. He has too much of the rebel, and not enough of the soldier. He questions all, watches everything and unsettles everyone. His tongue is that sharp ...' Daska shook his head. 'Even if he does take the Pledge, it would be a brave captain who took Sarin on.'

Nirias laughed. 'I knew Sarin's grandmother. A formidable woman who most certainly followed her own path. I would not expect anything less of her kin.'

Daska frowned to himself. The time Nirias had spent with the Aurum fell into the dark years; the times they did not discuss. A heaviness had settled on the room. He continued. 'As for Ash ...' What could he say? The boy was like a frightened kitten.

Nirias interjected. 'Do not concern yourself with Ash. Ash faces a greater challenge than any of us. There is something about that lad, Daska.' It was always the same. For Nirias everyone had promise. And everyone had a use. Nirias was gesturing with his spoon instead of eating. 'True he does not look like a League warrior, not by any means. But if Ash ever had a childhood, it is far behind him. By some strange quirk of Fate, which I am yet to fathom, this boy, this slave from Mildaresh has inherited the Song. All the histories of all the world reside in that head of his. Perhaps he may not survive it. And yet ...' Nirias paused, glancing at the book he had been reading. 'Ash has some strange destiny. I feel sure of it.'

Daska raised a brow. No wonder the boy looked so pale.

'I want Ash trained in the Breath, and self-defence, but little more. He has other tasks.' Nirias was distracted and his stew was going cold. 'The lore-stone Ash carries may hold knowledge of the Melk — knowledge from before T'al Jazure was locked. Knowledge that might help us eliminate the Melk once and for all. Unlocking those secrets, that is the key.'

Daska could not help sighing. It wheezed from him. In another man it would have held a whisper of despair. He had joined the League as a young man, with fuzz on his chin and barely a hair on his scrawny chest. This was his seventieth winter. His whole life had been spent hunting nulls, seeking out the Melk. But that was nothing compared with the centuries endured by Nirias. Daska understood his leader's capacity for hope — it is what he loved about the man. He just did not understand how it could flare anew after so many defeats. And lately … Daska worried. He had started to notice a shadow — not a darkness — never that, but something was amiss with Nirias. Daska sensed a tiredness that went beyond the physical, as if the man had pushed himself to the point of self-destruction.

In the long pause Daska turned his gaze to the triangular window with its view of shining turrets. He frowned. Even the windows were wrong in this strange city. He would have been happier in the labyrinth of caves beyond the hills. This place felt … watchful. Daska feared that so much luxury might weaken the resolve of his warriors. Would the pledges hold? Could he spur the warriors out from safety to once more face the madness of the Melk? Still, if T'al Jazure had not been found, could the League even have survived another winter? They were scattered. Disillusioned. The old warrior shook himself; there was no point dwelling on it. Nirias had followed his gaze, and apparently his thoughts.

'Daska, we have been given a miracle. A whole winter of respite. Time to recover, to rebuild, to restore minds and strengthen bodies.' Nirias's eyes went faraway in their focus, beyond the mountain peaks. 'Mildaresh will be a challenge my friend. Perhaps the challenge of this lifetime. Aranti is a clever and ambitious man. He will prove a formidable nexus, stronger than any we two have yet faced, I fear.'

Daska nodded. The jinn in Mildaresh was in disarray, that much could be read into the message which had come. Just a couple of shades left, no warriors. They could not prevail.

Nirias clapped his hands together, then rubbed them in tight circles. Once more, the man seemed to divine his thoughts. 'The spring thaws will bring the captains, and fresh news of how things lie in Mildaresh. In the meantime we will rebuild the jinns. Training will commence as soon as the Sorrow is done.'

Neither spoke of their losses. The madness at Zondra had claimed two of their very best. Raycha, the red fox captain, was a terrible casualty. A quick, sure fighter and brilliant strategian, she had also been a senseer — one of the rare people able to recognise the hosts of the Melk before they became nulls. And Daro … Daska closed his eyes. He would not let himself think of Daro. Now was not the time to weep. He would visit the Cryer this afternoon to tend to his grief. He coughed, staving off the emotion which threatened to overwhelm him.

'I want you to oversee everything, Daska — especially the training of the Seekers. And watch that Ash does not spend his time hiding in the kitchen. He is no longer a slave.'

Daska gave a slow nod. 'But the girl, Nirias. She will not be ready. Not by spring.'

'I understand your concern. The stakes are high. Kep is important as a symbol of hope. We will keep her safe.'

Daska's frown darkened. The indirect answer did not fool him. He knew when Nirias was dissembling. *Keep her safe?* If he had his way Kep would never leave the city, let alone go to Mildaresh — into the jaws of the most threatening nexus they had ever faced. The girl had all the powers of Calkinon baying for her blood, not to mention the Melk. The Melk had spoken her name! What was Narsis pondering? Daska knew that look. It was an argument that could wait.

He gave a deep sigh. He had known from the beginning that the girl would be trouble. She was too full of spirit, and far too beautiful. He had seen the way the young men looked at her, and a couple of the older ones, too; it was more than curiosity about her name. Just as well the Cryer's daughter was sharing her room.

Daska shook his head. A weakling, a mischief-maker, and a spirited beauty with a price on her head — Seekers or not, it was just what they didn't need. Of course there was no point voicing his concerns to Nirias. 'Eat your stew,' he grumbled.

❧

The second day of the Gleaning found Kep agreeing to a very odd request. One of the deceased warriors, Daro, had been Varlon. It seemed that Varlon people did not hold funeral fires for the dead. Kep was shocked to learn that they did not burn their dead at all. In this case a death bower was required, so that Daro might sleep in the ground. Kep had not been able to think of an excuse when the Cryer had asked for her assistance, so she had spent all morning bent over a stack of reeds, doing her best to soak and split weaves to Ordelle's exacting specifications. It was not as easy as it sounded. The reeds had razor-sharp edges when split, and Kep's fingers were stinging from tiny cuts. Perhaps Aechon had thought it would be a good chance for them to become friends. He was wrong. 'I expect we won't get on. I'm better with the dead than the living.' Ordelle had made the odd declaration on that very first night. Now the prophecy seemed as accurate as it was bizarre.

At the time, the Cryer's daughter had been unpacking her bag, laying each item on the bed in a row — exactly two finger-widths apart. Kep had not dared to ask about the curious array of implements and materials. When Ordelle had finished lining them up, she had simply packed them away again, apparently into the same pockets from which they had come. That done, she had shrugged herself into a nightgown, before lying herself flat on her bed, as stiff as a corpse. After Kep had put out the light she had made a second announcement. 'You don't have any books.' She had fallen asleep before Kep had managed to think up a response.

The Cryer's daughter was in the other room now, working with Gallin to embalm the two bodies. Kep was trying not to think about how they would curl the man's corpse into a foetal position. She was just happy to have some respite from Ordelle's company. The young woman was mostly silent, regarding everything with the same expressionless gaze. Then, without warning, she would volunteer information, delivered in outbursts, as if recited from a book. The result was that Kep knew far more about bodily fluids, decomposition and the extraction of organs than she had ever wanted to know. By Argess! What was wrong with the girl?

By the time Ordelle returned, Kep had built three piles of reeds, organised by length. There was a pile of cast-offs too, since it had taken a while to get the knack of splitting the material exactly down the middle. If Ordelle was pleased with her efforts, it did not show. She flipped open a small notebook. 'We have measured the body. The fit must be snug. We will need three times that many.'

Kep bowed her head to the task and they worked in silence. Kep's back was soon aching from sitting on the floor for so long. When she stood to stretch, she was surprised to see that a woven structure was taking shape. It shivered and waved as Ordelle twisted and wove the fibres. Kep was completely mesmerised by the deft working of those strong fingers. 'How many of these bowers have you woven?'

Ordelle did not look up. 'Six … and a half … One was for a child.'

Kep blinked. A bower for a child! Putting a child in the ground, with no bird to guide its soul. How horrible! Kep bit her tongue and returned to the floor.

⁂

'So, Ash. What have we gleaned about Raycha thus far?'

Ash jumped. Leaping forward, he used the tongs to grasp the burning brand which, thanks to Aechon's inept skills with the poker, had jumped from the grate and onto the rug. As he returned the brand to the fire, Acheon laughed. It was impossible not to like the little man. His charms worked on even the gruffest warriors. Perhaps their trust was related to the bird on his neck, the mark of his craft, or maybe to do with the man himself. Whatever it was, the Cryer's aura extended to Ash as well. He had received only a couple of curious glances during the Gleaning and mostly was ignored, which suited him perfectly.

Some of the warriors had visited them here in the cosy sitting room to share their memories in private. Others had been sought out by Aechon, lured into conversation by some snippet gleaned elsewhere. There had been weeping, and painful silences, but much laughter, too. And Heeda had brought anger. The red-haired woman had stormed and railed at the injustice of Raycha's death. The red fox jinn had been sent to Zondra partly because their captain had the gift of sight. Raycha had duly confirmed the nexus: a baker who had been poisoning the minds of others, stirring up hatred. Plans were in place for his elimination when, inexplicably, the Melk had swarmed. The warriors were caught between the avenging villagers with their hatred of strangers and the crazed hosts, abandoned by the Melk to madness. Trying to prevent the massacre, the captain of the foxes had taken a deadly stomach wound — her last act, defending the baker's children.

Ash had listened to Heeda's tale with growing fear, terrified he would faint again. Somehow the Cryer's calm presence, his quiet witness, made the terrible story bearable. And at last Heeda had been able to weep. Ash knew she blamed Nirias. In her mind, Nirias had sent Raycha to her death. And perhaps that was true.

Ash realised that Aechon was still looking at him, expecting an answer. 'Do you recall what Jakarmon Pyke had to say about Raycha?'

Blinky Pyke. That was Sarin's nickname for the man. And he had blinked a lot. It had taken all of Aechon's gentle persuasion to draw out his thoughts. 'He spoke of her strength as a fighter.'

'Good. And?'

'She was one of the best archers he had ever known. Could hit a cessrat at a hundred paces. And she led the advance in …' Ash tailed off, forgetting the name.

'Ah, yes. Gladinstoe.' Aechon jotted it down in a thin red notebook.

'She had a habit of humming when she walked, but only when she was feeling anxious, and … she had your back. Jakarmon kept repeating that … They all did. *Raycha always had your back.*'

Aechon nodded. 'Excellent! Another thread in the fabric of Raycha's Sorrow. Do you see?'

They continued working, with Aechon making notes and Ash chipping in with anything he could remember. Every now and again, Aechon would shoot the young man a keen look. Ash was quite sure the man was examining him, too; it did not feel uncomfortable, just a gentle probing.

Slowly a picture emerged of the warrior — the woman — that Raycha had been. Colour was important, Aechon said, and silence, too; sometimes beauty lay in what was left unsaid. Images, actions and mysteries, all must be given space, woven with emotion. Ash did not really understand. He did enjoy watching the Cryer, though. Slowly the man fell into a state of calm until at last he laid his notebook on the table. He smiled. 'Now is the time for mulling.'

Aechon reached behind him and plucked a dark-bellied lute from its stand. It was one of three. There were drums and flutes and harps, too. Handling the instruments seemed part of the process. Sometimes he played a few notes. Mostly he just held them. The sound of this particular lute was deep and earthy, making Ash think of forest shade.

'What do we think?' The Cryer's fingers tried out patterns on the neck. 'So important to find the right chord. That is the foundation of all.' His thumb stroked the strings. 'This for Daro?' He shifted his fingers. 'Or this?'

On the third variation, Ash leaned forward. 'That one.'

Aechon seemed pleased. 'I agree, Ash. A bright major chord for Daro. Of course his Sorrow may not be a song at all. A story perhaps, or a chant

...' he mused, staring into space. 'Still. We have found the right chord. Excellent! We should take a break. I should like to check on Ordelle's progress with the bower before going further.'

He seemed about to rise, then paused. 'Before we do, there is one soul left to glean.' Aechon wrapped his arms around the lute, as if he was cuddling a child. 'What chord do you think would suit your friend, Braig?'

Ash swallowed. Somehow, under the gaze of those gentle eyes, he found the words. 'I don't know. Something strong I suppose ...' Images of Braig lifting sacks of grain came to mind, muscles straining, and that smell he had ... earthy — not unpleasant, an honest farmyard smell. 'And ... cheerful, I suppose.' Ash frowned, remembering the times he had been on the receiving end of Braig's humour, back before Credé, before the Song, and before ...

Aechon nodded. 'Good.' He made no move to pick out notes. Instead he returned the lute to its place. 'I think we have enough to mull over for now, don't you?'

But still the Cryer made no move to leave. Instead, they watched the fire in companionable silence, each occupied by their own thoughts. When Aechon spoke again, his tone was thoughtful. 'I think of a shawl, you know.' He smiled shyly, as if sharing a secret. 'While I'm working a Sorrow. A shawl with tassels and ornaments, some threads hanging loose, and interwoven colours — or it might be one colour at one end and completely different at the other. My old nurse had such a garment. As the years went by, she would add patches and knit new sections. I remember holding it to my face to feel the different textures.' He laughed at himself. 'I wonder if I had never seen such a garment, how I might have visualised the process then.' The question seemed to intrigue him. 'And what about you, Ash? If you were to visualise the Song, what would it look like?'

Although Ash had never seen a shawl like the one Aechon described, he understood what the man meant — he could see how that might help him to think about the process. It was a comforting idea. Except when Ash thought about the Song it was just a chaotic mess. He appreciated what Aechon was trying to do. He was not trying to interrogate him, just help him to organise his thoughts. Nevertheless, the question made him panic. He was lost for words.

At that moment, something quite unusual happened. Tarlyn stretched, bounced lightly to the floor and up into Aechon's lap. The man gave a cry of delight. 'Ah! I am honoured indeed.' As he tentatively stroked the top of her head, Tarlyn blinked her eyes at Ash. It seemed even Tarlyn approved of the Cryer.

Ash wanted to trust him, too. The problem was he did not feel in control of the Song at all, he was not weaving or building anything, he was just being swept along. 'I … I can't really describe it.'

Aechon's eyes were wells of empathy. 'Perhaps there is something we might latch onto together. Are there particular images or patterns perhaps?'

Ash shook his head. 'Chaos, it is just chaos.'

'Perhaps if you think back to the very first time you experienced it? Would that help?'

Ash remembered singing with Credé quite clearly — how could he ever forget that? And the feel of the darkstone alive beneath his feet? 'It was fire,' he faltered, 'at first, it was traceries of fire, like golden script upon the black stone. It flowed and spiralled, in ribbons but … it was complicated and all interwoven with symbols.'

Aechon did not make eye contact, he just listened. 'And then?'

'I fell. And the symbols became images. It was like being in an extremely vivid dream.'

'Ah. How wonderful. And now? What does it feel like now?'

Ash frowned. He had spent all his time shutting the Song out and trying not to think about it. 'It is quieter here. There's a hush. It feels … like being at the centre of a storm.'

'And does that seem to make sense to you?'

It did. It made complete sense. 'I suppose so. If the Azuri created the Song, then its centre would be at T'al Jazure.' Tarlyn ruffled up her fur a little. Ash saw himself reflected in her huge, unblinking eyes.

'Then the answers must be here, too. It may take a little time, but you have a sensitive heart and a sharp mind, Ash. You will solve this problem, my friend.'

Ash could not help feeling a glow at the man's words. There was no guile in his expression, just an open, genuine smile. As incredible as it seemed, the Cryer really did seem to count Ash as his friend.

❦

Kep was up to her arms in water and reeds when the Cryer and Ash finally entered the workshop. The enthusiasm of her greeting spoke volumes about how relieved she was to see them. Ash was not surprised; he would not have liked to spend the morning with the Cryer's daughter either. Ordelle did not seem to think a greeting was required. She just kept working.

'Aha!' Aechon clapped his hands. 'What wonderful progress! I see you two have been very hard at work.'

Kep clambered to her feet and they all surveyed the half-built bower. Ash thought it looked more like a boat, until Aechon explained how the design would grow, making the shape in the air with his hands. Kep smiled warmly at the Cryer. But as he drew his daughter to one side to discuss some aspect of the decoration, she rolled her eyes and pulled a face that said 'Please … rescue me'. And when Aechon suggested that she had earned a break, she agreed readily. They left Ordelle to her weaving and scurried back to the warmth of the fire.

It was strange hearing Kep speak about Braig. In fact, Ash started to wonder if she had known a different boy altogether. To hear Kep talk, you would have thought Braig was perfect. She went on about his jokes and the pranks that he had played — Braig just made everyone happier, she said. The more she enthused, the more Ash shuffled in his chair. At last he simply had to say something.

'That's all true …' He stared at his feet. 'But Braig could be … well … a bit of a bully.'

Aechon's gentle smile remained in place as he turned his head, but Kep's eyes flew wide with surprise. 'How can you say that, Ash?'

Ash took a breath. 'You always stuck up for Braig, Kep. You always saw the best. No matter what. But Braig could be really mean.' Ash thought of all the times the larger boy had tousled his hair, the way he had punched him, or trapped him in a neck-hold. 'He called me "Weed".' When it came out like a whine, he winced. But if Ash had learned one thing from that morning, it was that stories of the dead come in shades, from the most wonderful to the least admirable. 'Braig became my friend. My only friend, apart from you. But he really did pick on me, Kep. In the beginning. I don't think he meant half of it, but … well, it wasn't always funny.' Kep looked so upset that Ash almost wanted to take his words back. 'I think he changed,' he added quickly. 'Maybe those days with Credé changed him. But maybe he only changed what he thought of me. Braig was so big and strong and confident … I don't think he realised that most people aren't like that.'

Kep was aghast, as if Ash had said something truly terrible. After a moment, though, her expression relaxed into a sad smile. 'Ash is right, Aechon. Braig could be … a bit boisterous.'

Ash spluttered, laughing at her choice of words. But she continued firmly: 'A bit boisterous in his treatment of other people's feelings.' Kep gave him a meaningful look, and he returned it with a smile. He could live with that.

On the third day, all was ready. The Sorrow began in the late afternoon, with Daro's burial in the orchard. His death bower was a thing of unusual beauty. The reeds had retained their greenish hue, with pieces of cloth and wooden beads woven in for effect. It seemed the sort of bower a bird might build. Aechon had decided on a chant for Daro after all, accompanied by a simple drum. He sang out the words as the bower was lowered into the ground, a call for a hero now returning to the earth.

Raycha's ceremony was as different from the Mildaren Fires of Passing as it was similar. Everyone who knew the woman had been invited to select coloured beads, signifying her importance to them. The necklace which Aechon had created would be sent to her village, in far-off Morgaine. When it arrived, her people would understand its significance, and they would weep for the woman and child they had known. Through the beads they would come to understand what Raycha had meant to the League. There were eighteen green beads, for friendship; three dark blue, marking sisterhood; five of amber, signifying admiration and respect; and a single bead of the deepest crimson — a lover's claim.

Raycha's coffin was open so that people might say their farewells. Ordelle had performed pure magic, erasing any sign of violence. The woman's hair was dressed and braided. She might have been sleeping, dressed in her warrior robes, her arms clasping her ebony bow to her breast. The fires were lit. A bird took flight. And Aechon sang. The Cryer's song lifted into the air as he led the procession back, towards the feast and a night of celebration.

Later, in the privacy of a quiet corner, there was a song for Braig, too.

Aechon had captured their friend's strength and enthusiasm to perfection; Ash could almost picture the warmth in those brown eyes. As he saw Kep smiling back at him through unchecked tears, he understood something profound. This was not death weaving at all: the Cryer was a weaver of lives.

Chapter 11

POISON

Karliana repositioned the awkward basket, trying to ease the spot where it bruised at her hip. She would have liked to swap arms, but the crowd made it impossible. As they drew closer to the heart of Mildaresh, things only got worse with the mill of bodies churning in all directions. There was apparently some sort of knack to avoiding others, and Karliana clearly did not have it. The steps of this dance were a mystery to her. Several times she caught a passer-by with her shoulder, and once nearly lost her basket altogether. When a farm slave approached, armed with a chicken, she misread his path and dodged the wrong way. The expression in his eyes, a quick flash of hostile interest, gave her a jolt. Hastening on her way, she adjusted her tattered shawl, tugging it closer around her face.

They were supposed to be attracting as little attention as possible, but Karliana did not seem to have the knack of that either. Twice, her companion had hissed a warning to walk less proudly, and now she sent her a glare. Karliana strove again to emulate the woman's posture, eyes downward, shoulders slumped, jaw slack. 'Don't see me,' her body said. It was an artform. Who said slaves were unskilled? Perhaps it helped to be born to it — that and a high tolerance to dragging skirts and the scratch of thin wool. Dodging a walking bundle of sticks, Karliana set her jaw against the chaffing of homespun cloth at her throat, cloth which was practically useless in protecting one from the winter chills. She was quite certain she would be left with a rash. Still. If she survived the day with merely a rash, it would be a pure miracle.

When they turned a corner, bringing the Squad headquarters into sight, the glimpse of the ugly, squat building made Karliana flush. Knowing she had behaved rashly was only part of her discomfort; the fact that the encounter had been utterly fruitless took the lion's share. She had gone in secret, against Pelor's wishes, seeking an audience with Rutholine Moagli. To beg. A letter. Just a letter. That was all she had asked. That he bear a letter to her father, to let him know she was well. And Rutholine had refused. Refused! How galling it had been to sit there, so thoroughly in the man's power. He had cradled the little note in that giant hand of his, staring at it for a long while, caressing it even, before handing it back. Such a strange refusal.

Those dark eyes so deep, like wells of … what? Sadness? Not remorse, certainly. Remorse was hardly part of the Moagli family's repertoire. Yet, if sadness, then for what? It made no sense, and Karliana liked things to make sense; especially people. Did Rutholine believe, like Pelor, that communication from his daughter would worsen Torland Lendri's torment? If so, why refuse? Was Rutholine not Aranti's henchman? His name was as closely associated with the Squad's nefarious business as his brother's. *It is too dangerous.* That was the only reason he had given. Dangerous for whom? Did he fear for himself? It made no sense. And it made Karliana angry. To think she had debased herself by grovelling to the man, only to leave in such confusion, and with the letter still in her keeping!

'Kel.' The reminder came more sharply this time. Brought back to the present, Karliana realised she had been grinding her teeth and scowling at folk. Responding late to the name they had agreed upon, she nodded. Her companion's concern was underscored by the tense lines around her eyes and mouth. 'We must be on our guard. It is not far now.'

Mara. That was the woman's name, and that was about as much as Karliana knew about her, except that she had once been a slave, bound to the House of Lendri. Freed by her father, Pelor had said. In his usual secretive fashion, the man had volunteered few details, apart from saying that Mara was now apprenticed to a jeweller, making her perfect for today's undertaking. Of course that had just set Karliana to wondering. Who was this woman? And who was she to her father?

She stole another glance. Tall and slim, Mara walked with a bit of a stoop. Her hair was cut very short, perhaps to tame the copper curls that clung to her head like a cap. Karliana had searched her memory for a tall slave with riotous red hair, and had come up with nothing. She seemed far too old for an apprentice. Karliana guessed Mara had thirty winters, although that was based on her confident manner rather than any physical evidence. Not once had she slipped up by calling Karliana 'my lady'. Mara was right, they needed to be on their guard, so Karliana put her musings to the back of her mind and paid attention.

They had entered the artisans' sector now, and were weaving their way into the heart of all its ramshackle clutter. If things went badly, Karliana at least wanted to know which way to run. Although she claimed never to have met the Alchemist, Mara did seem at home in this part of the city. She was obviously following clues: a blue door here, a shambling bridge, left at a waterwheel: the hidden signposts of those who frequented this locale. Karliana could not help thinking that this was a very different Mildaresh — stranger and darker than the one she knew.

As the streets drew in, Karliana sensed that Mara was growing even more cautious. Her eyes were urgent now, interrogating a movement at a window, peering sharply into shadowy entryways. She kept sniffing the air, too, making Karliana feel even more jumpy. Did she sense that something was wrong? Certainly there was a watchful air about the place. The boarded-up windows and empty streets belied the fact that this was one of the most densely populated areas in the city. So where was everyone? Hiding indoors presumably.

When they rounded a corner it was almost a surprise to see two lads leaning against a stained brick wall. The young men, both dressed in the anonymous garb of free-folk, carried on their conversation. Only the slight incline of a head suggested that their approach had been noted. Karliana held her breath. It seemed they might let them pass by, then: 'Hey! You!' The taller of the pair kicked his boot against the wall, pushing himself upright. Karliana cursed her stupidity. She should not have looked their way. 'Yes, you! Miss haughty-drawers. Where might you be heading then?'

In seconds the pair had drawn up close — too close. Karliana could smell the sweat on them, a harsh, masculine scent. Their thin faces and hard eyes frightened her. The smaller lad had brown hair that hung to his shoulders in ragged tails. Her eyes went to the frayed cuffs of his too-loose shirt and the mismatched buttons on his shabby green waistcoat. A thread hung loose where one button was missing.

'Leave us be,' growled Mara, hands on hips. Like a bushed-up cat, she suddenly took up more space. The time for being invisible had obviously passed. 'My brothers don't take kindly to boys taking chances.'

The lad in the waistcoat seemed to take stock at that, backing away a little. His partner just guffawed, sending hot breath into Karliana's face. His sawdust-coloured hair stood out from his head in odd chunks, as if it had been rubbed with dirty wax. There was something waxen about his skin, too, and those too-pale eyes.

'What about you? You got brothers, too?' Leaning in, he inhaled — deliberately, nostrils flaring. 'You don't smell like you got brothers. Too clean.' Karliana stiffened at his words. That was exactly what Mara had muttered, while helping her don the disguise. As the young lout squinted into her face she read his puzzlement. Did nobility have a smell? Was that what this lad sensed? Or was it her fear? Is that what emboldened him to pluck at her shawl? She was so transfixed by his audacity that she missed the other boy's hand shooting out. The shock of her buttock being squeezed made her squeal and drop her basket, sending the contents rolling.

Both lads whooped. 'Look at her hair! Pure-spun gold, that is.'

The shorter one grabbed at her skirts, preventing her from whirling away. 'And look! Did you ever see such a fine white leg?'

Mara went at them, spitting and scratching. She shoved the smaller lad, causing him to stumble, and landed a punch on the other. That only seemed to encourage him. Karliana found herself lifted clear off the ground in a sweaty embrace. She struggled, flapping and hitting, trying to break free. Then somebody shouted in a deep voice: 'Enough!'

The power of that cry put a swift end to the unseemly scuffle. Karliana found herself summarily dropped back to the ground. Both young men stood to attention, side by side, like soldiers, albeit very poorly dressed and ill-mannered ones.

'We think they're spies,' muttered Karliana's attacker. He had dropped his eyes, defensive, like a dog called to heal.

Karliana gathered herself together and snatched up her shawl. Disregarding the mud on it, she wrapped it around her chest before turning to discover the person who had spoken with such authority.

A woman stood there, grasping a staff taller than she was. The look in her black eyes suggested she would have no compunction using it should her words not be obeyed. Her skin was black and glossy, her hair bound beneath a bright yellow scarf. Bright green and yellow earrings dangled from her ears. Her apron was long, almost to her knees and covered in pinkish dust. Karliana could not help staring at the woman's feet, not just because they were large and broad and bare, but because she wore silver rings on her toes.

The stranger regarded them.

'Spies? Perhaps. But that does not give you two leave to act like idiots.' She gave a derisive snort. 'Pick everything up, and bring them inside.' Their rescuer did not give them a second look, nor wait to see if she was obeyed. She simply wandered back down the alley, hips swaying, and through the weathered blue door from whence she had come.

While Karliana gaped after her, Mara roused at the lads, shaming them into collecting the persimmons, bottles and assorted wares that had bounced away. When they were done, she led the way towards the open doorway, not waiting to confer with Karliana. As she followed, with the boys in her wake doing their very best to look like an escort, Karliana knitted her brows. She found herself doubting whether Mara had ever been anyone's slave.

The place they entered was both a workshop and a storage room in one. Karliana wrinkled her nose at the smell; the dusty, earthen tang grabbed at the throat. The whole back wall was made up entirely of small drawers — they rose from floor to ceiling, some tiny, and none bigger than a shoebox. The space on their right was taken up by three pottery wheels. Two stood empty, the middle was straddled by the woman they had followed. She was hunched over a large pot, working the wheel with her foot. She did not look up as they entered.

The sharper smells, acrid enough to make the eyes water, originated from the jars of chalky liquid lined up on a bench where a ragged child sat. He did not look up from his work either, he just continued stroking patterns onto a dish with his brush, his little pink tongue protruding from the corner of his mouth.

'Don't touch anything,' commanded the woman, in acknowledgement of their presence. 'Stand over there, and don't breathe too deeply. You two, back to your post.'

The lads bobbed their heads and slunk out.

Karliana pulled her shawl across her mouth, trying not to breathe and watching the pot turning. She was mesmerised by the woman's swinging earrings, and the way her sharp tool peeled the clay from the pot's base. Karliana realised she had never watched a pot being made. It was quite fascinating. She did not need the nudge from Mara to remain silent.

After a few moments, the wheel slowed and came to a stop. With a satisfied grunt, the woman detached the pot from her wheel, transferring it to a shelf. As she wiped her hands on a cloth, her attention was at last directed at her visitors. It was completely nerve-wracking.

Forgetting her agreement that Mara would take the lead, Karliana blurted out: 'We are not spies.' For some reason she wanted to impress the gigantic woman who was appraising them with such keen eyes.

Mara frowned and pushed forward. 'We were delivering supplies to our master, Belam the jeweller. You may have heard of him.'

The potter laughed, making her earrings dance. 'Not spies? That is just as well. For you do a terrible job of it.' She made a slow wink. 'Save your dissembling, I know Torland Lendri's daughter when I see her.' Her laughter made her bosom wobble. Then her eyes clouded with misgiving. 'It is a long while since Pelor sent me persimmons.' She paused, seeming to make a calculation behind those dark eyes. Then she nodded. 'You may call me Darlena. It is not my name, but it will suffice.' She winked. 'You can hardly call me the Alchemist.'

⁂

There was nothing for it but to accede to the Alchemist's will, that they wash their hands, eat herbed cakes and drink green cordial that tasted slightly of fish.

'For your eyes,' the Alchemist toasted, raising her own glass. A motherly finger waggled. 'They could be brighter.'

The same could not be said of the Alchemist's eyes. Despite deep wrinkles which congregated at the corners, her eyes shone with the clarity of raindrops. Taking a dutiful sip, Karliana looked around her, trying to absorb their totally unexpected surroundings. It made perfect sense when she thought about it — to hang out a sign declaring one was an alchemist was sure to invite trouble. Much better to pose as a humble potter. Although the work was hardly humble. Reminiscent of the woman's earrings, the finished pots were gorgeous in their design, a riot of pattern and rich colours.

The workshop was impeccably tidy, except for the large pile of broken shards that had been swept into one corner. The mix of shapes and colours suggested a whole shelf had come down. Was the young apprentice clumsy perhaps? The woman whose name was not Darlena followed Karliana's gaze.

'The Squad. They take exception to the fact that I will not pay them … for protection.' She thrust out her jaw. 'So they smash my windows and break my pots. They are children. Dangerous children. With sticks.'

Karliana felt her chest tightening. 'Protection? From what?' She thought she could guess at the answer. Only one thing could drive such fear. 'A slave uprising, you mean?'

To her surprise, both women laughed. It was bitter music, especially on the part of Mara.

'By Narsis. No, girl. It has not yet come to that.'

Karliana bristled. She did not much like being called 'girl', nor the way that Mara was looking at her, as if she thought her a fool.

The Alchemist explained as she refilled their glasses. 'No, the protection is from their own louts, of course … and those guardians who enjoy a bit of private bullying on the side. Guardians! Pah! There is not much of a line between them and the Squad.'

Karliana kept quiet.

'They mostly cause damage, petty breakages here and there, never enough to threaten a person's ability to pay, but there is looting, too. How much Aranti lets the Squad keep for stirring up trouble is anyone's guess.' The woman sniffed the air. 'And now, real danger is brewing. More of us are refusing to pay, and the consequences—' She stopped, as if not wanting to put her fears into words. 'But come. It is time for us to speak of what brings you to my door bearing persimmons and charcoal. An unusual combination, one might think.' She flashed her teeth. 'Do you wish to kill your husband?' Karliana could not help staring with wide eyes. 'That's how I got rid of mine. Instant death. No pain. He just collapsed. Like cutting the strings of a puppet.' She made a snipping motion with her fingers. Perhaps she was waiting to observe Karliana's reaction. When Karliana did not speak, she gave a slow nod.

'No. Not your husband,' she said softly. 'Another.' Her dark eyes glinted. 'We need not speak of it. There is no decision to be made. I will give you what you require.' Her shoulders slumped and her tone became weary. 'What *Fate* requires. Because sometimes poison is the only cure. And sometimes, as terrible as the consequences may be, violence can only be curbed by violence.'

Her eyes fell upon her small apprentice who was yawning over his work. 'Away with you, snotty urchin. I'll not have my boys nodding off. To your blankets now!' Karliana watched as she chased the boy from his seat. If her words were harsh, her movements were careful.

As if by magic, one of the previous lads appeared to claim the boy. As the child put his little hand into the older boy's outstretched one, he cast a sleepy but adoring look over his shoulder. Karliana frowned. She could not help herself. 'Is he not too young?' she ventured.

'Too young? Oh, yes, he is far too young to die on the streets. That is why he is here.'

Taken aback, Karliana turned to catch Mara's eye, only to be stunned by her intense expression. It truly looked as if the woman was about to spit! She resolved to keep her thoughts to herself.

If the Alchemist was perturbed by the unspoken criticism, she made no show of it. She crossed the room to the wall of a thousand drawers. None of them seemed to be labelled or marked in any way. Karliana could not imagine how the woman could keep track of what was in each, yet the Alchemist did not hesitate and opened one near the bottom. Whatever she took out of it was easily concealed in the palm of her hand. Rejoining them, she placed her fist on the table with a degree of ceremony. Drawing a deep sad breath, she opened her hand.

There, on the Alchemist's palm, was a small phial containing clear liquid. There also, to Karliana's surprise, was a pendant on a silver chain. She realised in a flash: the gorgeous purple gem was made of glass — the tiniest bottle conceivable, containing the most deadly of poisons.

'A sharp twist will suffice. But you must not touch the contents. Do you have the means to conceal these?'

Karliana nodded, reaching for the purse that was tucked away in a secret pocket beneath her skirts. When she tipped gold coins out onto the bench-top, the Alchemist let out a cry of alarm. She swiftly covered the pile with the rag her apprentice had discarded. 'Carrying gold on your person? By Telion! As if it were not enough that you came in person! Has Pelor lost his mind?'

Karliana answered her quietly. 'There was nobody else. It had to be me. Aranti's men watch every servant. But you need not worry: all believe that I am in my chambers, taking reflection as noblewomen do at the time of their womb's tears.' Karliana was not about to reveal the existence of the villa's secret passages. 'It was the only way,' she added firmly.

The Alchemist looked from Karliana to Mara, who confirmed it with a nod. She shook her head. 'Very well. But take back your gold. I know your quarry. I will not sully the righteousness of your cause through the exchange of gold.'

Karliana was about to argue, to urge the woman to take the gold, if only to distribute it to the needy, when Mara cut across her.

'Do you smell smoke? Is that your kiln?'

Once alerted, Karliana could smell it, too. Looking up, she saw that the lofted ceiling had become hazy. At that moment the two lads from before burst through the door, bringing the strong odour of burning with them. Their tidings delivered with the excitement of youth, they shouted over the top of each other.

'Fire! They've torched the shambles!'

'The folk are rallying! We've been called to the barricades! We are called to fight!'

In spite of the horror, both lads were grinning with the excitement of it all. All their bright enthusiasm was swiftly quashed by the Alchemist's response.

'Fight Aranti's thugs? You will do no such thing!'

Commands were issued. Before Karliana was even aware what was happening, benches had been moved out of the way. Stone flags were prised up to reveal a wooden trapdoor beneath. It flipped open as easily as the lid on her sewing box, revealing a flight of steps. The Alchemist's face was a picture of determination.

'Others will man the barricades. Oliver, I have a far more important task for you. One that will prove suitable penance for behaving like a complete oaf earlier. You will take the ways, and escort Lady Karliana and her companion out of danger.'

The lad who had grabbed Karliana's bottom gasped. 'Lady Kar—?' As he exchanged a look with his friend, his face wilted. It would have been comical had the circumstances not been so frightening. The Alchemist laid a large hand on his thin shoulder. 'By this dangerous task shall you renew my respect, and even win the respect of the lady. But listen: you are to avoid the fighting and are to report back here. Is that clear?' The boy nodded and shuffled his feet, his disappointment clear. 'Should it come to fighting, we will need you back here, and ready to give your all. This place and all that it contains must not fall into the hands of the Squad.' He nodded a second time, more vigorously, his eyes alive with the knowledge that he might not miss out on all the excitement after all.

The Alchemist tutted with disapproval. 'Sharrif, you are with me. Now, help me move these pots.' The shelf of unglazed pottery was quickly cleared and its backboards removed. The long cloth-wrapped bundle that

Sharrif retrieved from the space was covered in a light coating of dust. The Alchemist unwrapped the bundle, revealing a jumble of weapons. Sharrif received a short sword from her with proud eyes, and fastened it around his waist, working speedily lest she change her mind. The Alchemist had already tucked an axe into her belt. 'You,' she demanded. 'Can you wield a blade?'

Karliana was stunned when Mara nodded and selected a short sword. Watching the way Mara drew the blade, coolly inspecting its edge and weight, Karliana was left in no doubt: jeweller's apprentice or not, this woman was no stranger to swordplay.

As she followed their now highly attentive escort through 'the ways', Karliana realised she had never really known her city at all. Who would have thought that this secret system of alleyways and passages could exist? The whole thing suggested not just an underground community but an extraordinary spirit of co-operation — not to mention a hearty distrust of those in power.

'The ways' were like a rabbit warren, a haphazard mix of ancient tunnels and makeshift passages. Sometimes they even passed through shops and dwellings. There were more trapdoors, yards strung with washing lines, alleyways so choked with barrels that they had to climb up and over them, and a fenced-off terrace where a chained dog barked, its jaws slavering and snapping at Karliana's skirts.

To her horror, each time they caught sight of the sky it looked a darker grey, tinged with the glow of red. She could taste smoke now. The sounds of people screaming and shouting for buckets came to them more loudly at every pass. As they hurried on, Karliana had to fight the urge to run back, to try and do something. Anything! It seemed as if the whole city, her city, might be engulfed in flames. The guilt of leaving others to fight fed the anger in her heart. Was Aranti really prepared to sacrifice the city itself to gain power? It seemed so.

At last the sounds of chaos were dulled by their passage down a stone tunnel, an ancient remnant of the old city. The two women lifted their skirts as they hurried along, forced to share the path with a slow stream of water flowing down its middle. At the tunnel's end they were confronted by an iron gate, stark against the glare of a grey afternoon made more dismal by smoke. The water paid no heed to the gate; it slid underneath and ran silently down, over slimed rocks to join the river below. Karliana held her sides, trying to catch her breath and urging her heart to still its banging. The river! That meant they must be close to the Lendri estates — and the quiet tunnel that led to the refined hush of her father's library.

The lack of wind must have been a mercy for those fighting fires, yet the smell of smoke was surprisingly strong on the air, even this far from its source. Oliver was peering through the bars, still holding a finger to his lips. He motioned for them to flatten themselves even further against the sides of the tunnel. He had collected a swathe of cobwebs in his hair. Somehow it made him look even younger. Karliana wanted to reach across and brush them off.

A few heartbeats later he pushed the gate open, leading them out. They followed the thin river path for only a short way before climbing a steep flight of steps. Struggling with her skirts and the height of the steps, Karliana had no choice but to accept Mara's help. Then it was into the cover of trees. In minutes they had traversed the small copse and reached the edge of a formal terraced garden. The Montfane family were neighbours. Somewhere beyond those trimmed hedges was their comfortable villa. Karliana breathed in the scent of witch hazel. 'You may leave us now, Oliver.'

The lad shook his head. 'I promised to see you to the edge of your estates, my lady, and that is what I will do.'

Karliana smiled at his determined manner. It was rather wonderful to see how much it meant to this boy to follow his orders to the letter, and she certainly approved of the improvement in his manners. 'Very well,' she nodded.

They made easy passage through the gardens. Mostly, they were able to run along behind the curved hedges which demarcated the neatly trimmed order of the formal garden from the woodland. At this time of the afternoon, the only people they were likely to encounter were Lady Beatrice and her long-suffering gardener. It was the lady's habit to survey the gardens every afternoon, just to ensure that every plant was growing according to her exacting standards. The lady of the house would express grave disappointment that the roses had not bloomed in the colours she had imagined, and demand to know what the poor man intended doing about it.

Karliana could not help smiling to herself a little as they passed monstrous statues of sea creatures wallowing in beds that would be filled with bluebells come spring. And the astonishing pilat corner. Karliana doubted if anyone had actually been allowed to play pilat on its perfect triang. The brightest green and as plush as velvet, it was one of Lady Beatrice's quirky indulgences, as was her private amphitheatre.

Labelled a folly by most, the theatre was quite an ingenious structure. The stone seating could accommodate up to a hundred spectators on a summer's night, utilising the gentle slope of the land, with the façade of the villa and its terraces acting as an elaborate stage. The acoustics were quite remarkable. Perhaps if the performances had not been quite so tedious, Lady Beatrice's indulgence might have been looked upon more fondly. The amphitheatre was rarely used these days, so it came as a surprise to catch the faint sounds of shouting as they grew closer. Karliana frowned. Was Lady Beatrice rehearsing a play? In the middle of winter?

Although they had intended to avoid the villa, Karliana was beginning to sense that something was wrong. Very wrong. The smell of smoke had been getting stronger. With a shock she realised it was billowing ahead of them, rising from the northern side of the property, towards the boundary of the Lendri estates! Could it be possible for sparks to fly so far? And on a day with so little breeze? Something was amiss: she was sure of it.

Karliana deviated from her path, running towards the sounds that now came clearly to her ears. The screaming of horses. Men shouting. The stables! The Montfane stables were alight! She heard Mara's harsh warning, but she did not care. She had to see what was going on. The horses! In a few strides Mara had overtaken her, and all but dragged Karliana down behind a stone wall. Oliver flung himself down beside them, wide-eyed and panting. Karliana might have protested at the rough treatment, and the woman's impertinence in commanding her to stay down. But the crash of glass shattering dragged her attention away to the villa and the awful scene being played out on the terrace.

Lady Beatrice was at the centre of the group, clutching the basket she used for picking roses, standing very tall. She looked as if she was about to break into one of her tragic songs. A clutch of slaves was kneeling near her feet. At her side was her husband, Evin. Usually a cheerful fool of a man, there was something decidedly odd about his stance. He seemed frozen — they both did. Karliana squinted, and in a heartbeat understood. There were other players here: two men in black. Guardians! They stood to the side, swords drawn. Three Squad members were in the wings, armed with bows, their armbands lending flashes of bright orange to the scene. Whatever was happening? Was the pair under arrest?

Loud crashing from inside the villa suggested that the place was being ransacked. No! It was worse! As they watched, a chair came flying through one of the gorgeous stained-glass windows. Yet they all just stood there, a frozen tableau. Waiting. For what? Mara's voice croaked with fear. 'This is bad. We must leave. Now, Karliana.' She tugged at her sleeve. 'Come away.'

Karliana knew she should obey — especially when she recognised the large, dark-haired man who sauntered out through the doors. But she found herself incapable of movement. It was as if she had been fixed to the spot, her gaze glued to the scene unfolding below. Telion froze time, in a terrible moment of respite, until Castronon Moagli made a chopping motion with his hand. Lady Montfane fell to a sword, cut down like the tragic heroine in one of her own plays, followed by the collapse of her husband. Karliana screamed, heedless of their discovery. The slaves were screaming, too, and running.

'Run! Run!' the men shouted. Laughing and waving their swords, they hurled encouragement. 'Run!' And the slaves ran, towards the trees and straight towards their hiding place. It seemed some of them might escape into the woods. Then the arrows began to fly.

'Run!' Now it was Mara shouting, and Oliver, too. At last Karliana found the will to move. The last thing she saw was a young slave girl flying in their direction, her open mouth screaming. The arrow that struck her from behind seemed almost to lift her into the air. She hit the ground, writhing in agony.

❧

Up to her chin in hot water, Karliana hugged her knees, staring blindly at the water's surface. The old nurse was bathing her just as she had done when her mistress was a child. Making little clucking noises. Squeezing out the sponge. Smoothing soap across her charge's shoulders in small circles.

Karliana could hear comings and goings on the lower levels. The news had reached the villa, and the suitors had found a new competition. Who could be the most outraged? Karliana knew what was being said. The Montfanes, murdered by their own slaves! And on the stage of their own design! Their prized horses had been taken by the flames. Only the quick thinking of the guardians had saved the villa and its treasures. Some of the wicked, wicked slaves had been found with jewels and gold in their pockets. All killed of course. Put to death on the spot. Trying to flee towards the river. Just like slaves. Stupid! It was all you could expect. The Montfanes had always been an odd couple. Dressing up their slaves, giving them treats. Letting them take advantage. It was inviting trouble.

Then came a second wave of messengers. Their crashing news swept away all else. A slave uprising! And aided by the artisans. Fire! Fire in the city! Averted only by the quick actions of the Moagli Squad. The villa shuddered with fear and the sounds of people running hither and thither. Some paced from room to room, merely to match the agitation of their thoughts.

But the news had sparked more purposeful action, too. The sounds of carriages and harnesses jingling announced that some of the suitors had been recalled to their Houses. They had penned hasty notes of apology to the mistress of the house, before leaving in the same clattering manner in which they had arrived. Karliana cared not.

Although the water was already lapping at the top of the tub, the old nurse added another steaming kettleful. 'There now. Don't cry. Don't cry.' Perhaps she spoke to comfort herself. Karliana had no tears. Just numb shock. And memories that would never go away. Lady Beatrice. The sword at her throat. The way she had fallen — like a broken doll. And the eyes of that slave girl. The hot water could not wash those images away, nor stop Karliana from shivering. It felt as if she would never be warm again.

Chapter 12

COMBAT

The warriors were dressed alike for training, in linen shifts the colour of parchment, belted at the waist, with matching leggings, loose for easy action. Those with long hair had secured it in braids or topknots, and Kep wished she had thought to do the same. Her own hair was becoming far too unruly. The four captains stood to one side, their faces solemn. Nobody spoke. In fact, nobody interacted with anybody else. Some of the warriors had their eyes closed. The room almost crackled with pent-up energy. Kep did not dare look at Ash or Sarin. 'Just watch for now,' Daska had said. So Kep was taking in every tiny move, trying to control her excitement.

The Pine Lodge had the same layout as the others. Except here the wood panelling was blond, giving the space a brighter, more open feel, and instead of fish motifs on the parquet floor there were swallows, chasing each other in flight. As with the other lodges, the window was a huge glazed triangle onto the outer world. The sun was not yet up, so there was nothing to see, but the glass shook every now and then, shivering against the wind. A storm had battered the city all night, and it seemed there would be no respite today.

The hall had been entirely cleared. Thick rush mats were lined up along each side. All was ready. When Daska walked in, Kep felt a sharp thrill in her stomach. At last! She was almost bursting with impatience, aching to get started on her training. Even archery practice had been suspended for the Sorrow. But the waiting was over. One desire burned in Kep's mind: the next time she encountered those nulls with their awful, empty eyes, she would not just scream. Next time, she would fight back.

When the chime of a bell sent the warriors moving, six perfect circles formed like magic, or they would have been perfect, were it not for the gaps. Only one jinn had a complete circle: the white mouse jinn, led incongruously by Benjin Dale. The giant man really should have been with the bears. As she glanced at Sarin and Ash, Kep missed some sort of signal.

As one, the warriors bowed then sat cross-legged on the floor. It seemed wrong to remain standing, so the novices sat, too.

The warriors moved again, almost snapping into position. Kep caught her breath. She had never seen this version of the sign of the triangle. The two index fingers were pressed together as usual, but instead of bringing the thumbs to their cheekbones, they held their hands in front, as if the triangle was a frame through which to view the world. With perfect stillness, the warriors retained the shape, breathing together.

Outside the wind battered, driving snow at the windows. Inside — perfect calm. When the bell sounded again, the warriors rose and swirled, like a cloud of birds. As they paired off, Daska approached. 'Come, we will watch the Dance together.' He motioned for the novices to sit with him, on a long bench to one side.

Kep was utterly spellbound. Each pair seemed to be following the same patterns, some moving more quickly, all flowing without a break in the stances. Each movement obviously had a counter-movement and, although they never touched, it really did look as if they were dancing.

El had partnered with Pretalla Chanara. Kep watched intently, taking in how the women's feet moved, the stroking sweeps of their arms. Their faces revealed the intensity of their efforts. Every now and then Kep caught a flash of emotion, triumph, or a rueful twist of a mouth. She was not surprised to see Heeda partnered with Jakarmon Pyke. Was one partner leading the other? Perhaps Heeda? It was impossible to tell. The twins, Muku and Tuku, moved like mirror images, grinning, yet wary, too. Jaibari's partner was Reardon Galt, as lithe and muscular as she was. His hair had been shaved up the sides of his head. Sleek on top, and smoothed back, it reminded Kep of a dark bird's wing. Their movements were swift and compelling — ferocity in motion. As Kep concentrated, trying to interpret the moves, she suddenly understood. It was not a warm-up at all, but a fight sequence!

Kep could have watched for hours, but Daska rose and hit the bell again. This time the warriors did not halt as one; each pair finished whatever sequence they were performing. The effect was quite beautiful, like a gust of wind in the rushes. When the last couple came to rest, Daska rang his bell for a final time. The warriors bowed to each other and then to Daska — deep, respectful bows.

Kep's heart was filled with something like joy as she turned to the others.

Although Ash looked a bit dazed, he, too, seemed impressed. Sarin half-smiled, as unreadable as ever. The warriors were chatting quietly now, some repeating moves. Their arms and shoulders shone with sweat. Some took the chance to stretch out their muscles. Daska was shaking his head. As he turned, his concerned expression became a smile.

'So, what do you think of the Dance of the Blades?'

Ordelle fixed him with a stare. 'There were no blades.'

Kep cringed. It sounded as if she was accusing Daska of palming her off with last season's apples.

Sarin grinned. 'I think we were supposed to imagine the blades.'

'Then it should be called the Dance without Blades.'

Daska's tufty grey eyebrows came together in a perplexed hedge and he blew out his cheeks. 'Well, it is lucky there were no blades today. We'd have been cut to pieces.' He cast disapproving eyes over the warriors. Kep was startled; everything had looked so perfect. She wanted to see the whole thing again.

She turned to speak to Ash, but he was staring out of the window, once again distracted. He seemed to be listening for something. Or trying to follow another conversation completely. Perhaps he was just wondering where Tarlyn had slunk off to.

Daska was still tut-tutting, shaking his head and making his beard waggle. 'There is much work to be done.'

'Yes! There is work to be done.' Nirias had joined them, rubbing his hands together and smiling over his warriors like a proud father. 'So much promise is here before us, my friend. We are together, we have space, and we have time.' He beamed at the novices and repeated the words, 'So much promise.'

Kep blushed under her leader's appraisal. 'When can we start learning the Dance?' In the corner of her eye, Sarin was folding his arms. She ignored him.

'Today Daska and I will give some thought to finding each of you a partner who will introduce you to the Dance of Blades.' Nirias's eyes twinkled. 'For now, I think you will enjoy what we have prepared in the Rosewood Lodge. It will be a chance for you all to show us what you can do.'

Ash's eyes went wide with alarm. He looked as if he had been asked to swallow a frog. Kep could not contain her grin.

The hall of the Rosewood Lodge had also been emptied — of furniture at least. With the same layout, including the massive window, staircases and gantries, this hall had red timber panelling and a view of tall pines. The floor was inlaid with charming images of tiny mice, scampering after each other's tails. Kep barely gave them a second glance, she was so excited by everything else.

There were ropes hanging from beams, rings strung in lines, stacks of large wooden cubes, a rope net, ladders and beams, and upturned barrels. A wooden clacking came from one corner where Muku and Tuku were already trying to whack each other with quarterstaffs. Daska shook his head when a blow struck, hard enough to break a normal man's arm. Muku, if it was Muku, just whirled his staff to the other hand and continued as if nothing had happened.

Another area had been set aside for knife throwing, and a fan of weapons was laid out on the table. A blond giant of a lad called Polkin Dew was already hurling daggers at a timber post. Kep watched long enough to note that the first two stuck. The other warriors were forming up in pairs and groups. Some dangled from various apparatus, working muscles, others circled in pairs with wooden swords.

'Well,' commented Daska grimly, eyeing a pile of axes, 'Agnid is in for a busy winter.'

Nirias chuckled as if the old warrior had made a wonderful joke. 'Yes, indeed.'

Under Daska's watchful eye, the new recruits began their trials. Kep started well, easily conquering a narrow beam. The rolling barrel took more effort, but, while she could not direct it around the course, she did manage to keep her footing. Gamon Baze, another blond giant, older and broader than Polkin, nodded and gave a grunt. Handing her a pair of wooden rings, he pointed out the row of pegs that had been fastened to the edge of the high gantry.

'Start at the beginning, and work your way along,' he said.

Kep stared at the line of pegs, wondering how to get up to them. There was the staircase of course, but ropes dangled at either end, too. Kep frowned. She decided it was a test of strength and agility, so she was probably supposed to climb the rope to reach the pegs.

Gamon watched in silence as she threaded the rings onto each arm, clutched the rope and began hauling herself up. The rope was harsh on her hands, and by the time Kep reached the top her palms were already stinging. She managed to hook one ring onto the first peg. It shifted, but held. So she let go of the rope. Dangling from one arm, she refused to think about falling. She swung the second ring. It caught! Peg by peg, she advanced. Her muscles were screaming with pain now. It felt as if her arms would be pulled from their sockets.

Below, people were shouting. Kep did not listen. She fixed her eyes on the pegs. Once peg at a time. Swing and release. Swing and release. And don't look down. At last she hooked out a foot and caught the rope at the end of the line. Transferring her weight, she let the wooden rings bounce to the floor. Barely in control, she slid all the way to the ground. Her arms were like jelly, her hands raw, but she had done it. Benjin Dale gave a roar and smacked his mighty hands together. 'Well done, Kep!'

Only then did Kep realise how many people had stopped to watch. Reardon gave three slow claps of his hands as Gamon Baze shook his head. 'Thought I would have to catch you,' he laughed. Kep grinned at him. Even Jaibari's glowering face could not ruin the moment. In fact, if anything, her sour reaction made it all the better. Sarin spoke at her elbow. 'Yeah, I'd have gone that way, too. Those stairs look pretty treacherous.' He shook his head, woefully. Then he gave her such a smile. It entered the very heart of her.

❧

The midday meal was the usual dismal fare, there was just more of it. Salt was passed down the tables and everyone applied it liberally. Ash had disappeared; off somewhere with Nirias, no doubt. The novices ate heartily, discussing the morning's trials. Sarin of course had been good at everything. He ran along obstacles as easily as the floor. His knife-throwing was exceptional, too.

Ordelle was even worse at throwing knives than Kep, a few going so wide that people had to leap sideways. She was surprisingly agile, though, and had managed the barrels with ease. She also had ability with the staff, and was already assigned to Lakmorin Spink, one of the weapon's masters. He was a surly young man with long red hair and a pair of earrings in one ear. They would be evenly matched for disposition if not ability.

Nobody else had taken Kep's approach to the ring challenge. How was she supposed to know that you were meant to throw the rings? Even Pallin laughed out loud when Sarin related the tale. Of course Sarin did make it sound like some sort of wild circus act.

The meal break was too brief; Jen-Jay was already wheeling in a cart for the dishes. Jaibari rose first, shoving plates across the table towards Kep as she did so. When Kep reached out, meaning to stack them with her own, Sarin caught her wrist. Jaibari had already turned to walk away, only to find Jen-Jay blocking her path. The old woman's eyes were pale and icy-clear. 'Everyone clears their own plates here.' The young woman sniffed. Making a great show of reclaiming the plates, she dumped them on the cart. Jen-Jay met Sarin's eyes and grunted. Then she continued her journey down the tables. Sarin released Kep's wrist. 'If you act like a slave, they will treat you like one,' he murmured.

⁂

That afternoon, while everyone else trained for unarmed combat, the novices were initiated into the moves of the Dance. Their teacher was Kennid, an older warrior as grouchy as Daska was kindly. In the entire few hours, he taught them only three moves. A pivoting crouch, a standing posture, and a twisting thrust. Kennid offered very few tips on how they could improve. He simply scowled a lot and bid them repeat the movements, over and over. Sarin joined in for only a short while, before standing back. Kennid pounced.

'What's wrong with you? Why have you stopped?'

Sarin shrugged. 'I thought it might be fun. It wasn't.' Already belligerent, the old warrior's face hardened into disbelief. He seemed lost for words. 'So I'll just be taking myself off.' With that, Sarin did indeed take himself off, leaving Kennid spluttering.

When he turned his displeasure on Kep instead, she dropped her eyes and redoubled her efforts. It made no difference. If anything his expression became even more grim.

And so the Dance continued. Kep's neck and shoulders had been aching to start with; now they radiated pain. Her legs were wobbling, too. How could such simple movements hurt so much? She felt certain the others were also in agony. A quick glance confirmed that Pallin was trembling. His eyes looked panicked, as if he, too, was wondering how long he could keep it up. Ordelle's expression had not changed — not once. It did not even look as though she was sweating. When Nirias came to teach them how to breathe, Kep was so relieved that she did not question his strange announcement. Breathing? How hard could that be?

Breathing, it turned out, was a nightmare of errors. Although Nirias was a much more patient teacher, Kep still felt as though everything she did was wrong. Nirias explained that the flow of the Dance relied on the flow of the breath. Perhaps that is what Kennid had been scowling at? So they breathed. They stood and breathed, they bent themselves double to blow air at their feet, and they sat cross-legged, inhaling, exhaling. Breath in. Breath out. Ash had joined them from wherever he had been hiding, and Kep could tell he was just as confused as everyone else.

When Nirias announced that they would leave the warriors' triangle for later, she sensed he was not as pleased with their progress as his smile suggested. Though sometimes Nirias was as difficult to read as Sarin. She frowned, biting her lip. As the rest of the warriors filed in, Kep felt sure she had let her leader down. She would practise, she promised herself, for as long as it took, until she got it right. Right now, Benjin Dale was taking the floor.

The mood shifted at once. Smiles were passed around the room as Benjin boomed directions. Shouting seemed his only form of communication. Kep had never known him do anything else. He held two poles in his hands, from each of which flowed a silk banner. The day's training was to end with a battle. From what Kep could tell, the object was to secure the other team's banner. Benjin directed that the banners be positioned up in the eaves, at the far end of each gantry. There was laughing and jeering as he hollered rules. Kep suspected there were no rules.

The warriors were split into two teams, one commanded by Jakarmon Pyke, the other by Reardon Galt. Kep found herself on Jakarmon's team. After a quick huddle of strategy, the man barked instructions, blinking madly all the while. Paired with Pallin, Kep's job was to guard a barricade of barrels which blocked the stairs. When Jakarmon tossed a couple of staffs at them, Kep managed to catch hers. Pallin's clattered to the floor. As they took their position she wished she had paid more attention to Muku and Tuku. They had made it look so easy. How did you even hold the thing? She was still working out her grip, when Benjin boomed 'Go!'

The lodge erupted into chaos. People wrestled on the floor, scrambled up nets or dragged each other off, or, in Sarin's case, lobbed missiles in the form of rings and balls. Kep's team had an early advantage, with Ozu Mako making a sprint, vaulting barrels and dodging hits. He ducked defenders and, leaping to a rope, climbed with legs bent like a frog. He managed to cling on, even when Polkin Dew grabbed the end of the rope and shook it mercilessly. It took a flying staff to dislodge him. Even then, he flipped in the air and landed neatly.

Jarkamon and Heeda were leading a charge now, taking on the combined efforts of Muku and Tuku, who had somehow ended up on the same team. Meanwhile, Pallin and Kep faced their first challenge — in the terrifying form of Pretalla Chanara. Her eyes, made fearful by black paint and an even blacker tattoo, flashed as she laughed. Pallin swiped wildly and was promptly disarmed. For a split second, Kep wondered how hard she should hit the woman. The hesitation was fatal. Their staffs clashed. One brutal twist and Kep's wrists gave way, her weapon flying from her grasp. Pretalla laughed with a toss of her head, making ornaments fly. She made no move to leap onto the barrels, though. Urgent cries were calling her to the opposite end of the hall where the battle was surging anew. She cartwheeled away, joining the fray.

Pallin and Kep retrieved their staffs and stood shoulder to shoulder once more, breathing deeply. Within seconds there was a shout. Reardon's team had reached the upper levels! Kep craned her neck to look. There was a great thumping and commotion. Then Muku gave an almighty yell of triumph and the red flag came fluttering down. Victory for the other team.

The room erupted again, this time in a shouting mess of laughter, thumps on backs and uproarious ribbing. Kep grinned at Pallin. They had been triumphant in their own way after all, with the barricade of barrels remaining in place. She was rubbing her forearm, ruing that she had not been a little quicker, when she felt a sharp thwack on the back of her legs. Her hand went out to stop herself falling, and the wrist twisted. Her head hit the parquet floor with a thump. As she lay there, writhing in pain, Kep heard a sharp hiss in her ear.

'Just a slave.'

Everyone had been looking the other way, laughing at Muku's antics with the captured flag. At Kep's groan, Gamon Baze turned his head. 'Hey! Watch yourself there, Kep!' He laughed, clearly thinking that the game had been too much for a novice. When he grabbed her injured arm and hauled her to her feet, Kep wanted to scream. Instead she clenched her jaw and hugged her wrist to her chest. Gamon thumped her shoulder hard, making her grimace. Her wincing grin did not fool Daska. He took one look at her face.

'Off to Agnid with you, Kep.'

When Kep tried to protest, Daska scowled. 'We train again tomorrow, and that needs looking at.' She bit her tongue and nodded. The expressions on Ash and Sarin's faces made it clear that they had some inkling of foul play. They flanked her, shielding her exit from the room. As they left, Kep noticed that Daska was scratching his beard, his thoughtful eyes on Jaibari. On the opposite side of the room, the young warrior was laughing and jostling with Reardon.

❧

To her disgust, it was Kep's turn to take up a bed in the Curing House. Her arm was swathed from the elbow to her fingers in cloths so cold they seemed made of snow.

'So you tripped and fell? Just like that?' Sarin wasn't buying her explanation that Jaibari had just given her an over-zealous shove.

Ash looked sceptical, too. 'It does sound a little … boisterous.'

Kep shot him a glare. Jaibari was her problem and she would deal with it herself. It was time to change the subject. 'What about you, Sarin. What, by Argess, were you playing at earlier with Kennid? Were you trying to get punched? He was pretty riled by your performance, or lack of it.'

Sarin knew exactly what she was doing, and pulled a face and didn't answer. But Kep was not about to let it go. 'I don't think the training is optional around here.'

'Why not?' Sarin's eyes slid to Agnid, who was weighing some sort of crystalline powder onto a set of scales. Kep rolled her eyes. But they waited in silence until the nurse had bustled out of the room.

As soon as she had gone, Kep raised her eyebrows. 'Well?'

Sarin held her eyes with his. It was a topic they had been skirting around since arriving in T'al Jazure, and an argument had been long in the brewing.

Ash was shuffling his feet, refolding a blanket that did not need refolding.

'We are Seekers, Kep. We came to T'al Jazure to learn. Not to become assassins. Not to join any League. I have no intention of killing a man just because Nirias says so.'

'The nulls are not men: they have been taken over by the Melk. We've learned that. By Argess, Sarin! We've seen them for ourselves. They are pure evil, and the Melk is growing stronger. You know it is true.' Kep's anger flared. 'We have to train. We have to overcome the Melk. That is the purpose of the League.' She scowled at the way Sarin stood there, so calmly. How could he be so infuriating? 'We can't just hide away here, safe in the city and do nothing. Aranti will grow strong. And Nirias is right: he will be the worse nexus the world has seen. He was monster enough before.' She looked at Ash for support. 'Think about poor Braig.' Ash held her eyes for a brief moment before hanging his head.

Sarin's eyes glinted. 'And you think Nirias is going to let you leave, do you? He won't, Kep. He will keep you safe here in the city. So long as you remain here, the legend of Kep is safe, too. Remember, you are T'al Kep. Kep the Valiant.'

Kep almost spat her reply. 'As if I could forget that! As if I don't see the warriors sneering. I know what they are thinking. That I haven't earned those stupid names. Well, you just watch me. I'm going to learn how to fight. I'm going to master the Dance of Blades, and I am going to fight for freedom, for goodness. Because that is what is right, Sarin. That is what good people do.'

Sarin met her anger with that same infuriating calm. 'Perhaps. But following someone blindly is what stupid people do. You seem to think we owe Nirias our allegiance. We don't. And we don't have to do what he says. None of us. Not me, not Ash, and not you.' Sarin's eyes narrowed. Tilting his head, he dropped his voice. 'Continue training if you want. All I'm saying is let's find out more about what is really going on. Let's explore the city and see if we can discover why it was locked.' He shook his head. 'There are too many things that just don't make sense. Why would the Azuri leave? All the stories tell of how terrible the world was back then. But they marched off merrily into danger, taking their children with them and left all of this behind. Why? Why abandon the only place where they could be safe? Something is not right. Surely you can see that?'

Kep scowled. She did not know all the answers. All she knew was that they had to fight for justice. Surely that was the fate that Narsis had in store? 'You are making things complicated. None of that matters. The truth is simple: we have to do whatever we can to help Nirias destroy the Melk.'

Sarin shook his head and addressed himself to Ash instead. 'Tell me this, then. Why was Credé so adamant that the Taelstaun must never go to T'al Jazure? He could have lived out his days, in safety here; instead, he chose to live in the squalor of a hut. Why?'

Ash had that stricken sort of expression he always adopted when there was any kind of confrontation. He rubbed a hand over his face. His soft grey eyes were panicky. 'I don't know. Kep, Sarin makes some good points. And ... well the city does feel ... strange ... sometimes.' He made an apologetic face. 'I'm not saying we shouldn't do everything we can to resist the Melk.' He scrunched up his face. 'Well, I don't think I have a choice anyway.' He meant Rilka's vision.

Kep sighed. Why was she even arguing with Sarin? Fate had conspired to bring them here. They were part of the League, for better or for worse. 'It's our fate, Ash. Yours and mine.'

Ash's eyes were frightened. 'Perhaps.' Then he returned his gaze to Sarin. 'But Sarin is right, too. We should try to find out more. The city is supposed to be a place of peace, but ...' He shook his head, his eyes worried. 'It doesn't feel ... There's ... something.' Ash did not complete his thought. Kep knew there was more, but Ash had clammed up, and she knew him well enough not to push.

Sarin still had half his attention on the corridor beyond the room. He probably thought the old nurse was eavesdropping. Did he trust anyone? He measured people by his own habits, Kep supposed.

He spoke in a quiet but urgent voice. 'Think, Kep. Why was the city locked? What really stopped the Melk? I'm pretty sure it was not a bunch of assassins, taking them out one nexus at a time.'

Kep gave him the most furious stare she could muster. 'Nirias knows what he's doing, Sarin. He knows more than anyone!'

He gave her a level look. 'You think? I think that after a thousand years fighting these guys he might have done a better job.' He cocked his head again, frowned and changed the topic. 'So, the first thing we need to do is work out is how to stop Jaibari from beating you up.' He grinned. He actually grinned, as if they had not been arguing at all! 'I have an idea.'

'Really?' Kep flung the bedcovers to one side and swung her legs over the side of the bed. 'That's wonderful. I don't need to hear it, though. Because I have an idea too, Sarin. I'm going to become the best fighter you have ever seen and put Jaibari on the floor.'

Chapter 13

A BOY AND A BIRD

The air left Ash's lips in a frustrated blast. Controlling the urge to hurl the lore-stone at the window, he replaced it on its plinth and gritted his teeth. How long had he been staring into the thing now? And for what? He had discovered the trick of stilling his mind — entering that weird space between focus and drifting consciousness — yet every time he slipped into the realm of the orb he found himself in the same room. It had six panelled doors and no windows. Nirias had just chuckled when he told him his problem. Demara Cantoya had loved puzzles, and he had every confidence that Ash would pass the test. Except Ash had tried everything. He had tried all the doors. He had knocked. He had pushed with flattened hands, had stroked the wood one way, then the other. He had shouted and banged and pleaded like an idiot. Nothing had worked. The lore-stone had kept its secrets.

It sat next to Credé's now. Twin orbs on matching plinths, taunting him. It was no good. Ash was really terrible at this. How could he ever master the Song if he could not even learn to unlock his first lore-stone? He sighed and stretched his neck, hearing the sinews crackle. Going to the window, he pushed his hands against the pane and cast weary eyes over T'al Jazure. Such a frozen world — unreal. He was turning away when his eyes darted back, alert to something new. A figure!

Squinting, not quite believing what he was seeing, Ash threw the shutter open. 'Hey!'

The figure uncurled. Ash's heart was in his mouth as he watched Sarin negotiate the flying spur that connected the two towers. He moved like a dancer, placing his feet with purpose, his arms out for balance. Ash felt hot, prickling fear rushing through him at the sight. He could not help reaching out his hand to grasp Sarin's arm as soon as he was close enough.

'Mind out!' Sarin made a great show of tumbling, and somersaulted onto the floor.

Ash shut the window against the blast of cold. 'Sarin! What by Telion's breath were you doing out there!'

Sarin's hair was soaked with mist. He smoothed it back and shrugged. 'Waiting for a bird.' *Waiting for a bird.* Of course. Ash shook his head in disbelief. 'For a swift? You were waiting for a swift? In the freezing cold?'

Sarin grinned. 'Yeah. It was pretty cold. To be honest, I was not quite sure how I was going to get back down. It was more slippery than I thought.' As Sarin blew on his fingers, his eyes swept the room, taking in the soft couch and desk, his gaze lingering on the two orbs in their place. The cold had done nothing to dull his curiosity. 'Nice room. If you don't mind me asking, how exactly did you get in here?'

'Through the door,' replied Ash. 'You know? Doors? People don't usually somersault through windows, you know.'

Sarin smiled without showing his teeth. 'Funny. Seriously, though, Ash. How did you get in? In fact, how did you even know this room existed? I spotted it from the outside, but couldn't find the door. Trust you to have a secret hiding place!'

Ash felt a warm surge of pride. 'Tarlyn helped me find it,' he confessed. From that first day in the Knowledge Stores Ash had decided he needed a place to concentrate. Not Nirias's favourite nook; somewhere of his own. He had wandered about for a bit, sticking his nose into different rooms. Then Tarlyn had made that noise she does when she wants attention: a sort of clicking in her throat, followed by a muttering rattle. So Ash had followed her to a landing, halfway up a tower stair. He had not been particularly surprised when the panelling had opened to his touch.

Ash enjoyed showing off the secret. 'That's very impressive,' commented Sarin. As Sarin inspected the doorway from both sides, Ash wondered if he meant the craftsmanship or the fact that Ash had discovered the place. 'I can't see where the mechanism might be housed. Can you?' Ash shook his head. It was typical of Sarin. He just loved figuring out how things worked. Ash found himself under inspection, too, as those golden eyes narrowed with speculation. 'This city is full of secrets. I wonder how many other hidden doors there are? I suppose *you* can open them all. That's the deal, isn't it? Being the Taelstaun?'

Ash shrugged. 'Nirias did say something like that.'

'Hmmm. Well, if Nirias asks you to open any doors, I'd think carefully.'

Sarin's mistrust of the man had certainly not diminished. It was strange. Nirias was clearly loved by many of the warriors, and practically adored by

Kep. Was that the problem? Jealousy? Ash was not so sure. Maybe it was seeds of doubt sown by Nalina, Sarin's grandmother.

Back in the hidden tower room, Sarin checked the window before taking a seat. He picked up the small portrait of a young woman that sat on the desk. 'Who do you think this is?'

Ash leaned over his shoulder. She had blonde hair and a challenge in her eyes. He had peered into her face many times wondering the same thing. Now he had a theory. 'I think it was Leynore. She was one of the Council of Three when the city was locked. Nirias said Tarlyn was her constant companion. I think this was Leynore's room. She's young in this portrait, though.'

'It's lovely work.' Turning the frame over, Sarin spotted the initial carved into the back. 'C? The artist?'

Ash was about to agree, when a dark shape fluttered to the window ledge, making him jump.

'Aha!' Sarin leapt up and eased the casement open. The bird hopped onto his outstretched arm, giving three urgent-sounding chirps.

Tarlyn materialised from where she had been curled up on the couch and fixed her eyes on the bird. Strangely, it ignored her completely. It was like that with Tarlyn. For some creatures, she did not seem to exist. Sarin sprinkled grain on the ledge before unclipping a tiny tube from the bird's leg. The bird happily pecked away while Sarin unravelled the message.

Ash frowned. 'Sarin … Do you really think you should … ?'

'Probably not.' Sarin grinned and read the message anyway. *'Cats at play. Winter with Harper. Will send flowers in spring.'* He raised an eyebrow at Ash. 'Any clue?' When Ash shook his head, he laughed. 'Me neither. It's stamped with a captain's seal, though.'

Ash nodded, staring at the mark. The captains all held such seals: the sign of their jinn, set on a triangular base. They peered at the mark, trying to make out which animal was depicted. It was blurred, as if the writer had made their stamp in a hurry. Definitely some sort of feline. An otter maybe? Or a cat of some sort?

'I reckon it's a jarlycat.'

Ash nodded agreement. He had seen a jarlycat only once. Smaller and even more fierce than the mousers who stalked the Feyindi kitchens, the creatures kept to the wild. It made sense. 'And the message? *Cats at play?*'

Sarin shrugged. 'Must refer to the jinn. Still, it will be nice to get some flowers, won't it?'

Ash blurted a laugh. No doubt the code would mean something to Nirias. To Ash's relief, Sarin curled the message up and reattached it to the bird's leg, impeded somewhat by the bird itself, which was pecking eagerly at his pocket. Laughing, he pulled out a bundle of herbs. 'Sorry, little chap. Game's over.' He crumbled the leaves between his fingers and cast them into the air. The bird flapped, danced in a circle, and flew after them. After circling for a while, it made a line for the tower opposite. Fluttering to the landing perches, it disappeared into a nook.

Sarin pulled the window closed and gave Ash a sly look. 'You thought I called that bird with my mind, didn't you?'

'No,' answered Ash quickly. 'Well … a bit.'

Sarin hooted. 'Hickock leaves,' he explained. It was one of those Sarin explanations that did not really explain anything at all. 'Swifts love them. Works every time. If you can get close enough to the target, you can divert them.' Reminding Ash of the bird, Sarin cocked his head. 'Can I come again? It's certainly more comfortable than that ledge.'

Ash groaned. More comfortable and a whole lot safer, too! He was not at all sure that Sarin should be intercepting swifts meant for Nirias, and he dreaded to think what Kep would say — probably that it was against the gods. Ash knew he would lie awake worrying about getting caught. He found himself grinning anyway. He had to admit, it was exciting to be part of the deception. 'Of course you can.'

⁂

After Sarin had left, using the door this time, Ash sat on the arm of the couch just thinking. After a long while, he drew the heavy red drapes, shutting out the winter view. The room instantly became more intimate, like his own private cave. Taking a seat at the polished desk, he drew the lore-stone towards him. Closing his fingers around it, he searched for that strange space between absolute focus and daydreaming. This time the transition happened swiftly. His thoughts slid, and he found himself, yet again, in the room with six doors.

Ash turned in a slow circle. Everything was as it had been before. Just six dark doors, with large brass handles. He did not try the handles. That was the road to frustration. This time, he would follow Sarin's example.

Anything here is possible, he told his thinking mind. *Anything is possible.* So … I'm just going to slide under that door. Switching off his rational mind, he closed his eyes and imagined himself doing just that, fingers first, flowing like a ribbon. His intuition told him it was working, and he opened his eyes and laughed. At last!

Ash was in a sunlit garden, and a woman was walking towards him carrying a basket, full of flowers and sweet-smelling herbs. Demara Cantoya had skin the colour of chestnuts and honey-coloured hair, covered by a straw hat that looked as if it had been caught in the rain. Warm eyes sparkled at him. 'Hello, Ash. Welcome to my garden.'

'Um … Hello.' Although Nirias had explained that the Heartstone would calibrate the stone to his needs, it was still a surprise to hear his name. It was quite peculiar speaking to a woman who was not really there. The garden, its bees and butterflies — all just Demara's thoughts, imprinted on the lore-stone long ago. It felt very strange, and the woman was studying him very intently.

'You may call me Demara.' Her mouth quirked in amusement. 'Come, let us walk.'

Ash joined her side, and together they strolled in the gardens. 'So! We can count your first lesson as learned.' Her eyes twinkled at him. 'It is a truth that must be experienced rather than told. If you are to become a Keeper, the first thing to grasp is the power of the imagination. What my little trick teaches is that it is not enough to compose lyrics or relate stories. As a Keeper you must be inventive and think beyond all doors.' When she waved at the garden it almost seemed to wave back, the breeze lifting leaves in salute. 'That is the first lesson, and one of the most important. But not *the* most important.'

Her skirts brushed a hedge, sending butterflies into the air. 'There is one rule, a golden rule if you like, which will safeguard you against the dangers of the Song.' She caught his eye, and nodded. 'Good. I see fear in your eyes. The Song is a most perilous affair … Never fool yourself into thinking otherwise.' All of a sudden she sniffed. 'Ah!' Ash jumped at her exclamation. 'Hold this please.'

The basket was pushed at him and, drawing a sharp knife from her apron, Demara lunged into the garden bed. Ash blinked at the sight of her ample backside swaying among the bushes. He received the thorny stems of pink roses awkwardly, between finger and thumb, tucking them into the already overflowing basket. He was most relieved when she rejoined him on the path.

Completely ignoring the break in their conversation, Demara continued. 'You have been chosen, Ash. From thousands of possibles. Your talents make you perfect for the task.' Ash fought down rising panic. He had not been chosen; he was just a slave. 'Unfortunately, those very talents are precisely what will put you in peril.' The woman's eyes were like shining glass as she held him in her gaze. Ash bit his lip. Knowing about the dangers of the Song and hearing someone else confirm it were quite different things entirely.

It was almost as if Demara sensed his despair. She motioned him towards a garden bench, where they sat together, lulled by the sound of bees humming. Ash frowned to himself. Perhaps that is why she had created the scene, to soothe the listener. How many other terrified apprentices had sat with Demara on her garden bench watching imaginary bees?

When the woman spoke again, her words seemed to blend with the harmonies of the bees. 'Only those most sensitive to the melodies of our world can harness the mysteries of the Song. And therein lies the peril. As you sit here with me, enjoying the sound of my bees, some portion of your mind tells you that there are no bees. Am I right?' Her smile spread into a wicked grin. 'So, we come to the second lesson. The most important of all.' She gave a deep sigh. 'The Song is dangerous, Ash. That cannot be denied. It carries so much emotion, so much pure energy, it can easily overwhelm the human mind. If you do not keep your feet, it will sweep you from your own reality. And to be lost in the Song is to be lost forever.'

Ash stared at her in horror. How many times had he already been swept from himself by the Song's visions? How close had he come to being entirely lost? 'How do I control it?' he stammered.

Demara laughed, shaking her head. 'Oh, you cannot. The Song is uncontrollable. Wild. You may as well try to control the oceans.' She clicked her tongue. 'What do they teach you apprentices these days? No, you cannot control the Song. You can only control the way in which you sing.' Demara let her eyes wander, following the darting exploits of a dragonfly. 'And that is the most important lesson. It is your engagement, the framework which sits between you and the Song: *that* is what will save you from becoming lost, or driven to despair.'

Ash did not answer. He bowed his head in his hands. He could not help thinking about Credé's half-crazed eyes.

'Do not fret.' Demara gave him a shrewd look. 'You must work hard, Ash. Harder than you have ever worked before. I cannot teach you how to engage with the Song, because everyone thinks differently. If you are to become Taelstaun, you must find your own way.' She patted his knee. 'I brought you here, to my garden, because that is how the Song works for me. See my basket? I have selected herbs, flowers and branches for my bouquet. Do you understand?' Her eyes pierced him.

Ash cleared his throat, edging his way towards what he thought she meant. 'So, for you the Song is like a garden?'

She smiled. 'Very good. It is one truth. My truth.' She reached out to pat him on the knee once more. 'You will find your own way. Return here to me when you have had time to think.'

Chapter 14

THE STARDOME

Kep sat on her bed, watching Ordelle go about her nightly routine. Kep had never asked her why she unpacked the contents of her large square bag, lined everything up on her bed, then repacked it all again. She just did. Every night. That evening, as she watched, Kep had a sudden idea. When she asked her strange roommate whether she might have a pair of shears, Ordelle froze. She regarded Kep for a moment from those large protruding eyes before passing over a delicate pair of silver shears. Then she sat on the edge of her bed, tapping her thumbs together. The absence of a pair of scissors must have messed up whatever it was she was doing. No doubt she would just sit there until Kep gave them back.

Kep turned the scissors over in her hands. Pulling out a curl, she ventured a snip. The scissors caught, dragging at the hair, but a lock came off in her hand. She was staring at it, wondering what to do next when Ordelle spoke up. 'I can cut it if you like.'

Ordelle probably did not trust her with the scissors. Fair enough — Kep did not trust herself. She hesitated, before nodding. 'I just want it shorter.'

'Like a warrior,' stated Ordelle flatly.

'Yes … Like a warrior.' As Ordelle dragged a stool over, Kep wondered how much those watchful eyes had taken in.

Ordelle certainly handled the scissors with confidence. Kep bit her lip to see the black curls growing thick about her feet. Was there any hair left on her head? She felt a surge of panic. Female slaves in the House of Aranti were not allowed to wear their hair cropped short. Too late, she told herself. A fresh flush of anxiety came when Ordelle made an announcement. 'I've never cut a living person's hair before.' Kep closed her eyes. *It will grow back.*

The ordeal was over in a remarkably short time. As Kep ran her hands over her head, a slow smile formed. The smile widened to a grin when Ordelle produced a hand-mirror. The transformation was incredible. Kep's hair was clipped short at the sides, but longer on the top, with her curling fringe cascading down one side of her face. Ordelle supplied a second mirror so Kep could see the back. It was cropped very short, except for three tails.

'It's wonderful,' Kep breathed. 'I look like …'

Ordelle nodded. 'An Astran warrior.' She paused. 'Did you know the three tails are for the gods?'

Kep tugged them with her fingers. 'I do now,' she smiled. She laughed in delight at the feel of short fuzz at her nape. 'Thank you, Ordelle. I am in your debt.'

Ordelle nodded and returned to her task of lining up her possessions, as if it had been unadvisedly dangerous to leave it unattended for so long.

The chance to repay her debt to Ordelle came a lot sooner than Kep had imagined. Ordelle had buckled her last buckle and was preparing to undress when a shower of pebbles hit the window. Kep had half-expected the signal. A second shower confirmed that Ash or Sarin, or both of them, was outside. Kep rose, quickly adding layers of clothing and casting about for her boots.

Ordelle's eyes went to the window. 'Is that your boy?' Kep frowned, as if she did not know what the girl was talking about. 'Your friend with the yellow eyes — that Sarin.'

As she fastened her cloak, Kep blushed, wondering what the young woman was thinking. She did not want to give the impression of a lovers' rendezvous. 'I think so. It might be Ash. Or both of them.' Somehow that just sounded worse. 'We've arranged to meet up — all three of us — to explore a bit of the city.'

Ordelle got to her feet and took a couple of paces, her hands clasped in front of her. It was obvious that she wanted to come along. For once there was a light shining in her eyes. Kep spoke quickly. 'It's not something you would be interested in, Ordelle.' She caught herself and winced. Exploring the city in the dark? Of course Ordelle would be interested. 'I don't think …'

The girl's eager expression had already faded. She looked like a dog that had been scolded for no fault of its own and sent to its basket. Kep felt a pang of remorse. The poor thing was obviously no stranger to rejection. She ran her hands over her hair, and when her fingers found one of the tails, she gave a sigh. She would probably regret it, but it was only fair.

'Look, you can come along if you like,' she found herself saying. 'But we must be quiet.' The words were barely out of her mouth and Ordelle was already halfway into her coat. She probably thought if she did not move quickly, the invitation might be withdrawn. Kep took a deep breath. Dreading to think what Sarin would say, she opened the door and they crept into the hall.

⁂

The meeting place had been chosen for its proximity to the Sable Lodge. It could be approached from separate alleyways, meaning that the boys could take a different route. Ash and Sarin were seated at a table in a small room at the back of the workshop. Clear-lights cast fans of light against the deep red walls, and thick cream-coloured curtains decked the windows. Like many rooms in T'al Jazure, it was heated by the walls themselves and was already cosy. The young men looked up, surprised when Ordelle entered the room first. Their jaws dropped in astonishment when they saw Kep.

Kep knew she looked different, but their awestruck expressions made her blush. The tingling flush grew, until it felt as if the roots of her hair were on fire. 'It was Ordelle,' she explained, turning partly out of embarrassment and partly so they could see the tails at the back.

Recovering first, Sarin laughed in delight. 'That's brilliant! Why didn't I think of that? Ordelle, you are a genius!' The corners of Ordelle's mouth quivered a little. Kep decided it counted as the first time they had seen her smile. 'Her skin is darker,' mused Sarin, 'but that doesn't matter.' For Ash's benefit he explained: 'Astran warriors often have blue eyes and dark hair, just like Kep's. The braids, worn to honour the gods, form part of their complex battle ritual.'

Ordelle turned unblinking eyes upon Sarin. 'That is correct. The braids of an Astran warrior who falls in battle must be managed with particular care. Never burned, they are to be coiled, submerged in unctions pertaining to each god, and placed into small urns for burial; one at each hand and one at the crown of the head.'

Sarin grinned.

Ash was still staring at Kep as if he was not really sure it was her. 'So it's a disguise?'

Sarin nodded. 'And a brilliant one. It will be Astra that comes to mind first when people see Kep now, not Mildaresh.' Kep nodded happily, pleased that Sarin was so impressed. She cast a sidelong look at Ordelle, trying to catch her eye. The young woman had reverted to her usual disinterested demeanour and was staring at the curtains, but Sarin's eyes were thoughtful. 'That has given me an idea.' In that smugly secretive way of his, he refused to say anything further. 'You'll just have to wait. Tonight we have to get organised. And I have a couple of other surprises.'

Ordelle gave Sarin her full attention.

'Is Ordelle in on the plan, then?' Sarin's question was directed at Kep.

'The plan?' Kep looked to Ash, who seemed just as confused as she was. 'What plan?'

Sarin laughed. 'To uncover the secrets of T'al Jazure of course. The Taelstone is your province Ash, obviously, along with being the master of doors and Keeper of the Song.' Sarin dipped his head in mock reverence. Ash looked horribly uncomfortable, but Sarin's teasing golden eyes had already danced back to Ordelle. 'So, Ordelle. What are you good at?'

Ordelle answered him in a monotone: 'Embalming bodies.' After a pause she added: 'Organising things. And reading.'

Sarin lifted an eyebrow, his lips quivering. 'Well, here's hoping we don't need that first one, but the others will be perfect.' Ordelle agreed that she would be 'adept' at keeping the records, and accepted the black ledger that Sarin pushed across to her.

Kep gave an inward groan but she could not say anything, and Sarin was rubbing his hands together in that way he had — excited, as if coming up with a scheme. He proposed that they start by listing all of the questions they had, as well as any strange observations. They would meet up here, every third night to report on progress and investigate together.

'It is a suitable methodology,' nodded Ordelle as she opened the book.

Sarin laughed. 'You've been spending too much time with Gallin. You even sound like him.'

Ordelle cast a careful glance at Kep before answering, 'Yes. That is likely.' She frowned. 'Gallin is a scholar and engineer.' Sarin just laughed.

So they drew up their list of questions. Sarin went first, voicing one of the most worrying. Why was the city locked? As they progressed, Ash looked even more anxious than he had before.

Kep added one that was much in her mind: 'Why are there no altars to the gods?' Ordelle wrote it down without comment.

Then she raised the first of her own: 'Who cleans the city?' They all frowned at her. 'There should be dust.'

'Good observation.' Sarin ran his fingers along a ledge, then rubbed them together. 'This room should have gathered some dust since we opened the city. There are no cobwebs either.'

Kep frowned. 'Perhaps we should ask Nirias.'

'Ah. Which brings us to another question: can we trust Nirias?'

'Don't be ridiculous, Sarin. He is the leader of the League. Of course we can trust him.'

Sarin leaned forward. 'Ash?'

Ash answered slowly. 'I think we can trust him. Nirias doesn't have all the answers, but I think he is doing his best. It's just …' He avoided Kep's eyes. 'He just reminds me of Credé sometimes,' he muttered.

Sarin nodded. 'Nirias is Malshorne, and we don't even know what that means.'

Kep felt like hugging Ordelle when she chipped in: 'Aechon trusts him. With his life.'

'Yes. And Daska trusts him, too. In fact, just ask any of the warriors!' Kep could not help raising her voice a little. 'I don't know what you have against the man, Sarin. A little loyalty wouldn't hurt.' She lifted her chin.

Sarin held her eye for a moment. Then he shrugged. 'The list is long enough for now. We can keep adding to it.' He stood and stretched his arms behind his head. 'Okay: agreed? We meet here every third night to share what each of us has found.' Ordelle closed the ledger and nodded. Kep groaned. Every third night? She wanted to spend less time with Ordelle, not more. She wished Sarin had consulted with her first. He'd said he had something important to show them, but she had been training since dawn and was not at all in the mood for more mysteries.

Sarin had three surprises in store. The first was a life-sized painting. It was hanging in one of the many sitting rooms on the ground floor of the Knowledge Stores. It depicted a woman dressed all in blue. She held her hands out in front of her, as if grasping an invisible ball. On her shoulder was a creature with huge, mirrored eyes and a long tail.

'That's … That's Tarlyn!' exclaimed Kep, as they drew closer.

'Who is the woman?' asked Odelle.

Sarin turned to Ash. 'What do you think, Ash? Is it her?'

Ash stepped closer. 'She's older. But yes, I think that's Leynore. She was one of the Council of Three — at the end, when the city was locked.' Kep understood when he put his fingers out to the painted image of Tarlyn: it was incredibly lifelike. She stole a glance at the real Tarlyn, and looked quickly away when the creature swivelled her head. Kep had no doubt that Tarlyn was listening, and understanding everything. It was creepy.

'So,' said Sarin, 'this woman knew why the city was locked and why the people left. If we could find records or diaries, we might find some answers. It's a shame she can't speak.' They stood there for a moment longer, contemplating the proud woman in the blue velvet gown. 'Right. On we go. Ash, the next surprise is for you.'

Sarin was not joking, although Ash looked stricken rather than surprised. The mural took up an entire hallway. Astonishingly lifelike, the forms seemed to emerge from the walls, like a crowd coming out of the mist. The people were dressed in flowing garments, worn long over calf-length leggings. Their sandals were fastened in criss-cross fashion up their legs. Every single one of them, men, women and children, had pale skin, grey hair and matching grey eyes. Kep looked at Ash, then back again. It was uncanny. 'Who are they?'

Ash answered, almost in a whisper: 'Wimsari.' When Tarlyn muttered on his shoulder, his hand went up to stroke her tail. 'Nirias has told me a little about them. They are the ancestors of the Zari … and … he thinks they must be my ancestors, too.' He paused, staring at a boy who could have been his brother.

It could not possibly be true, but … the likeness was undeniable.

Sarin cocked his head. 'Ordelle? Do you know anything about the Zari?'

She shook her head. 'Aechon does not cry for the Zari. They see to their own dead.'

Sarin nodded. 'Fair enough. From what I know, the Zari are pretty reclusive. Barnham told us about the Wimsari. Remember? Their ancestral home was on the Isle of Baktar.'

Kep shook her head. She vaguely remembered something about towers that sang in the wind.

Ash broke in. 'Nirias showed me on a map. They live on smaller islands now, near the mistlands. The Singing Isles. That's where El's mother is from. El sang to me because I look like them. Her greeting was in their language, in Zari.' A muscle twitched under his eye. Kep knew exactly what he was thinking. It was all very well, but how on earth could Ash have known how to reply? She held her tongue. Poor Ash. He sounded and looked exhausted.

'I think we should head back now, Sarin. Some of us need to sleep.'

Sarin blinked as if he had forgotten the fact. 'One more thing. I promise. Ash did you bring the dopple-stars?'

❃

Kep was soon cursing Sarin. The tower was tall and narrow, with no windows either — just a staircase, climbing ever upwards. Kep was the last to reach the top. Her tiredness and irritation with Sarin for dragging them all up there had been building with every step. Almost on hands and knees, she staggered onto a platform, more than ready to give him a piece of her mind.

Her annoyance vanished in a blink.

It was as if they had climbed right up among the stars. The moons looked close enough to touch. The whole room was a hexagonal dome: crystalline, with the barest hint of silver netting. Sarin's eyes reflected in the moonlight. His teeth flashed. 'Ready, Ash?'

Ash fumbled in his pocket for the cube which held the dopple-stars. He tipped the spiky cluster out onto his hand and handed the crystalline box to Sarin. Before Kep could ask what they were up to, Ash gave the object a sharp twist, splitting one star in two. Kep had seen him do it before, of course. This time he did not return one star to its box, though, but instead held a star in each hand. They pulsed brightly in his fingers, humming at a frantic pitch. Their light dazzled the eyes! Then Ash opened his hands.

Everyone gasped. The stars blazed and shot up into the air. They circled each other, spiralling, spinning faster and faster. It was the most wonderful thing. Kep laughed for joy at the sight. Everyone did. Even Ordelle. As the stars settled into a bright rotating dance, Ash turned, eyes shining. The gyrating stars spun close, nearly brushing his head.

It was Sarin who had discovered the tower, naturally. 'The dome was built just for them.' Ash's voice wavered. 'So they could be together. Sarin found pictures of this tower in a book. The dome is the only place they can live together as they were meant to in their world.'

'Their world?'

'They are not of this dimension. The book says their world was destroyed.' Ash swallowed. 'And … Kep. We tortured them, every time we created the shield. They can't bear to be alone like that.'

Kep felt sick to her stomach. 'But we didn't know, Ash. How could we have known?'

Ash sniffed. She saw him wipe a sleeve under one eye. 'Credé must have stolen them, but that doesn't make it any better. I still feel terrible.'

Kep nodded. It was terrible. 'Well at least they are together now.' When Ordelle let out a loud yawn, Kep could not help yawning, too. All her tiredness seemed to come flooding back at once. Sarin laughed and announced that they'd probably had enough excitement for one night. So, after a few more minutes watching the stars, Ash started down the stairs with Ordelle close behind. Kep was about to follow when Sarin caugh her hand.

It was the briefest moment — a stolen moment — made eternal by Telion's light. Under the starlight, they lingered. Just the two of them. First came the brush of fingertips. Then the brush of lips. And the sweetest caress — lit by dancing stars under a crystal sky.

⁂

Dragging the covers right up to her nose, Kep smiled into the darkness, eyes wide. It felt as if she had brought a piece of burning starlight back with her, buried deep in her belly. Ash had kept casting her curious looks on the journey back. She was not surprised: it felt as if she was giving off a glow. Had he noticed that secret smile at the corner of Sarin's mouth, too? Had Ordelle noticed anything, she wondered? Kep doubted it. She was probably already asleep. Kep was closing her own eyes, knowing she would never sleep, when her peculiar roommate made an observation.

'Sarin does not wink when he is joking. Some people do, but not Sarin.'

Kep smiled into the dark. 'No. Not always.' She considered. 'He does sometimes, though.'

'When he said that you could be my chaperone, he was joking, was he not?'

'Um. I think he was making fun of Nirias for putting us in the same room.'

Thankfully, the girl moved on. 'And he does not really think that your new haircut will make Jaibari more friendly?'

'No.'

'Good. That is unlikely. Jaibari is not disposed to friendliness.'

'No.' Kep had a sudden revelation. She turned her head on her pillow. 'Ordelle, would you like me to wink if I believe Sarin is joking? I mean … when it's not clear.'

'That would be helpful.'

'All right. I'll try.' Kep could not help chuckling. 'So long as you understand I'm not exactly an expert where Sarin is concerned.'

'He is very confusing.'

Kep nodded, closing her eyes again. 'He certainly is.'

Chapter 15

THE HERATI

Karliana was not at all surprised to hear the sounds of a dulcimer and loud giggling coming from the topmost chambers of the eastern wing. It was all too frequent an occurrence these days. The whole place reeked of incense and musky perfumes. She wrinkled her nose. Tindelfion Aranti had certainly made himself at home. Professing himself completely unable to live without herati, the young lord had brought with him a veritable flock of the creatures, all dressed in the brightest, most sheer garments imaginable. The gorgeous women, and a couple of astonishingly handsome young men, seemed to take it in turns attending to his every thoughtless desire, while others fluttered about in the carpeted corridors, toying with instruments and chattering.

Of course Karliana did not care one jot: she had never liked the boy, and all these lavish entertainments kept him out of her hair. In her opinion Tindelfion more than lived up to his reputation as the most boring young man in Mildaresh. It was quite a relief that he had made no effort whatsoever to woo her. Unfortunately, it was more than she could say for the rest of her guests. Some days she wanted to beat them off with a broom. As she set her slippered foot onto the first step of the spiral staircase, she let out a sigh.

The person who was waiting had a languid loveliness that was completely out of place in the stone tower room. Dressed in a scarlet gown that barely contained her curves, and with a mouth painted to match, Belle was the most unlikely League warrior a person could imagine. The sign of the herati was stencilled in ochre on one of her perfect cheekbones. Her chestnut curls bounced as she turned, but her eyes were deadly serious.

'All is in place,' she murmured in that ridiculously sultry voice.

Karliana blinked. Perhaps the woman had not been putting that tone on after all? Heart racing, she worked her fingers into the silk purse attached to her sash. She took another quick glance about the room. Pointless of course, the tower was completely empty of hiding places. That was why it had been chosen, and for its proximity to Tindelfion's quarters. Karliana handed over the phial with a sense of dread and watched as Belle tucked it into her bodice. It was a terrible risk. True, Tindelfion was probably sodden with wine by now, busy composing another one of his awful poems, no doubt. But any one of the other herati might alert the guardians before Belle had a chance to smuggle the poison back to the Aranti villa, whether by accident or design. There was no knowing which of Tindelfion's pretty playmates were Aranti's spies.

There was nothing more to be said, and it was far too dangerous to linger. Belle already knew how to administer the poison: just a couple of drips into a glass of wine or onto a morsel of food. Karliana pursed her lips and frowned. How shocking it was to become the type of person who knew of such matters. She dreaded to think what other dark things she might learn now that she was part of the League.

It was quite terrible to be standing here, coldly conspiring. And she was cold. Coldly certain that it was the right thing to do. The voice in her head, the one that had whispered that taking a life was a crime against Argess, had fallen silent. The Montfanes' deaths. The heads of innocents on spikes outside the Squad headquarters. The boy who dangled from a scaffold, his faded green waistcoat missing a button. Those things had hushed that voice. Aranti was himself no longer. He was Melk — and he had to be stopped, at all costs. When the image of her father's face came to mind, Karliana pushed it away.

'Let it be done.'

The herati made the sign of the triangle and bowed her beautiful head. 'Let it be done.' The echoed words seemed even more terrible when whispered.

Chapter 16

THE TAELSTONE

It was morning, and Ash was alone. Alone and once more standing at his tower window. Overnight snow had created new drifts, softening sharp edges, hiding some things, transforming others into alien, unrecognisable shapes. The only things untouched by winter's hand were the soaring wings of the city. The shimmering blue sails seemed even more miraculous against the dazzling white. They tilted slightly as Ash watched, catching the sun. It was so hard to believe there was not a mind involved.

Looking towards the northwest, Ash could see the dopple-stars' dome. That the Azuri would build such a structure just to house the pair was astonishing. Somehow it made Credé's act of theft and imprisonment all the more shocking. Ash pulled his gaze away. The last thing he needed right now was to dwell on the late Malshorne's capacity for cruelty.

The day had begun in the same way as every other — long before dawn, with the Breath. Ash had sat cross-legged with the other novices, forming the triangle and breathing. Pretending he was doing his best, as usual. He hated the pretence. But Ash did not dare let go completely. If he surrendered himself to stillness, he was too afraid of what might happen.

That morning he had excused himself from the Dance of Blades, too, telling Aechon he was making progress with Demara's lore-stone and wanted to continue. Another pretence. A downright lie. But that morning Ash was not just hiding from the judgement of others. He had set himself a task. The thought of it sent him into a trembling sweat. Just a few more minutes, he told himself. At once, fear was replaced by a hot prickle of guilt. Guilt for being weak. Guilt for hiding away here in his tower. But most of all guilt for dragging Kep into such an awful situation.

The warriors had probably moved to their combat phase by now, meaning Kep was already taking a beating. It seemed the better she got, the harder they knocked her down. And Kep just kept getting back up. That was Kep. Ash felt a wave of shame and despair. Taking on the Melk should never have been Kep's fight. He turned from the window with a new look of resolve in his eyes. If there was something he could do, some knowledge he could discover that would prevent Kep ever having to become a warrior, then he had to try.

Seating himself at the desk, Ash planted his feet on the floor. He took a long, steadying breath. The two lore-stones sat before them, alike but so very different. Demara Cantoya smiled from the stone on the right, a woman inside a bubble. On the left the Taelstone glowered like a dark moon. Ash wet his lips. He pressed both palms onto the desk. Nirias was right: he was not ready. But the winter was slipping away. One day Kep would leave to take on the Melk. Perhaps not in the spring, but one day, no matter how hard Sarin tried to talk her out of it. Credé had known secrets — secrets that might help them defeat the Melk. And Ash was the only person who could uncover them.

Tarlyn was perched in the sun on the window's casement. When Ash reached out, drawing the Taelstone towards him, she sat up, prowled along the sill and leapt onto the desk. Shining eyes regarded him, whether in support or warning, he could not tell. 'I have to try, Tarlyn,' he murmured. The creature settled on her haunches and then down to lie on her belly. Ash stroked her silken body. It was a comfort to have her close. He was almost certain the stone would take him straight to the fountain at Eeroktan, to that awful scene of destruction. This time, he told himself, he would be ready.

He took the Taelstone in his hands.

The orb surged at once, responding to his touch. Blue flame ignited at its core, lighting his fingers with a weird shine. Out of the corner of his eye, Ash could still see Demara. The sight gave him a sudden thought. He rubbed one palm over the top of the Taelstone, in the polishing motion he had seen Nirias use. When a face appeared Ash was so shocked he nearly dropped the thing. It was not Credé staring back at him, but a young woman. Tarlyn's gentle mutter confirmed it. It was Leynore! Ash sucked in air. Ignoring the pulsing in his temples, he cupped the stone with both hands and closed his eyes. Following the rhythm of his breath, he let himself drift.

❧

As the room wavered, Ash reminded himself to relax, surrendering himself to the memory. His next breath was heady with the fragrance of fresh flowers. A summery breeze caressed his face, warm with honey scent and the hum of bees. He was walking through a garden — but not Demara's garden. This one was walled. Flowers tumbled down the brickwork, others nodding in profuse clusters from shaped beds and urns.

He glanced at his hands. They were long-fingered, and cuffed with crisp white linen. It was the strangest sensation. He was both Credé, and himself; free to observe, but walking with Credé's purpose, seeing through Credé's eyes. The pathway was encrusted with shells, making it sparkle with a pearly lustre. Credé kept looking off to one side, his eyes drawn towards a willowy tree, white with blossom. When a flash of blue caught his eye, his heart fluttered. Ash felt the weight of Credé's uncertainty for a long moment. At last he left the path and made his way across the lawns towards the tree.

The tree's foliage formed a swaying skirt that almost touched the ground, creating a magical space inside; a secret world hung with tapestries of green. Through the leaves he spied a low wicker lounge, set on a white rug, amidst a scatter of fringed cushions. A cast-off sandal peeped from beneath the pile. Its owner, a tall, young woman, was reclining on the lounge. Her chiffon gown was pale blue. A diaphanous scarf of a deeper hue, a perfect match for her eyes, floated up behind her shoulder. Her blonde hair fell in waves. One hand twirled a bright lock in and out of her fingers, the other held a small book. She chewed her lip pensively as she read, her brow creased into a tiny, perfect frown.

Credé drew a quiet breath before parting the shimmering curtain and stepping into the bower of her world. Her eyes lit up when she saw him, then, just as quickly, she adopted an expression of deep, affected sorrow. She pouted prettily over the edge of the book, her eyes imploring and her voice low, and unexpectedly thrilling. 'Have you come to rescue me, Credé? Please say you have. I am dying from boredom.'

Credé laughed softly. 'Good afternoon, Leynore.' He eyed the green leather-bound volume. 'And what has Master Merrin set for your edification this time?'

'Levante.' One slender eyebrow lifted into a perfect arch. 'It's dreadfully profound. Listen … This one's about a hare.' She made her expression solemn. *She thus rejoices at the view, marking tracks in plashy dew.'* Tilting her head, she repeated the words. ' "Plashy dew". Have *you* ever seen "plashy dew", Credé?

He chuckled. 'I can't say I have.' He waved an admonishing finger. 'You are mocking one of Merrin's favourite poems. I believe the theme is the fleeting nature of youth.'

'Precisely! And isn't that just the most ironic waste of a young person's time!' Leynore tossed the book aside and, yawning, reached pale arms to the sky, fingers splayed. Then she turned her head and smiled. 'How cool you look, all in shining white. Like a prince from the west. Are you a prince in disguise, Credé? If it is true, you must act swiftly. Rescue me! Else I will languish where I lie. Hark! I feel myself grow faint!' She closed her eyes with a flutter, the tiniest smile playing upon her lips.

Credé laughed, shaking his head. He was overdue elsewhere, but nevertheless he settled himself on the rug at her side and played along. Dropping his voice into a conspiratorial tone, he murmured, 'My lady. All is arranged. We leave tonight ...' He smiled. 'We'll flee beneath the moonlit skies and none shall see us pass.'

The corner of Leynore's mouth quivered a little as she caught his parody. The little bow on her bodice rose up and down, curving sweetly with the motion of her breath. She did not open her eyes. After a moment, he continued. 'And as we reach the river fair, the dawn shall kiss thy golden hair.' The verse earned him a wider smile still. 'The waiting craft has wings of white, with shining prow and raindrop bright, we'll draw it from its plashy dell and float along the Elanelle.' Leynore giggled quietly. 'And river folk will laugh and sing, at beauty borne upon the spring, and flowers toss upon a whim, until the boat is o'erbrimmed.' At this Leynore contributed a sweetly dramatic sigh and cast a hand across her brow.

Credé reached up to pluck blossoms from the hanging branches. As he threaded them into her hair she remained entirely still, breathing quietly. The white blooms shone like stars upon the golden halo of her hair. 'And so surrender, thee and me, as rivers flow unto the sea. And as the waves of evening sigh ...' Credé faltered then, overcome by a sudden aching melancholy. A lump came into his throat, preventing him from uttering another word.

Leynore opened her eyes at last. Her fingertips caressed his face, her voice a thrilling murmur. 'And as the waves of evening sigh ... we'll sail unto that spangled sky.'

In that moment Credé knew. Leynore saw him as nobody else ever could. She saw him entirely.

❧

Ash dropped the Taelstone onto its plinth as if it was on fire. His face certainly was. He clamped his hands to his mouth, trying to regather himself. The memory had been so unexpected. So deeply intimate. Finally he stumbled to his feet, scanning the bookshelf. He recognised the book at once. Drawing the dark green volume from the shelf, he read the name on its spine. *Levante.* The book broke open and there, pressed flat, obscuring the words, was a single star-shaped flower.

❧

'Well, that *is* unexpected!' Kep's dark brows were perplexed. 'Credé was in love with Leynore?'

Ash shrugged. It was impossible not to blush. He had stammered a recount of Credé's passionate encounter, leaving out the most embarrassing details. 'I think so. I fell straight into the memory. Nirias said bonded stones work a bit differently, that strong emotions draw the mind. I think that memory must have meant a lot to Credé.'

Kep nodded. 'If he was in love with Leynore he would have thought about her a lot … I mean … I suppose.' She seemed flustered. She had gone bright pink and kept touching her hand to the back of her neck.

'It's a great start, Ash.' Sarin clapped him on the back, beaming. 'I think we can safely say that the investigation into Credé's deep, dark secrets is officially underway. You've certainly made more progress than the rest of us.'

They had already run through their initial list of questions, sharing what they had found out. It was precious little. Ordelle had found out virtually nothing about the Malshorne, just a few vague references. Everyone agreed it was surprising, given the Malshornes' long lives.

The origins of the city itself were proving just as elusive. It seemed the Azuri were philosophically opposed to origin stories. There was nothing in their art or stories or histories that told where they had come from, or why. If the Council of the Azuri had kept records, they had hidden them well. Only one thing was clear: the Azuri were not a race of people. Anyone could become an Azuri — in theory. The Heartstone seemed to be at the centre of it all, but they had found no information about the strange orb, who had made it, and how it worked. It seemed the city was reluctant to give up its secrets.

Ash was silent. As he listened to the others, he became more and more miserable, hugging his failure to himself. He had avoided the Heartstone since that first awful encounter; he just could not bring himself to go anywhere near it. The thing terrified him. Now he felt horribly guilty. What if it held answers that could only be revealed to him — to the Taelstaun? He felt as if the others were thinking the same. He was relieved when Sarin shrugged.

'Come on. We are wasting our time here. Besides, I've got something to show you.' When Kep grumbled about climbing stairs, he laughed: 'Don't worry, it's not far.'

⚘

Snow, Kep had decided, was not quite so wonderful after all. The ground was icy and treacherous. Fortunately, Sarin was true to his word; the workshop he was taking them to was only a couple of doors down from what he insisted on calling 'the red lair'. They piled into a narrow porch, stamping snow from their boots. Workshops like this one were everywhere in T'al Jazure — spaces of light and imagination, filled with all manner of shining tools and rare materials. This was by far the messiest, with half-finished projects scattered everywhere.

Everything looked as if the owner had left in a hurry, which might have been a reasonable assumption, had the clutter not been so general. Kep smiled when Ordelle began to straighten things. It was a fruitless task. Sarin steered them towards a bench. It was strewn with pens and paintbrushes, half-filled bottles and thin books with wide pages. The book Sarin wanted them to see was held together by metal clasps. A flat piece of wood stuck out from around the halfway mark. Sarin flipped it open to that spot. 'I found these. They are ancient Astran designs.'

Rendered in black ink, the designs were beautiful. Stylised depictions of vines, birds and animals of all kinds flowed across the pages, crowded to the very margins. There were snakes and lizards, spread-winged eagles and tiny mouse-like beasts.

'They're wonderful,' Kep murmured.

'Your slave marks are set more on an angle than Ash's. A simple band wouldn't hide them. And it might raise suspicions.'

Kep swallowed. She knew why her brand was wonky. She had wriggled, jerking her little arm away from the cruel needle. Kep would never forget the coarse hair on the back of the tattooist's hands, the stench of his breath, and his barking laugh. *Pretty little thing. I should of bought you myself. You and me could of had loads of fun.* He had dragged her even closer, leaving bruises on her arm. Shoving the memory away, Kep flipped a sheet, and another, before realising she had not really been seeing the images at all.

Sarin put out a hand, brushing hers ever so slightly. 'Here. Go back a couple.' He helped her manage the pages. 'Look. These are the ones I worked from … and …' Drawing a folder from under the bench, he laid a sheath of drawings in front of her. 'I thought … something like this?' All of a sudden, Sarin seemed unsure of himself. He kept smoothing his hair back, frowning at the papers and reshuffling the order. Finally, he stood back to give her space, his arms wrapped across his chest, quietly tense.

Kep's eyes grew wider as she inspected the drawings. Those were her hands! Sketched in soft pencil, but incredibly lifelike. Sarin had placed the slave marks with precision, with each drawing showing his attempts to incorporate them in different ways. Inspired by the ancient designs, her new tattoo would wrap around her wrist, obliterating any link to the House of Aranti. No … not obliterating — those cruel marks of ownership had been reclaimed, set to work as part of a new design.

Kep could sense bridled energy in Sarin as he waited. There was one design that he preferred, she was sure of it. Would he be disappointed if she chose differently? Her eyes kept returning to one drawing, but she ran her eyes down the line again. They were all wonderful. They would all work. But really there was no decision: that one design was absolutely perfect. Proud, bold and utterly fierce. A falcon. The page shook as she picked it up. Her eyes welled so suddenly that she could not prevent the tear which splashed onto the paper. She pressed a hand to her lips to stop them trembling and looked at Sarin. His grin said everything as he nodded his approval.

Chapter 17

JEN-JAY

Kep grunted, catching sight of a small figure out of the corner of her eye. She kept whirling her staff, though, refusing to let the woman intimidate her. The surly cook seemed to have made it her business to prowl the training rooms, long before the sun was up, before the warriors were awake. Kep had no idea what Jen-Jay thought she was doing. The woman would flit by shadow-like, or stand under the arches watching — as if she did not have anything better to do! She never came any closer, she never spoke. Kep kept working her wrists, keeping the staff spinning in a smooth, whirling motion. The chime calling everyone for the Breath could not be far away, and she had not finished her exercises.

The little woman haunted the training sessions, too, always shaking her head in disdain. She was full of muttered opinions. Really! What would a cook know about fighting? Kep could not understand why Daska tolerated Jen-Jay's eccentricities, but they spent so much time in grumbling conversation that Ash had proposed they might be a couple. Sarin had laughed uproariously at the idea, nearly choking on his food. Poor Ash. Kep could not imagine any man wanting to be with such a woman. Even Nirias seemed scared of her! You would think that as their leader he might take her to task about her cooking. The food had improved recently, but only because Sarin had been sneaking herbs into her stews. Kep pivoted, confirming her suspicions. Yes. She was still there! Lurking and watching.

Kep's staff whirled faster. What was wrong with the woman? Sometimes Kep would look up from her meal and find Jen-Jay staring, skewering her with those ice-blue eyes. When she had noticed Kep's new tattoo, she had made a startled choking noise. Perhaps she was a bit unhinged? Sarin found it all hilarious of course — he took a weird delight in everything to do with Jen-Jay.

Kep swore. Her rhythm broken, the staff clattered to the floor. She snatched it up, scowling. She always seemed to lose concentration or make a mistake when Jen-Jay was present. The woman was a menace! Enough was enough. She pressed her lips into a determined line and decided it was time to say something.

Kep stalked across the room and took up a stance, the staff firm across her body. 'What is it? Tell me! What do you want?'

The pale eyes regarded her for a long moment. 'Complete commitment, total secrecy, and no answering back.' The woman jerked a nod. 'If you can promise those three things, I will agree to train you.'

Kep would have laughed, except that Jen-Jay's expression was deadly serious. Something about her stance made Kep think of Tarlyn, utterly still but ready to pounce.

'You?' Kep could not hide her incredulity. '*You* want to train *me*?' The woman *was* unhinged. Train in what? Surely not cooking?

Jen-Jay's grimace made the lines around her mouth even deeper. 'Nirias will send you into the world.' She sniffed. 'But you are weak. A weak child. You must be trained.'

Kep frowned. 'I *am* training.' Her hands on the quarterstaff were as firm as her words. 'I am learning to become a warrior.'

Jen-Jay let out an impatient *tsk*, heavy with derision. 'A warrior, is it?' Kep was caught again by her eyes. Pale blue irises ringed with deeper blue. 'Show me.' Kep lowered her staff, puzzled. The woman had been creeping about for weeks, watching. Surely she had already seen how Kep had improved? 'Strike at me, girl!'

Kep gave a firm shake of her head. She was certainly not about to whack a little old woman with a stick. The little old woman laughed. A swift dart, a sharp wrench and Kep was disarmed — just like that. Jen-Jay had moved with such speed! Kep blinked at her empty hands, feeling completely foolish. It was like one of Sarin's sleight-of-hand tricks.

'So.' Jen-Jay tapped the staff on the floor. 'You demand a demonstration.' Her eyes narrowed in displeasure. 'I am not a performing monkey, but …' With a shrug of her thin shoulders she began to wield the staff. It spun so quickly that it seemed to disappear entirely, like the wings of a dragonfly. And Jen-Jay moved with it, in a rapid flurry. Kep thought she recognised sequences and stances, but the flow was so swift she lost track. None of the other warriors moved like that, not even Rodine Gametale. When the whirling came to a stop, Kep gasped. The blunt pressure of wood pressed into her throat. She had no doubt that Jen-Jay could have injured her very badly, had that been her intention. The woman's eyes had a steely focus.

Only when Kep gave a submissive nod, did she snap upright, her back as straight as the staff itself.

'Do you agree to my conditions?'

Kep made the deepest bow of her life. 'Thank you, Jen-Jay.' She swallowed, blushing at some of her earlier thoughts. 'I apologise for my lack of respect. And for my doubt. I agree to your conditions. To anything. I am willing to learn.' Although she spoke with humility, her heart was jumping for joy. She would have promised anything to learn to move like that.

Chapter 18

WINTERDEEP

How long had it been snowing? Forever? Ash would not have been surprised. He was finding it hard to remember a world without snow. Layer after layer had fallen, day after mind-numbing day. Sometimes it seemed the city might be buried entirely, hidden once more from human eyes. Perhaps that would be a good thing. Ash pressed a hand to the window pane, feeling its cold resistance, then bowed his head so that his forehead rested against the hard surface of the glass. The snow kept falling.

A part of Ash welcomed the ever-deepening drifts — a large part. So long as it kept snowing, nobody could leave. Not Sarin, not Kep and, most importantly, not Ash. The snow was a safety blanket, keeping everybody safe from peril. Yet with every fall came another layer of tension, too. The sense of waiting grew stronger. The city seemed to ache, as if its very soul was yearning to leave.

Not surprisingly, the warriors were beginning to niggle at each other. Despite their discipline, more than one sparring session had resulted in real injuries. Agnid was kept busy with sprains and bruises, dislocated shoulders and cracked heads. The warriors watched each other like hunters now; fighting and training were all they seemed to think about. Few had bothered themselves with the wonders of the Knowledge Stores. Not all could read, and what was the point of thousand-year-old knowledge anyway? Even if there had been books or stones about fighting, Ash doubted the warriors would be interested. For that knowledge they had each other. They talked and breathed fighting — quite literally if you considered the morning ritual of the Breath.

Kep was one of the worst. Ash barely saw her these days. She spent all of her time training, either with the others or in secret sessions with Jen-Jay. In the evenings she was so exhausted that she nearly fell asleep in her food. Kep had always been single-minded, for as long as Ash had known her. But this was a whole new level of determination. She rarely came to the red lair now, and did not seem to care about uncovering the secrets of the city. All she cared about was joining a jinn, taking on the Melk, and leaving. Ash sighed, misting the window pane. With the tip of his little finger he traced the shape of a triangle on the glass. Then he turned back into the room, back to his books.

How many hours had he spent in this tower alternating between searching for answers and staring out at the snow? It had all been fruitless. He was no closer to understanding. Credé's stone seemed to contain a single memory — his lovestruck mooning over Leynore. Every attempt to read the stone had taken Ash back to that garden and the scene beneath the tree. Credé's secrets were as safe as ever.

Ash ground his teeth as he stared at the hated stacks of books. He was tired of puzzling out long words and clouded explanations. Telion knows how many hours he had spent, struggling to improve his reading, mouthing out words syllable by syllable. And the result? The books had told him nothing. Oh, yes. He knew all about the theory of the Song. He could probably reel off the names of every Taelstaun who had ever lived. The history was all there: where they came from, their diplomatic endeavours, the instruments they had played, even titles of worthy compositions. All that was nothing. It told Ash nothing.

When his eyes fell upon Demara Cantoya's face, smiling at him from inside her lore-stone, he scowled. All those conversations in her stupid garden had just made him even more afraid of losing his mind to the Song. The woman had been reassuring at first. She had even chuckled at his questions. *Do not concern yourself. Your mentor will help. Nobody becomes Taelstaun without the fullest preparation.* At last, she had set her basket aside, leaning forward to pat his knee. *You are too full of fear, my boy. Perhaps you have the talent, but in my opinion it would be dangerous for you to continue. I am sorry, Ash. You are simply not ready.*

Not ready. Ash wanted to laugh, or spit, or throw something. Of course he was not ready! He wasn't the Chosen One! Credé had chosen Braig to learn the stupid Song! And now Braig was dead. An unfamiliar surge of anger coursed through Ash. His hands jerked at his sides and he gritted his teeth. His thinking mind registered the strangled roar that escaped his lips with a flicker of surprise. Then he lashed out at a stack of books. A second swipe sent still more tumbling.

Tarlyn whirled upright, uncoiling like a spring, her ruff bristling with quills. At the same time Demara Cantoya's orb flew into the air, smacked against a shelf and rolled under the couch. A single book remained open on the table. Ash shoved that one off for good measure, then cast about for something else to throw.

When his eyes fell on Tarlyn, he froze mid-action and groaned. She was watching him in utter stillness, her eyes dark lakes of unfathomable meaning. Holding his hands over his ears, Ash crumbled. 'I'm sorry. I'm so sorry.' As he sank to the ground, she made a soft burring sound and came closer. Her muzzle nudged his face as his tears welled, spilling down his cheeks.

'I can't do this … I can't do this, Tarlyn.' Gathering the creature into his arms he bent his head and wept. He understood now. He was trapped, as surely as a memory within a lore-stone. He could never leave the city. If he did, the Song would drive him insane.

❧

The tap at the door came later. Ash was not sure how much later. He had fallen asleep with Tarlyn in his arms. Raking fingers through his hair, he scrambled to his feet and let Sarin in.

'You look terrible.'

Bleary-eyed, Ash rubbed his face with the back of his hand. Sarin's eyes made a lazy sweep of the room, taking in the chaos. He made no comment. Instead he strolled to the window. 'Do you know what day it is?' Ash stared. What possible difference could it make? 'It's Winterdeep, Ash. You know? The deepest day of winter?' Picking up one of the fallen books, Sarin scanned its spine before returning it to the table. 'Don't they celebrate Winterdeep in Mildaresh?'

Ash gave a tired shrug. The nobles did. The slaves just worked all the harder, trying to get the feasts prepared.

'I know you've been busy,' Sarin's eyebrow quirked, 'but really, Ash … do try to keep up. There's going to be a celebration. They've even cancelled this afternoon's training. Fancy that!' Sarin snorted, his eyes glinting with amusement. Moving to the window, he watched the swifts' tower for a few moments, then raised his brows at Ash. 'No sign?'

'Oh … um …' Ash wrung his hands. He had completely forgotten he was supposed to keep an eye out for swifts. 'I didn't really …'

Sarin just laughed. 'Too busy?' His eyes fell once more on the dishevelled mess. 'You need to get out of here, Ash. Come on! I'm taking you hunting.'

'Hunting?'

As Ash scratched his head, staring at the snow-laden landscape, Sarin laughed again, enjoying his confusion. 'Here, you'll need this.' Ash caught the silver band which Sarin tossed at him. *Beyond the rim? Seriously? They were going beyond the rim?* 'Don't look so worried. It's not that sort of hunting. We're after bloodberries — for the feast.'

⚜

Ash had to admit it, Sarin was right. It was good to be outside in the fresh air, even if the snow-reflected glare made his eyes stream. Most of his attention was on his feet and the odd contraptions strapped to his boots, which Sarin called snowfloats. Sarin had brought a pair for each of them. He demonstrated how they folded into tear-shaped rafts, and helped Ash clip them onto his boots. Walking took a little more care: you had to lift your feet to avoid scooping up snow. They quickly got the hang of it, though, and picked up speed as they moved across the bright landscape, leaving strange-patterned tracks behind.

They came to the rim sooner than Ash expected. While there was no visible trace of the perimeter that ringed the city, there was no doubt that they had reached the limits of the realm of T'al Jazure. Halting in his tracks, Ash put his hands to the sides of his head and made a yawning motion to pop the sudden pressure in his ears. Sarin was holding out his palms. 'Let's see what it's like to walk through,' he suggested with a sideways grin.

Ash sighed. It sounded like a horrible idea, but he was too tired to argue. Copying Sarin, he removed the silver band from his wrist and settled it over his brow. No longer marvelling at the way the circlet changed its size, nor the odd pressure it created at his temples, he stretched out his hands, as if feeling his way in the dark.

Passing through the rim was a most disturbing sensation. Movement became lethargic, as though time had slowed. It felt like they were pushing through a bubble, one made from thickened glue. The sudden release made Ash stagger. Looking over his shoulder, he took a sharp breath. It stunned him every time. The city had vanished. All that could be seen were trees and snow.

'That was fun. I reckon that's what hatchling turtles feel like.' Sarin grinned. 'Let's do it again sometime.'

Ash pulled a face. He was definitely not doing it again. And there was nothing fun about the Enigmata. Wearing the circlet helped, but the trees still seemed to waver, as if you could pass your hand through them. He shuddered, hoping that the bloodberries were not far away.

Sarin stretched his arms over his head and took a deep breath of forest air. He seemed perfectly at home, and perhaps he was. He was no stranger to the Enigmata; what with all the hunting he had been doing, he had probably spent more time out here than anyone. He grinned. 'Come on, then!' Ash wished his friend wouldn't clap his hands like that. It seemed unnecessarily loud. 'Let's see what's about.' Ash had no wish to see what was about, but he followed anyway.

The forest was rich with the scent of conifers. It was still and silent, except when a bough shivered and shook itself free from snow. Sarin related how he had discovered the secret of snowfloats as they trudged along. 'Hirimus Stell!' Sarin seemed oblivious to how his words echoed. Could he not hear that strange ricochet through the trees? Ash shivered. 'That was her name! Her lore-stone was organised by colour, would you believe?' Sarin pointed at their feet. 'I found her explanation of these in the pink section!' Ash frowned. Why would you organise a lore-stone according to colour? It made no sense. Sarin caught his eye. 'I know, it seems crazy. I suppose it made sense to Hirimus. To be fair, there was a kind of a pattern, once I puzzled it out. Anyway, she was an extraordinary inventor, Hirimus Stell—' Sarin seemed about to say more when he held up a hand. His eyes widened as he tilted his head to listen. 'Did you hear that?'

Ash froze in his tracks, desperately hoping it was not wolves, or something worse.

'There!' When Sarin clutched at his sleeve, Ash stared in dismay at his feet. There was no way he could outrun anything in those contraptions, and certainly not a wolf. But Sarin seemed more excited than scared. His eyes were shining as he shaped his fingers at his mouth. He emitted three quick notes, rising up and down and ending with a metallic sort of click. Ash had no idea how he could achieve such a sound. Eyes sharp, Sarin scanned the trees and whistled again. They strained their ears. Then a fluttering shower of snow announced that something had landed in the branches above. 'It is! It's a redwing!' breathed Sarin. He circled the trunk to get a better look, and Ash craned his neck, too.

The bird's tail feathers were twice as long as its body, falling in thin scrolls and tipped with bright scarlet. A fan of feathers stood up on its head, like a tiny coronet. It surveyed them with shining eyes, and parted its beak. The redwing's song cut the air; bright and silvered. For breathless minutes the bird sang on, its cascading shower of notes sending a thrill through Ash's body. The sound was so true and so clear, it seemed to draw his heart into his mouth. Then with a twitch of wings and a shower of white it was gone.

Sarin gave a little caper of joy in spite of his snowfloats. 'A redwing, Ash! A redwing — and at Winterdeep, too!' Ash was stunned to see that his friend's eyes were glistening. As Sarin stepped forward, placing both hands upon the tree, Ash saw his lips moving. Was he speaking to the tree? Perhaps praying. To Argess? Ash wanted to ask. But somehow the moment seemed too intensely private.

Neither of them spoke, it was enough to just stand there breathing. The bird's song had imbued the place with a lingering magic. When the bird called again, Ash's heart swelled at the beauty of it and he went to catch Sarin by the elbow. Then he realised the truth. That was no bird! It was a cascading melody. Ash reeled. The Song was back! It flitted at the edge of his mind, just like a bird hiding in the canopy. He only had to reach out and the Song would come to him. He swayed, holding his head. What terrible visions might it bring? What if he lost himself again?

Sarin had started walking on. When he turned back, Ash covered his panic by crouching and fiddling with the straps on his snowfloats. It didn't seem to fool Sarin. Ash looked up into his friend's concerned eyes. 'Are they much further, then?' The question came out as a squeak, causing Sarin's frown to deepen. Ash cleared his throat, and made an effort to drop his voice. 'The bloodberries. Are they far?'

Sarin studied him for a moment. 'We're not really out here for bloodberries. There's a tree much closer to the lodges — well inside the rim.' He did not take his eyes from Ash. 'I thought you needed a break from the city. And there was something I wanted to try.'

When Sarin was being mysterious Ash usually just waited, knowing that sooner or later his friend would reveal whatever surprise was entertaining him. But Ash needed distracting, anything to help keep the Song at bay. As they retraced their oddly-patterned tracks, he said, 'So ... these work. The snowfloats, I mean.' A sudden realisation made him pause. He searched Sarin's profile. 'You're not ... You're not leaving, are you?' The possibility filled him with dread.

Sarin responded with a rueful look. 'No. Not yet. You'd need more than a pair of snowfloats to negotiate those passes in the heart of winter.' As he stared at the far peaks, his eyes had a wistful look in them. He gave a resigned sigh. 'Not yet.'

Ash knew his friend was wishing winter away. Sarin was Aurum — he was not used to staying in one place for too long. But there was another reason, too. 'Are you worried about Rilka?' It was a clumsy thing to say, and Sarin did not bother answering. Of course he was worried. 'Will she be ousted, do you think?'

Sarin's face had taken on the tense, chiselled look it always did when anyone mentioned his sister. 'Probably.'

Ash gave an awkward nod, as if he understood. But he didn't really. The Aurum's custom of ousting made him uncomfortable. Every spring Sarin's clan voted, and if an individual received enough votes they had to leave the clan until the following autumn. Rilka was younger than Sarin by a couple of winters, but she always got more than her share of the votes, because … Well, she made life uncomfortable with her strange trances and visions of the future.

Sarin's plan was to bring Rilka back to T'al Jazure, and it seemed he had Nirias's blessing. Nirias had shown great interest in Rilka's visions: he thought she might even be a senseer, someone able to detect the presence of the Melk. Ash shivered.

He needed to change the subject — he didn't want to be reminded about Rilka's foretelling, that his destiny was bound to the Melk. He latched onto the first thing that came to mind. 'Kep will be happy when the spring comes. She can't wait to leave.' Just saying the words made his heart feel like lead.

Sarin scowled. 'True. Kep can't wait to go off and get herself killed. She is nowhere near ready. But …' His face creased with worry. 'I can't see her being accepted by a jinn. Can you?'

Sarin's eyes dared Ash to say otherwise, so he shook his head.

'I'm worried about her, Ash. Every time somebody mentions a mission to Mildaresh she gets a dark look in her eye. You don't think she's seeking revenge, do you?' The side of Sarin's mouth twitched a little, and he cleared his throat. 'For your friend … Braig, I mean.'

Ash frowned. He was hardly the expert on what Kep was thinking. Perhaps she did blame Aranti. His decision to sacrifice Braig as an eternal gift to Mascellion Feyindi had certainly been the move that had set everything else in motion. But Aranti had not killed Braig. Realising that Sarin was waiting on his answer, Ash shrugged. 'I … I don't think so. I don't know … Maybe.'

Ash put his head down. *Braig didn't die because of Aranti. He died because of me.* Those were the words he wanted to say. The confession he had never made. He wanted to tell Sarin that it had been his fault. If he had been able to fight off Feld that day, Braig would still be alive. A hot, guilty flush swept his body.

Sarin was staring at him so intensely that for a moment Ash felt as if Sarin could read his mind and see the guilt written there. He spoke quickly. 'I don't think Nirias would send Kep to Mildaresh. I think he wants to keep her safe.' Sarin gave him a slow nod.

They trudged on, each deep in his own thoughts, until the tracks they had been retracing came to a sudden stop, marking the place where one world became another. They stared at the pristine white surface.

Sarin drew his brows together. 'You can come with me, you know.'

Ash bit his lip. 'Thanks. But …' As he answered, the wings of birdsong brushed his mind, making him feel sick. 'I … can't,' he stammered. 'I can't leave the city. Not until I master the Song.' If he was honest, he could not wait to get back inside the rim. Swallowing hard, Ash dragged one of his gloves off with his teeth — he needed bare hands to create the door. To his surprise, Sarin stopped him.

'Wait.' There was mystery in his smile. 'Let me try.' Sarin had been rubbing his hands together. Now he held them out for Ash to see. Ash gasped. The moons on Sarin's palms were intricately decorative now, overlaid in blue lines. Sarin gave him a grin before reaching up, inscribing the shape of an arch. Ash caught his breath when the air shimmered. It was working! Sure enough, a solid archway materialised from thin air. The space within its frame wavered for a moment, a sheerest curtain of light. Then it dropped away, revealing T'al Jazure — a frosted miracle within a sea of white.

Ash was weak with wonder. 'Sarin … you … That means …'

Sarin was staring at his hands. 'Yeah,' he said thoughtfully. 'Guess that makes me an Azuri.'

⚶

Kep folded her arms, surveying her reflection once more. The dress was better than the others, she supposed. It still made her feel like a foolish girl. If Nirias had not ordered everyone to dress for the occasion, things would have been so much easier — she would have gone to the feast in the same outfit she wore for training. She heaved a sigh, but Nirias had made things more than clear: this was to be an evening of peace — all thoughts of fighting were to be put aside. As Ordelle moved behind her, stepping into the mirror's frame, Kep screwed up her face. 'How do I look?' she asked, wrinkling her nose.

Ordelle ran a critical eye over Kep's reflection. 'Like a warrior — in a dress.'

Kep snorted. It was true. The midnight blue gown was made of gorgeous fabric that sparkled faintly like the night sky, yet it was cut simply. It did not drag along the ground. Its sleeves, like the bodice, were comfortably fitted, without flounces or hampering trailing bits. Deep pleats in the skirts allowed for easy movement. The beginnings of a smile formed. Turning so she could see the straight-laced back of the gown, Kep nodded to herself; perhaps there would be no fighting, but if there was, she was dressed for it. She turned to get a better look at Ordelle's costume.

Her roommate had cast only the most cursory eye over the endless racks of garments in the share stores. She had opted instead for clothes of her own. As always, Kep wondered if Ordelle's outfit was typical of what the people wore in Calkinon — with Ordelle you could never be too sure. Kep was not even sure if it was one garment or several. The outfit consisted of several overlapping squares, brightly coloured in pink and orange, with concentric patterns and gold-trimmed edges. The stiffened shoulder-line, squared sleeves and straight trousers all contributed to the sense that Ordelle was wearing a set of boxes that had been stitched together. The sharp edges of her trousers hovered incongruously above a pair of sleekly contoured ankle boots in mauve.

Kep smiled. 'And you. You look very ... colourful.'

Ordelle swivelled her head in that odd way she had, owl-like, without moving a muscle in the rest of her body. She gave a slow blink of her large, serious eyes and nodded agreement. Impossible to tell if she took it as a compliment. Her eyes went to the woven casket that Kep was turning over in her hands. 'Have you decided to wear Sarin's token?'

Kep chewed on her lip, dragging her mouth out of shape. 'Yes.' She paused. 'I think so.'

'Sit down, then. I'll weave it in place.'

Perching on a stool, Kep handed over the token.

Ordelle held the ornament against Kep's hair, checking the position. The feathers, one iridescent green and the other an impossible shade of blue, stood out like a bright flash against her black curls. Kep nodded at Ordelle, trusting her judgement. She still had no idea of the feathers' significance. Sarin would not have just chosen them randomly, she knew that much.

As Ordelle began to separate strands of hair, weaving the token into place, Kep wondered again about Sarin's gifts. Ordelle knew only a little about the courting rituals of the Haelrum clans. She was more interested in their treatment of the dead, and was most disappointed that Sarin had kept his silence on the matter. As for courting, she said the braiding of hair was important, as was the giving of gifts. Kep was sure that every single one of Sarin's gifts meant something. But what?

She frowned at herself. She spent far too much time thinking about that young man. Why did he make her feel so confused? Sometimes he would ignore her for days, or tease her mercilessly. Then he'd give her such a smile! A smile that struck at the centre of her being, as if she was the only person in the room, and her insides would turn to molten fire.

Ordelle's hands had paused. 'Kep?'

Kep flushed a little, wondering if the girl had caught her thoughts. Then she realised Ordelle had been asking her something. Her mind tracked back. Something about stepping out? 'I'm sorry, what did you say? I wasn't paying attention.'

'It is nothing. It does not matter.'

The way that Ordelle brushed her hair from the side of her face made Kep certain that it did matter. 'No. Ask me again. Please,' she insisted.

'In Comity Reel. Would you step with me?'

'A reel? Is that a dance?'

'Yes. First known instances date from the reign of Lord Isel, in Darlington. The Comity Reel is one of the oldest known.' Kep could tell that Ordelle was resisting the urge to tell her more. 'It is a friendship reel, danced only at Winterdeep.'

'I can't dance the steps with you, Ordelle.'

'I understand.' Ordelle poured her attention into the working of her fingers.

'Oh, no! I don't mean—' Kep could have kicked herself. 'I'm sorry. Not because I'm not your friend. I just … I've never danced a reel. I don't know the steps.'

Ordelle's fringe shifted, revealing a pair of hopeful eyes. 'It is a very basic dance. Even village idiots know it.' Ordelle's eyelids fluttered. 'I mean, everyone just does the same thing at the same time.'

'Well, if idiots can do it …' Kep laughed. 'If you show me the steps, I would be proud to dance with you.'

Ordelle's smile was the widest Kep had ever seen her give. It completely transformed her face.

Chapter 19

THE HALL OF THE BARDS

The Hall of the Bards was a completely round building, and hung with so many tapestries that it seemed more like a large tent. The walls, painted a rich purple, swooped upward into an onion-shaped dome. Suspended from that was a huge central ring, hung with lamps. Like crystal pears they dangled in clusters, spilling golden light onto the circular stage. Matching pear-drops hung from sconces affixed to the walls, lighting everything with a soft glow. Most of the works depicted gardens, inhabited by people dancing, playing music or conversing over wine and food. Spirals of incense rose from fat-bellied pottery vessels wafting the scent of sandalwood and cinnamon through the room. The whole place radiated warmth and comfort, from its deep burgundy rugs to the fat cushions and low-slung chairs.

Tonight, the windows and doors had been festooned with boughs of bloodberries. It was traditional, according to Ordelle: the vivid red clusters were both a symbol of rebirth, and a ward against evil. Ordelle was elucidating the origin of the practice and comparing it with customs across the lands. Kep had already stopped listening. Selective ignoring was an important strategy in keeping your temper when Ordelle was around.

Her eyes found Sarin, balanced halfway up a ladder, reaching up to fix the last decorative bough. An uncertain Ash was watching on, one hand on a rung. Perhaps he planned to catch Sarin if he fell. Neither event seemed likely.

Kep's smile dissolved. Ash seemed so lost these days. Gauntly pale and more evasive than ever, he barely seemed to know what was going on from one moment to the next. As for this new paranoia, his insistence that something was watching him ... Kep sighed. She just wished there was something she could do. His head was all messed up, with that Taelstone and the Song. It would help if he wasn't just ... so sensitive. When Ash looked her way, she gave him a merry wave and crossed the floor. Ordelle trailed after her, still lecturing on the traditions of Winterdeep.

Sarin gave the large green ribbon a final tweak and dropped from the ladder, landing neatly. His quick eyes went at once to Kep's hair and his secret gift. When his lips curved into a smile she looked quickly away. Her discomfort was made even worse when she saw how Ash was staring at her. No wonder! Under the lights her dress had become a galaxy of shining stars.

When Ozu Mako approached with a tray of silver goblets, he gave her an appreciative grin. Kep took a goblet, avoiding his eyes. In her blushing confusion she missed hearing what it contained, so she spent the next few moments just swirling the contents and looking about.

Ozu looked different, too. His pure white tunic was the perfect foil for his acorn-coloured skin and flowing black hair. It made her feel awkward to see the warriors in their finery, and it seemed she was not alone. Spending most of their days slamming each other into the ground, they knew each other's fighting style intimately. Now they eyed each other shyly, like strangers.

Fortunately, Nirias did not waste any time in making his way to the centre of the room and leaping up onto the stage. The lights caught the gold embroidery at his collar and the edge of his red tailored coat. It seemed to Kep that the grey in his beard was shining, too.

'My comrades. My dear friends. We have reached the heart of winter!' A couple of people raised a cheer, and Nirias lifted his goblet in salute. 'It gives me great cheer to see you gathered here tonight, not as warriors, but as men and women. It is, I fear, an event all too rare. But tonight we take a sweet interlude.' His wide smile included them all. 'Here at Winterdeep, we draw breath.' Kep took a deep breath and felt others around her doing the same.

'Yes, my friends. Tonight we allow ourselves a breath. The breath that comes before the storm.' Nirias took a few paces, quickening his words. 'I do not deny it, nor would I have you forget: a storm is surely brewing. Events in Mildaresh run on, as yet unchecked.' He lifted a finger. 'But we have earned this breath, this pause, because Winterdeep marks a moment in time. It marks the beginning of a new phase in our training.'

A low murmur, barely discernible, rippled through the audience. Nirias nodded, smiling.

'Yes. Now it is time to choose new captains to fill the places of those we have lost.' The murmuring became a little louder. 'Tomorrow the tournament of skills begins. Each of you will have a chance to prove yourself worthy. My friends, tonight Marki hangs full in the sky,' Nirias pointed to the little moon peeking in through the window; 'when he waxes again, all will be in place. Sweet Telion has granted us the greatest weapon against our enemy — time.' His voice grew louder. 'We will use that gift of time to its full advantage. We will select our finest warriors. We will create our finest teams for the battle that lies ahead. And come spring…' He paused. 'Come spring … we will prevail.'

Nirias allowed the cheering to grow, then quelled it with a motion of his hand. 'But tonight we speak of other things. I ask you to embrace the moment — bask in the sweet breath of peace. Because it is just a taste, my friends. A taste of what we are fighting for. Peace! The Melk has stalked these lands for long enough! We will take our fight to the Melk in the spring with renewed vigour, with renewed resources, with renewed hope. And we shall overcome!'

Kep cheered with others, her face growing warm. Nirias had looked straight at her when he said those words. She swelled with pride to think that she was part of his plan, part of the battle to rid the world of the Melk. Looking around she saw many others beaming and nodding, too — all except Sarin. With arms folded, and one eyebrow lifted, Sarin was the very picture of disdain. When he caught her looking, he rolled his eyes. Actually rolled his eyes. By the gods! What was wrong with that boy? Shooting him her best glare, Kep returned her eyes to Nirias.

He was bringing his speech to an end with a gentle reminder that wrestling bouts, knife tosses and any other sort of roughhousing were suspended for the evening. When Benjin bellowed that he would clobber anyone not dancing or making merry, everybody laughed.

Kep raised her goblet with the others. When they drank, she took a large swig and gulped it back in surprise. The liquid was sweet and a little fiery, stirring warmth in her belly. After the initial shock, she laughed, adding her voice to the resounding cheer.

There was a great deal of laughing that night, along with dancing, juggling — thanks to Sarin — and raucous singing. It turned out that Lakmorin Spink was a fair demon on the fiddle, and with Aechon on the lute he turned out one merry jig after another. Gamon Baze produced a flat drum, which he proceeded to hit with something that looked like an old spoon. He had a mean talent for a quick beat. The trio's rollicking rendition of common tunes, mixed in with cheerful mistakes, soon had everyone dancing and falling about laughing.

When it came time to dance the Comity Reel, Kep took her place eagerly, muffing only a few of the steps and skipping happily through the tunnel of arched arms. It did not matter to Kep that she was partnered with the most solemn person in the room — if anything, that made it more fun. Ordelle even seemed to enjoy the dance. 'That was enjoyable,' she confirmed glumly when it was over.

The only thing that took the edge off the night was Sarin. Kep accepted another goblet of mead and resolved to avoid him completely.

❧

As the night wore on, Ash withdrew further into himself. Unable to slink away entirely, he found the next best thing: a couch in a shadowy corner where he could watch undisturbed. He had to admit it was heartening to watch everyone become rosy-faced. He even laughed once or twice at the antics. Muku and Tuku performed a hilarious dance together involving perfectly synchronised movements and rude gestures. Eventually things got a little too raucous, so Benjin Dale hopped up onto stage bearing a wooden stool. Everyone roared when he stood on it, casting his arms wide as if about to sing. The big man laughed, fended off a couple of cheeky quips and announced that, as talented as he was, Aechon had agreed to a request.

There were cries of approval as the Cryer made his way onto the stage. Benjin slapped him on the back so hard he nearly knocked the short man off his feet. The big man beamed. 'This is for you, my friends. For my friends in arms.'

The Cryer had swapped his lute for a harp. Small enough to be held in the lap, the instrument was as black as a raven's wing, with a curved back that rose up over Aechon's shoulder like the stern of a ship. The lights dimmed as he settled himself on the stool. The harp had an ancient tone, almost jangling but deeply beautiful. At the first note Ash pressed his hand to his heart. When the Cryer ran his hands over the strings again it felt as if the man was plucking at the strings of his soul. 'Hear now, "The Lay of Eregil and Mendolas",' the Cryer intoned.

Ash caught his breath. He'd already known what the song was called, from that first exquisite chord. As Aechon began to sing he had to resist the urge to murmur the words. It was like the call of an old friend. Ash could see the faces of the two heroes: one so dark and the other so bright. He saw their bronzed shields, the clasp of their arms, bracelets of hair entwined about their wrists. As Aechon's clear voice rose, the story unfolded as Ash knew it would. Shoulder to shoulder the heroes fought, joyful in victory. With each chorus Ash became aware that others were joining in, some stamping their feet as they sang the refrain. *And all prevail, and none shall fail* … Some of the lyrics varied — 'flaxen locks' had become 'flaxen hair' — but the essence remained: the joy of loyalty, two brothers-in-arms, bound by adventure.

Ash's heart burned at the strident beauty of the notes, but something was missing — the counterpart. A female voice was supposed to rise from the fourth verse, balancing the melody's deep march. When the chorus came around again — *And all prevail, and none shall fail* — Ash braced himself for the final verse. Instead Aechon launched into a repeat of the chorus. Ash reeled in confusion. But the audience was already laughing, embracing and clasping arms. Aechon was bowing and smiling.

Ash gasped. It felt as if an iron band was contracting around his chest. The more he gasped for air, the dizzier he became. Blood pounded in his ears. He gulped, trying to breathe. Why couldn't he breathe? Almost instinctively, his hands grasped for the Taelstone. He clutched it to his chest. In moments, his panicked gasping subsided. The blood in his ears started to abate and his breathing slowed. Closing his eyes in relief, Ash fell into memory.

❧

Credé was sitting on a stool at a high bench, in a workshop flooded with light. The space was brightly clean. Tools hung where they belonged; labelled jars stood in lines; and materials were stacked in cubbies and under benches. A sharp smell hung in the air, making the eyes water a little. Credé had a fine paintbrush balanced between his long fingers. Every ounce of his being was focused as he stroked a clear substance onto the object before him. The model was superb. The little boat's prow had all the grace of a swan's neck; its wide hull had sweeping lines, dovetailing at the stern like the wings of a swimming bird. Tiny feathers had been carved in the most exquisite detail — the effect enhanced by each stroke of Credé's brush. He worked in rapt silence.

Then, after inspecting the craft from every angle, he picked up a metal canister with tiny holes punched in the top. Holding it above the model, he tapped the side with two fingers, releasing a shower of fine white powder. His breath had been slow and careful; now he held it completely. When a presence in the room registered as a cold shiver along his spine, Credé ignored the sensation. One last tap, a dusting of white, and there! It was done.

Breathing once more, Credé took a moment to contemplate his work. The craft shimmered, as fragile as frost, impossibly white. A dream made real. He sighed. Only then did his eyes slide sideways, acknowledging the form in the doorway. His mouth twitched, dragging at his cheek. He did not turn. 'You've been absent a long time, my brother.'

The man who entered the room moved with powerful grace. Everything about him suggested restrained energy. Bear-like in his furs, he approached, arms flung wide.

'I've been in Therak.' The man's voice rumbled, low and sonorous. He shed his fur-lined cloak and tossed it over a stool. His vest, the colour of claret and richly embroidered, was open slightly at his chest. It was caught in by a wide belt with a huge buckle. Credé raised a brow at the freshly-tanned scabbard which hung at the man's side. Dark hair, unkempt from travel, fell in tangled waves to his shoulders. His beard was untrimmed. He leaned over the bench, framing the little boat with splayed hands. Grey-green eyes beneath intense brows swept the model before fixing on Credé.

Ash could sense Credé's wariness. He was trying to hide it, by making his tone lazy and unconcerned. 'Another visit to an unauthorised dimension, Artus?' He stirred his brush in a jar of solvent and left it spinning there. 'Your insistence on testing the Council's patience grows stronger.' Credé was moving deliberately, tidying his workspace and returning things to their places, not meeting the other's gaze. 'And Therak. Of all places. A hot, filthy world where people scrape out miserable lives, fighting for paltry riches in the dust.' He sneered. 'I don't see the attraction, Artus. Really, I don't. Why waste your time with such a place?'

Artus towered over the little boat. His growled response was thick with menace. 'And I might ask you, my brother: why do you insist on wasting your time making trinkets for a woman who will never be yours?'

Credé reciprocated his glare. Pointedly gentle in his actions, he lifted the model out of harm's way, placing it safely upon a high shelf to dry.

Artus let out a rumble, banging his fists on the bench. 'Credé!' Ash felt fear wash through Credé — real fear. It was as if the Malshorne expected to be struck. Artus had drawn himself up to his full, imposing height. 'Yours is the greatest intellect T'al Jazure has ever known. You know how it pains me to see—' With an abrupt shake of his shaggy head, he halted mid-sentence. 'But I do not come to renew old arguments.' His expression softened as he unbuckled the scabbard at his side. 'I have brought you a gift.'

Credé feigned disinterest in the item laid before him. His arms had wrapped themselves in a protective shield across his body. 'How terribly kind. A contraband item, more than enough to get me exiled.' Ash could feel his struggle. He dearly wanted to ignore the gift, but his curiosity was just too great. With a disdainful curl of his lip, he opened the leather casing and drew out a long, thin knife that shone greenly. Ash recognised it at once. It was Kep's knife! The one he had found in Credé's hut. The same knife he used to kill the yaggluts! It was so strange to feel Credé's curiosity growing as he examined the blade. He stroked the unusual script and ventured a thumb across the edge. 'It is barely sharp.' He set it down. 'No more than a pretty trinket,' he sneered.

Artus did not react to the taunt. He just smiled, raising his eyebrows. 'Why don't you try it?' He tossed a thick scrap of coarse leather onto the bench. When Credé shrugged, making no move to pick it up, Artus chuckled. Reaching into a pocket, he produced a thumb-sized lump of greenish rock. With great ceremony, he placed it next to the knife. 'Perhaps you'll be more interested to hear that my gift has two parts.' His hands came together at his beard so that his fingertips brushed his lips. His eyes were unblinking, like a hawk's. 'Try it,' he urged. '*Will* the knife to your bidding.'

Credé's lips parted at those words, and Ash felt his curiosity flare. His eyes flicked, from the rock to the knife and back again. He was unable to resist. As he set the blade to the leather, strong tingles coursed up his arm. The blade sliced through the thick leather so easily that it slashed the hardwood bench as well. Credé nearly dropped the blade. He drew several quick breaths. 'Mind-sync!' he whispered. He was staring at the rock as if it were alive.

'Precisely.' Artus smiled a darkly wicked smile. 'The ore has innate capacity — even in its own dimension.'

Credé stroked the blade of the knife, completely entranced. 'It is an alloy then.'

'Yes.' Artus nodded. 'I met a man in Therak; a brilliant man, misunderstood by his own kind, and deeply undervalued.' He gave Credé a pointed look. 'He shared a few of his secrets, and has promised to teach me more. He made this knife, using the silver of his own world.' Artus barked a laugh. 'Ha! I see your face, brother! Yes! Imagine the possibilities. What if the ore could be melded with a metal from our world? What magic might then be ours?' He paused. 'But there is an even greater secret.' He ran his eyes along the labels on a nearby shelf. 'Do you have red sands? From the shores of Beal?'

'Of course.' Credé found the jar and poured the sand into a stone vessel as directed.

Artus made a small depression in the mound. 'Watch!' He dropped the rock. Hitting the sand it burst into life, filling the vessel with a blue flaring light.

Credé cried out. He held out a hand to the miracle. 'How long? How long will it burn?' he stammered.

'A very long time. Almost eternally, it seems.'

Credé was shaking. He shook his head. 'But, Artus. Inter-dimensional craft: it is forbidden.' He pressed a hand to his forehead.

'Yes.' Artus grasped his brother's shoulder in a talon-like grip. 'That is why we must work in secret. We cannot show either of these discoveries to the Council. Not yet. Not until we can prove their value. Think of it, Credé!' He gestured at the flaring bowl. 'Energy like this could change the world! And imagine: objects that obey the mind! Be brave, my ingenious brother, and together we will create miracles. And we will force the Council to see sense through the sheer brilliance of our discoveries.'

Credé nodded, still transfixed by the flames. 'And Nirias? What of Nirias?'

'Ash.' Beyond the memory, somebody was patting Ash's face. 'Come back to us, Ash.'

The scene wavered, collapsing in on itself. Breaking out of the memory was like coming up from deep water. Ash's vision swam. He took a mighty gasp — and there was Nirias. The Malshorne's gaze held him, keen and probing.

❦

Ash was bewildered and a little alarmed to find himself in Nirias's small sitting room. The two had walked back together on Nirias's insistence, leaving the others to their laughter. A place had been cleared for him, among the books and maps and lore-stones. Now Nirias handed him a cup.

'A tonic,' he murmured. His mouth twisted into a rueful smile. 'Don't be concerned: it is just a tincture of herbs to calm your nerves. The base is valerian and chamomile, if it interests you.' He poured himself a cup, took a sip with a meaningful glance at Ash, and sighed. 'Now. Tell me what happened.'

Nirias seemed under the impression that Ash had fallen into the memory by mistake, and of course he had — this time. Ash did not confess that he had been trying to unlock the stone's secrets, nor did he feel inclined to tell him about Credé's lovestruck encounter with Leynore. Ash hesitated. Yet he had little choice but to trust the man. He spoke slowly, trying to relate the memory as accurately as he could.

As he spoke, Nirias held him with intent eyes. When at last he was done, the Malshorne still did not speak. It was Ash who broke the silence. 'It's the same knife … I'm sure of it.'

Nirias nodded. 'Undoubtedly. And now its dark origins are confirmed. I'm not surprised that Credé would have cast this memory into the stone in an attempt to dull its edges. It was the beginning of a great betrayal.' He sighed. 'A betrayal that caused terrible dissent. For the Malshorne, my kin, did indeed break the code. Using knowledge and ore from another world, they created objects that obey the mind. Credé crafted a set of arrows. Beautiful. Blue-shafted and lethal, they could be directed to their target — with the mind.' Nirias nodded at Ash's start of recognition. 'Yes. He bequeathed them to me, and I … to Daska.'

A shadow of pain crossed the Malshorne's face. His mouth trembled. He downed the contents of his cup and set it aside before continuing. 'To this day I cannot imagine what Credé was thinking. To demonstrate a weapon to the Council.' He shook his head. 'It would never gain sanction. But the discovery of dymiril — that divided the city. Who could deny the benefits of such an energy source? And Artus was cunning. He made gifts of dymiril lamps — yes, like yours, Ash — and he distributed them to those most likely to take his side. It led to great conflict within the city of peace.'

Ash swirled the liquid in his cup. 'What happened?'

'In hindsight, the worst thing possible. The Council refused them, point-blank. Inter-dimensional craft was outlawed. My brothers' discoveries threatened to rock both worlds — T'al Agria and Therak — to their very foundations. The Council demanded that they reveal their sources and relinquish the craft. Despite their wisdom, they did not anticipate that Artus was prepared for just such an outcome. He fled, taking the secret of dymiril with him, choosing exile over the code. Credé followed him soon after.'

Ash had been watching Nirias carefully. 'And you? Did they not ask you to go with them?'

The Malshorne's expression clouded. 'I would have refused. My loyalty was to Leynore, and to my city. The Council was probably concerned that, like Credé, I would follow. They probably thought that my nature and youth would lead me to rebellion.' His mouth twisted into a smile. 'But no, I did not betray my city. Not then. Leynore had bound me too close. I was a foundling, you see. Abandoned.' Ash watched the tiny muscle that flickered beneath the older man's eye. 'It was Leynore who found me and raised me according to the Azuran code. No, I would not betray Leynore for my brothers' dreams. Not then.' His lips pinched together in an expression of regret. 'My own rebellion, my betrayal, came later — when I joined the Azuran League.'

Ash sat up in his chair. 'The League? It … it was formed back then?'

Nirias nodded. 'The Council clung to words of peace, even when the threat became clear. But the Melk could not be defeated by diplomacy and soft words, no matter how subtle.'

As Nirias brought his eyes to rest on Ash's face, it was as if a curtain had parted. Ash caught a glimpse of a man who was fraying at the edges, utterly beaten-down. Then the impression passed. Nirias sighed. 'Not to act, can be as terrible as taking the wrong action, Ash. Especially when it comes to the Melk. That is why I broke my oath to the Azuri. That is why I joined the League.'

Ash formed a terrible question. 'Was it Artus and Credé, then? Was it their fault?'

Nirias rubbed hands over his tired eyes. He blinked at his books. 'I did not know then what I suspect now. But yes, I believe that my brothers brought the Melk into our world. The Melk takes its name from the first nexus. A man named Mellik. It seems likely that he is the very same man of whom Artus spoke.'

Ash held his breath. He did not say anything. He could not.

When Nirias leaned forward in his chair, Ash recoiled. His hazel-green eyes seemed to burn with purpose. 'Ash, I have a confession to make.' Ash's heart raced. What dreadful revelation was coming next? 'I was arrogant. I thought I could discover the answers. But, I confess, I am no closer to discovering why the city was locked. I had allowed myself to hope that whatever weapon the Azuri released upon the Melk would be here, in T'al Jazure. That the Council would have left some clue.' The Malshorne's eyes flashed with impatience. 'I have failed. The city holds its secrets just as tightly as it ever did.'

Then his tone softened. 'But you, Ash ...' Ash wanted to wriggle out from under that gaze. 'I despise myself in burdening you with such a dangerous task. But if you have unlocked one memory ... If the answer is not here, in the city, it may lie with Credé. And,' he spread apologetic hands, 'with you, Ash.'

When Ash made no reply, Nirias rubbed his head. He sighed and sank back into his chair, then gave his chin a thoughtful scratch. 'Tell me, how are you getting on with Demara?'

Ash felt trapped. The man seemed haggard, tired and desperate. So desperate. He was nothing like the confident leader who had given that rousing speech earlier. He dreaded telling Nirias that he had failed. So he lied. 'Um. Good. She's a very interesting woman.'

Nirias smiled fondly. 'That's wonderful. I knew Demara would be able to help. And I am certain that mastering the Song will help you with Credé's stone as well.'

Ash just nodded. There was nothing he could say.

Chapter 20

DEATH AT BREAKFAST

The news of the death came at breakfast. Arriving as it did, between the smoked fish and coddled eggs, its timing was particularly disturbing. These days, Karliana partook of her morning meal in the small feasting hall overlooking the ornamental lake. Its tranquil view over the water had once provided a pleasing sense of calm; now she could barely remember what it was to feel calm. Nothing had been changed in the room since Karliana's birth. It had been her mother's favourite space; a gentle room, with a faded elegance, it made one think of dried flowers. Karliana did not mind that the tapestries had softened with age, nor that the upholstery sagged. Of all the rooms in the house, this was where she felt most safe — relatively. Safety, too, was a thing of the past.

There were a number of reasons why breakfast had become Karliana's favourite meal of the day. Very few of her young guests were enthusiastic about early morning events, unless they involved hunting or some other sport. Since breakfast was the only meal where wine was not officially served, that deterred others. Happily, the majority of her would-be suitors preferred to sleep off the revels of the night before. All of which was most agreeable. Karliana was joined only by her most ardent admirers, and those sensible young men who professed to enjoy seeing the sun rise.

On the morning that the messenger came from the House of Aranti, Karliana was joined by one of each, as usual. The presence of a third guest was rather a puzzle. It had given them something to ponder while they dissected their sweet smoked herrings.

Berin Skagali, always at the table first, was sitting in his usual spot, to Karliana's right. If there was a prize for being Karliana's most doting wooer, Berin would win it outright. He reminded her of a spaniel, with those pale eyelashes and baggy brown eyes, and he looked even more like one when he had just woken up, with rheum still in his eyes. Since the imprisonment of his uncle, Guardulian, and the scandal hanging over his family's name, Berin's disposition seemed even sadder. Nevertheless, Karliana found it difficult to feel sorry for the boy. His insufferable doting was bested only by his tenacity, and he had the bothersome habit of happening upon her in the gardens, armed with a poetry book and lavish compliments about her complexion. Now he was gazing at her with adoring eyes, waiting for the right moment to pass the cream. If he *had* been a spaniel, Karliana would have sent him to his basket.

Seated on Karliana's left was Mateus Sanarson, of whom, she had to admit, she was becoming quite fond. In fact, had she actually been seeking a husband Mateus would not have been the most terrible choice. Level-headed, and able to dance a reel without stepping on one's toes, he was not wholly unattractive either. Mateus was attempting to grow a little pointed beard, which was quite off-putting, mostly because he kept stroking it, as if it were some sort of pet. It put Karliana in mind of a fox's tail, which seemed quite out of keeping with his gentle disposition.

That morning, both young men were perturbed, because to everyone's surprise, and undoubtedly not of his own volition, Tindelfion Aranti had decided to join them. It was most strange. Tindelfion had made it clear on his arrival that he had no intention of wooing Karliana. Under the influence of rather too much fruit brandy, he had added with a slur: 'I prefer my women taller, and less opinionated.' Karliana had born the insult with grace — she was not *that* short. Anyway, Tindelfion's lack of interest suited her very well indeed.

She studied him over her teacup. Those late nights had certainly done nothing for his looks. Dark rings about his eyes accentuated his already pasty complexion. If his gloomy expression was anything to go by, his presence that morning was at his father's command. Karliana let out a little sigh. The last thing she needed at breakfast was Aranti's sulking heir.

The conversation had been horribly stilted, in spite of Mateus's gallant attempt to engage everyone in a discussion about trout and his thoughts on breeding ponds. Karliana had just popped a slice of lemon into her tea, more to thwart Berin's efforts to furnish her with cream than any liking for lemon, when the tureen of eggs arrived. They all looked up, with the sense of anticipation that always greets the arrival of platters when conversation is lagging.

The messenger in Aranti green loomed behind the serving man with a tray of his own. When Karliana's eyes took in the black-edged note on his silver platter, the sight made her stomach lurch. She had the horrible feeling that she was about to part ways with her breakfast.

Tindelfion rose, his face even paler. Snatching the missive from the tray, he bore it out through the delicate patio doors, careless of how they shuddered at being flung so wide. Motioning for the others to remain, Karliana followed him. Wrapping a fur stole tightly about throat, she hastened down the flight of steps. Tindelfion had fled all the way to the water's edge and was standing in the little stone rotunda.

It was horrible to assail the young man in his grief, under the cold midwinter sun, especially in her mother's special place. Ghoulish even. But Karliana had to know. Tindelfion still clutched the message, his hands on the balustrade. As she approached, she could not help feeling sorry for him. All his posturing had dissolved. His shoulders slumped, as if he was folding into himself somehow. Observing his profile, she realised for the first time how very unlike his father he was.

Tindelfion turned with the distraught look of a child who has been struck. Karliana could not work out what to do with her hands. 'I'm so sorry.'

Tindlfion's expression changed then. A bitter smirk washed across his face like a wave on the shore taking his vulnerability with it. He actually laughed. 'Ah, Karliana,' he said softly, 'if only you knew. There is no need to be sorry. My mother is at peace now. For the first time in a very long while.'

Karliana gave a little start. Had she heard correctly? 'Your mo— mother?'

Tindelfion's eyes narrowed, making him seem every bit like his father. One cheek jerked in an odd little twitch, just below the eye. 'I know what you were hoping for …' Karliana felt an icy chill at the back of her neck that was nothing to do with the wintry breeze. 'But no, it is my mother. My mother is dead.'

'Oh! I'm … I'm so sorry. Sorry for your loss, I mean.' Karliana knew she was stammering. Her mind skittered, bounding here and there like a frightened rabbit. His accusation wore the sheerest of veils. He knew! Karliana clasped her hands together at her chest to stop them trembling. She wanted to ask how Capricia had died, but could not find the words.

'She dropped dead, Karliana. At dinner it seems. Over a plate of steamed cuttlefish, I am informed.' His watery eyes flickered with emotion. 'It was not even her favourite.'

Karliana froze. Tindelfion had already known. He had suspected her involvement, and now he was letting her know it. Her heart raced. Had he discovered evidence? Had she been betrayed? Is that why he had come down to breakfast?

Karliana could not speak. She felt as pale as Tindelfion, who was a good match for the alabaster pillar beside him. Gazing out at the water was far preferable to meeting his eyes. The lake's surface was ruffled now, as if it, too, had been disturbed by the hand of death.

'I am recalled to the villa. To take my place at my father's side.' He recited the words, as if that was precisely what his father had written.

'Of course, Tindelfion. And, please, avail yourself of my help should you need it.' Karliana barely knew what she was saying. Her tongue seemed frozen in her mouth. Capricia Aranti, dead at her table! And Maliagne … alive.

Tindelfion nodded. 'A small wagon for my surplus belongings would be most welcome.' He turned his face towards her. 'Thank you, Karliana.'

Something in his expression gave those final words extra weight. His mouth was drawn, as if he had come to some decision. The look in his eyes frightened her.

❦

Karliana kept to her chambers for the remainder of the morning. For some reason, no matter how much wood was added to the fire, she simply could not get warm. A steaming hot bath, liberally scented with rose, did nothing to remove the chill that had invaded her very soul. Wrapped in her warmest robe, she paced in her private parlour, sat for a while, then paced again. A quiet knocking sent her heart racing. At her command, Pelor entered, closing the door behind him.

'Tindelfion has left, Lady Karliana.' Karliana nodded. From her windows she had watched the carriages departing, bearing away his ridiculous furnishings and equally ridiculous hangers-on. 'I mean to say …' Pelor coughed, a dry, apologetic sound. 'Tindelfion has left the city.'

Karliana closed her eyes. She should have guessed. Pelor's spies had discovered the truth: the carriage returning to Aranti's villa had not been bearing his grief-stricken son at all. The young man, it seemed, had had no intention of returning to his father's house. He had seized his opportunity. Now he was jolting his way towards the Felian Pass and beyond, to freedom.

In a wagon bearing the crest of Lendri! A number of trinkets were missing from the eastern wing: small items, but valuable enough to secure safe and secret passage. Aranti would be furious. And, if he thought her complicit in the boy's escape, he would be furious with Karliana.

'It is unfortunate,' Pelor murmured. Karliana drew a breath made up of a series of tiny shudders. Unfortunate. 'There is a chance he may be stopped at the border and sent back. The troop presence at the pass is very strong now. Regardless ...' Pelor locked his long fingers together. 'We must tread very carefully.'

Karliana was tempted to point out that stating the obvious was of very little use. She did not. Because Pelor was right. There was a funeral to attend, and things must be managed very carefully indeed.

Chapter 21

THE VESSEL OF TRIALS

In the Rosewood Lodge all eyes were on the tiles, in anticipation of the final draw. There were eight terracotta triangles left, face-down on the shuffling table. One was Kep's, imprinted with a leaf and etched with her initial. Daska shuffled the tiles about for another moment, then used a finger to push them together in pairs. Above each pair, he positioned a square tile, also face-down. Kep tried to moisten her mouth with little success. The past weeks had all come down to this: one last shuffle, a final chance to prove herself worthy of selection.

The captains had been rigorous in their testing, giving no warning of what might be assessed or when. Rope work, bucket hauls, sprints, balance bars, birdcalls, wrestling — if there was a skill, then they had designed a challenge. So far, Kep thought she had acquitted herself quite well, although there was no way of knowing for sure. Nobody really knew what the captains were recording in their notebooks. Her only downfall had been the stealth challenges. She was terrible at pickpocketing, and had only once managed to trail her partner without being discovered. Now all her training with Jen-Jay would come into play — the armed one-on-one combat challenges had been saved until last.

The eight remaining contenders stood in the semi-circle around the shuffling table. Kep's mind was scampering, calculating possibilities. Please don't let it be El. Or Reardon. She frowned at herself. Such a thought would have earned her a swift smack from Jen-Jay. Any opponent could be beaten according to Jen-Jay. You just had to pit your own strengths against their weaknesses. Only it was hard to see that Eliayliah Larien or Reardon Galt had any weaknesses, regardless of which weapons were drawn.

When Daska flipped over the image of an axe, Kep's heart raced. She had no experience of axes at all. To her relief Daska then flipped over Reardon Galt's and Polkin Dew's tiles. The two grinned at each other. It would be a good match, but Reardon would come out on top. The quarterstaff was flipped next. Kep glued her eyes to the adjacent pair of red clay triangles, willing one of them to be hers. It was not to be. She was pleased for Ordelle, though, who had drawn her favoured weapon and the easiest opponent in Pallin. And that left four.

When the rapier was turned up next, Jaibari's face split into a wide grin. Today the young woman's swinging braids were complemented by a topknot that dragged her hair back, accentuating her high cheekbones. Of course Jaibari was smiling — she had good reason. The only thing the girl spent more time on than polishing that sword of hers was practising routines. But Jaibari's face quickly fell when Daska flipped the tiles. A fox head on one, and three scratched lines on the other. El laughed and put an arm around Lakmorin Spink, giving him a shake. She would go easy, she told him as she patted his cheek. As Daska flipped the two remaining tiles, Kep's heart sank. She was to fight Jaibari. And not only that — they would face off with knives.

As Kep took up her position on the cross marked on the floor, other warriors started filing in, eager to see the last bouts. Jaibari was poised, hands at her sides, somehow managing to glare and smile at the same time. She stood a little taller than Kep, but they were of similar build. Kep knew Jaibari would relish the chance to humiliate her — again.

Ozu Mako stepped forward. As master of knives, he would oversee the fight. Kep formed the triangle and made her bow, trying to find the stillness of the warrior. It was impossible. Jen-Jay had taught her just one lesson about fighting with knives: don't get into a knife fight — ever. Kep grimaced and set her jaw, visualising her panic as a force that flowed out through her fingertips.

Ozu swept a cloth from a tray. 'There is no need to draw lots. The knives are identical.' Frowning, Kep picked up the nearest as directed. It felt heavy, the hilt slightly soft. Jaibari's puzzled expression indicated that she, too, was curious about the bright orange blades. Ozu's lips curved into a smile. 'These are not real blades, of course not. These are lethal only to your honour. The slightest contact with skin or clothing will make a mark, costing you points.'

Kep looked down at her thumb. Realising that it was coated with a bright orange powder, she closed her hand into a fist. Jaibari had made an identical movement, at exactly the same time. It was like looking in a mirror — until the woman ruined the impression by baring her teeth and growling.

'Fighters, ready.' Ozu held his hand high, his palm flat like a blade.

Kep gripped the knife that was not a knife and planted her feet. *A firm footing is the basis of every victory.* There was barely a moment to pull her mind into focus. Ozu's hand came down, as sharp as his command. 'Fight!'

※

For Ash it did not matter that the blades were not real. That did not change the horror of watching Kep fight. It seemed that nothing remained of the friend he had sought out every morning in the Aranti dairies. That girl had been replaced by this dangerous new creature, all muscle and sinew and flowing resolve. The pair circled like dancers, bound by a shared intent to violence. It was as if they had been reduced to fragmented pieces of themselves: two pairs of eyes, two firm mouths, two bodies that moved and jabbed, in the pull–push of advance and retreat, light on their feet, dancing the fatal Dance of Blades.

As the fight continued, Ash's heart became an ice-cold stone in his chest. He was not sure if it was his vision blurring or the fighters' movements. Unable to watch, he closed his eyes.

At last a cry rippled through the spectators, signalling that it was over. The tableau that met Ash's eyes should have brought him joy. It did not. Jaibari was pinned, her arm twisted behind her back to breaking point, the cruel grip making her eyes bulge wide in their sockets. Her weapon was still spinning where it had skittered away. Kep's elbow was pulled back, her dagger frozen in mid-air ready to strike at her opponent's kidneys. The look in her eyes was so terrible that Ash wanted to weep. Jaibari gnashed her teeth against a strangled whimper. Only when Ozu shouted 'Break!' did her tormentor release the bind.

An awful sadness swept through Ash as he watched the young women disentangle themselves and stagger to their feet. Shoulder to shoulder, chests heaving in synchronised rhythm, they waited for Ozu Mako to announce the win. When Kep's eyes sought and found him, Ash dropped his gaze to his feet.

Aware that he held the attention of all, Ozu let out an audible sigh before flicking his long, black hair over his shoulder where it cascaded down his back. He swept the crowd with a slow gaze before announcing his decision. 'It is a draw.'

A couple of the onlookers nodded knowingly; most exchanged confused glances. Kep and Jaibari stared in mirrored disbelief. Ozu pointed first at one, then the other, bringing attention to the orange marks on their clothes and skin. 'You are both dead.' He gave a woeful shake of his head. 'Yes, you put your opponent down and disarmed her, Kep, that is true. But flesh is a poor exchange for a shield. And that wound on your arm …' He shrugged. 'If it was real, you would bleed out in minutes.' Kep stared at the bright slash of colour across her forearm as if surprised to see it there. Gesturing with strokes of the knife which he had retrieved from the floor, Ozu put a point on his warning. 'Let this be a lesson to you all. Never get into a knife fight. Frankly, you are better to run.'

Ash felt the muscles in his mouth jerking. He clenched his jaw, fighting the wave of helplessness, trying to shut out images of Braig. Ozu had returned his dark almond-shaped eyes to the two young women. 'It is a draw.'

Surprisingly, it was not Kep but Jaibari who protested. 'No!' She tossed her head making braids fly. 'I refuse the draw. I call arrows.'

Ozu narrowed his eyes, but he nodded. 'The challenge is within the rules. Kep, do you accept?'

Ash sighed at the expression on Kep's face. He knew what it meant when her eyes flashed like that.

'I accept.'

⁂

When Daska presented Kep's bow to her already strung, she wanted to throw her arms around the old warrior. The last thing she needed was an audience while she struggled to bend the weapon. His expression was quizzical as he handed the quiver over. Kep wondered why, until she saw the bright blue arrow sitting there like a cuckoo among a flock of starlings. Beyond cleaning it up to show the others, Kep had not given the arrow a further thought. Kep hesitated, wondering whether it was wise to select an untried arrow. But the blue fletches seemed to draw her somehow. She plucked it up and held it tightly in her fist.

As challenger, Jaibari chose to go first. She swaggered to the line and, barely pausing to aim, sent her arrow flying. Applause erupted at the result: the arrowhead was buried deep and true, just to the right of bullseye.

Jaibari's dark eyes glittered like polished gems. Arms wide, she spun about, singing out a challenge loud enough for everyone to hear. 'Can you beat that?' Her next words, hissed beneath her breath, were for Kep's ears alone.

Kep's heart sank. She did not think she could beat Jaibari's shot. But her fingers closed around the shaft of the arrow anyway. Oddly cool to the touch, it sent a strange sort of shiver up her arm. Her brow puckered; it felt familiar somehow. Her heart racing, she nocked the arrow, sensing at once that something was different. As she stretched the bow, she detected a peculiar tension: it felt as if the arrow was singing, vibrating of its own accord. Kep inhaled, setting her jaw, searching for stillness. As soon as the arrow released she felt a sharp pang of joy. Her eyes followed its tingling, sizzling flight. Somehow, even as it curved towards the target, she knew it would hit. Everyone else stared in stunned surprise. The blue arrow was buried deep — at the dead centre of the target.

⁊

Several of the warriors came up to clap Kep on the back, congratulating her on the extraordinary shot. Even tight-lipped Reardon favoured her with a terse nod. 'Nice shot, Kep.'

Kep accepted the praise happily, her heart still racing with exhilaration. When Daska gave her a puzzled smile, she beamed back. She promised herself she would find him and explain later where she had found an arrow so uncannily like his. Right now she had to talk to Jen-Jay. The tiny woman had caught her eye, signalling with a jerk of her chin that she wanted a word. Kep waited until the others had left before joining her in the storeroom they used for training. Kep was bubbling with excitement. A word of praise from her mentor would top it off. Why was she so silent? 'Did you see the fight, Jen-Jay?' Kep knew that she had.

The woman snorted. 'I saw.'

Kep felt suddenly cold. Her smile faded.

'Tell me. What you were thinking as you held your knife, ready to smite your opponent? Think carefully before you answer.'

Kep bit her tongue, thinking. What had she done to deserve such a look of contempt? 'Triumph. Joy and triumph, I suppose.'

'Try again. What do you think I could see in your eyes, even from the back of the hall?'

Kep ran her hand up the back of her hair, brushing at the little braids. She wanted to drop her eyes. Jen-Jay's expression was like steel.

'Anger,' she confessed. 'I was joyful, but angry, too.'

Jen-Jay nodded. She pointed a bony finger. 'That is what I saw. A young warrior full of anger, and possibly hatred, too.'

Kep frowned. She wanted to argue. She was struck dumb. Uncertain.

'And that is why you are not ready. What happens to those who fight the Melk with anger and hatred in their hearts? Tell me!' Kep was silent. Jen-Jay spoke so softly that her words could barely be heard. 'No? Then I will tell you. They become enthralled. Overcome by the enemy. They lose themselves to the Melk.'

'I'm sorry, Jen-Jay.'

The woman brushed the apology aside.' You think Jaibari is your enemy? You have seen nothing.'

'I'm sorry. I'm sorry, Jen-Jay. I will work harder. I promise! I will master the Breath. I will find stillness.' Kep's heart was racing now. Jen-Jay looked so angry. So disappointed. 'Please don't give up on me.' She would have fallen to her knees if she thought it would make a difference.

Jen-Jay sniffed. 'Tomorrow. An hour earlier. Regardless of tonight's nonsense. Tomorrow.'

Kep made the sign of the triangle. 'Tomorrow. I promise. Thank you, Jen-Jay.'

❦

Kep noticed the Vessel of Trials as soon as she entered the hall of the Sable Lodge. It was impossible to miss. Set on a table of its own, the urn was bathed in a soft halo of light. Holding her breath, Kep stepped closer, fascinated. The vessel was made from unglazed red pottery. Its top had a wide flange, stoppered with a flat wooden lid and secured by silver casings. It was unadorned save for the frieze around its middle. Kep's heart leapt. All of the jinns were represented. She could not help wondering whether one of them might soon be hers. She peered at the tiny pictures. A couple of the signs were unfamiliar. Was that a hawk? It looked like a bird of prey of some sort. Another looked like a small cat. Kep wanted to run her fingers over the images for good luck.

At the sound of El's melodious voice, she turned and smiled.

'That was excellent work today, Kep. In fact, well done for the whole tournament. You've learned quickly and pushed yourself hard.' Kep flushed at the compliment. Winning El's approval meant a lot — her secret hope was to join her in the red fox jinn.

El's smile faded a little. Kep read concern behind her eyes. 'But remember, there is no obligation to take the Pledge. There are other ways of contributing to the battle against the Melk. Once you place your tile into the urn you are bound. You must go wherever Nirias and the captains decide you must. And the Pledge is for life.' There was a long pause, one loaded with unspoken meaning. El frowned. 'You are young, Kep. And you are a Seeker. If anyone has a right to the city's protection, it is you.'

Kep controlled her impatience. Not El as well! Why did everybody think she needed protecting? She had made her decision long ago. If she passed the trials she would place her tile into the urn, and into the hands of the gods. It was not a choice at all. It was a question of Fate — and what was right.

How dare El assume that motherly expression? She was not that much older than Kep herself. Kep lifted her chin, speaking clearly. 'I trust in the gods, El. If my tile is drawn, whatever the mission, then that is the will of the gods. I do not need protection from my fate.'

El was opening her mouth to reply when Sarin sidled up beside them. Whatever he was munching smelled wonderful, making Kep's mouth water. Something savoury, with spice, and garlic. 'So, this is it …' said Sarin, his expression solemn. 'The Vessel of Trials.' He licked his fingers. 'How very theatrical. Nothing like a bit of ritual to encourage compliance.'

El's brows went up, registering her shock at the remark. Kep scowled. She wanted to kick Sarin — she really did want to kick him.

❦

That night there was dried meat and herbed bread — dense and green-looking, with a thick nut paste — all accompanied by wine and quietly speculative conversation. People sat in small groups discussing past tournaments and possible outcomes. Who had done enough for selection? Who had excelled and might be a contender for the two vacant captain positions?

'The best captains are those who can teach,' said one. 'People who can transfer skills to others — those are our leaders.'

'Yeah, but they have to be able to fight.'

Muku tore his bread in two, handing half to his twin. 'Fighters just hit people. Nirias will choose teachers.' As he chewed on his mouthful he seemed to reconsider. 'But hitting people is good, too. And every jinn needs big strong men — like me!' He flexed a mighty muscle.

Lakmorin Spink laughed loudly. 'Yes, strength would come in handy, if you plan to drop boulders on the Melk.' He rolled his eyes.

Kep laughed with the others. Everyone knew Muku was a brilliant strategist.

Heeda, who was sitting next to him, scoffed. 'Shows what you know. The best fighters make the best captains.' The woman was full of spiky comments, though she rarely explained any of them.

Kep wondered to herself before asking, 'Who is the best fighter?'

Polkin guffawed. 'Nirias. Obviously.' Kep blinked in surprise, but everyone seemed to agree with the blond giant. She had expected them to say Rodine Gametale or Pretalla Chanara.

'Nobody has ever beaten Nirias in a trial.'

'Nobody? What, never?'

'Never.'

'Well …' Lakmorin Spink cut in with his characteristic drawl, flicking back his long red hair. 'That's not entirely true. They say Grey Wolf bested him once.'

It was as if the name held some sort of magic. It cast a spell of awe over the conversation. Even people at the adjacent table turned their heads. Kep was intrigued by their reverent expressions. 'Who is Grey Wolf?

Jaibari snorted over the top of her mug. 'Grey Wolf was a legend. A real one, who made her name from actually *doing* something. You know, instead of relying on stories and gossip.' She rolled her dark eyes. 'And fancy arrows,' she added under her breath. Kep bristled, wanting to bite back, but El was explaining.

'None of us has met Grey Wolf. She was a warrior long before our time. By all accounts she was the greatest fighter the League has known. Her jinn was legendary. So much so that the mark of the Grey Wolf has never been handed on, to honour her memory.' Everyone nodded. 'She was lost during the siege of Lamont.' El's eyes were full of pain. 'The League lost many during that mission.'

Kep stared. Even Mildaren slaves had heard of the siege of Lamont. Everyone knew the story of the tribune city that had revolted against Calkinon rule — and the terrible price they had paid. Lamont's blinded children and salted fields were a grim lesson for every realm. The retribution had been swift and cruel. Kep felt a nauseating chill at the base of her skull. What madness demanded payment in the eyeballs of children? It made sense if the Melk had been involved. It was terrible to think that humans could act so evilly on their own.

The warriors were starting to tell a story from one of their own past ventures. Kep had already heard it several times before, and saw that Lakmorin was lighting his pipe. Since pipe smoke made her throat burn, she took the chance to stretch her legs and find Ash.

Kep visited the washrooms and returned a couple of dishes to the kitchens. It was good to have something to do; it was nearly time and she was feeling even more nervous. For once, Ash was easy to locate. He sat with Pallin, at one end of a long table, his back to the high windows. Ordelle was there, too, along with Aechon and Gallin. Kep stayed where she was for a moment longer, just watching the room. The lights had been dimmed, making the illuminated vessel seem even more compelling. Kep retrieved her tile from her pocket and rubbed it between her fingertips, enjoying the feel of its rough surface. Her eyes did not move from the urn, not even when she heard a voice at her side.

'So, you're absolutely sure about this.' Sarin's eyes were on the vessel as well.

Kep sighed. 'I'm not changing my mind, Sarin. Surely you've realised that by now? I can't just cower here in the city, like a coward.' Cower like a coward? Why did she always mange to sound stupid when Sarin was around? She frowned as she turned. She did not mean to imply he was a coward. Sarin was many things — irreverent, rude and impossible — but not cowardly. She lifted her chin. 'I can't just stand by and do nothing. Somebody has to fight Aranti. He was bad enough before, when he was just an arrogant nobleman. What he had planned for Braig … it was terrible.'

She felt a familiar rage welling up inside. Not wanting to draw the attention of the nearby tables, she kept her voice low, but her words burned with passion. 'You don't know what it's like to be a slave, Sarin. And to be one for all eternity? I know Aranti. Nirias is right. He will grow to become the most terrible force the world has ever known. And I won't just stand aside. I have to be part of the response.' Her fist was holding the tile so hard that the points dug into her palms. She turned her eyes to Sarin's face. Why couldn't she make him understand?

His expression was indecipherable for a moment. Then he nodded and shrugged. So casual. As if the topic meant nothing to him.

He nodded. 'Just thought I'd check.' Kep raised her brows. Had he actually decided to let the matter go? He gave a sideways grin, cocking his head at Ash and the others. 'You had better come over and sit with us, then — before you get too important.'

Seeing them coming, Pallin hurriedly shuffled his chair back, making room so that she and Sarin could squeeze in beside Ordelle. Across the table, Ash responded to her smile with a weak nod. 'Good luck, Kep.'

She wished he meant it. She knew Ash agreed with Sarin, that she should stay in the city — forever. She watched how his hand trembled as he toyed with his goblet. How could a person manage to look so desperately sad? Part of her wanted to grab his hand and give it a reassuring squeeze; the other part wanted to shout at him and tell him to start pulling himself together.

At last the conversation petered out. Chairs creaked as people adjusted their view. Kep placed her tile on the table in front of her, hoping against hope. She learned forward to see Daska making his way towards the urn. His grey hair was glinted under the lights. As he cleared his throat and made a quiet show of unrolling a long scroll of paper, Kep realised that she had become very fond of the old man. He obviously had the respect of everyone in the room. There was complete silence as Daska began to speak. 'It is my honour—'

At that precise moment, someone squealed. 'A mouse!' In a wave of movement, people reacted, throwing up their arms and pushing back their chairs. Kep caught a fleeting glimpse of a small brown shape scampering down the middle of the table. Its run was shortlived. A mouse stood no chance against Tarlyn. In one pounce it was dangling from her jaws. Just as quickly, both Tarlyn and the mouse were gone.

There was momentary laughter as everyone recovered from their surprise and embarrassment. League warriors, caught off-guard by a mouse! At once all eyes turned back to Daska and the business of the hour. Daska made a good-humoured quip about Tarlyn's fitting display of athleticism, then, without flourish or preamble, simply stared reading out names.

Looking around, Kep realised she was not the only one who was nervous. Even the most seasoned warriors had their attention fixed on Daska, for he was not just naming the novices who had passed the trials, but also those who had demonstrated mastery in a particular field. One by one the warriors took their place around the urn to the cheers and applause of their peers. As she watched on, Kep started to feel her heart sink. However could she have fooled herself that she might be good enough to join such a group? Then Daska looked towards their table and her heart pounded faster.

'Sarin of Aurum ...' Daska gave a rueful shake of his head. 'League Warrior ... and Master of Stealth.'

Sarin made his way up, to the sound of appreciative laughter, scattered applause and a few good-hearted curses. Kep knew she should not have been surprised. After all, Sarin was not only a brilliant archer, he was good at everything he bothered to focus his mind on, and he made pickpocketing look like magic. Her heart sank a little when she realised Daska had come to the end of his scroll. His pause seemed terribly long. Was he finished?

'And ...' Daska's beaming smile was possibly the best thing Kep had ever seen in her life. 'Kep of Mildaresh.' Taking her place next to Sarin, Kep was so overwhelmed that she nearly cried from joy. Then Ordelle was joining them, too — the very last person to be called.

Daska made a low bow. 'I give you ... the League's newest warriors and her honoured masters.'

It was time for those willing to take the warrior's Pledge and place their tiles into the vessel. While Ordelle and Sarin both stood back, Kep did not falter. On one knee she swore to abide by the warrior's code unto death. Her tile made a slight chinking noise as it joined those already inside the urn.

Chapter 22

A WHISPER IN THE DARK

Ash sprang awake, certain that someone had whispered his name. Jerking into an upright position, he grappled with the dymiril lamp, nearly knocking it from its stand. The room was empty. Sarin's bed had not been slept in. Although that was hardly unusual, Ash felt certain that something was wrong. Something felt … different. Shoving covers aside, he struggled into clothes, pulling on warm socks and dragging boots from beneath the bed. A quick look through the window revealed that the moons were high and bright. Morning was still a long way off. The fire was slumbering in the empty common, red and glowing in the warm silence. As he crept to the door, Tarlyn appeared as if by magic and leapt to his shoulder.

With no idea where he was going, or why, Ash eased the solid outer doors open and let himself out. Sniffling, he rubbed his nose, wishing he had thought to bring a handkerchief. The stars looked sharp, the cold companions of indifferent moons. Ash turned worried eyes toward the city's spires. That watchful feeling had shifted, he was sure of it. Now it registered in his mind as an urgent hum, calling him to action. The last thing Ash wanted was to venture into the city on his own in the middle of the night, but something was drawing him on. It was stronger than mere curiosity. It was more of a compulsion, as if he did not have a choice.

Eyes wide, searching the shadows, Ash crept along. Nothing was moving in the gardens, unless you counted the water. The fountains, which winter had transformed into ice sculptures, had started to play again. The snow only hung on in places now, reduced to shrinking continents of white. Ash felt as if he was walking through a dream. His mind rebelled against the strangeness of it all. He desperately wanted to turn back, but he could not. Every time he slowed, something beyond his consciousness drew him on. So he followed, until cold fear stopped him dead.

Something else was moving, just up ahead. Tarlyn shifted her weight. Ash felt her claws in his shoulder. She muttered a growl, deep in her throat.

Ash trained his eyes on the patch of shifting shadows, his heart banging. At the edge of the trees, a figure floated into view. Human-shaped, it glowed, weirdly luminescent. As Ash watched, the figure wavered, like a cloak billowing in the wind — except there was no wind. Again came the terrible tugging at his heart. Against his will, Ash tottered forward. As if in response, the figure started flowing, coming straight towards him, growing larger as it came.

His heart flipped when it uttered his name.

'Ash!' The voice was thin, unnatural. It made his flesh crawl. 'Why are you sneaking about by the light of Telion's moons?'

Ash was so scared he thought his heart might stop altogether. His tongue seemed stuck to the roof of his mouth. The figure grew closer, and closer. It was within a few paces when he heard a laugh from deep within the shadowy cowl. 'Sneaking about is *my* job.' The hood fell back, revealing a decidedly human face, and a wide, flashing grin.

Ash spluttered and gawped. 'Sarin! You … you bloody idiot!' Pressing his hand to his chest, Ash reeled with the sweet sickliness of relief. 'You … you absolute nightmare, Sarin!' He cursed and moaned, hugging his arms across his chest. Realising his feet had gone completely numb, whether from cold or fear, he stamped them back to life. It also helped enormously in keeping him from punching Sarin on the nose.

Sarin just chortled more loudly, throwing his arms wide, delighted by the prank. His strange cloak billowed out again, becoming even more voluminous. Sheer, like patterned silk, the fabric moved very oddly, bending the light and confusing the eye. The effect was bizarre, especially when coupled with Sarin's gleaming, golden eyes. 'Whatever are you wearing?' asked Ash, in spite of his annoyance.

Sarin looked even more pleased with himself. 'It's odd, isn't it?' He held out an arm and laughed when the fabric floated up into the air. 'I found it in one of the workshops and thought I'd try it out.' His brows made a quizzical shape. 'I'm not entirely sure of its purpose.'

Ash scowled. 'You mean apart from frightening people out of their wits?'

Sarin grinned. Then he sobered, studying Ash's face. 'More importantly, you didn't answer my question. What are you doing out here?'

Still annoyed, Ash did not reply for a long moment. Now that he was over his shock, he realised that the insistent pull was still there. It was obviously nothing to do with Sarin.

'I heard—' Ash shook his head, reconsidering. 'No. Felt. I felt something. Something peculiar. And I thought I'd better come out to take a look.'

Sarin gave him an incredulous look. 'You're joking? You got out of your warm bed and trundled out here to "take a look"? Just because of a feeling?'

Ash nodded. He knew it must sound completely ridiculous. He was searching for words to explain the strange compulsion when Sarin poked him in the chest, hard.

'Hey! That hurt.'

'Just checking you're not sleepwalking.'

Ash scowled. 'I'm not asleep. And it wasn't a dream. I'm sure of it, Sarin.' Ash was shivering now, less certain of his conviction. Why was he standing in the middle of the courtyard in the freezing cold? Was he losing his mind?

To his relief, Sarin did not argue, nor ask him if he was feeling all right, which would have been worse. He just rubbed his hands together and grinned. 'Well, then! An adventure. Where are we going?'

As Sarin fell in beside him, Ash felt a surge of relief. Relief, intermixed with a deepening sense of doom. He could not deny his intuition — the call was coming from the very heart of the city.

❧

If walking through the moonlit gardens had seemed unreal, the paths to the Knowledge Stores were even more so. The sculptures and murals looked so different at night; darkly dramatic. The whole journey was like a macabre dream, and Sarin's strange light-bending cloak did nothing to help. Ash was relieved when he took it off. The strange garment folded into a remarkably small bundle and disappeared into one of Sarin's pockets. Sarin had assumed the lead, of course, and was moving and ducking through passages. Ordinarily, Ash would have been bewildered by the unfamiliar route. He was not. The pull of the Heartstone was stronger now. As they entered the main chamber of the Knowledge Stores, it pulsed, like a sun, beating at on his forehead.

As Ash stepped reluctantly onto the dais, the orb surged with light. His heart swelled with a strange mixture of fear and awe. Tarlyn had already jumped down. She circled the Heartstone once, thrashed her tail a couple of times and sat by Ash's feet, perfectly still.

Sarin murmured beside him. 'That's weird.' He met Ash's eyes for a moment before gesturing at the globe. 'I've never seen it like this. It glows when I put my hands on it, but this … It's like a firestorm in a bubble.' It was a good description. The centre was roiling with purple fire, sending up spurts of light. Hitting the surface they dispersed, in clouds of violet energy.

Sarin circled the globe, his eyes worried, studying the thing. Returning to Ash's side, he folded his arms and frowned. 'Well? Can you still feel it?'

Ash nodded. It was a vibration, humming in his bones. Sarin did not reply. His face said everything. Be careful! Ash swallowed, hard. His scalp was prickling with dread and his knees felt weak. But slinking back to bed was hardly an option, so he stepped forward and held out his shaking hands.

As before, Ash was drawn in, his palms fused to the orb. There was no escaping those searching tendrils. His heart throbbed, hammering at the cage of his chest. It felt as if it was about to burst. Inside the orb a maelstrom whirled and erupted. Ash cried out at the sudden surge. Then the flames began to peel back, like the petals of a burning flower. And there, at the stone's heart, was a face.

It was the face of a warrior, battered and worn, bearing the marks of battle. The mouth was dragged into a flat line, through pain or exhaustion or both. But those eyes! Fierce yet despairing, beneath an anguished brow. The man had a group of three stars tattooed on his cheek and — Ash cried out in recognition — he wore a silver band across his forehead. The image remained for only a moment, before vanishing, consumed by currents of light.

The sudden release of his hands made Ash gasp and stumble backwards. He swayed, light-headed.

Grasping him by the elbow, Sarin helped him to the edge of the dais, worried that Ash was about to faint. And Ash did indeed feel faint. 'What was that? What does it mean?'

Ash stared back at the Heartstone, which was now just a pretty bubble, set on an ornate stand. 'Someone is at the Stone. We have to find Nirias!'

⁂

Ash did not question Sarin's swift assurance that he knew exactly where Nirias would be. Sarin had taken it upon himself to find out as much about the Malshorne as he could, and it seemed this extended to his nocturnal activities as well. They raced through the alleys like a couple of rats. On reaching the Curing Houses they saw that lights glowed in a couple of the windows. A blurred shadow revealed that somebody was moving about in the western wing. They did not stop to kick off their boots. As they entered the inner halls, Sarin spoke softly, almost as if to himself: 'This could be interesting.' The only answer he gave to Ash's querying look was an enigmatic smile.

They found Agnid writing notes as she bent over her patient. Ash knew him by name only: Homer Baldwig. The poor man had been in the Curing House since his arrival.

'Nirias!'

At the sound of Sarin's voice, the nurse turned her head sharply. When she saw the pair of them standing there, her eyes narrowed. With a frown she brought a finger to her lips. As she ushered them into an adjacent room, Ash felt himself blush. The old nurse was obviously vexed by their abrupt intrusion into her domain.

'Sarin?' Lips pursed with arms folded over her ample bosom, Agnid was the very picture of displeasure as she gave Sarin a level stare. A flicker of her eyes acknowledged Ash where he hovered. 'And Ash.' Her lips puckered into a wrinkled purse. 'What brings you both here so late?' For some reason, Sarin seemed to find the response amusing. He actually smirked. Then he folded his arms and pouted, mirroring her stance. Was he mimicking her intentionally? Ash winced. Sarin really could be incredibly rude. And this was no time for disrespect. He shot his friend a warning look and blurted out the news.

'We're sorry to disturb your work, Agnid. We need Nirias — urgently! Somebody is out there. At the Stone!'

Agnid's brows shot up into high arches. Without pausing to ask how Ash might possibly know such a thing, she began unlashing her apron. Bustling over to a cabinet, she began selecting phials and bandages, at the same time issuing a command over her shoulder. 'Sarin, go to the door at the end of the corridor and rouse Pallin. He is overdue for his evening shift.' She half-turned her head, her jaw twitching a little. 'I'll fetch Nirias … just as soon as I've finished here.'

Ash was about to ask what he should do when Sarin let out a snort. 'Right.' For some reason his eyes were full of challenge. 'Or … you can change here. We don't mind.' He smiled cryptically.

Ash blushed, hot with embarrassment. Why was Sarin teasing the old nurse?

Agnid turned her head. As she fixed Sarin with a long, hard stare, Ash held his breath. He had no idea what was going on, he just knew the air was crackling with tension. The nurse's words were as crisp and starched as her apron. 'Nirias will be along shortly.' Her eyes had none of that kindly twinkle — they were icy cold and dangerous. 'He will handle the situation. But later, I'm quite sure he will have some words for you, Sarin.'

Agnid turned her gaze upon Ash, who quailed at the threat in her eyes. With a look fit for slaughter, she rapped out a command. 'Ash, stop gawping! Go and raise Pallin. If there's a man in danger, then the pair of you can help!'

Leaping to obey, Ash found Sarin blocking the way. His feet were planted, arms still folded, one eyebrow raised. 'I rather think the game is up, *Agnid*, don't you?'

Agnid had turned away as if to sweep out through an adjoining door. She halted, drawing herself upright. She did not turn to face them. She just stood there. The fingers of one hand twitched at her side. 'Very well.'

Ash glanced at Sarin, baffled by his friend's bizarre behaviour. All of Sarin's attention was fixed on Agnid. He seemed to be holding his breath. Whatever was happening? Even Tarlyn had abandoned her exploration of a bureau. Her eyes glowed, trained on the motionless figure of the nurse. What were they all waiting for? There was a man's life at stake!

Ash half-opened his mouth to protest. The utterance died on his lips.

Agnid was … glowing! Her body was outlined in a halo of light. Ash rubbed his eyes. No. The rest of the room was clearly in focus. It was just Agnid who wavered. Ash stifled a cry. He took a step back. The old nurse was no more! In her place was a shining column of multicoloured particles. The shimmering dust moved like sands spinning in an upset hourglass. Then, all of a sudden — in a snap — the particles coalesced. No longer Agnid, the figure turned.

Nirias's tone was coolly dangerous. 'Naturally, you are both compelled to secrecy.' His glowing eyes reminded Ash horribly of Credé. 'Sarin, you needn't look so smug. I have been quite aware of your skulking. I guessed you would discover Agnid's true nature eventually. We will speak of her importance later.'

Nirias had already started shoving bandages and bottles into a haversack, taking up where 'Agnid' had left off.

Ash jumped when the Malshorne snapped at him: 'Ash, tell me!' Weak-kneed and barely coherent, he stumbled through a recount as best he could.

Nirias's expression grew increasingly concerned as Ash told of his encounter with the Heartstone. When Ash described the warrior, his eyebrows shot up in startled alarm. He paused in his hurried preparations and made Ash repeat what he had said. His expression was grim. 'The man you describe is Skarlon de Bree. It can be no other. But he should be in the Elgrave with the jarlycats.' Nirias shook his head. 'Skarlon would not brave the mountain passes in these conditions unless ...' The thought was left hanging, overtaken by Pallin's sleepy arrival and a barrage of instructions.

⁂

By the time the small search party had reached the Stone, clouds were veiling the stars and dulling the light of the moons. A foggy vapour had settled into the treetops. It created scarves of mist that swallowed the light of lanterns, causing feet to stumble. The smell of smoke on the air led the rescuers on. They discovered the man not far from the Stone itself. Too exhausted to make the climb to the high refuge and its labyrinth of caves, he must have used the last of his energy to build the pitiful fire.

He was propped upright, as if he had been battling to stay on guard. A blanket formed a dark cowl around his face. Nirias rushed forward. As he cradled the man's face, the cover fell back to reveal three dark stars on one cheek. The man's eyelids fluttered. At the sound of his name, he tried to stir, and failed. Then his lips moved. 'Nirias?' His voice was a papery whisper. Fingers fumbled, patting blindly at Nirias's sleeve. The man slumped again, eyes rolling closed. 'It is you. Thanks be to Argess.'

'Thanks indeed, Skarlon. Thanks indeed.'

While Nirias turned his attention to the man's leg, inspecting a makeshift bandage and rummaging for salves, Ash held a flask to Skarlon's lips, urging him to drink. Whatever the medicine was, it seemed to do him good, because his eyes became more focused. After a few more sips, he pulled a face and shook his head, so Ash squatted back on his heels. Although Nirias had told him to get as much down their patient as possible, Ash was not about to insist. The warrior's face was a grizzled mess of age lines and scars. A hard man. And no stranger to killing. Ash quailed under the man's scrutiny.

'One thing. In case I don't make it … Is it true? Is the girl here?'

In the time it took Ash to blink, Nirias was back at the warrior's side. He brought his head in so close that their foreheads were nearly touching. 'You are not about to die. Save your strength, my friend. There will be answers, all in good time. Save your strength.'

The man coughed, a rasping rattle that made Ash want to pull away. But Skarlon's eyes were insistent, not leaving Nirias's face. His fingers clutched a handful of his cloak. He winced in pain. 'Nirias. The girl. Is she safe?'

Nirias's tone was firm, to the point of being curt. 'She is safe, Skarlon. But hush. No more questions. We must get you warm and down to the city.' Skarlon's mouth twitched into a half-smile as he slumped, succumbing at last to exhaustion.

For a moment Ash thought that Nirias was scowling at him for not administering enough medicine. Then he realised the man was looking past him. Turning, he saw that Sarin was standing there, stock-still. In his hands he held the reins of the largest, shaggiest horse Ash had ever seen. Its great head was bowed in exhaustion. Sarin held Nirias's gaze for a long moment. Then, without speaking, he turned and walked away, leading the stumbling beast down to T'al Jazure.

Ash lowered himself onto his bed, not bothering to change his clothes. What was the point? There were only a few hours until dawn. He stared at the panelled ceiling for a while, eyes tracing the grooves in the wood, then he let his head fall sideways to watch Sarin. Apparently not tired at all, Sarin was sitting cross-legged on his bed with a dark green knapsack in his lap. Unfolding the kit that he had retrieved from one of its many pockets, he selected a needle and threaded it. Ash pushed himself up onto an elbow. He watched as Sarin examined the small rip and started his repairs.

'How did you know? About … about Agnid?'

Sarin kept his head over his stitching. 'I didn't really. It was a guess.' He squinted. 'Can I borrow your lamp?'

Ash nodded as best he could with his neck propped the way it was. It was funny how obvious it seemed now. Agnid had never eaten with the others, she rarely left the Curing Houses, and was never seen in the company of Nirias.

Sarin concentrated on his work. 'It is a clever trick ... making her so reclusive.'

Ash frowned. Nirias had everyone deceived — and now they were part of that deceit. Would it be better not to know?

'You have to admire him.'

Ash opened his eyes wider. 'But he's lying, Sarin. To everyone.'

'Yes, but it is a useful lie. One outweighed by good.' Looking up, he caught Ash's shocked expression. 'Think about it, Ash. Agnid can do things that Nirias never could. Who do you think these tough warriors want to see them at their weakest — at their most vulnerable? Their fearless leader? Or a reclusive old woman who barely speaks to a soul?' Sarin nodded and returned his attention to his work. 'It is an admirable deception.'

An admirable deception? Ash blinked.

Sarin formed a few more stitches, before looking up again. 'What is more interesting is why Nirias finally decided to reveal his secret to us.' He paused for a long moment, considering, his eyes resting on Tarlyn. She just stretched and settled herself into a ball. 'That is the real question, Ash.'

Ash turned the puzzle over in his tired mind. Sarin was right. Why *had* Nirias transformed before their eyes the way he had? He could easily have denied Sarin's guess by leaving and coming back in as Nirias. Yet he had chosen to trust them with his secret. Why?

Ash groaned and let himself flop back on the pillow. Did Pallin know, too? He frowned, trying to recall the expression on Pallin's sleep-creased face. And Daska. Did Daska know? It hurt his head just thinking about it.

It was not until Sarin pulled his last stitch tight, cut the thread with his teeth and inspected the strength of his patch, that Ash had a sudden flash of understanding. He pulled himself upright.

'You're leaving!'

Sarin's rueful smile confirmed the guess. 'I have to, Ash. Skarlon made it through the pass. I think I can, too. If I go now while the weather holds, I can follow his tracks and catch the Aurum in Jerra Bal, well before the ousting.'

Ash watched his friend packing items into the bag with a growing sense of horror. He understood that Sarin had to find the Aurum before they began their travels. It wasn't just about Rilka — he planned to speak with the seed-keepers, too. T'al Jazure needed seeds. Its numerous glass domes were designed to grow all manner of crops, but the few seeds they had discovered had turned out to be unviable. Ash frowned. He was not convinced that either of these were sufficient reasons for Sarin to leave straight away.

Ash rubbed his tired eyes, wishing there was something he could do to stop him. Skarlon had very nearly died coming over the mountain paths. But this was Sarin. Ash knew better than to try and dissuade him. 'Have you got everything you need? I mean … food and …' Sarin just laughed and nodded. Ash felt completely helpless. 'Well, can I do anything? Do you want to borrow the dymiril lamp?'

Sarin's expression was suddenly grave. 'No. The lamp should stay here. But I do need you to give something to Kep. Will you do that for me?' Reaching under his bed, he pulled out a long article wrapped in cloth.

'You mean, you're going right now? Won't you wait for Skarlon's news?' Ash felt a stab of alarm. 'Won't you even say goodbye to Kep?'

Sarin shook his head. His eyes seemed to glimmer. 'Look after her for me.'

Ash stared. As if he could look after Kep. He frowned. 'Sarin, what is wrong between you? I mean … You should say goodbye yourself.'

Sarin half-turned away. 'You don't understand. It's complicated. There's something I should have told her. And I didn't. But I should have done … I missed my chance.' Ash had never seen his friend look so anxious and confused. 'And now …' His eyes seemed to plead, begging understanding. Ash was at a complete loss to understand why.

'I can't explain, Ash. Not now. Just know … I'm sorry.' He pushed the wrapped item towards Ash: 'Please, give Kep this. Tell her to practise, and—' He grimaced. 'Look after her.'

Ash found himself holding the parcel. 'All right, I'll give it to her,' he promised. 'But what can I do? If Kep's selected, she'll be leaving, too.' His heart filled with misery at the prospect of losing both of his friends.

Sarin shook his head. 'She won't be,' he answered. 'Not this time.'

Ash frowned. How could he be so certain? But Sarin was already hoisting his pack over one shoulder. He took Ash by the shoulders and looked into his eyes. 'Do your best. Keep trying to find out why the city was locked. It's important. And don't trust Nirias. I'm going to make Nalina tell me everything she knows.'

Ash nodded, although he doubted Sarin's grandmother would tell him anything she did not want to.

Sarin frowned. 'One more thing … Well, just don't do anything stupid, kin.' He gave a grin. 'Not until I get back.' Ash was taken by surprise when Sarin stepped forward and caught him in an embrace. And with that he was gone.

Once again Ash lay on his bed, staring at the ceiling. He felt totally miserable. Yet, in spite of everything, his mouth curved into a faint smile. Sarin had called him kin.

❧

'Ash! Sarin! Wake up!' Kep's voice sounded muffled through the door. 'Let me in! There's news!' More pounding on timber. Then: 'Oh, for Telion's sake! I'm coming in! You had better be decent!' Kep burst into the room bringing a basket and an aura of excitement.

'Your breakfast, my lord.' Making a quick curtsey, she set the basket on the side table before flinging the shutters wide. Dazzling light poured in, making Ash squint and cover his eyes with an elbow.

'Nirias said to let you sleep, but it's long past midday. And it wasn't humanly possible to wait a moment longer.' Kep's eyes were brimming with excitement. She began unpacking the basket, rattling on all the while. 'You can tell me all about the rescue in a moment. Nirias told us you were involved.' She rolled her eyes, but could not hide her smile. 'But my news first. You won't believe it: they've named the captains!'

As Ash sat rubbing his eyes and yawning, Kep went on in a rush of breathlessness. 'Everyone is in a stir. Daska called us together and announced it! Just like that! And who do you think's been chosen?' Even if Ash had had the wits to answer, she gave him no time to get a word in. 'Muku's leading the bears. That's not a surprise. But El! Just imagine, Ash. El is captaining the red fox jinn! She'll make a brilliant captain, don't you agree?'

Ash mumbled a response and accepted the bowl of porridge. It was still warm in its pottery bowl and faintly pink. Sweet potatoes found in the forest were making their way into most of the food these days. Ash didn't mind. He liked the sweet, nutty taste. He swallowed a couple of quick mouthfuls in case it slopped with Kep's bouncing.

She was still singing El's praises. Of course — Kep was hoping to join the foxes. If they had named the captains, then the draw would not be far away. Ash wanted to give the saddest, deepest sigh. He managed to hold it inside. 'And who was the third?' he made himself ask.

'Reardon! Reardon Galt's been named for the blackhorns. So Sarin was right.' She rolled her eyes. 'A stag for the stags.' She laughed. 'Where is Sarin anyway? I thought he must be here, so I brought extra food.'

Ash froze, his spoon halfway to his mouth. 'He's gone.'

Kep popped a sliver of salted venison into her mouth and licked her fingers. 'Obviously. But where did—' The look on Ash's face had caught her full attention. 'Ash! What is it?'

Ash struggled to make his tone light. 'He's gone to find the Aurum.'

'What? Without even saying goodbye?' He could see she was upset, her eyes seemed more blue somehow and her mouth quivered.

'I think … maybe he didn't want to wake you.' Ash cringed at the hurt behind her eyes. 'But he asked me to give you something.' Ash would have risen to collect the parcel propped in the corner had his legs not been pinned beneath blankets and plates of food. Instead, he pointed to the package.

Kep weighed the object in her hands before sitting back on the bed. Ash half-smiled. From its shape it could only be one thing. Kep shook her head, frowning deeply as she unfastened the ties. She let out an audible gasp as the covering fell away.

It was the most beautiful bow that could ever be imagined. Similar in style to Sarin's own, it was of Aurum design and much shorter than a longbow. Carved from wood the colour of chestnuts, its flowing curves were accentuated by carvings that wrapped like curled leaves around its tapered ends. And, naturally, there were falcons — with fierce eyes — identical to the one Kep now bore on her arm. Ash shook his head, marvelling at Sarin's skill. If ever there was a bow for Kep, this was it. 'He said to tell you to practise,' he said quietly.

Kep's fingers stroked the three arrows that had been tucked into the wrapping, their fletches a perfect match for the blue-and-green feathered token that dangled from one of her braids. Kep's eyes squeezed back tears. Her mouth was soft. Trembling. 'Of course he did,' she whispered. 'He's such a strange boy.'

Ash nodded. It was a fair point. Attempting a smile, Kep pulled a small package from her pocket and unwrapped a brand-new bowstring. 'Well.

At least I know what this is for now.' Ash guessed her scowl was an attempt to hold back tears. 'It's so … so typically Sarin. Honestly, Ash, why would he dash off like that?'

Ash gave a helpless shrug. He wanted to point out that he wasn't any better at working out Sarin than she was, but he held his tongue. 'He said he needed to speak with Nalina.' Ash hesitated. 'And I think Skarlon's arrival might have had something to do with it.'

Kep sniffed. 'Nobody's seen or spoken to him yet. He's still in the Curing Houses with Agnid.' She missed how he frowned at the mention of the nurse's name. She was staring at her new bow. She stroked the wood, as if she could not quite believe it was real. Ash did not blame her — it was like something one of the Azuri might have created. He blinked at the thought.

Kep lifted her eyes, studying his face. 'Ash … Nirias said they knew where to look because you had a vision.' Ash winced at the word. *Wonderful.* The last thing he needed was people thinking he was seeing visions. The truth was even more alarming.

Kep was looking at him in that insistent way of hers. She would not rest until he told the story, so he related what had happened. He felt awful leaving out the part about Nirias's transformation, but he needed time to think. What exactly had Nirias meant by the phrase 'compelled to secrecy'? It was all so disturbing. And Kep looked disturbed enough already. Her earlier buoyant excitement had all but dissipated. Her hands were restless, fiddling with the bow string. He thought she was worrying about Sarin until she gazed at him with those solemn blue eyes. Her question made his chest tighten. 'Do you think the Heartstone is dangerous?'

There was only one answer. It came out with a squeak. 'I … I don't know.' Ash cleared his throat. He felt horribly pinned down by the blankets. The back of his neck felt clammy and his mouth was stale. 'Um … Can we talk about it later? I should get up.'

Kep shook herself. 'Yes, you really must.' She hugged her beautiful bow to her chest. 'You have to get ready.' Her eyes were wide and serious. 'We've been summoned, Ash.' As Tarlyn sat up and stretched, Ash felt an urgent flutter in his chest. Summoned? Where? Kep's gaze held his. 'To the Captains' Council. They are meeting this afternoon. Nirias wants both of us there in case there are questions about Aranti. And Mildaresh.'

As she rose, Ash realised just how much his friend had changed. He saw nothing of the fresh-faced milkmaid he had grown up with. The woman who smiled at him had the eyes of a warrior. 'This is it, Ash. Things are about to change.'

As Kep closed the door softly behind her, Ash knew in his heart that she was right. This was it — the beginning of something new. He wanted to pull the covers over his head and hide.

Chapter 23

THE CAPTAINS' COUNSEL

'Maliagne Aranti.'

Ash shivered at the coolly deliberate way that Nirias said the name. 'Potentially the most dangerous nexus any of us have faced.'

As everyone at the table watched, Nirias leaned across and placed a small black obelisk on the map. Mildaresh. Right at the ragged edge of the map. Ash's home, he supposed. But Mildaresh seemed vague and distant now. How strange that a place could be reduced to a mere dot on a map.

There were twelve people in the tower room. Nirias had referred to the meeting as the 'Council of the Captains'. Half of the attendees were indeed captains. Daska Kindleman, Rodine Gametale and Benjin Dale — all seasoned campaigners — had an air of calm. The freshly named captains, Eliayliah Larien, Muku Tor and Reardon Galt, were understandably less composed. Their eyes kept flicking to their companions, and they sat forward on their chairs, expectant.

Ash was uncertain where Gallin fitted in. Presumably he was there, like Aechon, as an expert on Calkinon politics. Ash cringed. He and Kep were supposedly the experts on Mildaresh and Aranti. Of course Nirias had already questioned them at length, taking copious notes in his tiny handwriting. Ash doubted there was anything left to tell. The twelfth person in the room was a complete mystery: the stranger, whose sudden and impossible arrival at T'al Jazure had been the catalyst for bringing the meeting forward. Ash knew he was not the only one trying not to stare, wondering what dire news the stranger had brought.

The man had been introduced simply as Skarlon de Bree, of the jarlycat jinn. From the glances the other warriors shot him, he was a stranger to everyone in the room — except Nirias. How he had made it through the mountains in deep snow was anyone's guess. He was certainly not giving anything away. A silent presence, he sat stolidly in his chair with feet planted, arms folded. Nirias's introduction was acknowledged with the curtest of nods.

Skarlon's thick leather garments seemed designed for combat over comfort. Ash thought there was something dry and husky about the man, as if he had slept too long under unfriendly thickets and had taken on their personality. His silvered hair straggled to mid-length. Slate-grey eyes watched proceedings with tired disdain. Perhaps he was simply exhausted from what must have been an arduous trek. Ash was not sure, but his gaze seemed to rest on Kep the longest. Ash tried to catch her eye, but all of her attention was fixed on Nirias, who was starting to speak about her former master.

'The man is highly intelligent, charismatic and hungry for power. For these reasons alone we had him under our watch.' Nirias placed his hands on the table, frowning at the map. 'Unfortunately, by some quirk of fate or some dark destiny, the Melk swarm has found the perfect host. Aranti is no local warlord, no thug to be taken out by simple assassination. Even before he became a nexus of the Melk, Aranti had his mind set on seizing power. He has an uncanny knack for self-advancement. Not only that, the man now has a private army at his disposal, recently granted legitimacy by the Senate. And, from what Ash and Kep have told us of the Moagli Squad, many of those may already be under his thrall.'

Nirias fixed the captains with his eyes. 'The man is astute and extremely wary.' He shook his head. 'Our first attempts to curb the threat have met with failure.' There was a long silence. A couple of the captains exchanged looks. It seemed Nirias was not about to elaborate on the point. Instead he gave a deep sigh and steepled his hands beneath his chin. 'We must act with great care in this case.' In the pause that followed, all eyes followed his — to the black token on Mildaresh. 'Aranti could plunge the world into war.'

At Nirias's signal, Gallin cleared his throat and leaned forward. His voice was rich, resonating with the confidence of one accustomed to oratory. For a man who seldom spoke, it came as quite a surprise. 'Aranti is playing an extremely dangerous game of brinkmanship. As we all know, Calkinon does not brook dissent from any of her tribune states. Now that Mildaresh dominates the elpha supply, eyes will most certainly be turned on Aranti's manoeuvres. Of particular concern is the murder of the Calkinon ambassador. He most certainly visited Aranti at his villa. League stealths have ascertained that Aranti was the last person to see the man alive.'

Gallin paused to let his point sink in.

'Moreover, the Calkinon generals will undoubtedly see the rise of the Moagli Squad as a private army, undermining the presence of the city guardians. Assurances have been received from Aranti that the measure was merely aimed at putting down the slave rebellion, but doubts will remain. This year, it is rumoured that the elpha tribute has not yet been made. Of all the tribune cities, only Mildaresh grows noikos pods in significant quantities to be processed as the highly-prized elpha fuel, and every year fifty per cent of the elpha they produce is sent to Calkinon as a tribute. Anything that threatens the elpha supply will of course lead to swift retribution.'

At this point Eliayliah interjected. 'But surely the man cannot be so reckless as to take on the might of Calkinon! No city would survive such a conflict!'

Nirias leaned back in his chair, his expression bleak. 'That, I'm afraid, is the problem, and one of the reasons we must act swiftly to curb this danger. Mildaresh is uniquely positioned to withstand an attack. The Irian Range is impassible, elpha-birds cannot fly that high, and the Felian pass is easily held. Nor can an army advance by sea. Even the smallest boats would get mired in the marshlands. If Aranti were to dig in his heels, then Mildaresh could withstand even the might of Calkinon.'

Ash stole a glance at Kep. She looked just as horrified as he was.

Nirias dropped a word into the grim silence. 'But ...' He produced a second token from his person. 'I'm afraid the problem deepens.' Leaning across, he placed the token right in the middle of the map, on the lake city of Calkinon. A gasp went around the table. Nirias pulled a sour face. 'We have evidence of another nexus.' When he gestured, Daska cleared his throat.

'The nulls that tracked Kep into the Enigmata wore Calkinon uniforms. They were wholly under sway. The exact link to Calkinon is unsure at this point. But we have to consider the strong possibility of a Melk presence within the Calkinon forces.'

As Nirias resumed, Ash felt a shiver of fear, remembering the hollow eyes of those nulls.

'So, with Aranti flaunting the dictate of the Calkinon Peace, and a Melk presence within the ranks, or worse ...' Nirias spread his hands, an expansive gesture taking in the whole map. 'For the first time in hundreds of years, we have a situation that could spill over into war. A war driven to madness by the Melk.'

Aechon spoke up at this point, his voice gentle. 'But surely we are a long way from that? What of the Mildaren Senate? Are the nobles so fully cowed as to allow such recklessness?'

Nirias shook his head. 'There are people who would oppose the man, but with every day Aranti is consolidating his power. It is becoming harder to get information. No, his grip upon the city is closing — fast.'

'So!' Benjin Dale slapped his mighty hands down upon the table, his booming voice making the windows shake. 'Nothing changes. We move on Mildaresh as soon as the spring thaw allows. Cut the head off the nex before the poison can spread!'

Nobody spoke. More than one person turned their eyes to the man at Nirias's side. The stranger had not spoken. He had listened to everything without his expression changing once. Surely his arrival had some bearing on the reason they had been gathered together so hurriedly?

Kep nudged Ash with her foot, reflecting his frown back at him. He completely understood the question in her eyes. Why were they here?

Impatient with the brewing silence, Benjin Dale thumped the table again. 'Why are we here, then? If we have been gathered for a vote, then let's take it!'

Nirias held up a hand, quelling the muttering that went around the table. Drawing a folded parchment from his tunic, he held it aloft. 'This missive arrived last night, born here by Skarlon de Bree.' Ash drew a breath. All eyes were on the paper, as if staring hard enough might reveal its contents. Nirias bowed his head to the warrior at his side. He did not move a muscle. 'Skarlon has undertaken a perilous journey to bring us this news — a journey that few could endure.' Ash felt a rippling flush of anxiety. *Sarin.*

With slow ceremony, Nirias unfolded the paper. It rustled crisply in the intense silence of the room. 'This letter is from Pharni.'

There was an instant wave of interest. Ash sat up, too. He knew at once that the seal bore the image of a small cat. He shot a look at Kep. At last they would learn the identity of the mysterious captain who had Sarin so fascinated.

'I am pleased to report that Pharni is alive. She escaped Mildaresh, making her way to the Elgrave Peninsula, here …' Nirias pointed on the map to a thin piece of land. Ash blinked. He knew of the place. Or at least he knew of Idira. The bustling port at the top of the peninsula was a cornerstone of Mildaren trade.

Nirias went on. 'For those few who do not know of whom I speak, Pharni is captain of the jarlycat jinn, which she has been running out of Mildaresh for the past five years. An exceptional shade, she has gathered invaluable information about the workings of power in that realm. As Aranti's mistress, she was ideally placed.' Nirias rubbed at his forehead. 'Little did we know how important, and how dangerous that relationship would be.'

At Kep's very audible splutter Nirias caught himself. 'Oh, yes. You two would know her by her slave name — as Matapharni.' Ash felt his blood rushing. He knew Kep would be beside herself.

Nirias resumed his calm narrative. 'At the beginning of Aranti's recent rise to power, Pharni was imprisoned. We are still not sure why; the jinn was compromised. Her rescue, along with a group of nobles, cost the League dearly — not least because it exacerbated the political turmoil in Mildaresh. It was Aranti's first display of the considerable power he had gathered to himself.' Nirias raised a brow. 'And the first signs of his tyranny. Lord Lendri himself, the previous Mildari, was accused as a traitor and taken captive.' Ash did not dare meet Kep's eyes. He knew they were full of fire. 'Fortunately, although Lendri's situation is unknown, part of the jinn is still in place. Unfortunately,' Nirias held up a finger, 'there are no fighters in play. Only shades.'

The news sent a ripple of alarm around the table. Nirias had to raise his voice above the outcry. 'However ...' He raised the letter a little higher, waving it to refocus their attention. 'This missive does not just concern Mildaresh. It contains tidings of great import. Tidings that have precipitated this gathering.'

Ash held his breath. What possible news could be more urgent than what they had just heard?

'As I said, Pharni fled Mildaresh to our refuge in the Elgrave. There she set herself, once again, to discovering the whereabouts of our long-time foe.' Some of the captains leaned forward, others let out quiet exclamations. Nirias nodded. 'And thus we find ourselves with a rare opportunity.' Moving with slow intent, Nirias placed a third token upon the map, on a group of islands. 'My friends, the lair of the pirate Kara-fell has been discovered.'

Ash could barely take it in. He was not over the shock of learning

Matapharni was a captain of the League, let alone able to take in news of a third nexus. Several people had risen to their feet and were staring excitedly at the map. Muku had reacted the most violently of all, shoving back his chair. Now he stalked up and down the room. Ash could almost hear his teeth grinding. 'Kara-fell!' he stormed. 'Tell us Nirias! Where is the fiend?' The cheerful giant seemed transformed, the muscles in his face twisted by anger.

Nirias shook his head. 'Muku, please. I understand. But … please … be seated.' He made a soothing motion with his hands and Muku obeyed. He clutched at the arms of his chair, though, as if holding himself in. Nirias waved the letter. 'Skarlon has risked much to bring this news here in time. Kara-fell never stays anywhere long. But if we move quickly, as soon as the season allows, there is a chance.' Nirias did not table the letter. Instead he tucked it safely into the breast of his tunic. 'So, we cannot move upon all threats at the same time. Each is perilous. To strike has consequences. Not to strike, or to strike and miss the mark …' His mouth screwed sideways. 'That can be worse.'

'Enough!' Having been so silent, Skarlon's exclamation gave Ash quite a shock.

As the man pushed himself up with the help of the table, Nirias made a motion with his hand. 'We would hear your thoughts, Skarlon. But, please, there is no need to stand.'

The suggestion was ignored, with a growl. The man's grimace distorted his already broken features. 'I'm no fancy orator. But some things are better said standing.' Although standing clearly cost him an effort, he looked ready to throttle anyone who argued otherwise. Nirias deferred to him with a nod.

The man growled. 'The jarlycats have wintered hard.' A dismissive wave of his weathered hand revealed just what Skarlon thought of the room's thick rugs and brocade furnishings. 'In colder, harder places.' He did not say places more suited to warriors. It was most certainly implied. A few of the warriors shifted in their seats, their eyes narrowing. 'We have not had the luxury of rest. And cosy fires.' His lip curled. 'We have held our vigil. And more. We have paid for hard-won gains. In blood. The blood of warriors.'

His scowl took in everyone in the room as if they were all somehow responsible. 'I hear Nirias speak of this man, Aranti. This most terrible threat. And, yes, perhaps he may become the monster we fear. But what of the monster we already face? The pirate Kara-fell has wreaked destruction that would make your marrow freeze. She is blackest scourge. If you had seen what I've seen, you would not sit here warming your toes and staring at maps!'

Skarlon jabbed a finger at the air. 'You speak of evil? Kara-fell is the most vicious, most insane nexus that ever drew breath. Her raids have spread poison in the Elgrave, like black ink in those once sweet waters. Now her ships plague the Singing Isles, too. Are we to wait? Squandering our one chance? Chasing this … what? This politician? A phantom of what might be? I say no! We have bought our chance … with blood. Are we not warriors?' He held them with his eyes. 'I say we strike at the monster who is already sinking ships, murdering babes, torturing good men and women, driving despair into every soul. We strike now, at the monster we can see. We take out Kara-fell.'

A careful silence fell as Skarlon sank back into his chair. His breathing was laboured, his gaze no less intense. For a long moment Nirias did not speak. When he did, there was no emotion in his tone, his voice was completely level. 'What say the captains?'

Around the table came the refrain as the captains answered one by one. Some voices were more strident than others, and some eyed the other two markers on the map. But all spoke in agreement. The name was repeated around the table. Six times, for six captains: 'Kara-fell … Kara-fell.'

'So be it.' Nirias brought his hands together. 'Kara-fell is our primary target. We move as soon as the weather allows. Daska, arrange the draw. I will take thought as to what might be done in Mildaresh. Skarlon, I thank you for your words. I believe Agnid has a pledge upon your presence. The captains will stay. Everyone else is free to leave.'

As Ash rose to file out with the others, he felt a touch upon his arm. Nirias spoke under his breath. His eyes were grave. 'Ash, we must speak. I will find you, just as soon as we are finished here.'

Chapter 24

THE HIGH SEAT

Ash still had no idea what Nirias wanted with him. They had walked, apparently at random, chatting about nothing — it was completely nerve-racking. 'Ah, of all the archways in T'al Jazure, this is my particular favourite.'

Ash nodded politely. From recollection, Nirias had said exactly the same thing of at least one other. As the Malshorne stood back to admire the form, Ash did his best to look enthused. This arch was elegantly simple. Wrought from bright silver and smooth as burnished silk, it twisted upon itself, like three interwoven ribbons. Set beneath a dome, at the juncture of several corridors, the archway did not seem to lead anywhere. It made no sense. But then, many things in T'al Jazure made little sense.

After a while Nirias turned his head to Ash. His expression was as difficult to read as ever, but there seemed to be an odd tension about the man. Ash shivered. Then the impression was gone. With a smile, Nirias gestured that they should pass on, through the arch. Ash stepped forward, relieved to move on. As he did so, the frame of the arch changed, from silver to a pale blue. There was an odd tearing sensation, then everything vanished.

Ash threw his arms wide to stop himself falling, staggering at the shock. His first impression was that they had been transported onto a saucer suspended in the clouds. As he straightened, he realised that the space did in fact have walls; they were just made of clear crystal.

Nirias laughed. Throwing out his arms, he called out in grandiose tones: 'Welcome, Ash. To the high seat of the Azuran Council.' He chuckled drily. Perhaps it was because the room was literally high. Or perhaps he saw some private irony that Ash did not understand.

Ash did not care. His throat was making strangled noises. He felt as if he had swallowed a nest of lizards. It was impossible to find words as he struggled against the turmoil in his stomach. Not sure if he was about to vomit, he tried to breathe.

Fortunately, Nirias was happy to supply both questions and answers.

'Where are we? Far above the city. If you move closer to the edge, you will see the tops of turrets.' Ash had no intention of going anywhere near the edge. 'You could think of this place as a secret pocket, within the secret pocket that is T'al Jazure — it is obviously more complicated than that.' Ash closed his eyes, swallowing and breathing deeply. 'As for how. The archway brought us here — because of you. You brought us here, Ash.' Nirias gave a little bow and pulled a painful face. 'Which brings us to why we are here.'

Ash was still gathering his wits. As his dizziness subsided, he took a careful look around. Apart from the still glowing archway, the only other thing in the room was a huge table, surrounded by high-backed chairs. Set on massive silver claws, the table was round and topped with a shining glass surface. Edging closer, Ash realised that it was purpose-built to house a map, although to call it a map was rather insulting. The cities and towns were depicted in exquisite relief, the rivers so lifelike they seemed to flow down from the sharp-cut mountain ridges. The map's coastlines were familiar, yet unfamiliar. Looking for Mildaresh to the north, beyond the peaks of the Irian Range, Ash caught his breath to see the miniature towers of Eerok-tan. Of course. This was a map of the ancient world. On the Isle of Baktah stood the fluted spires of the Wimsari. They were pink, just as Barnham had described. Where the mighty city of Calkinon should have been, at the edge of the great lake, there was nothing — just a name that Ash had never heard of.

Looking up, Ash caught a curious expression on the Malshorne's face. The man was circling the table, his hand brushing the tops of the blue high-backed chairs. When he caught Ash's eye, he pulled a chair out. His eyes glimmered as he gestured for Ash to join him and Sarin's words came back. *Don't trust Nirias.* Ash eyed the archway. Presumably it led back to where they had come. Could he make a dash for it? *Don't trust Nirias.* Sarin's words kept repeating in his head, but what could he do? He edged himself into the chair. When he glanced again at the arch, Nirias's eyes seemed to follow.

After an excruciating silence the Malshorne sighed. 'Your shock is understandable. I guessed the archway would work for you, Ash.' He sighed. 'Of course it would. You are the Taelstaun.' His mouth twitched. 'Doors will open for you that neither of us know exist. Even doors to the most secret of places.' Nirias spoke so softly. Was he angry? Bitter perhaps? Was that what reminded Ash so uncomfortably of Credé? 'Few of the Malshorne have entered this place. Those who were invited came as advisors. The Azuri did not trust our kind to be on the Council.' Nirias smiled. 'Trust is hard to come by, for those of our abilities.'

Ash swallowed, hard. Once again, he had the horrible feeling that Nirias could read his mind.

'Yet I have been here before. Just once. Leynore brought me, when I was not much older than you. I think she wanted to teach me something about the workings of power. Something I was far too young to learn.' His expression clouded. After a moment's thought, he went on. 'I remember thinking this place was like a crystal eagle's nest. Oh yes, I was impressed. Who could fail to be impressed? Here the Council deliberated, wrapping themselves in subtle arguments about the pains of the world. All judgments, all decisions, to act, or not to act were made here — upon high. Far above the city, and far, far removed from the realities of the world outside.' Ash sensed his bitterness. 'Now, I think perhaps that Leynore wanted me to understand a terrible irony. The seat of power, was ultimately powerless to act.'

Ash frowned at the map. So much had changed. Cities, rivers, even the coastline had been cast into new shapes. But one thing had not changed: for all that time, Nirias had been fighting the Melk. It was a terrible thought. Was it any wonder the man seemed close to unravelling?

'Are you worried that the captains have made the wrong decision?' Ash asked quietly.

Nirias turned his head, almost as if he was a little shocked to see Ash sitting there. 'No. Not at all. The captains have made the only decision they could. No …' He seemed to shake himself. 'I did not bring you here to speak of strategy. It makes sense to begin with Kara-fell. Do not be alarmed, Ash. I will keep Kep safe. You have given us a great gift. For once we have the advantage. We are rested, we are trained, and we have information.'

Up until then, Tarlyn had been prowling along the edge of the table. Now she turned. She stared at Nirias with limpid eyes. Her ruff went up, sending spines out, quivering. Her ears opened out like black fans.

Darkness cannot drive out darkness, Nirias. The way of violence leads only to despair.

The woman's voice was gentle, remonstrating. Ash was wide-eyed. Tarlyn spoke so rarely, it always came as a shock. Nirias had gone white, his hands gripped the edge of the table. Ash felt his heart pulsing in his temples. He had almost forgotten the weird quality of Tarlyn's utterances. This time he thought he could hazard a guess as to whose voice that was. 'Was that her? Was that … Leynore?'

Nirias sighed. A weary, defeated sound. 'Yes. Leynore. She said those words to me in this very place.' His face crumpled with pain. After a moment he took a shaky breath, composing himself. 'Tarlyn seems to think a reminder is in order.' He lifted an eyebrow at the creature. Tarlyn gave a quivering shake and shrank, resuming her usual sleek form. Her eyes continued to stare at him, dark and unblinking.

Nirias scowled. 'If only Tarlyn knew what torture those words bring. I think of nothing else, Ash! But,' he spread his hands, 'this is my fate. I am a man caught between two codes. The oath of peace and the warrior's pledge. There is no choice. We must resist the Melk.' The Malshorne's eyes flashed. 'There is no choice. And Leynore … Leynore discovered that, too. The warriors will leave as soon as they are able. And I, I must go with them. But you, Ash. You are Azuri now, and your place is here.'

Ash felt suddenly cold. Nirias must have seen the panic on his face, because he added gently. 'You will not be alone. Gallin is staying, too, and he is as much a master of the mind as Aechon is of the heart. They will help you. You are bound to the city, Ash. Your relationship with the Heartstone … I do not begin to understand it, but it is like no other.' He leaned forward. 'Ash, this is your fate. You are the Taelstaun. I believe that you may succeed in finding answers, where I have failed. After all,' he chuckled, 'you and your friends have shown yourself to be surprisingly good at uncovering mysteries.'

For the first time Ash realised how truly alone he would be when the warriors left. If he was going to say something, it was now. 'But, Nirias … I think … I think there is something dangerous here. In the city.' Ash bit his lip. He knew it sounded childish. It was not exactly that the presence felt evil. It just felt … alive.

'Danger? Of course. T'al Jazure is full of danger. Dangerous secrets.' Nirias smiled, perhaps in an attempt to take the fear out of those words. It had the opposite effect. 'And dangerous people, too. At the moment your friend Kep might be the most dangerous of all. Why do you think Calkinon fears her? Why do you think the Melk tried to recruit her?' Nirias leaned back in his chair, his elbows on the arms. 'And you, Ash.' He spread his hands. 'What of you? You have the ability to open doors and unlock secrets,' he lifted a brow, 'perhaps even secrets that should not be revealed.'

Ash caught a glint of warning in his eyes and understood. Nirias was talking about his own transformation.

'I won't tell anyone about Agnid,' he said in a rush.

The Malshorne stroked his chin. 'Not even Kep?'

Ash took a breath. 'No. I … I agree with Sarin. It is an honourable deceit.'

Nirias tilted his head. 'Sarin …' His expression was troubled. Ash found himself wondering if he was aware that Sarin had left. 'An honourable deceit, you say.' Nirias's lips formed a smile that did not touch his eyes. 'Yes. Perhaps it is that.'

Chapter 25

LEAGUE WARRIORS

'That woman!' Kep pushed the shovel along the ground so hard she risked splitting the handle. The muck hit the bucket with such force that it nearly tipped over. Ash did not have to ask which woman. Kep had been raving since the meeting of the captains. It even seemed to have taken her mind off the selection. She fairly spat whenever she said the name.

'Matapharni! I still can't believe it. How could she? Spying for the League is no excuse to do what she did! Just think about it, Ash!'

Ash had thought about it. Of course he had, how could he not? And he understood the reasons for Kep's anger. But he was not actually sure Matapharni had been given any choice in preparing Braig's body for Mascellion Feyindi's funeral fire. He was not about to argue with his friend, though.

As he forked hay into the manger, he could not help marvelling at the beauty of its carved design. In T'al Jazure, even objects as lowly as mangers were crafted to last and give pleasure to the eye. The stables were more suited to housing nobility than animals. The building had proper glass windows, and carved panels depicting running horses. Of the twenty-odd stalls, only two were occupied. The lone mule now had the company of Skarlon's enormous horse. Both beasts were watching Kep as she raved, their ears pivoting.

'I mean! The woman ran the herati, Ash!'

Ash nodded. He knew that, too. And he knew how sorely Kep must feel it. After all, Kep herself had been recruited by Matapharni. If things had worked out differently, if Braig had not died, Kep would be herati now — serving at Aranti's pleasure. It was hard to get used to the idea that Aranti's dazzling mistress had been a League warrior all along. You had to admire the woman for infiltrating his household and slipping into a position of such power. Of course Matapharni, or rather Pharni, could not possibly have known that Aranti would be taken by the Melk. Who could have predicted that the Melk swarm would choose him for its host?

'And his mistress! To share the bed of such a man!'

Kep was not showing any signs of simmering down. Ash replaced the pitchfork on its hook and dusted off his hands. He rubbed his itching nose with the back of his hand. 'Are you ready?'

Kep pushed her curly fringe out of her face and scowled. 'Yes! I have never been more ready!'

Ash suppressed a sigh. It had been the same since the Captains' Council. If Kep had been single-minded before, she was even worse now — she seemed unable to think of anything other than the draw. She was convinced she would be chosen: it was the will of Narsis, according to Kep. This new flush of anger had Ash worried. He did not know which outcome would concern him most. Although he was relieved Kep would not be sent to Mildaresh, the mission to assassinate Kara-fell sounded just as dangerous. But, if Sarin was right, and Kep was forced to stay behind, well, she would be a complete nightmare to live with.

'I meant are you ready to get cleaned up?' he said quietly.

Kep scrubbed at her face with a sleeve and sniffed. 'No, it's nowhere near time. I need to keep busy. I'm going to rub down Twinkle. You can help if you like.'

Skarlon's horse could not have had a less appropriate name. Uncannily like her owner, the creature had scars on her face, a ravaged mane, and ears that looked as if they'd been chewed on by a large dog. Although she no longer seemed about to drop dead on the spot, Ash had never seen a more flea-bitten and bad-tempered animal. Her eyes held the same expression as Skarlon's, too — restrained violence. Ash had no doubt that the beast was plotting to bite him as soon as he got within range. As Kep began brushing out tangles, murmuring that Twinkle was a lovely girl, Ash muttered something about kitchen chores, and left her to it.

As he passed through the carved portico, and out along a narrow pathway, the whiff of pipe smoke caught his attention. Then voices. Tense voices. Instinctively, Ash flattened himself against the wall.

'I'll keep my word, Nirias. But I don't think it's right, that's all I'm saying.' Skarlon's gruff voice was unmistakable. For a horrible moment, Ash thought the men were going to round the corner and catch him eavesdropping. Should he walk on past, and pretend he had happened upon them naturally? Something about Nirias's tone made him think the better of it.

'Your intentions are admirable, my friend. No harm will be done. They will be told. All in good time. You have my word on it, Skarlon. But that time is not now. We must not jeopardise …'

As the men moved further away, the remainder of Nirias's sentence was lost in the babble of a fountain. Ash frowned, intrigued. Jeopardise what? Peering around the corner, he saw that the men had already passed out of sight. Sarin, no doubt, would have found a way to spy on the remainder of the conversation. Ash had no intention of trying. He stowed the matter away to fret about later.

⚹

The rumbling rose to a thunder. Kep drummed her own fists on the table, adding to the din. With each tile drawn, her fervour had grown stronger, if that was possible. So far, ten warriors stood side by side to Nirias's right. They made a proud and fearsome group. Only one was a novice — Polkin Dew. Nobody had shown any surprise whatsoever when Rodine Gametale had spoken to claim him. It was a formality really. Not only had he been travelling with the snakes since his recruitment, his strength and skill with the axe perfectly complemented the talents of others in the jinn. The pounding grew even louder as Nirias put his hand into the urn. Then it ceased, leaving Kep's heart to pound on alone. Nirias held the tile aloft. Kep was certain Nirias was looking her way. He smiled as he called out a name. 'Jaibari Selenka of Manas.'

To the sound of cheering and the slapping of hands on tables, Jaibari took proud ownership of a place in the line. Kep clapped, too, battling disappointment. She looked away, unable to bear the dazzle of Jaibari's grin. A few seats down, Ash was making an attempt to look disappointed and sympathetic — a poor attempt. Relief was written all over his face. He wanted her to stay behind, safe in T'al Jazure. Safe in her cage.

As Jaibari kneeled in front of the urn, waiting to be claimed, Kep kept her eyes on Reardon Galt. There were several places left in the stags, and Reardon had never hidden his friendship with Jaibari — in fact, Kep suspected it might be something more. Was that what Jaibari hoped for? To join the stags? Reardon remained silent, his arms folded across his chest. Nobody moved. Kep was just starting to entertain the possibility that Jaibari might not be claimed at all, when a quiet cough drew everyone's attention.

221

Daska rose from his seat with a smile. He knuckled his moustaches, eyes twinkling. 'The scorpions claim Jaibari Selenka of Manas.' The barest flutter of Jaibari's eyelids gave her away. So, she *had* been worried. As Jaibari accepted the claim and swore her allegiance, Kep heard Sarin's voice in her head. *A scorpion for the scorpions.*

Eleven warriors chosen. One left to draw, and a place still open with the foxes. When the drumming began for the final time, Kep closed her eyes. Her own fists remained clenched in her lap. Only one place left. *May it please Narsis.* When the drumming thunder rolled into silence, Kep opened her eyes. Nirias was holding the very last tile between his fingers. The captain of captains let the moment stretch into a long, torturous silence. Then he spoke the words that would change everything.

'Kep of Mildaresh.'

Kep was not even sure how she had made it to the line. She was transported there magically, upon a wave of cheers. As she bent her knee, she cast hopeful eyes at El. Her heart sank when the warrior looked away, her brows knitted. The other captains were shuffling their feet. Even Daska looked uncomfortable. A lump was rising in Kep's throat. To her surprise, Reardon Galt cleared his throat. He seemed about to speak when there was a loud thud. Then another.

All eyes turned to the back of the room. Jen-Jay thumped her staff down again. 'Enough!' Reardon and everyone else froze, no doubt wondering why the little cook was disrupting proceedings. Jen-Jay marched forward. 'I claim the right to speak!'

As Jen-Jay made a spritely leap onto the stage, a shocked murmur went around the room. To say that mouths dropped open was an understatement. Kep gasped, too. Jen-Jay ignored them, all except for Nirias, whom she pinned with one of her stares. Was she going to object? Would she tell everyone that Kep was not ready? On her knees, Kep wanted to clutch at the woman's skirts, to beg her not to speak.

Nirias, it seemed, had been turned to stone. His eyes flickered. Had he gone a little pale? There was something oddly flat about his response. 'By what right do you speak?'

Kep had never seen Jen-Jay so angry. She snorted in derision. Not once had she taken her eyes from Nirias's face. Now she thrust out her arm and opened her fist. A silver object dropped to the end of a leather cord. Those closest let out a gasp. The pendant was triangular. It flashed as it spun —

silver-blue like Jen-Jay's eyes. 'By what right?' Jen-Jay raised her brows. As proud and as straight as her staff, the tiny woman cast her eyes over the gathering. 'By a captain's right.'

Confused and outraged expressions gave way to excited muttering.

Jen-Jay's next words struck everyone dumb with shock.

'Kep, of Mildaresh is hereby claimed by Grey Wolf ...' She glared at Nirias. 'For the wolves.'

Chapter 26

THE FIRES OF PASSING

If anybody needed further evidence of just how much Mildaresh had changed under the rule of her new Mildari, they needed to look no further than Capricia Aranti's Fires of Passing. It was a well-known fact that Aranti had held his wife in poor regard. Nevertheless, in the history of the city there had never been a funeral more extravagant.

The Great Court was crammed with people in spite of the bitter weather. Many were there to partake of Maliagne Aranti's considerable largesse, others, like Karliana, were bound by obligation. There was something debauched and unseemly about the whole affair to Karliana's mind. The highly-charged crowd became even more volatile each time the Mildari motioned for more coins to be tossed. In the scramble, wild cheers were intermingled with the cries of people trampled in the melee.

The inevitable green banners were everywhere. Karliana would not have put it past Maliagne to hang them from the temples themselves. Many of the free-folk were wearing green, too. She noted with horror that a significant number had embraced the new fashion of 'taking the dye'. In a desperate attempt to show allegiance to the most powerful lord the city had ever known, since the time of the monarchy at least, they had coloured their faces with vegetable dye. Most often this took the form of a single green stripe across the forehead, but Karliana had spotted more than one child with a completely green face. It transformed the infants into inhuman frog creatures. She shuddered to imagine what drove a mother to do such a thing to her children.

It was not a surprise when a veritable flock of birds was released for the soul of Aranti's wife. Forty-three, it was rumoured. Without being able to count them, Karliana believed it to be true. One soul bird for each of Capricia Aranti's winters, and the brightest green one could imagine. Nobody in Mildaresh had seen the like, nor would again. Captured far from these shores, the gorgeous creatures would not survive a single night of the Mildaren winter. The crowd laughed and cheered when the birds spread their exotic wings and flew squawking into the darkening horizon. There was something macabre about the sight.

Although Karliana had held Capricia Aranti in low regard, it made her sad. It was as if Aranti had not been able to resist the temptation to mock his unfortunate wife one last time.

If there was one thing more frightening than the proliferation of green, it was the garish flashes of orange. The Moagli Squad members were not the only ones flaunting armbands. Now most of the guardians wore them, too. Karliana shivered at the sight. Slave uprising or not, Calkinon's retribution would be swift when she heard tales of such dissent. The guardians' enduring allegiance to Calkinon, over and above their tribune cities, was an iron-clad law under the terms of the peace.

Karliana was relieved when the seers' final cry went up, signalling that the debauched rites were over. Seeking refuge from the awful spectacle as much as the drizzling rain, she made her way to her carriage. She was handed up by a tight-lipped Pelor, who settled himself on the opposite seat, drawing a fur across his bony knees. 'You are right to look dismayed, my lady. But do not fear. The League will not abandon Mildaresh, I assure you. We will be foremost in their plans.' Karliana gave him a shaky nod as they joined the line of carriages, heading down to the Aranti estates.

By the time they reached the bridge of Assan, where the Nochier Way began its long journey south, the rain had set in, sending people scurrying back to their homes. There were no spectators lining the streets here. No banners waving. Nevertheless, the road was lined. Karliana drew her furs across her mouth, gagging at the stench. The Traitors' Row they were calling it. The heads of the so-called enemies of Mildaresh were here, on display as a lesson to all.

Karliana had been warned but nothing could have prepared her for the sight. There were so many! Slaves, free-folk, nobles. The rain fell on their faces, plastering their hair to ravaged skulls. It was cruelty beyond all imagination. Each refused a funeral, each denied a bird to guide them to the After. Pelor spoke, his jaw tight: 'Look away, Karliana. He is not here.' Karliana knew it to be true. Pelor's spies brought him an account every day. Yet she could not drag her eyes away. What if he was wrong? What if one of these poor souls was her father? She could imagine how it would please Aranti to inflict such ignomy on his hated rival.

As they made the long approach to the Aranti villa, her heart dragged, laden with grief.

Chapter 27

ARANTI'S FOOL

Once, there had been silver birches lining the long approach to the Aranti villa. The pale-limbed beauties were all gone now, burned in great piles. Instead, stone pillars marched on either side, linked with iron chains. To Karliana's mind, the Aranti villa had always had pretensions of grandeur; now it was thoroughly ostentatious. A new marble atrium had sprouted at the front of the building, supported by over-large colonnades. It yawned, like an enormous mouth, doors pinned back despite the cold. Inside, the walls gleamed black as obsidian. Karliana shivered at the sight of her own dark reflection as she passed through, into the heart of Maliagne Aranti's domain.

The cloistered entrance hall now boasted a series of massive emerald urns. Karliana recognised the maker as none other than Ragalini, the most esteemed artist in the land. Poor Ragalini. She dreaded to think by what means Aranti had wrested the reclusive artist from his retirement. The urns were gorgeous, admittedly, but so enormous as to be grotesque. The gilding alone would have cost a pretty fortune. One thing was certain: Aranti was not short of gold.

The banqueting arrangements had undergone changes, too. An entire new wing had been annexed to the great hall. It seemed incongruous, like a freshly-grown limb on an old body. There, the newly wealthy jockeyed for place. Karliana caught glimpses of garish waistcoats, puffed silks and buckled satin shoes. Ebullient, self-conscious laughter spilled into the main hall, causing many a high-born spine to stiffen.

Those guests deemed worthy would dine in the great hall, at two banqueting boards. Swathed in the inevitable Aranti green, they ran down the length of the room. Karliana had no time to ponder the lavender runners because a footman swooped, intent on whisking her to her place. All the noble families were represented since failure to attend a noblewoman's funeral feast was an unforgivable slight, no matter how low the lady's regard, nor how far one had fallen from favour.

As she followed the footman, Karliana wished she could take notes. The seating arrangement was an accurate representation of those who had risen with the new regime, and those who had been cast off. She recognised the long neck and ornately braided hair of Madalinelle Skagali at the very lowest table. Karliana fully expected to be relegated to the bottom half of the hall herself. So she was surprised when her usher led her on. When the footman motioned her towards the top table itself, her heart did a somersault.

Perpendicular to the others and elevated on a raised platform, the top table was decorated with huge bouquets of flowers and rafts of candles. Karliana stepped up, endeavouring to look honoured and delighted. She was neither.

Most of the other seats were already occupied. A rather stout priest was presiding over the conversation to the right, nodding sagely while stuffing olives into his mouth. Father Keller had certainly done well for himself by Aranti's ascension. She had never laid eyes on the second priest, but vaguely recognised the merchant to whom he was speaking. He had a sharp nose and an even sharper smile. Karliana nodded, avoiding his eyes and those of his excited, rosy-cheeked wife. On the left-hand side of the table was Serenitia Moagli, with her son Castronon. They looked up from a private conversation, like a pair of crows disturbed from a carcass. Their knowing smiles sent Karliana's flesh crawling. By this point, her own smile was so brittle it might shatter at any moment.

There was an empty space next to Castronon, and two more right in the centre of the table. The servant pulled out a chair with a flourish. Surely there must be some mistake? Karliana had been placed next to Maliagne himself! Seeming to anticipate her confusion, the footman gave her a swift reassurance that all was as the Mildari had instructed. So, with a tightening in her chest, Karliana Lendri took her chair.

The guests at the tables below sent her surprised glances. Some whispered behind their hands. No doubt they were trying to fathom why such an honour had been bestowed on Torland Lendri's daughter. When she caught the confused look of Mateus Sanarson, Karliana forced a smile. What else could she do?

Within moments Maliagne Aranti swept in, imposing an awed hush on the room. Karliana was not at all surprised to see that he was flanked by Rutholine Moagli. The rumours were true, then: the man accompanied him everywhere. Aranti strode towards her, the green of his doublet shining, as iridescent as a peacock's tail. Every now and then, when he paused to acknowledge some acolyte or another, the garment flared, revealing a flash of deep purple lining.

As he approached, Karliana realised that her hand had fluttered to her chest, and the amethyst pendant lying there. Trembling at her error, she patted her hair instead. Then she secured both hands in her lap, lest they betray her. The Lendri custodian had made every assurance that the necklace would go unremarked; perfectly at home with the deep purples and mauve of her gown. Karliana was suddenly far from certain. It felt like a beacon around her neck. As she forced herself to take a breath Aranti was upon them. He mirrored her acknowledgement with a dip of his own dark head. Karliana's body arched away as the Mildari seated himself. She could not help it. Had a snake been coiled beside her, just at the edge of her vision, she would not have been more on edge.

Karliana had expected Aranti to give a speech before the feast. He did not. Nor did he speak during the meal. He ate efficiently from several small plates. Each was presented to him by a woman; his taster, judging by her terrified expression. As the meal drew out, Karliana had the distinct feeling that the man was waiting for something. It was entirely nerve-racking and she barely touched her food.

The noble houses had sent the very best they could offer, either to appease Aranti or honour his wife. Along with stuffed grouse, roasted boar, pigeons stuffed with blue cheese, walnut and pumpkin soup, and honey-roasted turnips, there was an assortment of wondrous delicacies. After much discussion with Pelor, Karliana had decided the House of Lendri's contribution would be a barrel of cherry liquor. Not only was the vintage highly valued, it had also been Capricia Aranti's favourite. Karliana had no idea if Aranti knew that, or even cared. It seemed fitting. And, besides, the wine would otherwise only have been quaffed by her troublesome suitors.

Course after course was paraded and the wine flowed ever more freely, and still Maliagne Aranti did not speak. Mostly he stared out over his guests, with a composed air of ownership. But every now and then his eyes would flick towards the ceiling, as if he was distracted by some urgent thought. It was most disconcerting. She became more and more convinced that he was waiting, or listening, for something. Once or twice he half-turned to Karliana, his mouth curving in a smile. She pretended not to notice.

The pendant was a burning brand on Karliana's breast now. She told herself repeatedly: Aranti could not possibly know what it held. It did not stop her heart from racing. How foolish she had been. To think that she might pull off an assassination! And at a Feast of Passing! Although Aranti did partake of wine, his goblet was never far from his hand. Karliana began to doubt if Capricia *had* been the unfortunate victim of poison slipped into the wrong drink. She could not imagine how Belle would have got close enough.

Seeking distraction from her thoughts, Karliana turned her attention to the enormous tapestry which took up most of the left-hand wall. It depicted a battle scene. The man wielding an oversized sword was presumably supposed to be one of Aranti's ancestors. *Ridiculous.* Near the border, a horse was standing, having thrown its rider. It was jet-black, with strong hindquarters and a proud, straining neck. Karliana frowned a little. 'Tell me, Rutholine. The stallion you were riding today. Is he of a Malvern line?' She had been quite impressed by Rutholine's horsemanship in controlling the feisty animal.

Rutholine stopped cutting his meat, clearly startled. 'You have a good eye, Karliana. His sire was indeed from that region.' With a little prompting, Rutholine was drawn into a stilted conversation. Karliana was surprised by his depth of knowledge. Who would have thought she would find herself discussing horse breeds with Rutholine Moagli, of all people? And who would have thought the man's solid presence would bring her such comfort? Their conversation was cut short when Maliagne Aranti rose to his feet.

There was no ringing of bells, nor shouting from the Master of the Table. Yet the effect on the room was instantaneous. Everyone's attention snapped to their host and forks clattered to plates. Aranti began in the usual manner, thanking his guests for their attendance. However, that was as close as the evening came to obeying convention. He did not call for eulogies, nor speak of his fondness for his wife. Perhaps he understood how disingenuous that would seem. His guests looked puzzled. Perhaps the speeches were coming later? Announcing a break in the feasting, Aranti directed them to stretch their legs and indulge in the entertainments laid on for their pleasure. Later, he promised, the feast would recommence, with delectable treats such as Capricia herself would have approved. Karliana was not the only one who noticed how his mouth quirked.

For a moment the guests did not move. It was all too much of a novelty. Then the Master of the Table called out in his squeaky voice: 'Come! To the games! To the games!'

As he spoke, a band of musicians and cartwheeling jugglers entered the hall, bringing with them a reckless gaiety. The herati arrived, too. Wearing glittering masks, they cavorted among the tables, enticing and flirtatious. Some guests were lured away to dance, others towards games of amusement, and opportunities to gamble one's wealth away. There were fire jugglers and exotic beasts paraded on golden leads, acrobats and games of dice — even a pair of twins who performed a writhing dance with seven bright green snakes. Karliana arched a brow. It was certainly shaping up to be a night to remember. Her young suitors seemed entranced, caught up in the excitement. She worried that many might find it a night to regret.

Aranti's smile lurked; a furtive thing in the corners of his mouth. He held out a hand. 'Come, my dear. Let us resume our own little game.'

Karliana fluttered her lashes, making it clear that she had no idea what he was talking about. If Aranti was annoyed that she refused his hand, he did not show it. His earlier dark mood seemed much changed. He gave a throaty chuckle.

'I must confess, I am finding you to be a most enjoyable adversary. That last move was triumphant — spiriting off the heir to the House of Aranti no less. Inspired. Quite inspired. But, alas, Tindelfion is safe.' Maliagne tilted his head. 'Intercepted at the pass and returning as we speak. Tonight it is my turn. And Karliana, I think you will find that I have saved my best moves until last.' A shadow crossed his eyes. Even more than his quiet laugh, it made Karliana shrink from him. 'Come, I have arranged a private viewing. Come and see my gallery.'

As a child, Karlina had always been intrigued by the galleried room that looked down into the Aranti feast hall. She had imagined all sorts of figures living up there, hunchbacked spies maybe, banished from sight and sequestered in the shadows. That evening she had no desire to satisfy her curiosity. As they climbed the stairs, shadowed by Rutholine Moagli, Karliana's mouth was dry with trepidation.

Tucked beneath the high rafters and slightly hazy with smoke, the space was indeed perfect for spying. Devoid of spies, it was empty — except for three large box shapes, set in a row under one of the beams. Like three roofless shopfronts, each had a window at the front, with curtains secured to the outside. All were closed. Karliana frowned at the tasselled ropes which dangled in front of each box. The cords went up to a pulley system suspended from the overhead beam, then down into the boxes. Karliana's sense of dread deepened when Aranti began to rub his hands in slow, circling motions. She could feel his anticipation. The man was like a thunderstorm in a jar. 'Come.'

Drawn by a dreadful fascination, Karliana approached the first box. Maliagne stepped up and with a performer's flourish parted its bright yellow curtains. Karliana gave a squeak of horror. Inside was the dangling body of a man! His head was bowed to his chest. This was quickly remedied when, obeying Maliagne's signal, Rutholine pulled on a rope. Pulleys squeaked. The head jerked up. Stifling a cry, Karliana recognised the contorted features of none other than Guardulian Skagali. His body moved grotesquely, yanked this way and that by the cruel ropes. Maliagne Aranti folded his arms in smug satisfaction. 'You see, my dear. All of my enemies learn to dance to my tune, one way or another.' He sniggered. 'But wait! This one speaks as well. Speak, puppet!'

It was hard to tell whether it was fear or the ropes making the old nobleman jump about. 'Traitor,' he rasped. The ropes jigged more urgently, tugging at frail knees and elbows. Lord Skagali cried out, more loudly this time. 'I am a traitor!' His face was gaunt, his jaw set square with pain. His skin was so unhealthy a colour that he might well have been wrought from paper and glue. Karliana suppressed a whimper. Nobody would have described Guardulian as a pleasant man — she herself had thought him a lecherous old fool — but he did not deserve this. Karliana clenched her teeth, fighting back tears. 'You are a monster!'

Maliagne made a neat little bow. 'Ah, but I mustn't claim all the credit. The puppet gallery was Castronon's idea.' He nodded thoughtfully. '*He* is a monster, I grant you. But a terribly useful one.' He glanced sideways at Rutholine, as if expecting a reaction. It was futile. Rutholine seemed neither gratified nor insulted on his brother's behalf. He just stood there. Dumb and expressionless.

Karliana's eyes shot to the other two boxes. Maliagne would see how she clutched her hands to keep them from trembling. He had planned this, of course. He guessed at her hopes and revelled in her fears. When she lifted her chin in defiance, Maliagne smiled. 'Would you like to see the others?'

Karliana glowered at him, using her outrage to brace against tears. 'Of course you would. Let us walk on.'

Taking up his position at the next set of ropes, Rutholine's face was a mask. Perhaps his movements were too deliberate, his shoulders too tense. Karliana did not know the man well enough to tell. Certainly, he was avoiding looking in her direction. Just following orders, his body seemed to say.

The curtains drew back. The second box held a man, too, and the answer to a puzzling mystery. Now Karliana knew exactly where the High Protector had disappeared to — and that he most definitely had not sanctioned the guardians' new oath to serve the Mildari exclusively. Carlton Enegi could not speak. His mouth was gagged. His scowl was eloquence enough, underscored by the smothered but perfectly audible sounds of his anger. He was trussed tight. Rather than animating his body, the ropes seemed designed to stop the tenacious little man from escaping. His fluffy eyebrows, which Karliana had always thought quite comical, went up in startled recognition. There was nothing funny about the sight, nor his costume of feathers and frills.

Maliagne adopted an expression of pained regret, as if considering a poorly wrought artwork. 'I'm afraid our High Protector has yet to embrace his new role ... as you can see.'

Karliana was so affronted that such a well-respected man should be treated with such indignity that she could not hold her tongue. 'You have no right! This man — he is the Head of the Guardians! The Protector of the city itself!'

'Ah ... uh.' Aranti made a tutting noise and held up a hand. 'Karliana, dear Karliana, I think you will find I have every right. I am the High Protector now, as granted by the Senate when they accepted my rule as High Commander. To be Mildari in such ... uncertain ... times is to assume the high command, in its entirety.' His tongue came out to taste his lips, as if savouring the words.

Then he blinked rapidly. 'All of which renders this little man quite superfluous. I should have him put to death for insubordination of course. But I just can't bring myself to do it. Those eyebrows and that shining pate; it is altogether too amusing.' Aranti screwed his face into a wry expression.

From the murderous look on Carlton Enegi's face, Karliana had no doubt the man would die before naming himself traitor. The realisation sent a sharp chill of terror through her. What of her father? Would he capitulate to save his life?

'I think I'll keep him where he is for now. Wave goodbye, my little fellow.' Karliana looked away as Rutholine reached for a rope.

The final box smelled of fresh paint. Deep lavender, it was dressed with gold curtains and a purple ribbon, as if it contained some special gift. It would contain her father, of course. Torland Lendri — Maliagne Aranti's sworn rival. Who else could it be? Karliana desperately wanted to walk away, to refuse to look. Except she could not convince her feet to move.

She mustered the courage to speak. The words felt clumsy in her mouth. 'This is madness. Dangerous madness! You cannot dissolve the office of the High Protector. Calkinon will shake the foundations of our city. You will bring her armies upon us — and they will not be merciful.'

Aranti seemed to contemplate her words. 'Do you know?' He raised a finger as if considering her point. 'I would have thought so, too. Yet they insist on sending fresh ambassadors: I've barely killed off the last one before they send another.' Karliana's mouth fell open. He said it so casually!

'Mind you,' he continued, 'I did think Calkinon's interest would have been piqued long ago … when our elpha tribute failed to arrive.'

Karliana spluttered. Surely she had misheard the man? His smirk said otherwise. 'You withheld the elpha quota?' She was barely able to give voice to the words. The covenant of Mildaresh's annual tribute was ancient, and inviolable.

'Requisitioned, my dear. For purposes better suited to a city as proud as our own.'

'What have you done? You will shatter the peace.'

'Peace!' Maliagne scoffed, flicking out a hand. 'Such a word! The stealthiest of words. A word fit only to hide behind.'

Something dark slid behind his eyes. Too furtive to be seen properly, it was there then gone again. Karliana was reminded of a hawk blinking.

'Come, Karliana. Relinquish your fond notions about peace. You are too old for such childish dreams. Calkinon is stretched. If we were ever at peace, we are not now. The wizened empire clutches at her vassal provinces more tightly every year, squeezing every last drop to feed her futile campaigns. Ever does she lust for new territories. But our mistress is spread thin … like a whore's nightgown.' He chuckled. 'Her generals are divided, the jilted lovers of an aging harlot. War, my dear, is only a matter of time. I've simply, shall we say, taken the initiative.'

Karliana sputtered and fumed. 'You would crown yourself king!' She spat the word, as an insult.

Maliagne just smiled, infuriatingly calm. 'You misunderstand. I have no need for a crown.' His eyes glinted darkly. His voice was so soft he might have been murmuring to a sleepy child. 'I am more powerful than a king.' Karliana wanted to deny it. She could not; she knew it to be true. Maliagne put on a rueful pout. 'Oh, look at that sad face. I know, you grieve for your precious Senate. I'm afraid that, too, is an empty dream. You must let it go. The Senate is a mockery. It keeps us weak and makes puppets of us all.'

He arched his brows. 'Who do you think benefits from a system that keeps us arguing amongst ourselves? Debating sewers and water-pipes?' Since Karliana just scowled, he answered his own question. 'Calkinon of course. Our charmingly overextended empire, intent on making us puppets — on keeping us enslaved.' He paused, a smile quivering on his lips. He extended his hand. For a horrible moment Karliana thought he was about to touch her face. 'Well, I am no puppet. And you, Karliana, you are no slave. To my everlasting delight, you have proven yourself to have the heart of a queen.' His words, and the formal dip of his head, actually seemed sincere.

Karliana gulped, grasping after the meaning behind those black eyes. Then he waggled a finger at her, as if teasing a child. 'But come. Don't you want to see the last of my puppets?'

It took all of Karliana's courage to take those few steps towards the last box in Aranti's ghastly show. Maliagne was watching her even more closely now. His will was a dark thread, pulling her toward the curtain. Get it over with, she told herself. Bring an end to his horrible gloating. Ignoring the tears which tumbled unchecked down her cheeks, she stepped forward and swept the curtain aside.

Her body reacted to the shock before her mind could catch up. The sight was enough to make anyone stagger. A mighty sob erupted, wrenched from her very soul. Relief! Such relief. And such horror!

Belle's face stared back at her, framed by those gorgeous chestnut curls. She was beautiful, even in death. Karliana wrapped her arms around her chest, closing her eyes against the sensation that the room was spinning.

'One of my own herati,' mused Aranti, 'daring to poison the Mildari. Now that, that is the work of a traitor, wouldn't you agree?' Karliana could not stop her jaw from jittering. 'Oh yes. An assassination plan is more than sufficient to earn a place in my gallery. Clever girl. She saved some poison for herself, and when the phial was discovered took her own life. A shame. I would have liked to have her dance for me, one last time.'

Maliagne jiggled a rope, then heaved a sigh. 'It's just not the same.' His expression slid from feigned sorrow to indifference. 'She cannot stay here long of course. The stench will grow too great. Sadly, that pretty head must join the others on Traitors' Row.' He turned his dark gaze on Karliana once more. 'As a warning to anyone who dares lift a hand against the Mildari.'

He closed the curtains with a sunny smile. 'Ah well, her departure will leave a vacancy in my gallery. Do you know, Karliana, that poison was wonderfully swift? Capricia collapsed, just like that!' He snapped his fingers in her face. Karliana gasped as his dark smile turned suspicion to conviction: Maliagne Aranti had murdered his wife.

❧

Karliana was not sure how long they stayed in that high gallery. She remembered clinging onto the balustrade, staring at her knuckles while Aranti raved on. The slaves bustled silently below, clearing plates and refreshing tables. Karliana saw none of it. Aranti's words became an incoherent jabbering in her ears. No doubt he was making further justifications of his tyranny. He need not have bothered. All of Karliana's attention was pinned to a single purpose — trying not to faint.

At last, the whispers of quiet preparations gave way to murmurs, then the rising hum of excited conversation. The guests were returning to their seats, preening and posturing, oblivious to the horrors above their heads. By some miracle, Karliana's body acted of its own accord, transporting her back downstairs without incident. Rutholine must have shared her belief that she might fall. He kept very close to her side until they were safely on the bottom step.

As they re-entered the feast hall, Aranti piped up again. 'Did you notice my fool, I wonder?' With a weary sigh Karliana turned her head in the direction he was indicating. Yes, she had marked the figure earlier. Dressed in black and white silk, tucked almost in a corner, he sat on his own little dais. 'Come a little closer.' Karliana had no desire to comply, yet she could hardly refuse, especially with so many of the guests now looking in their direction.

As they approached, the figure struggled to his feet. She saw then that his face was painted white. A hat with many points and tiny bells was screwed down over his brow. 'Since he made a fool of me,' Aranti was saying, 'it only seemed fair to return the favour.' The fool's mouth was painted in a wide exaggerated smile — completely at odds with the terrible sadness in his eyes. He inclined his head in such a familiar manner …

Karliana held a hand to her swelling heart. Tears sprang in her eyes. In that moment, nothing else mattered. Her father was alive! She did not care that Aranti had made him the object of ridicule. His sneers and jibes mattered not. 'He's a terrible juggler. I've been telling him to practise more.' All that mattered was that Torland Lendri was alive and gazing into her face. 'He mostly sits about looking sad. Still, he does seem to have perked up a little now. Let's hope that he stays that way.'

Her father gave a tiny shake of his head, sending an all-too-obvious warning. Karliana sobbed and smiled. He was alive! And if she had to play Maliagne's games to keep him safe from harm, then so be it. She gave the fool who was not a fool a deep curtsy.

As she walked away, Karliana marvelled that nobody else had recognised the fool. Perhaps it was not so surprising. Torland Lendri was much thinner, and with that costume and all that make-up it would be hard to be certain, even for those who knew his features as well as his daughter. For now, Aranti was certainly enjoying his little secret. Karliana cared little.

She resumed her seat with her chin high. She could bear a betrothal to Tindelfion. If she had read Maliagne's hints correctly, then that was the price, and if that was what it took, then so be it.

'Thank you,' she murmured. Aranti gave her an enigmatic smile.

The guests were already gorging themselves on tiny cakes, sumptuous cheeses and confections encrusted with sugar. Many were red-faced and laughing rather too loudly. When Maliagne Aranti rose to his feet there was a hearty cheer. In fact, it took quite some time for the enthusiasm to settle down. He spoke very briefly about his 'dear Capricia'. How she would have enjoyed the feast — especially those little cheeses that were her favourites.

He moved on quickly to say that he had a happy announcement, one that would turn sadness to great joy. Karliana's skin prickled. She flushed with a cold sweat. Surely not tonight? But Aranti was continuing. She could feel his gaze on the top of her head. It made her scalp crawl. Every platitude tightened the band around her heart. *Life should be lived to the full. Enjoyment should be seized while one was young.* Then came those awful words.

'I feel certain that my dear Capricia would forgive me for sharing my joy with you tonight. Please celebrate with me now. Raise your glasses and your voices. For tonight I am happy to announce a betrothal!' More cheers. People had caught on. Some even banged the tables. 'There has been much speculation as to the man who would capture the heart of this beauty beside me.' Laughter and excitement ensued. People leaned forward in their chairs. The reason for Lady Lendri's seat at the high table had become abundantly clear.

Karliana stiffened. When Maliagne held out his hand she gritted her teeth. She willed herself to stand. Placing her hand in his sent a shudder of ice down her spine. Her stomach recoiled. 'It gives me great joy to announce that the House of Aranti has been most honoured. Karliana Lendri has, this very night, agreed — to be my wife.'

With applause crashing around her and cheers hurting her ears, Karliana hid her shock by fixing a smile to her face. The performance she gave in that moment was surely her best ever. She knew her father's face had turned white beneath that ridiculous make-up. But he was alive. For that reason she smiled. Yes, she would smile and nod, and bear it all.

Her free hand stroked the pendant at her throat. The game was not over yet. And it was her move next.

Chapter 28

THE INQUISIUM

The knock on Ash's door was strangely regular. Three raps, followed by two, then one. It could only be one person. Groaning, he eased the door open and blinked at Ordelle.

'You're all creased.'

It was probably true. He'd just woken up, after all. 'What is it?'

Her eyes bulged in a stare. 'It is the third night.'

Ash scratched his head. Really? Did Ordelle think they were still going to meet? Without Sarin? Without Kep? His heart sank another notch. He just could not believe that Kep had gone. Sarin had seemed so convinced that her name would not be drawn. And now Ash was alone. Left behind. To worry about the pair of them.

'You should come now.' Her foot was tapping. A repeated rhythm: three taps, then two, then one. Ash shrank behind the door. Why couldn't she leave him to his misery? The last thing he needed was an evening with Ordelle and her strange routines. He was grasping for an excuse, when she added in that flat voice. 'Aechon wishes to speak with you.'

'Right.' Ash scrubbed his head with his knuckles. 'Give me one moment.' If anyone could dissuade Ordelle from insisting on three-nightly meetings, it was Aechon. Finding his shoes, he pulled them on, before trailing after Ordelle, with Tarlyn at his heels.

A short walk brought them to one of the workshop complexes. Following Ordelle down a hallway, Ash rehearsed in his head what he would say. By the time they stopped at the brightest red door imaginable, he felt more prepared. But nothing could prepare him for the world beyond that door.

If ever a room reflected its occupants, this was it. There were books, lots of books, and several fat armchairs in which to read them. Plants set on either side of the fireplace were competing to invade the room. Their broadleaved vines scrambled up the walls and across the mantle, caressing the candlesticks with their tendrils. Red flowers stared like faces, poking out their yellow tongues.

Aechon had his own province. He sat cross-legged on the floor, plucking at a fat-bellied lute, a pen between his teeth and squinting at a sheet on a carved music stand. Papers, some scrunched into balls, surrounded him like a nest. A couple of instruments hung on a rack, although most had found alternative homes around the room. Ash recognised lutes and harps, and an enormous horn. A stuffed owl stared from the corner, vastly annoyed at having to share its territory with several wooden puzzles, a broken puppet and a half-dismantled clock.

In stark contrast, the rest of the room was neat and orderly. At one end of a long wooden bench something bubbled in a flask, over a gentle flame. At the other was Gallin. He was tinkering with a complicated-looking machine. His only greeting was a slightly raised eyebrow and a curl of his lip. Aechon, however, gave a cry of delight, pushing his lute to one side. When the Cryer hopped up, Ash saw that he was wearing a pair of long, bright pink socks. Ash gave him a grin. It was shortlived, dying on the spot when Ordelle made an announcement.

'Aechon says we should meet here now. He does not want me to get pregnant.'

'Wha—? What?' Ash spluttered, wanting to back out of the door.

'Ah…' Aechon seemed equally caught by surprise. He scratched his head. 'Oh. Um … I didn't exactly …'

Gallin looked up, hiding his amusement extremely well. 'Welcome, Ash,' he said smoothly in his deep, resonant voice. 'Welcome … to the Inquisium.' The man's mouth twitched slightly.

Taking pity on the bright pink and highly flustered visitor, he gestured towards the hearth. 'Take off your coat. And sit by the fire. Ordelle, for Telion's sake get Ash some mulled cider. You never know, it may calm his nerves.' Gallin's expression suggested that he doubted that very much.

And that was how it began: with Ash clutching a pottery goblet, sipping mulled cider spiced with cinnamon and cloves, stealing glances at the strange marvels in the room and trying to comprehend Aechon's enthusiastic explanation of his latest composition. To his great relief, he was completely ignored by Ordelle, and nobody ever mentioned her previous assertion again. True, Gallin was still smiling to himself, but the man seemed to do that a lot.

It was remarkable how quickly Ash adapted to the nightly routines of the Cryer's quirky little family. His days were so dreary now, filled with loneliness and anxiety. The Inquisium, with all its eccentricities, became a haven. Most nights Aechon played for them, or tinkered with an instrument. He delighted in taking things apart to discover the inner workings. You could never really understand a thing until you understood its parts, he claimed. Ash was pretty sure it was Gallin who eventually collected the scattered parts and pieced them back together again.

The dark-browed man spent all his time hunched over something at his bench, like a great brooding crow. He was a silent presence on the whole, but always listening, dropping in an occasional quip when it amused him. While Ash often failed to understand his deadpan remarks, Aechon clearly thought the man very droll indeed. He would laugh uproariously, continuing to chuckle for a long time afterwards. The more time Ash spent with the pair, the more they seemed like two parts of an intriguing whole.

As for Ordelle. She was just … Ordelle. Mostly she was absorbed in her studies, her fringe swinging above a book. Every now and then she would sit up unexpectedly, interjecting with some snippet of information or a flatly worded observation. After a while Ash got used to it and smiled with the others.

One evening, lulled by the mellow warmth of the Inquisium, Ash told Aechon about the missing verses of 'The Lay of Eregil and Mendolas'. 'They die,' he explained. 'The heroes. Eregil falls first, in battle. So Mendolas cuts a lock of his friend's bright hair and weaves it with his own. He wears the charm into battle, hoping the magic will endure. But when the bracelet snaps, he is overcome.' Ash's voice caught. 'They die. That's the whole point. They don't prevail. There is no glory. They all die.' Seeing the shock on Aechon's face, Ash almost regretted his decision to share the true end of the story.

But Aechon was nodding. 'Ah, that makes sense. The lyric never quite sat well with me. There is a vein of melancholy towards the end. I've always wondered at that.' He gave a wry smile. 'This is often the case. Songs change with the times, and "The Lay of Eregil and Mendolas" is ancient — the oldest that I sing. It does not surprise me that whole verses have been lost.' He sighed. 'Telion guides our songs, but it is human to wish for joy and to bury pain. We tell the stories we think others wish to hear … and those we yearn to believe.'

After a silence he cleared his throat. 'I don't suppose … ?'

It was impossible to resist the plea in the little man's eyes. So, in a hesitant voice accompanied by the jangling beauty of the jet-black harp, Ash sang. He kept his eyes on his feet the entire time.

When he did lift his head, after the last note had fallen, he saw that Aechon's head was bowed over the ancient instrument, his hands still upon the strings. Gallin was motionless at his bench. It seemed they would sit there forever, while the fire crackled on. It was Ordelle, of all people, who broke the spell.

'It is a better song,' she declared with a nod.

Aechon laughed through his tears. 'Yes. It is a better song.'

⁂

After that night, Aechon became even more enthusiastic about teaching Ash to play an instrument. Since many of the Zari who left their secluded communities were minstrels, Sarin had designed a guild band to hide Ash's slave marks. Now Ash regretted going along with the idea. How could he pose as a musician's apprentice when he had so little talent? His fingers were clumsy on the strings of the lute, and he did not seem to be improving for all that he practised. If he was honest, he knew what the problem was: he was afraid. Afraid of losing himself in the music.

One evening Ash was listening to Aechon play, foolishly wishing that he could absorb the skills just by watching the Cryer's fingers. Unaware that he had drawn the Taelstone from his pocket, he began turning the orb between his fingers. All at once he found himself in a red carpeted hallway.

⁂

'Credé, stop! Listen to reason!'

Credé spun, awaiting his pursuer. The corridor was soft with tapestries and tasselled carpets. Crystal lamps hung at intervals, sending showers of dancing light onto the ceiling. Set on tall stands of twisted glass, vases of flowers seemed to hover in mid-air.

Ash noted that Leynore was older now. Her face was sharper and her bright golden hair was swept into an elegant fold at the back of her head. It made her pale neck look even longer. Over a blue gown, she wore a dove-grey cloak overlaid in silver thread. It was pinned at her throat with a long silver clasp. The blue sash of the Azuran Council crossed her breast. She was breathless from the chase.

Credé stood his ground, rigid, hands balled into fists at his sides. His chest heaved, too.

They stood there, eyes locked. Adversaries.

After a long moment, Leynore advanced. Just one step. 'Credé.' Her palms fell open, imploring. 'You and Artus have made your arguments, and the Council has been more than patient. Now you must abide by the wisdom of our decision. Both of you.' Her brow tightened. 'Where is Artus?'

Credé let out a huff of air. His hands twitched at his sides. 'Patient?' His mouth stretched into a sneer. 'Oh yes, the Council has been patient. Eternally, paternally, patient.' He lifted his hands. 'And so very benevolent —after their own patronising manner. Patiently thwarting every worthwhile endeavour, stifling any invention that promises progress, anything that would better the lives of the people outside of this!' He pivoted, sweeping his arms around. 'Their perfectly precious cage.'

Leynore's chin jutted, her eyes flashed. 'Credé, you are angry. I understand. But the decision cannot be faulted. It is entirely consistent with the Azuran code. You must see that.'

Ash felt Credé's fury as a rush of fire. It burned so intensely that he nearly broke free of the memory. Credé's jaw worked as he struggled to speak. His heart hammered at the betrayal. 'Leynore, you voted with Oden! You stood with your father!'

'Yes!' Spots of colour grew on Leynore's cheeks. 'Yes, Credé! I stand with Oden. Not because he is my father, but because he is right. Your inventions are too dangerous. Yes, they are marvellous, wonderful things. But we cannot risk the impact on this world were they to leave the confines of the city.'

'Pah! Listen to yourself! Parroting the fears of the Council. You would take us back to the age of isolation!'

'Yes, yes I would.' Although Leynore's eyes flashed, her words were steady. 'Rather that than unleash the uncertainty, the power shifts that such inventions would bring. We must live by the code, Credé. It was created to protect the peoples of this world. For thousands of years we have brokered peace. We cannot risk that now.'

'Leynore, Leynore.' Credé turned her name into a sneer. 'The Council has surely worked its tricks on you. How you have changed. Playing with the toys of your new-found authority.' He was choosing words carefully, seeking to wound. 'Leynore … the daughter of doctrine and duty. I barely recognise you. Where is the girl who took joy in miracles? Who embraced the adventure of discovery?'

His laughter was a bitter, scathing weapon.

'The woman I see before me is a mere husk. A cold, sterile husk.' It was a heartless barb, cruel beyond measure. Credé cared not — not even when her lips trembled, revealing that his aim was true.

But Leynore was made of sterner stuff. Her eyes hardened to steel. She asked again, very slowly this time: 'Credé, where is Artus?'

Ash shivered at the malice in Credé's laugh. The Malshorne dragged his lips into a triumphant smirk. 'Ah! And there it is.' He stabbed a finger. 'There the question comes again … The real reason for this unseemly pursuit. It is too late, my dear. Artus is gone. He has chosen exile over life in a cage.'

At his words Leynore's eyes flew open. Picking up her skirts, she turned on her heel and strode away from him. His anger building into a furnace of fury, Credé watched until her fluttering form had disappeared. His hands had become shaking claws of rage. His jaw was clenched so tightly it threatened to shatter. With a terrible roar, he unleashed his wrath and smashed everything within reach.

Ash pulled free from the stone with a mighty gasp. The orb tumbled to the floor, bouncing under Aechon's stool. Ordelle, Gallin and Aechon all gaped at him. Aechon's fingers were frozen on his lute. He frowned at the Taelstone, seeming about to reach down to pick it up. Uncertain if the Cryer knew about bonded stones, Ash leapt from his chair, scooping it up before the man could touch it. With a mixture of concern and curiosity, Aechon watched Ash return the stone to his pocket. He covered both with a chuckle. 'Let me guess. If that gasp is anything to go by, I'd say … swimming lessons?'

Ordelle lowered her book, suddenly engaged. 'Did you drown?'

Ash gulped. Did she always have to be so morbid? 'No, it was nothing like that.' But it was exactly like that — escaping Credé's memories always felt like coming up for air.

Aechon returned his lute to its stand, lovingly, as if placing a child in a cradle, and smiled. 'I've played enough for one night. I wonder if you might indulge me in a game of cards?'

Although it was late, Ash accepted gladly. His blood was still pulsing with Credé's rage. He could not bear to go back to his empty room. Sadly, the distraction did not work, and he played even more poorly than usual. He could not block out the question that burned in his mind. *What had Credé done?*

Chapter 29

SORE HEADS

Kep woke to a blurred world. She frowned. What was wrong with her eyes? Squeezing them shut, she eased them open again. The same blank stone confronted her. Still slightly blurry. Her tongue was dry in her mouth. Wrinkling her nose at the smell of rotting leaves, she pulled herself upright. The bedding roll on which she had been lying stank of mould. She had never seen it before. Nor the leather band encircling her wrist. It was locked; not cruelly tight, but tight enough, and impossible to slip her hand through. Fastened to the band was a long chain. It ran to an iron ring, high on the wall.

Her heart racing, she gave the chain a tug. It jingled. There seemed no chance of escape. Yet her captors, whoever they were, had been oddly considerate of her comfort. A wooden bowl was set beside her, with a few pieces of bread, already broken into pieces. She eyed the water pouch for a long time before thirst won out over her fear of poison. She took small sips, trying to stay calm. The pouch was only half-full, so she drank little — just enough to wet her mouth — before turning her attention to her prison.

The stone room was huge, but in ruins. Roots and trees grew from the crumbling walls. The flagged floor was covered in mosses and scattered debris — green tiles, broken chunks of cornices and carved pediments. The nook where Kep was kneeling was sheltered by the scant remains of a roof. It seemed ready to tumble in, too. A pair of swallows had nested in the highest corner. Dragging herself to her knees, Kep yelled as loudly as she could. 'Hey! Hello? Hey! Is anybody here?'

No human response. But when she hollered again, a horse whickered. Berry! She was almost sure of it. The chestnut mare, that had been her mount since their party had left the trading town of Farndale, was somewhere nearby. Kep did not shout anymore — her throat was dry, and shouting hurt. Instead, she squatted, her back against the cold stone wall, trying to think. Whatever, by Telion's grace, had happened?

After crossing the river and parting from Nirias and the others, their group of six had ridden for three days, along the flats, then into the forests of the Kenting district. It had been pleasant-going. But riding all day was hard work; when the scouts returned, everyone had been pleased to hear of a small township up ahead. Kep remembered how Jaibari had scoffed, saying they might as well push on. It was all a show, of course. Kep had seen how Jaibari shifted in her saddle. Her back and legs were just as stiff as anyone's.

The scouts, Polkin and Ozu, had brought a stranger back, whom they had met on the road. He hailed from Bixdale, one village short of Ferridale where they were heading. A cheery sort of chap, with a balding head and a long apron, he had certainly not seemed dangerous. Ran the finest establishment in the Kenting, he said. Kep remembered promises of a bright fire and roast meats, and even stories from a travelling minstrel if that took their fancy — all of which had sounded perfectly wonderful. Even Rodine Gametale had cracked a smile.

So the innkeeper had become their guide. There was only one safe track, he had told them. The hills in the Kenting were made of limestone, and hidden pits could swallow rider and horse. There were wonderful caves if the visitors had time and the inclination to visit, but it was dangerous to stray from the path.

Kep frowned more deeply, working her thumbs in circles at her temples. It must have been a trap. But why was she alone now? Where were the others? She forced herself to recall every detail. The stranger had seemed desperate to please. Perhaps more eager than an innkeeper simply seeking custom? And why had he been wearing his apron in the forest? Was that a clue? Had they been set upon? It was just so frustrating not being able to remember. Kep had no memory of any commotion. She brushed absently at her sleeve. It was dusted with fine yellow pollen. No. There had not been a fight, she was sure of it. Her last memory had been peaceful: trotting in single file through the trees. And the heady scent of honeysuckle.

None the wiser, and her legs getting numb, she hauled herself to her feet. Her captor had left the chain long, giving her freedom to walk about. Another consideration.

On shaky legs, Kep walked as far as the chain would allow, working her way around a broken wall and partway into an adjacent room. Once it must have been a grand entryway; now the space was mostly open to the weather. The view through the doorway revealed nothing. Just treetops and stone steps leading down and away.

Kep stumbled back, over piles of stone, then stood eyeing the broken wall. True, it would be dangerous, but if she climbed to the top she might be able to see out through one of two high apertures. Tall and arched, they must have been very impressive in their day.

Kep was already halfway up the wall when she realised the stonework was far from stable. The mortar had crumbled, loosening the blocks. She inched her way up, feet scrabbling, her cheek pressed against the stone, praying it was not about to collapse. As she hauled herself over the top, she sent a couple of chunks crashing down. Her heart racing with fear and exertion, she swivelled on her stomach and managed to sit up, legs straddling the wall. Pointless. There was nothing to see. Just treetops, tossing in the wind. She could be anywhere.

Kep gave a deep sigh. She was wondering how she would get down again, when she heard a sound. A horse whickering. It was Berry, she was sure of it. This time the horse's gentle neigh was answered by another. Kep froze, eyes wide. A rider was approaching!

A frantic investigation revealed a loose piece of stone. She broke a nail wiggling it free. Then, shaking out the chain and clutching the chunk of stone in her free hand, she waited. Jen-Jay's voice spoke in her head. *Breathe. Find your poise.* Hooves stamped. Footsteps announced the person's arrival. Heavy boots scraped stone as someone climbed towards the entrance. *Breathe.*

The man who entered wore a filthy wide-brimmed hat. That was all Kep could see — all she had time to take in. Heart in mouth, she dropped from her perch, knocking him flat. When the man's body broke her fall, she grunted, feet scrabbling and struggling against the drag of the chain. Unable to find her feet, she lashed out. Surprise was her best weapon. The rock struck hard, connecting with her captor's face. He cried out. Putting up his arms to shield his head, he gave a strangled, incoherent shout. Kep pulled back her arm to hit him again. Then, the rock suspended in mid-air, she saw something that made her freeze. On his face were three dark stars.

※

Kep rinsed the cloth, wrung it out and passed it to the man who sat opposite. The side of his face was swollen now. She was not about to apologise. If anything, he owed *her* an apology. And an explanation.

'I can't believe you were tracking us all that time! I suppose it was Nirias's idea.' She sniffed and glared. 'I don't need protecting!'

Skarlon winced, dabbing the cloth at his face. He growled. 'Reckon I'm the one who needs protecting — from you.' If his lip had not been split, Skarlon might have smiled. Kep doubted it; he did not seem the type of man who smiled often. He paused to wiggle at a tooth and spat blood. His level gaze met hers. 'Good thing I did come along.'

Kep scowled. It was true, but it did not stop her fuming. Apparently Skarlon had been tracking them ever since Lowford, where, crossing the river, they had parted company with Nirias and the others. He was good at his craft, Kep had to admit. Unless of course the scouts had known he was there, too. She scowled. Imagine tying her up like that!

It had been a jellin dust bomb, according to Skarlon. Hanging in the canopy and released by tripwire. The debilitating gas accounted for the strong floral smell Kep remembered, and for the yellow dust on her clothes — not pollen after all, but jellin. An unusual mineral, it was stable until mixed with a catalyst — then it exploded. The whole party had been struck down in seconds, toppled from their horses into the brushwood, even the innkeeper.

Happening upon the scene a short while later, Skarlon had bundled Kep onto his horse, spiriting her away, with Berry in tow. There had been no choice but to tie her up, he claimed, to keep her safe while he scouted things out. The party had been taken — where, he did not know.

Kep ground her teeth. What if Skarlon had not returned? She would have been left here, starving, with no water and chained to a wall with absolutely no idea why. She sniffed and folded her arms. She did not need a guardian! But there was no point dwelling on it. The man was right: if he had not been following, she would have been captured, too.

She took a sip of water and studied him. He was not a large man, but wiry. And tough, like the hardened leather of his clothes. He was strong enough to overpower her, that was certain. She could tell he was stubborn, too, no doubt set on his own ways.

But they needed to rescue the others. And no matter what ridiculous arguments Skarlon came up with, Kep was not about to be left behind.

Chapter 30

MARTA AND APPLE

Skarlon had insisted that they take no chances, so they had watched the little farmstead for a long time, waiting for the sun to disappear. A smallholding, well outside of the village, the place was well-kept. Fruit trees stood in orderly rows and the paddocks were ploughed, though not yet planted out. There were pens for animals — all curiously empty. Nobody came out to feed the chickens. There were none. There were no dogs either. The only movement had been that of a lone figure. An old man, by his hunched posture and slow movement, he had shuffled from the house to the barn, then back again, bearing a sack over his shoulder.

At last the light had faded, revealing two warm squares of candlelight, shining like eyes beneath the deep-browed veranda. They crept closer. Skarlon had his bow ready, an arrow already fitted. His eyes glinted over the top of his mask as he positioned himself against a tree trunk. He nodded. Leaving the safety of the trees, Kep glanced back just once; he was completely invisible in the gloom. She walked on alone, making her way down the path. Her own bow bumped against her back; she would much rather have been holding it in her hands, with an arrow fitted.

Kep crept past a scarecrow, onto a winding path lined with flowerpots, and with a banging heart reached the cottage. Stepping up onto the veranda, she called out the words they had rehearsed: 'Hello? Is anyone there? I'm lost. Can you help me?' Her ears picked up a scraping noise inside. It was followed by silence. Ignoring the lump in her throat, Kep called out again. 'Hello? Can you hear me?' She was almost certain that she heard footsteps then. Her heart thumped, drumming out a warning. The door did not open. The curtains twitched, though, just a fraction.

A man spoke, his words muffled by the door, or perhaps by fear. 'There are no travellers here. You must go. It is dangerous in this village. You must leave.'

Kep took another step, bringing her face into the light. 'I know it is dangerous. But I can't leave; my friends are in trouble. My name is Kep. I mean you no harm.'

More voices. At least two people, arguing in quiet tones. One was a woman. Kep wanted to put her ear against the door. But not as much as she wanted to run.

After a few more moments, Kep's heart jumped and began to patter even faster: the door was opening! Just a crack at first, then wider. The woman who peered out had grey hair, curling in wisps at the sides of her face. Her eyes were sunken and tired, but full of curiosity.

'No harm? Well dear, that *will* make a nice change.'

❧

One of those tireless little women, Marta Appleton looked utterly exhausted. Like her husband, she was achingly thin, with bony wrists and skin stretched too tight over her face. She called her husband Apple. He reminded Kep of an apple, too — wrinkled, with ruddy sun-kissed skin, and eyes like brown pips. Kep had no sooner stepped inside than he lowered the chunk of wood he had been wielding, casting her an apologetic smile. His wife gave a stern nod, as if he should be ashamed of himself for having picked up the weapon in the first place. It was Marta who asked the questions, with bright, searching eyes, Marta who welcomed Skarlon in, and Marta who bade them sit and rest.

The room was tiny, furnished with simple chairs and a bowed table. The rustic dresser looked strangely bare, holding just a few pieces of pottery, some baskets and a cracked pitcher filled with wooden spoons. A curtain was partially drawn across an opening into the adjacent space, which served as a small larder and workroom. Kep caught glimpses of empty shelves and the chunky edge of a bench.

She was refusing the couple's offer to share a meal — from their appearance they had little enough to eat — when Skarlon interrupted her with a swift agreement. Her glare got no response. But when he drew a sizable chunk of cheese and some flatbread from his pack, Kep understood. The food was obviously a welcome supplement to the couple's thin soup. They ate with barely restrained eagerness. After a while they began to relate the awful tale of what had befallen the village of Bixdale.

Using the same dirty trick, a jellin bomb, a gang of ruffians had struck when Eldar was full. A wedding was underway, it being the first auspicious day of spring. The whole village had been celebrating in the village hall. One moment they had been dancing and making merry, the next they had awoken to a nightmare of pain. Anyone who showed the barest hint of resistance was carted off in a wagon.

When the gang knocked the blacksmith to the ground, his loyal dog ran out to protect him. The poor beast met a brutal end. It was the first lesson. The leader of the ruffians, a cruel fellow in a red hat, had laughed. Laughed uproariously. Then, he had ordered that every dog in the village be destroyed. Marta paused for a moment. As Kep's eyes went to the empty basket near the hearth, Marta's mouth trembled. It was a long moment before she was able to resume her story.

Any villager deemed strong enough had been shackled and led to the abandoned mine. An ancient source of jellin, the mine had almost been forgotten; the villagers had little use for jellin. Somehow, the gang of brutes had known of its whereabouts. The bridegroom, still in his best clothes, and half the village was up there now, trapped underground, toiling and crushing the yellow ore.

As for the young women and children, they had never left the wedding. They were there still, locked in the village hall and surviving on whatever scraps the other villagers were allowed to take them. Every now and then a few of the children would be let out for a while, to 'play' in the square, under the anguished eyes of their elders. It was a cruel reminder to those left free to serve the ruffians. A cruel reminder of what was at stake — as if anyone could forget.

'They made us stack wood around the hall, and tuck kindling drenched in fat into the gaps,' said Apple in a quiet voice. 'When that was done they set a guard. There are always two men, with torches at the ready. That is what they have over us. The terrible cost of rebellion.' He pointed a gnarly finger at Skarlon. 'And they will! They'll do it! They have no hearts. They will set fire to it! So don't you …' the old man's voice cracked and broke. His eyes spilled tears. 'Just don't you be making any trouble!'

'Now, Apple,' Marta's mouth trembled, too, but she spoke firmly. 'These folk are not about to do anything stupid. Anyone can see that they know what they are about.' Her sharp eyes had been summing up Skarlon. Now she gave Kep another appraising glance, her thoughtful eyes lingering on the tattoo that wound about the young woman's wrist.

'We promise, Apple. We'll be careful.' Kep's voice shook a bit as she replied. How could anyone do such a thing? To threaten good people like these? It was unthinkable. She caught Skarlon's eye. He gave her a warning look, accompanied by a slight shake of his head. She frowned. It had to be. It just had to be the Melk. It was too terrible to think that humans might act like this on their own.

As Marta took up the tale again in her quiet voice, they learned that the villagers had been reduced to slaves, obeying the ruffians' every whim. Good beasts had been slaughtered, even pregnant beasts. The red-hatted leader demanded that they call him 'Simbab' and bring him tribute, in a ceremony that he called the Gifting.

'Simbab?' Skarlon sat up in surprise. 'That is a pirate word. It means "Master," or "Leader".' He snatched at his chin. 'Or something along those lines.' Kep frowned. They were a long way inland for pirates.

Marta sniffed. 'Pirates. Yes, that is exactly how they behave.'

She explained that every evening the villagers had to line up, bringing what little they had left. And if the gifts weren't sufficient—

Marta stopped then. Her husband bowed his head. A long moment passed as she wrung her hands, jaw clenched. She never finished the thought. Now, there was little left to give. The winter stores were depleted and there was nobody to tend the fields.

Marta jerked her head at the workspace. Apple had slaughtered their last goose, just that afternoon. They planned to roast it in the morning, to present at tomorrow's Gifting. The goose was the only thing they had left, their last chance to avoid Red Hat's displeasure, and certain punishment. Kep shuddered as the couple exchanged frightened glances. It seemed the gang kept some of the gifts for themselves, but most were driven away in wagons, along with any passing travellers. Incapacitated, robbed, bound and carted off. That was how it went.

Kep swallowed, fighting down a hot rush of panic. She asked the question that had been sitting like a stone in her stomach. 'Do you know what happened to our friends?'

Apple gave a slow shake of his head. He answered gruffly, with downcast eyes. 'All taken, I heard.' He bit his lip, staring at his trembling hands. 'All save one. An old woman. Too scrawny to have any value to slavers. Too weak for the mines. She'll be in the hall.' His mouth fell open in surprise when Kep gave a shout. It sounded awfully loud in that small space — as did the joyous pealing of her laughter.

The old couple sat up, stunned, as if they had forgotten the sound of laughter. Skarlon raised his grizzly brows.

Kep laughed again. Suddenly it felt as if anything was possible.

'Jen-Jay is in the hall!'

Chapter 31

FIRE AND ROAST GOOSE

Kep was in position — if you called hiding in a bush being in position. She had wanted to go with Skarlon, to take on the two guards at the hall and release the captive villagers. However, the old warrior had insisted on her playing a safer role. Now, she could not help twitching with impatience. The bush grew in a thicket at the edge of the blacksmith's yard. It was suitably dense, but prickly. She sucked at a scratch on her arm. The discomfort was worth it, though. She had an excellent view across the village square, straight towards the inn where the gang was holed up.

The Plough Inn was a cheery-looking establishment with a bright red door, thatched roof and window-boxes full of flowers. A squat chimney puffed smoke up into the late afternoon sky. Inside, the Gifting was already underway. The villagers had formed up in a despondent queue outside. They shuffled forward in silence, awaiting an audience with Red Hat, the leader of the gang. Some held baskets or pottery jugs, one had a scrawny chicken under his arm.

Kep watched as Marta approached, wearing her battered hat and walking slowly with her burden. The old woman had barely joined the end of the line when one of the men, no doubt catching the delicious aroma of roast goose, hustled her inside. Kep bit her lip. So far, so good. She trained her eyes on the line of villagers. Watching — poised for action. Nothing happened. She stretched her neck a little, one way then the other, but not once did she take her tired eyes from The Plough's entrance. It would be any moment now.

They had spent half the night preparing, forming plans and discarding them. At last Skarlon and Apple had gone out into the darkness, leaving Kep to try, unsuccessfully, to catch some sleep. The pair had returned just before dawn, grey-faced and filthy, but bearing the prize.

It had taken the rest of the day to prepare the feast. Kep smiled to herself. The goose was golden brown and cooked to absolute perfection, complete with a very special stuffing: a crust of sage and onion for show — but otherwise packed with jellin powder. Deep inside was the hidden pouch, which, once pierced, would create a stupefying gas, giving the thugs a taste of their own medicine. The red-hatted bully was bound to make Marta carve; apparently he liked nothing better than forcing the starving villagers to serve him. And Marta would obey, biding her time until the right moment to plunge the knife into the bird.

Kep's hand went up to the rope, which was coiled in readiness over her shoulder. Her job was to watch and wait. When the gas had dissipated, she would enter the inn to bind the incapacitated men. She sucked in deep breaths of air, blinking weariness from her eyes. Her head felt so heavy, it would be easy to nod off.

When a bug crawled inside her collar, Kep flicked it away. It had been an awfully long time since Marta had entered the inn. Yet the villagers were still coming and going, shoulders slumped, heads hung low in defeat. Surely by now? Doubt crept into her heart. Then a figure appeared in the doorway. It was Marta! The old woman staggered at the threshold, putting her hand to the frame. Looking straight to where Kep was hiding, she shook her head.

The plan had failed. But that was the least of Kep's concerns. The fellow who had been slouched against the wall drew himself up. Kep's heart raced. 'Oi! What are you doing there?' Arms folded, he stared directly in Kep's direction. Marta sank at his feet, bringing her hands into the shape of a triangle. 'Stop your grovelling, woman! Get along!'

To Kep's horror he started across the square in a swaggering saunter. As he approached, Kep could see his suspicious eyes darting. He was a most alarming person. A glorious tangle of black hair, hanging in tight ringlets to his shoulders, was matched by a huge black moustache. A gold hoop hung from one ear. An assortment of teeth, medallions and trinkets were strung about his neck on leather cords. His waistcoat and leggings were black, his shirt, blood red. A long sword was tethered at one hip, a curved knife at the other. All of a sudden, the thicket in which Kep was hiding did not seem anywhere near dense enough.

The man stopped just a short distance away, scowling, his eyes scouring the ramshackle stables, the smithy and the paddocks. The wind brought the sharp stink of him straight to her nostrils. After a while he grunted, and his scowl relaxed. To Kep's disgust, instead of turning away he fumbled at his trousers. When he began to pass water she turned her face away, trying not to breathe. Thorns found her face, but she grimaced and held still. The brute obviously had no idea she was there. When he began to whistle a tune, Kep sensed that he had tucked himself in and was starting to move away. Then his whistling faded. Something about his stance made Kep freeze, too. The sight of a second thug approaching made her want to shrink even further into the bush.

This man was short and thickset. His bald head was etched with green ink, in crude patched designs. A wicked grin split his broad face, revealing teeth that flashed with gold. Like the other, he wore a bright shirt. Mustard yellow, it billowed over his belly, caught in by a wide belt over short buttoned breeches. Kep was not sure why, but this man was much more terrifying. Perhaps it was the expression in those cold piggy eyes.

'Hey, Curly! How about that! A whole roasted goose. Stupid old crone. You should have seen her pawing at Grady's feet. Bag of old bones. I'd have given her more than one kick.' The man guffawed, a dry sound bereft of humour. 'Pathetic!'

'Yeah. These people are peaches, ripe for plucking.' The man called Curly laughed, too.

The newcomer made an obscene gesture, thrusting out his groin. 'Yeah, ripe for plucking!' His exaggerated wink made his face even uglier. 'Grady reckons they're pretty squeezed-out now. Time to move on. But first we feast! Roast goose! And then ...' He paused, running his tongue over his lips. 'Grady says we'll have ourselves a nice fire to celebrate the occasion.' He inclined his chin towards the hall.

The first man tugged at his ear. 'He means to fire it, then?'

'Sure he does! Punishment for the old lady. A lesson, Grady says, for keeping that fat goose to herself all this time.' He cackled, rubbing his hands together as if warming them at an imaginary flame. 'There will be more than goose roasting tonight! I'm heading up there now. Just to check out the womenfolk. You're to get Ratskin and Spike. Grady's orders are to seal the mine.'

'With the villagers inside?' The man with curly hair seemed to lean forward on his toes a little.

'Of course. Nice and easy; no loose ends. That's Grady's motto.' He leered at his companion. 'Sure, we'll have ourselves some proper fun now! What type of woman do you like, Curly? Redheads? I bet you like redheads. How 'bout a nice chubby redhead with lots of curves?'

Curly seemed to shake himself. Hooting, he gave his companion a whack across his shoulders. 'Just make mine a pretty one, Greigo! In fact, bring me two or three. All light on their feet. I've a mind for dancing.' Spreading his arms wide, he took a couple of steps, making his sword swing against his thigh.

'Dancing?' A string of obscenities followed, intermixed with laughter. Kep was glad when the bald man moved off, taking his coarse jokes with him.

The man called Curly did not seem in any hurry to carry out his orders, though. He stood there for a long while, watching as the other man strolled away toward the hall. Tugging at his moustaches, he seemed suddenly fascinated by his boot laces. Kep thought he was muttering to himself, though she could not make out any words. He shot several glances at the inn. Then he crouched into a squat. His fist shook and he cast something onto the dirt. Two black stones by the look of it. He stared, then brought up his hand to smack his forehead. Rising, he shoved the stones in his pocket and stalked away.

Kep let out a slow, controlled breath. Her stomach churning, she was on the verge of being sick.

Curly, if that really was his name, had veered away, heading to the right of the hall and towards the sawyer's yards. She knew the path to the mine started there, behind the yards. Apple had said the entrance to the old mine was not far, through patchy, forested hills. It would take the lout no time to get there and deliver his awful message. How long would it take for the gang to seal the mine? With hot goose at stake they were not likely to dawdle.

Kep put her aching head in her hands. It was beyond belief. The plan to bury innocent villagers alive was not even the worse part. They actually planned to set fire to the hall! Her immediate instinct was to head straight there. Skarlon would be completely outnumbered. She doubted he could take on the wicked-looking bald man as well as the two others on guard. And what of the men still inside the inn? Not to mention their leader!

The thought of his terrible orders caused a deep rage to well up inside her. She could barely think straight. She wished Sarin was there, or even Ash. Sarin would do something clever. She bit her lip. *Sarin is not here*, she told herself. *You are. And you have to do something — fast.*

Kep wormed backwards out of the thicket, emerging into a clump of rough grasses. She popped her head up. On this side of the town the buildings were arranged in a friendly muddle, along the curved bank of a chattering brook. Running along the edge, where little jetties jostled with slime-covered rocks, was a thin, muddied path.

Kep ran in a low crouch, keeping to the cover of reeds where possible. When she reached the churning wheel of the mill house she halted. After a moment's panic, she opened a side door and crept inside. The place was noisy with creaking wood and rushing water, but empty. It had been ransacked; its floors swept clean of grain, probably by scavenging villagers. Kep raced through and out the door on the opposite side. Vaulting one wall, clambering over another, she found herself in a yard full of broken carts. There, surrounded by half-wrought wheels, with her back to a ramshackle fence, she caught her breath.

A gap in the timbers gave Kep a narrow view into the neighbouring yard, enough to see stacked barrels and brick outbuildings. The stink of malt gave the place away. It was the yard of the Plough Inn. As Kep watched, the frantic notes of a fiddler came to her ears intermixed with somebody weeping. A wild scream rose, only to be drowned out by raucous laughter.

Kep pressed a hand to her forehead, trying to control the flush of panic that swept her body. If Apple was right, there were eleven members in the gang altogether, with two guarding the hall and three up at the mine. After accounting for the two that Kep had just encountered, that meant there were still four pirates inside the inn — including their remorseless leader. Somehow, Kep had to reduce the odds, or at least keep the men busy until Skarlon could come to her aid. By now he would have guessed that their plan had failed, since nobody had rung the village bell to signal that the men were unconscious and safely tied up.

Kep gave a small shake of her head, wondering if she should try creeping into the inn through the back door. Her only hope was to trigger that jellin bomb — she could hardly fight four heavily armed pirates. But where was the goose? And where were the pirates?

Kep came to a decision and set her jaw. She had wasted enough time worrying — she needed to find out what was happening inside the inn. Adjusting her bow over her shoulder, she ran along beside the fence. Then, blessing the cooper for his untidy habits, she clambered onto the remains of a wagon. It had been left to rot against the rickety lean-to at the back of his cottage. With the help of a plank, it was easy enough to scramble onto the roof. The cottage was a shaky, unstable sort of building with crooked, mismatched tiles. Kep grinned. It was just like being back in Mildaresh. Quick and sure-footed, she crept up and over the ridge, tucking herself behind the fat chimney.

There were two large windows on this side of the inn, their red shutters thrown open to admit the fresh breezes. Kep could still hear music, faint and manic, coming from somewhere at the front of the building. She could not see the fiddler. The only person she could see was the innkeeper, wiping at plates behind his bar. She crept around the chimney. Better! Now she could see straight into the front room. And there he was! A heavily built man, dressed in a dark frock coat, wearing a red feathered hat.

The gang leader was sprawled in one chair, his cuffed boots propped up on another. As Kep watched, he raised his glass with a jeer. A knife blade shone as he flourished it in time to the music. A small boy was at his elbow, holding a jug of ale almost as big as himself, no doubt waiting for the command to refill the ruffian's glass. The child was staring at the knife with huge, terrified eyes. The sight sent a hot flush of anger through Kep. She repositioned her quiver, her fingertips brushing the flights. She hesitated only slightly before selecting the blue-shafted arrow.

As she watched, a villager wearing a headscarf came into view. Kep could almost see the poor woman shaking as she placed a basket on the table in front of the pirate leader. Presumably the gift was acceptable, because he dismissed her with a flick of his hand. A burly fellow in a bright orange shirt collected the basket and stashed it somewhere out of sight as the next villager crept forward, cowering and bowing.

Breathing deeply, Kep nocked her arrow in place. There was nothing for it. She would have to kill the man in the red hat. A clean shot to the heart. After that … Well, she had ten arrows. The chimney gave good cover, and she would make every arrow count.

Kep pulled her elbow back, feeling the beautiful stretch of her bow. When Skarlon's quiet warning came back to mind — *Remember the code, Kep* — she shoved the words away. The man in the red hat was obviously evil — his actions had proved it. And he had to be stopped. She drew all of her focus to a single point, right at the man's heart. Then, just as she was about to release the arrow, somebody lumbered across her view. Kep exhaled sharply. Cursing her luck, she let the bow return to its natural curve. Then her eyes flew wide. She realised why the man blocking her aim had moved so awkwardly. He placed his burden on the end of the table, in clear line of sight. She could almost smell that glorious, golden mound. Roast goose!

Kep closed her eyes, finding her breath. It was a difficult shot, not impossible. But if she missed the spot where the pouch was buried … She could not miss. She sat there for a long moment, head bowed. Then she lifted her chin, whispered an entreaty to Narsis, and took position once more. In one fluid movement Kep pulled the drawstring to her cheek, trained the arrow to her will and sent it flying.

There was no sound. Or at least none that Kep could hear. But the goose, the boy, and the leader in his red hat, they all vanished in a cloud of mustard-coloured dust. Kep wasted no time, scampering as fast as the jittery slates would allow, no longer caring if she was seen. Up and over she ran. Then she launched herself from the edge of the roof, across the gap, into the canopy of a tree.

The line of villagers was in complete confusion. Those nearest the entrance had been overcome by gas and were sprawled on the ground. Those still upright stumbled about, coughing and clutching at their throats. When Kep swung to the ground they reeled away. Perhaps they thought she was part of some new torment.

There was no time to explain. Kep selected the person who seemed most in possession of his wits, a gristly-looking character with a thin beard, and flung her rope at him. Pointing at the prone villagers, she yelled. 'As soon as they stir, go inside. Tie them all up!' There was no time for clearer instructions. 'Marta will explain!' The old woman had regained her hat, and was limping over, grinning. Kep caught the man's astonished nod, before sprinting away.

The scent of smoke came to Kep's nostrils as she ran. Its terrible significance spurred her on. The hall had been torched! In this breeze the flames would quickly spread. Her thoughts flashed ahead. She darted left, towards the forge. The blacksmith's yard was empty, the fires cold, but everything was in its place. It took only seconds to find a hammer. It was large and heavy; Kep needed two hands to swing it up onto her shoulder. Then, as she was leaving, she spied a staff leaning against the wall. She snatched that up for good measure and pelted out, as fast as she could, towards the smoking hall.

The thick doors at the front of the building were heavily barred. Nailed shut. Ignoring them, Kep scooted around the corner. She could hear commotion now. Fighting — at the rear of the building. Skarlon! She could not help. There was no time. The windows on this side of the building were too high to reach. There was a door, though. Sturdy, with a large black lock, it was obscured by logs and kindling. Spurred on by screams coming from inside the building, Kep threw herself into dragging, hauling, rolling logs. Her thumbnail caught and tore away. She ignored it. Then she raised the mighty hammer.

As Kep began pounding at the door, smoke billowed from beneath the rafters. It caught at her throat, making her choke. Still she battered at the lock — hammering and bashing until her arms ached. It was taking too long! The villagers had built their hall with pride. More screaming. Kep roared and smashed the hammer down again. At last timber splintered. Another crash. The lock broke free!

Now banging was coming from the other side, too. Casting the hammer aside, Kep tugged and strained at the iron ring of a handle. The stubborn door would not budge. But nor would Kep surrender. She would not let those people die! With blood pulsing in her head, she screamed, hauling at the ring with every last vestige of strength. Then, without warning, the door burst open, releasing a tumult of smoke and bodies.

The villagers spilled out, gasping and choking. Some crawled. Some dragged children, their little mouths red screaming caves. Others clutched babes to their chests. And in the midst of it all was Jen-Jay. The warrior burst through the door in a whirl of seething fury. With one hand she caught the staff that Kep tossed to her. Ice-blue eyes flashing, and with a grim nod, she disappeared around the corner. Kep almost felt sorry for the ruffians: they had no idea of the wrath that was about to descend on them.

Many of the people were retching and vomiting. Some staggered, fainting, needing to be dragged away. Beyond the doorway was an inferno of roiling flame and smoke. A blast of heat made Kep stagger backwards, eyes burning. 'Is that everyone?' she choked, hoarse with the smoke. 'Is anyone left inside?'

A young woman dressed in a filthy white dress was shouting for everyone to run into the forest to hide. Sensible advice. She nodded at Kep, wiping her streaming eyes with her arm. 'It's everyone.' Her expression was one of deep anguish. 'Except … Beryl. One of the men … He took her.'

A beam crashed down inside the hall. Kep felt her purpose harden to steel. She picked up her bow and drew her knife from its sheath. It glinted green, sending a shiver up her arm. 'Hide! I will signal when it is safe.'

The young woman stared, wild-eyed. 'Who—?' Kep was already running.

Rounding the corner, Kep ran straight into a wall of heat. She gasped. This end of the building was well alight. Flames were licking from the rafters. Black smoke belched into the sky. Jen-Jay was whirling, dancing like a demon, driving at one of the ruffians with her staff. When his weapon, a curved scimitar, went flying into the air, his face twisted into a picture of fear and surprise. Jen-Jay jabbed again. The blow hit, under his jaw. He went down in a heap.

A disarmed Skarlon was swinging at a second thug with a tree branch. Kep was going to his aid when she noticed a third. Unconscious, he had fallen near the flames. Too near. Kep ran forward and grabbed his arm. He was heavy for his size, but she managed to drag him towards the bushes. When Kep saw the cruel lines of his face, she scowled. There was no time to regret her decision. The sound of cursing and breaking twigs made her turn. Somebody was crashing through the trees! Kep shrank beside the body. She dared not move. She dared not breathe.

'Stop! Drop your weapons or I'll slit her pretty throat!'

Two figures had moved into sight. The young woman's head was dragged back by the hair. The skin of her throat was stretched, pale against her captor's blade. She was weeping silently. The lout had been none too careful — her neck was already running with blood. The bodice of her dress was dark with it. Kep glowered.

The bald man's tattoos were no more attractive from behind. He gripped his victim tightly, pushing her along in front. Jen-Jay's staff whirled to a halt. Her cloak caught up a moment later. Skarlon froze, too. Holding up his hands, he dropped the branch. His opponent laughed in surprise and struggled to his feet.

The bald-headed lout dragged at the girl's hair, making her whimper with fright. 'That's right. There'll be no more of that.' Kep froze where she was crouched. If he glanced back, he would see her. He did not. All of his attention was on the others, and on his hostage. 'Everyone is going to do what I say.'

As the pair staggered forward like drunken dancers, Kep took a steadying breath. Her fingers found the hilt of her knife. She could hear Ozu Mako's advice in her head. *Never throw your knife. Not unless you are dead certain of hitting the mark.* It was good advice. It was the perfect way to disarm yourself. It was also the only plan Kep had. She gripped the hilt, sensing the weapon's tingling response.

The code, Kep. Remember the code.

She stared the rolls of fat at the back of the man's head. Then she cursed silently. Calling on Narsis, she caught up a rock and took aim, right at the base of his skull. Kep was not sure whether the girl's scream came before or after the rock found its mark. The poor thing kept screaming, even as the bully lost his grip and dropped like a sack of wet wheat. Jen-Jay whirled like a spinner seed. With a loud crack her staff found a skull.

Kep sank to her knees. She pushed her hands into the fragrant earth, trying to centre herself. As she looked up at the smoke-filled sky, the bells began to toll.

Chapter 32

KEP-VÁLI

The innkeeper's name was Barley. Barley Meek. And he could not have been more aptly named. He stammered through his embarrassment. 'I … I think this belongs to you … Kep-Váli.'

Kep sighed. She had no idea who had coined her new name. It seemed the villagers had already heard rumours of 'Kep the Valiant' and had devised their own version. Apparently 'Váli' still meant 'brave', but it clearly also meant something like 'our protector'. She suspected Marta might have had a hand in it. The chants had begun almost immediately, intermingled with the joyful tones of the village bell.

Sounding the bell had certainly been Marta's idea, to let everyone know that it was safe to come out. It had caused jubilant chaos as the villagers converged in the town centre — flying into the arms of their loved ones.

The poor innkeeper still blamed himself for the deception. But there are only so many times a person can apologise. He had been lucky to escape the effects of the jellin bomb, thanks to a timely trip to the cellar. Kep bet he would have preferred to be laid out unconscious with the others.

Taking the arrow, Kep gave him her best smile. He had certainly given it a thorough polishing — the shaft was an even brighter blue than before. 'I'm sorry I splattered your walls with goose.' Kep's expression grew even more remorseful as she looked about. It was not just the walls. Tiny shreds of meat were stuck everywhere. Barley would be picking them off his furnishings for some time to come. And, although the jellin powder had been wiped clean in places, the Plough Inn still looked like the scene of a golden flour fight.

The innkeeper bounced on his toes. 'It was a mighty fine shot,' he beamed. 'And don't you worry: plenty of folk are setting about to help clean up.'

It was true. The villagers were scrubbing away as they chattered, sharing news. The mood was decidedly festive, despite the fact that most people had not yet washed or changed. Those from the mine were grimy with sweat, their hair tinged yellow with traces of jellin. Nobody seemed to care.

Kep suspected that the entire village had squeezed into the little inn.

Dressed in the filthy remnants of their finery, the bride and bridegroom clutched each other still, as if they were determined to never let go again. Kep understood. When they looked her way, she smiled — covering a sudden wave of sadness.

An ancient healer was taking care of those with injuries. Some looked as if they would be better off in their beds, but nobody wanted to miss the news, or be alone. So people took rest where they could, tucked up in blankets, with mugs of hot tea and mulled wine at their elbows. Even those fighting the fires had come in now. The hall was beyond saving. However, all thanks to Narsis, it was pouring with rain, drowning mischievous sparks.

A huge cauldron of soup was bubbling over the fire, sending out the comforting aroma of onions and bacon bones. Cobbled together from whatever people had to share, Kep believed it was the best soup she had ever tasted.

There was weeping and exhaustion, of course, but mostly tears of joy. Since the fiddler was still out cold, a young woman with yellow hair had found a lute. She was playing one merry tune after another. Although nobody had the energy to dance, there was singing and laughter in abundance. A litter of black and white puppies, which Apple had managed to keep hidden in his barn, added exuberance to the overall gaiety and feeling of release. The puppy that had been presented to the blacksmith was cradled, squirming, in his brawny arms.

'Thanks to the gods!' somebody cried again. Frothy mugs of ale were raised once more. 'And Kep-Váli!'

Needing little encouragement, the children took up the chant and began capering about the room, chased by the excited puppies. 'Kep-Váli! Kep-Váli!' they piped in their high voices.

Jen-Jay barked a laugh at Kep's elbow. 'And so the legend grows.'

Ignoring the innkeeper's broadening grin, Kep hid her nose in her mug. She wanted to point out that she was not the only one to have a legend, but she kept her silence. Jen-Jay humphed, tapping her tumbler for a refill. The innkeeper poured eagerly — vintage rum, the very best he had.

Still trying to piece events together, Kep took a mouthful of the rich, dark beer. Her eyes darted once again to the little snug, where Skarlon had Curly bailed up. Curly really was the man's name, it seemed. At least that was the name he went by — if he had another, he had not shared it.

Apparently, Curly was happy to admit himself a thief; a pirate no less. But he was less thrilled about Red Hat's methods.

'Burying men alive,' he kept repeating. 'It just wasn't right. And the children, the little children. I just had to do something.' Kep frowned, trying to reconcile his words with what she had witnessed of the man. There was no doubt Curly had done a good thing by releasing the prisoners in the mine, betraying his own gang in the process. But things might have turned out rather differently. If 'the red-hatted fiend', as Marta called him, had been in any state to fight back, people would have lost their lives. Pickaxes and pitchforks were no match for cutlasses and crossbows.

Kep scowled, rubbing at her neck. When she stifled a yawn, Jen-Jay's quick eyes lit upon her. It was as if the little woman had picked up her thoughts. An accusing finger stabbed the air. 'That one bears watching. Perhaps we should have put him in with the others.' Jen-Jay jerked her head in the direction of the adjacent building.

The village had neither courthouse, nor prison cells. The stoutest door belonged to the weaver, so that is where the unconscious gang members had been taken — 'all trussed up like pigs for market,' according to Barley. They had been joined by the pair from the mines, both of whom had been rendered insensible by Curly during his surprising turnaround; a third had been killed in the struggle by the blacksmith. The man Kep had dragged away from the fire had been tossed in with the rest of them, along with the bald-headed thug.

Jen-Jay sniffed, as if she detected the smell of a rat over the warm scent of her rum. 'Perhaps he's not the worst of them. But, mark me, that Curly plays his own game.' Tossing the rum down in a single draught, she pulled a face. 'I fully expect to find him Curly by name and curly by nature.'

Kep's second yawn drew Jen-Jay's close attention once more, and this time a frown. 'You need to sleep, girl. You look terrible.'

It was true. Kep was struggling to keep her head up. But she could not sleep. Not yet. Not before they found out what had happened to the others.

Jen-Jay's lip curled in disapproval. Kep fully expected a lecture on acknowledging the body's needs. 'Stubborn.' The old warrior clicked her tongue. 'Very well, let us find out what these thugs have to say for themselves, starting with our friend, Curly. Then it's straight to bed with you. Assuming we can find a bed in this mess of a place.'

Kep followed the petite warrior, leaving the innkeeper wiping down his bench. They took care crossing the room, stepping around unconscious villagers. They had all been laid together, on rush mats near the fire. Concerned friends and relatives sat with them, adjusting blankets, holding hands and stroking cheeks — picking fragments of roast goose from their hair. Grateful eyes looked up as the warriors passed. Kep's ears picked up a quiet refrain in their wake: *Kep-Váli. Kep-Váli.*

The little corner was certainly snug: just large enough to contain two round tables, not much bigger than dinner plates, with two seats at each. The man hovering at the entrance shifted his bulk to let them through. Kep could tell he was wondering why this ruffian had not been tossed in with the others. It was a fair question. Skarlon and the curly-haired man looked up. The air in the snug was thick with tension. Skarlon clearly did not trust the man as far as he could throw him. Good.

Curly was sitting on a three-legged stool. His heels danced up and down, making his knees jitter. One hand tapped out a rhythm on his thigh. When Jen-Jay sent him one of her stares, he caught both hands between his knees.

Drawing up a chair, Kep took the opportunity to study the stranger. He did not seem as frightening now — though he smelled worse. She shoved her chair back a little. If you ignored the smell, his flamboyant shirt and outlandish jewellery, he was actually quite a handsome fellow. A pale scar under one of his brown eyes was shaped like a tear. Combined with his large drooping moustache, it gave him a rather mournful look. He looked like a naughty puppy, caught in the act of killing chickens. Kep responded to his imploring expression with her best scowl.

It was nothing compared with Jen-Jay's baleful countenance. Looking every bit the Grey Wolf of legend, she snapped. Two words. Sharp and menacing. 'Start talking.'

The man twitched and flinched; he was cornered and he knew it. He spoke with a lilting accent, jumbling his words in places. They were indeed pirates. Or had been. It was Grady who had cooked up the idea of coming inland to raid. Somehow he had learned about the mine. Smuggling jellin had proved a lucrative sideline in the past, and Grady was pleased at discovering a new source. The jellin and anything else they could pillage was sent in wagons back to the ship.

'We care nothing for your loot,' snapped Jen-Jay. 'The captives. What of them? Were they sold for slaves?'

Curly's legs were jiggling once more. His eyes slid away. 'Maybe ... I don't know …' The nervous way he licked his lips suggested otherwise, but Jen-Jay did not get to press him. At that moment the inn was filled with cries of joy. The villagers were waking! Curly's eyes widened. His knees stopped dancing.

Jen-Jay's expression was stony. 'I think you do know. But let us see what your leader has to say.' The man's moustache wilted.

To their alarm, the door was opened for them by the very farmer who was supposed to be guarding the prisoners. He used his large backside to hold it open — his hands were taken up with a pottery tankard and a large piece of pie. 'Allow me, Kep-Váli.'

'It's just Kep.'

The man did not seem to hear. He was too busy trying to bow while keeping hold of his pie. 'You'll want the key, Kep-Váli. It's here on my belt. If you'd just like to …'

The farmer beamed at them cheerily, not at all cowed by Jen-Jay's dark muttering.

The weaver's workroom was a welcoming space, rich with the smell of lanolin. The wholesome scent filled Kep with a sudden longing for her little flock of bug-eyes. How simple her life had been, back when her only concern had been looking after the creatures in her care and making sure they gave good milk. As she rubbed wearily at her forehead, Jen-Jay shot her a look of concern. Did the woman miss nothing? She was tired, that was all. Blinking away memories, she stared about her.

The loom had the air of quiet anticipation, waiting for somebody to bring it chattering to life. The baskets near the spinning wheels had been tipped out and their contents abandoned. Skeins of linen and wool were not valuable enough for pirates it seemed.

The locked storeroom was at the far end of the room. Kep's eyes were drawn to the long table that had been shoved hard against one wall. Although she had been warned of the extent of the pirates' looting, nothing could have prepared her for the tragic sight. The villagers' treasures were simple things. Necklaces of beads. Carved trinkets and painted candlesticks. Handmade bottles of ointments and soaps. A wooden puppet. There was little value in most of them — the pirates had simply taken the things because they could. Kep turned furious eyes on Curly. The man was staring at his feet, doing his best to pretend the table and its humble treasures did not exist.

'We confiscated these, of course.' The farmer shoved at the pile of weapons with the back of his hand. His distaste for the crossbows and cutlasses was obvious. His eyebrows went up when Kep let out a gasp. She knew Jaibari's sword from its scabbard — its twinned snakes gleamed as she drew the blade. Kep felt her jaw clench.

'You recognise it, Kep-Váli! Good sword that.' The farmer beamed as if he knew all about blades. 'He kept that one for himself, he did. Red Hat.' He went to spit, thought better of it and wiped his mouth. As he rattled the key into the lock, Curly spoke up. He had been looking over the weapons, closely watched by a scowling Skarlon.

'Did you not find a dagger? Black with a filigree hilt?'

The farmer ignored him. It was as if he had not spoken. Like Kep, he probably had no idea what filigree was. 'Come, see. There's no danger. All tied up, they are.'

Kep understood the impatient tutting noise that escaped Jen-Jay. The pirates were not 'trussed up like pigs' at all, but had been placed in chairs. Their hands were bound behind the chair backs, their feet tied together. It was all rather polite, given what they had done. For some reason the chairs had been arranged in a semi-circle. The seven pirates were in various stages of coming to. The two at the end on the right were already wide awake. Judging by the thick coat of yellow on their boots, they had been on guard at the mine. Kep's guess was confirmed as soon as they caught sight of Curly. They would have jumped out of their chairs had they been able to.

'Curly! You hit me! An' … an' Ratskin here, too. Smacked us fair hard, you did!' The boy's eyes — for he was little more than a boy — were hot with betrayal.

'I know, Spike. It was for your own good.'

Kep surveyed the unlikely pair. She wondered if Spike had been named for his nose — it was so pointed it looked as if it had been sharpened. His chin was pointy, too. He thrust it out at them, the only weapon he had left.

The fellow beside him, Ratskin apparently, was the complete opposite. Blunt of nose and round-shouldered, he was a little older but much broader. There was something mangled about him. A grubby, misshapen giant, with potato fists. He was dressed in the strangest assortment of clothes, as if he'd put on every garment he owned. Some actually did look as though they were made from the skins of rats. Like his companion, Ratskin was staring daggers at Curly.

A couple of the other pirates were stirring, too. They blinked and scowled, their eyes furtive as they took in the change in their situation. Kep could not imagine a more ugly and frightening bunch. They made the poachers at Senna seem friendly by comparison. Some flexed their muscles, testing their bonds, making their chairs creak. One ran his tongue over his teeth and spat in Curly's direction. Kep looked away from the glistening gob, frowning instead at the large red hat. It had been placed on the floor, in front of the man closest to her, at the end of the line.

'That was my idea.' The farmer sniffed. 'Thought it best to mark him out. Just so's there was no mistaking him.' The leader's head was still sunk to his chest. But Kep felt a cold shiver, deep in her being. By some instinct she knew he was awake. Then his shoulders stirred. They curled forward. The crown of his head started to move, too. Then his head snapped up.

His eyes! His eyes were a vortex of whirling darkness! Kep reeled. It felt as if her heart was being squeezed in an icy vice. A wicked black knife flashed in the pirate's hand.

'His boot! Didn't you check his boot?'

Kep was only vaguely aware of Curly's cry. She was struggling to move, mesmerised, enthralled by that terrible, empty gaze. Everything moved around her. Two of the pirates burst from their chairs, fists flailing. Skarlon swept out his sword as the farmer cried a warning: 'Kep-Váli!'

Too late! The pirate leader lunged. In the same instant Curly dived — a flying arc of red silk and black curls. 'For the *Lady Lee!*' A dagger flashed. Curly's blade sank deep. Deep into Grady's neck. Grady roared. He should have fallen. A normal man would have; Grady did not. Instead, he staggered forward. The sound that escaped his mouth was truly terrifying.

Jaibari's sword shook in Kep's hands, as if trying to escape her grasp. She had heard that voice before. It vibrated — a chorus of voices twisted into a ghastly inhuman thread. 'Kep-Váli! Come, Kep-Váli! Find me. Fight … me.'

The pirate leader gave one last lurch. Jaibari's sword found its home and he fell.

⁂

'Never trust a man with a knife in his boot.' As Curly grinned, folding his own knife and tucking it back into his boot, Kep could not help thinking of Sarin. Then Curly gave her an exaggerated wink. *Honestly.* This man was nothing like Sarin. The rest of the pirates had fallen into confusion. The death of their leader had had a profound effect. A couple were weeping, shaking and shivering. Ratskin and Spike were stock upright, staring at Kep with wide eyes. 'Simbab! Simbab!'

Kep questioned Curly with her eyes. He nodded. 'They would prostrate themselves at your feet if they could. You killed Grady, their leader.' He bowed. 'That makes you Simbab.'

Kep spluttered. 'That … that's ridiculous!'

Curly nodded and folded his arms. 'Don't be stupid,' he told the line of quivering pirates. 'She is not Simbab. She is Kep-Váli.' The boys' eyes went even wider. Curly flashed a grin at Kep, as if he had fixed everything. Jen-Jay snorted, loud as a horse. But it seemed the man was completely serious. 'They will swear to you, Kep-Váli,' he said, with solemn brown eyes. 'Under whatever oath you care to name.' As crazy as it seemed, the pirates were all nodding.

Jen-Jay spun about, as if she would like to strike him. 'And you? What oath would bind a man such as yourself?'

Curly's moustache twitched. 'Not an oath. A bargain.' To Kep's horror, the man kneeled at her feet. 'I, too, will follow you, Kep-Váli. If you will not accept my oath, and I understand why you would not, I hope you will accept my pledge. If you are to find your friends you will need a ship, and I have one. The *Lady Lee*, stolen from me by Grady.'

Kep frowned. She was swaying from exhaustion and confusion. 'Why would …? Please get up. Why would I need a ship?'

Curly stayed where he was. 'Because your friends are fighters.' He caught Jen-Jay's eye. 'They have been sold. Not into slavery — but worse.' He gestured at Jaibari's sword, still red with blood. 'The woman who can wield a sword like that, she is worth more than jellin.' His sigh was a great gust. His shoulders sagged. 'Your friends, they will be sold to Kara-fell. For the arena. Kept in cages. Forced to fight. They fight and die. Or become her creatures.'

Kep stared at him for a long moment, forcing her tired mind to absorb the terrible information. She barely needed to consider her reply. Refusing to look at Jen-Jay and Skarlon, she thrust out her chin. 'Not an oath, then. A bargain. Help us find our friends and you can have your ship.' The pirate's face melted into an expression of joy. He did not prostrate himself. There was no room on the floor. To Kep's great surprise, he kissed her hand instead.

※

'Kep-Váli! The pirate leader!' Jen-Jay had stormed and scoffed and banged her staff. But that was how it was. They could not leave the pirates with the villagers. Piled into the wagon they would pass as slaves, bound for market. Perhaps they could find Nirias and his team. If not, they would make plans of their own. So after a half day's rest, they left the villagers of Bixdale to their tasks — sharing out confiscated food, planting fields and tending to their hurts. Kep smiled when a bell rang out, tolling in farewell. It was a remarkable little place. The people were already making plans to build a new hall. It would have been a good place to stay.

Kep was once more riding Berry. The chestnut mare jogged along happily, apparently enjoying the company of Skarlon's Twinkle. They rode abreast, the wagon trundling behind, loaded with surprisingly cheerful-looking pirates. Curly had been given the job of driving the team. It would keep him out of trouble, Jen-Jay said, and right where she could keep an eye on him. Kep almost felt sorry for the man. He might be holding the whip, but there was no doubt who was in charge.

'So much for keeping you out of danger, Kep.' Skarlon squinted into the sun and pulled his hat down over his eyes. 'Nirias would skin me alive if he knew our plans.'

Kep's words were quiet but clear. 'The gods oversee my fate, Skarlon. Not Nirias, and not you. If it is the gods' will that I rescue my friends from Kara-fell, then that is what I must do.'

As Skarlon fell silent, she lifted her chin. If she was honest, she was terrified. For a moment she wished that Ash could be there with her. And Sarin. She wondered what Sarin would make of them taking up with pirates. Reckless, he would say. And he would be right. No, it was best that Ash was safe in T'al Jazure. And Sarin? Kep half-smiled. Sarin could take care of himself.

Chapter 33

THE MESSAGE

The sensation of Credé's searing rage stayed with Ash for several days. His mind could not stop returning to the fight with Leynore and that awful moment of destruction. The memory ambushed him at odd times, but especially during the Breath. It made finding stillness even more impossible.

He did not dare pick up the Taelstone again — not until he could control his emotions. He had given up on Demara Cantoya long ago. What was the point? The problem of the Song had settled like a leaden ball in his heart. He might as well accept it. He would never have the courage to leave the city. All he could do was keep himself busy and made himself useful — anything to shut out the worry he felt for his friends.

In Jen-Jay's absence, Benjin Dale had taken control of the kitchens. The resulting improvement in the meals had lifted spirits considerably — even if he did run the kitchen like a battlefield. One sunny morning Benjin decided it was time to reorganise. The spring would bring new people to T'al Jazure and they would all need feeding. Ash was helping him set up a second kitchen, in the Rosewood Lodge.

'Hey! Ash!' Ash jumped, still not used to Benjin's great blasting commands. 'Take these beans to the domes: they've sprouted! Who knows? Maybe they'll grow.' The man clapped him on the shoulder. 'And some fresh air might cheer you up, eh?' Ash doubted it, but he nodded anyway.

He inspected the bowl of dried beans as he walked. They had obviously been soaked and forgotten about. Fat and purple, each had a curling white shoot. Ash had no idea whether they would grow. Probably not.

He walked quickly, his collar up against a stiff spring breeze. The beans were not the only things sending out shoots. The garden beds were bristling with the blunt tips of bulbs. He scowled. T'al Jazure's flowers would probably sparkle, or change colour at different times of the day. The wooded groves were carpeted with swathes of tiny purple and yellow flowers now. Ordelle reckoned they were crocuses. She had given a lengthy explanation about fabric dyes and trade routes, to which Ash had paid little attention.

Now as he approached a small bridge, Ash's frown deepened. A pair of strangers stood in the middle, staring. People did that a lot when they arrived in T'al Jazure. These two were goggling at the splinter of crystal that rose from the centre of the lake. They did not look like warriors. Scholars, perhaps? Ash bobbed his head and scurried past. Catching their puzzled smiles, he knew at once what they were thinking. Where, by Telion, did the skinny boy with grey hair fit in? It was a good question.

Three groups had arrived so far. Along with their dumbstruck awe, they had brought pack animals loaded with supplies, milking goats and even chickens. If Ash was honest, it was nice to see a few more people about. It made the city feel less … unreal. Just so long as they did not expect conversation.

The newcomers were being housed in the Rosewood Lodge. But when the day's training and chores were complete, everyone congregated, as usual, in the hall of the Sable Lodge. Aechon was clearly enjoying a brand-new audience and fresh people to quiz. And where Aechon went, so did Gallin. Which meant that these days Ash frequently spent his evenings alone with Ordelle, in the Inquisium, dipping into books and plucking half-heartedly at a lute. He did not really mind, as her indifferent silences suited his dark mood. This was his life now: staying behind to worry.

࿓

The path leading to the gardens chased about according to the whims of the river. This part of the city was laced with waterways: bridges bounded gaily from one island to the next. Set in the middle of small lakes, the buildings twisted and curved in impossible shapes. Most intriguing of all were the gigantic domes. Grouped together, like a clutch of shining eggs, they were made of glass panes supported by silvery scaffolds. Each dome was unique. A couple were constructed entirely from patterned triangles, but most featured flowers with interlocked petals of glass. The largest boasted an enormous spider's web. It was there that Ash headed, hoping to find Baldwig Homer. Ash looked up as he entered, trying not to think about giant spiders.

Baldwig Homer was a frightening-looking character. Ash doubted anyone made jokes about his name, despite the fact that the man was completely bald. He had a prominent brow, a huge jutting chin, and a large bulbous nose. His thick neck, thick forearms and thick legs all added to the impression of a completely unbreakable individual, which made the fact that he was still recovering from a long illness hard to believe. 'Agnid is a magician,' he told everyone who had time to listen. 'Simply a magician!' If only he knew the truth.

Baldwig's ongoing recovery, and his past life as a farmer, made him the obvious person to oversee the domes. But the poor man was just as baffled by how the structures worked as anyone.

That morning Baldwig had been joined by Gallin, and was scratching his head and gesticulating as Ash approached. 'Nirias says this one should be the warmest. But blow me if they don't all seem the same—' Baldwig scowled at Ash and his bowl of beans in such a hostile manner that Ash wilted.

'Benjin thought—'

'Thought we might grow some beans, did he?' Baldwig growled. 'Well, I hope they're magic beans, 'cause we only grow magic beans here!'

Ash did not need Gallin's warning glance to know to back away; it was obviously bad timing.

Then Baldwig softened. 'Oh, all right.' He blew out his cheeks. 'No harm in trying. Take them to Ordelle, in that butterfly dome. There's trellises in there, so that should be a clue. Perhaps Ordelle will help you plant them.' Ash caught the twinkle in Gallin's eye. He obviously thought it most unlikely.

Leaving the men to their frustrations, Ash headed for the butterfly dome, where he found Ordelle raking soil in a long, narrow bed. Wearing wide orange trousers with an odd sort of waistcoat, she looked as if she would rather be anywhere else. Turning a sour expression on the beans, she shrugged. 'Bury them, I suppose.' She went back to her raking, making it clear that Ash was on his own.

Ash found a bed with fan-shaped trellises and picked up a bean. Was that white thing a root or a shoot? He decided it must be a shoot. So it would want to be in the air. Wouldn't it? He sighed. They would probably die anyway. He formed a row, burying the beans just beneath the surface of the soil, white tails sticking up.

Tarlyn, who had followed him in, was busying herself hunting for insects.

When she gave a chirrup, Ash turned his head, wondering what had caught her attention. At once his heart leapt. He grinned and got to his feet. It was Sarin! Ash's delighted shock at seeing his friend striding towards him faded in an instant. The expression on Sarin's face shot him full of fear. Whatever had happened?

Sarin was not alone. He was followed closely by his sister, Rilka. Peeking out from behind her brother's back, she blinked in surprise at the higgledy-piggledy line of beans.

'Where is she, Ash? Where's Kep? Pallin said she's not here. Is it true? Where's Kep?'

Ash stared into Sarin's face. He had never seen him look so exhausted. 'She's gone.' He frowned. 'Her tile was drawn.'

Rilka clutched at Sarin, hiding her face in his shoulder. Ash heard her whimper. Sarin looked as if he wanted to whimper, too. 'No. It's not possible.'

'Hello, Sarin!' Ordelle's greeting was so unexpected that everyone blinked. Sarin closed his eyes, composing himself. 'Hello, Ordelle. Rilka, this is Ordelle.' He managed a tight smile. 'It is good to see you, Ordelle.' Sarin returned his attention to Ash. He shook his head. 'Kep's tile can't have been drawn.'

Ash exchanged a frown with Ordelle. He was about to protest, when Sarin's next words stopped him short. 'It's impossible.' Opening his palm, Sarin revealed a terracotta triangle. 'Because I have it here.'

❧

Ash turned Kep's token over in his hands. There was no mistake: it was Kep's mark. Sarin had spoken the truth; Kep's tile had never been in the urn in the first place. Ash could not help feeling shocked at Sarin's audacity. Swapping it with his own, and under everyone's noses. He almost laughed to think of how that mouse had startled everyone. Kep would be furious when she found out! But now they were faced with a serious question: why had Nirias lied?

The Red Lair felt strange during the day, with light peeking through the gaps in the drapes. Rilka had not joined them at the table. Instead she hovered, touching her fingers to things in the room as if testing whether they were hot. Ash caught her watching him with an intent expression on her face, her head on one side. She seemed puzzled by what she saw. Then her gaze flitted away and the impression passed.

Sarin wanted to know everything that had happened in his absence. Oddly enough, he did not seem at all surprised to hear that Jen-Jay had turned out to be Grey Wolf, nor that she had claimed Kep for the wolves. That was the one thing he seemed pleased about. Pleased, not surprised. What most interested him was Skarlon. He made Ash recall every detail of the man and the news he had brought. Then he sat there, in deeply troubled silence. Ash had never seen him look so worried.

The longer his friend kept to his dark silence, the more Ash felt panic rising in his chest. 'It's not so bad, Sarin. Jen-Jay won't let Kep come to any harm.'

Sarin stared at him for a long moment, then turned his eyes to his sister. 'I'm going to tell them, Rilka.' Tilting her head, Rilka nodded, pale-faced. Her thin arms hugged at her tiny frame.

'Rilka has had a vision. '

Ash felt his stomach contract. 'What ... what sort of vision?'

'She is sure that it is Kep. And she is convinced of the danger. Kep was imprisoned in some sort of cage.' Sarin's golden eyes held Ash in a vice-like gaze. 'When Rilka first told me, I dismissed her claims. I was convinced Kep was safe, here in the city. But the dreams kept recurring. And ...' Sarin hesitated, waiting for Rilka's frightened nod before continuing. 'It's worse, Ash.' Ash groaned. How could it be worse? 'Rilka thinks ... She says Kep is not herself.' He bit his lip. 'She says there is something wrong ... something wrong with her eyes.'

Ash gripped the edge of the table. 'You don't think ...' He could not bring himself to say the words. 'But she was not supposed to go anywhere near Kara-fell. The novices were only going to check out some rumours in the Kenting. It was just reconnaissance. For training. It can't ... it can't be the Melk.'

Sarin scowled. 'Kep wasn't supposed to leave the city at all. I don't care what the captains said: she wasn't ready, Ash.' He clenched his fists. 'Nirias has sent her into danger.'

Ordelle had been packing up her things in her usual precise manner. She refastened the claps on her folder of notes. As she rose to her feet, she appeared much taller.

'What time are we leaving, and where do we meet? I have things to prepare.'

Sarin held out his hands. 'No, Ordelle. You can't come. Think of Aechon. He would never allow it.'

Ordelle swivelled her head, owl-like, unblinking. 'I am coming with you, Sarin. Kep is in need of rescue.' Although her tone was as flat and measured as ever, there was no doubt that she was immovable. 'I am coming with you.' After a pause she added, 'You are not the only person who loves Kep, Sarin.'

Abandoning whatever arguments he was about to make, Sarin closed his eyes. He rubbed at his forehead as if struck by a sudden crushing headache. He moaned. 'All right, all right. You can come. But you'll leave a letter for Aechon to find, and you'll follow instructions.' Ordelle nodded. She promptly sat back down, apparently waiting for instructions.

With a deep sigh, Sarin turned his eyes to Ash. The question in his eyes was left unspoken.

Ash took a deep breath. It felt oddly inevitable; the decision to leave the city was not a decision after all. This was how it would happen. For Kep. He nodded slowly. 'When do we leave?' Ash was certain he felt a tremor, just as he said the words. He blinked and looked around. The others seemed not to have noticed.

Sarin gave a grim nod. 'Tonight.'

Following Sarin's worried gaze over to Rilka, Ash frowned. Surely he was not considering bringing Rilka along? Ordelle would be impossible, but Rilka? She was a whole different kind of unpredictable. Rilka seemed to have lost interest in the conversation and was fiddling with a small ornament of blue glass. She pored over it with a strange focus, holding it up to the light. Ash stole a glance at Sarin. There was a pallor to his face and shadows under his eyes. Ash had never seen him that way. It was deeply unsettling. He realised that, for once, Sarin did not know what to do.

Rilka must have felt the intensity of everyone's eyes. She turned a pensive frown on her brother. Her quiet words made it clear she had been listening all along. 'I'm staying here, Sarin. The seed-keepers have been generous and there are many seeds to plant.' Her eyes brushed Ash's and she smiled. It was a good point. If anyone knew which way up to plant beans, it was Rilka. It made sense that she should stay. The problem was how to convince Sarin. To Ash's complete surprise it was Rilka who took quiet command of the situation.

'Sarin, you need to sleep. There is no point setting out in the dark. Ash can deal with the preparations.' Rilka gave Ordelle a nervous smile. 'And I think I would like to meet the Cryer.'

Ash did not know which surprised him more, the fact that Rilka had sent Sarin to his room, or the fact that Sarin had obeyed. That left the job of organising provisions to him. To his relief, the kitchen was deserted, as he had expected. Benjin Dale was holding a session on swordmanship and almost everyone had gathered to watch. Ash made quick work, packing dried fish, hard cheese, flatbread and salted meat into a bag.

Expecting Sarin to be sound asleep when he returned to their room, Ash was surprised to see him standing at the window. He was turning something over in his hands, a paper of some sort. Ash frowned. His friend looked so haggard, why was he not resting? 'Don't worry, Sarin. Get some sleep. We'll find her.' It felt like the most bizarre thing he had ever said. Since when did Ash tell Sarin not to worry?

Sarin nodded wearily, but still he did not take to his bed. As Ash began dividing the supplies into three piles, he prowled restlessly about the room. He kept folding and unfolding his arms. At last he stopped his pacing, and stood completely motionless, head bowed. He turned to meet Ash's worried gaze.

'Ash, I have to tell you something. Only I'm still not sure if it's true. But now I think it might be … and … I think I should have told you before — and Kep, both of you.' He held his head. 'I don't really know why I didn't. Maybe … I suppose part of me didn't want it to be true.'

Sarin's obvious distress was making Ash feel sick.

'It's about your friend. Braig.' The lines around Sarin's eyes tightened. 'I'm still not sure, but … I think he might be alive.'

Ash had no idea how to respond. It was so ludicrous. 'That's … It's impossible. I was with Braig when he died. I … There was a funeral fire.' Ash's hand went to his mouth as memories of the horrible scene flooded back. Why would Sarin say such a thing?

'I know.' Sarin shook his head. 'But it was Gooel — something he said before he died … I assumed he was lying, that it was some cruel trick. They are wicked souls, trackers, and they do wicked work, hunting down slaves. And there was no time to tell you. Not at first, with everything that happened, and then … then, it was too late.'

Feeling sick, Ash sat down on the edge of his bed. Gooel? What could Gooel possibly have to do with Braig? 'Well, tell me now. What did he say?'

'It was hard to make out his words, but he said something about a boy. That he had a message. And that the boy lived …'

Ash's reply was faint. 'A message? Gooel?'

Sarin held up the envelope. 'He had this on his person … And I kept it secret. I didn't believe him, not then, but …' His frown twisted. 'I thought Kep might. And I thought she might do something stupid.'

Ash took the stained envelope with trembling hands. It was blank, but the seal: 'That's …'

Sarin nodded. 'It's a jarlycat.'

Ash could barely breathe. 'So Gooel …' His eyes opened even wider. 'Gooel was working for the League?' Sarin shrugged, silent. 'You think he was trying to give Kep this? A message?'

Sarin was staring at the wall. 'Maybe. I don't know.'

'Why didn't you open it?'

There was a long pause. 'I don't know. It's complicated. Now I think I should have, straight away. But I thought Kep might blame me for Gooel's death. I thought she might think—' He started speaking in a rush. 'I really did try to save him, Ash. And I tried to find the right moment to tell her. But I'd left it too long.' He rubbed at his neck. 'And then that swift came. Remember? I recognised the seal, the jarlycat, and I started to wonder if the Matapharni you had spoken of and Pharni might be the same person. But I figured that if Braig was alive, there would be news. Do you see? And if the news came I wouldn't have to confess to keeping the letter. No news came. So I convinced myself that I must have been wrong. But now …'

Ash shook his head. 'Braig can't be alive. It has to be a mistake. If he was, we would know.' Ash suddenly understood why Sarin was so interested in Skarlon. 'Skarlon said nothing about it, and Pharni is his captain.' It could not be true. If it was, Skarlon would have brought the news. Unless Nirias … Ash knew Sarin was wondering the same thing he was. Had Nirias known and said nothing? The overheard fragment of conversation came back to Ash with a rush. *They will be told. All in good time. You have my word on it, Skarlon. But that time is not now.* Perhaps Skarlon had known but he wouldn't, or couldn't, say!

Ash's eyes fell again on the letter, then went back to Sarin's face.

'You do it,' Sarin almost whispered. So, with shaking hands, Ash broke the seal. He read the words aloud, stumbling over the phrasing.

My brave young friend,

These words must necessarily be oblique, and for that I apologise. To write otherwise would imperil us both. Know this. The bearer of this message can be trusted with your life. Charged with your protection, he will deliver you to friends ~ and to sanctuary. There, you will receive news to gladden your heart, news that I dare not write here. Be brave, my valiant friend, until we meet again.

There was no signature. It was a hope so impossible that for a moment he dared not speak. Ash pressed his hands to his face. 'What do you think?'

Sarin gave a wry smile as he read the script for himself. 'Oblique indeed.' He rubbed his forehead before letting out an exasperated sigh. 'Taken with everything else, and with Skarlon's strange silence …' His grimace gave way to regret. 'I have no idea how. And I'm truly sorry I didn't tell you. But, yes, I think your friend is alive.'

EPILOGUE

The archway shimmered, reflecting the cool light of dawn, welcoming the mystery of a new day. Ordelle and Sarin had passed through quickly, their eyes already searching out the horizon. Ash was bringing up the rear, still worrying if he had packed everything they would need.

All at once he faltered, rocking on his feet, before stopping dead. The pulse of emotion was so strong it knocked the breath from him. *Sadness. Terrible, lonely sadness.* Ash staggered, clutching at his breast. The call was compelling. So terrible in its beauty. It resonated in his chest, pulling at his soul. It was the Heartstone! It was calling. Calling him back.

Sarin turned, framed by the archway. 'Ash? What is it?' His golden eyes narrowed. 'Have you changed your mind?'

Ash gasped for breath. He could not respond. The sense of a presence at his back was so palpable. It was as if somebody was standing there, reaching out a hand. *Loneliness. Despair.* Ash turned his eyes back to the city, back to the miracle of T'al Jazure. His heart swelled with yearning. It almost overwhelmed him. But he could not stay: Kep needed him. He closed his eyes. He breathed. Three long breaths. 'I'll be back,' whispered Ash. At his words the city seemed to sigh. A soft breeze caressed his face, like a silent echo.

Ash turned to meet the concerned eyes of his friends. When Tarlyn nudged his face and curled her tail around his neck, he nodded. It was true. He would be back. The Taelstaun would return to T'al Jazure. There was just something he had to do first. He was not ready to brave the Song. But he understood now: he would never be ready, he just had to try anyway. As Ash passed through the archway, T'al Jazure vanished behind him.

*In another dimension, in a faraway world, something was whirring —
just waiting to be discovered.*

Thank you for purchasing Heartstone. If
you enjoyed the book, I hope you'll consider
spending a few minutes posting a review. Your
feedback and support is greatly appreciated. You
can leave a review on Goodreads or Amazon.

ACKNOWLEDGEMENTS

What a strange and difficult year 2020 has been. I certainly did not think I'd be publishing *Heartstone* as late as December. Writing the second book in *The Stones of the Azuri* series has been quite a journey. As our own world got more complicated, so too did Ash and Kep's world. Around April I realised that a major structural edit was in order: a large chunk of what I had written now belonged in book three, because Karliana's story insisted on being told first.

A huge thank you goes to the wonderful people who kept me sane this year, and especially those who encouraged me to keep writing, no matter what. Thank you especially to my lovely partner, Keith for his proofreading and general moral support. It can't be easy living with a writer, especially an indie who is also coming to grips with running a creative business. Diva, our rescue dog, who arrived just before lockdown, also deserves a mention: for keeping my feet warm and prodding me with a wet nose when I sat at the computer for too long.

My daughter Nikki and her partner Nopera, at NOKNOK Studios, have excelled yet again, creating a stunning cover and beautiful formatting. Thank you so much guys! NOKNOK is also responsible for my fabulous website and for support with all things technical. I have no idea what I would do without you two!

As always, my gratitude goes to my daughter Katie for listening to all my half-formed and crazy imaginings. Katie always gets to hear everything first and is an invaluable sounding board. I sometimes wonder how she manages to make any sense of my tangential flights of thought. Somehow, she always manages to restore my calm and confidence when I get panicky.

My youngest daughter Lara is quite simply the inspiration for the *Stones of the Azuri* series. Lara's gift for music and her extraordinary ability to move audiences never fails to astound me. Her feedback and suggestions are always spot on — like the design for Kep's tattoo.

For the map of T'al Agria, I am indebted to Dan Breton, my daughter Katie's partner. Thank you so much Dan for transforming my first attempt at a Wonderdraft map into something beautiful, not to mention readable.

Once again, Kate Stone has done an outstanding job as an editor.

I feel so lucky to work with such an experienced professional. Kate really is a magician with words, and I always learn a great deal from her careful editing.

I also owe a debt to my beta readers — thanks especially to my sister, Annette Whitehorn, Jenni Komarovski and Dan Breton for their detailed and thoughtful feedback. Special thanks goes to my good friend Jenny Vollmer, who somehow managed to make sense of the first draft of *Heartstone*, even though there were crucial chunks missing. I did not quite have the hang of compiling from Scrivener back then.

A big thank you goes to all my readers who have written reviews and embraced the series, and to all those who have made a difference in supporting me as a writer: Jessica Le Bas for coffee in the library and wonderfully enriching conversations; The New Zealand Society of Authors, especially the Top of the South Branch; Jenny Hager, for her encouragement and words of wisdom; Lynnette Evans at Scholastic; Gaelynne Pound and Stuart Batham for hosting me on their radio shows; Jonathan Moffat for his inspiring work on the audiobook of *Taelstone*; The Wishing Shelf Awards for heartwarming and well-timed feedback, not to mention a gorgeous medal; The Alliance of Independent Authors; and to all my fellow creatives. Writing can be a lonely endeavour and I feel honoured to be part of a vibrant creative community that stretches right across the world.

If you would like to find out more about my writing, you can visit my website:

ROBYNPROKOP.COM